Praise for Elaine Everest

'A warm tale of friendship and romance'
My Weekly

'Captures the spirit of wartime'
Woman's Weekly

'One of the most iconic stores comes back to life in this heartwarming tale'
Woman's Own

'Elaine brings the heyday of the iconic high-street giant to life in her charming novel'
S Magazine

New Horizons for the Woolworths Girls

Elaine Everest, author of bestselling novels *The Woolworths Girls*, *The Butlins Girls*, *Christmas at Woolworths* and *The Teashop Girls*, was born and brought up in north-west Kent, where many of her books are set. She was a freelance writer for twenty-five years and wrote widely for women's magazines and national newspapers, both short stories and features. Her non-fiction books for dog owners proved very popular and led to her broadcasting on the radio about our four-legged friends. Elaine was also heard discussing many other topics on the airwaves, from her Kent-based novels to life with her husband, Michael. She passed away in 2024.

Also by Elaine Everest

The Woolworths Girls series
The Woolworths Girls
Carols at Woolworths (ebook novella)
Christmas at Woolworths
Wartime at Woolworths
A Gift from Woolworths
Wedding Bells for Woolworths
A Mother Forever
The Woolworths Saturday Girls
The Woolworths Girl's Promise
Celebrations for the Woolworths Girls
A Christmas Wish at Woolworths
New Horizons for the Woolworths Girls

The Teashop Girls series
The Teashop Girls
Christmas with the Teashop Girls
The Teashop Girls at War

Standalone novels
Gracie's War
The Butlins Girls
The Patchwork Girls

Elaine Everest

New Horizons for the Woolworths Girls

PAN BOOKS

First published 2025 by Macmillan

This paperback edition first published 2025 by Pan Books
an imprint of Pan Macmillan
The Smithson, 6 Briset Street, London EC1M 5NR
EU representative: Macmillan Publishers Ireland Ltd, 1st Floor,
The Liffey Trust Centre, 117–126 Sheriff Street Upper,
Dublin 1, D01 YC43
Associated companies throughout the world
www.panmacmillan.com

ISBN 978-1-0350-2051-5

Copyright © Elaine Everest 2025

The right of Elaine Everest to be identified as the
author of this work has been asserted by her in accordance
with the Copyright, Designs and Patents Act 1988.

All rights reserved. No part of this publication may be reproduced,
stored in a retrieval system, or transmitted, in any form, or by any means
(electronic, mechanical, photocopying, recording or otherwise)
without the prior written permission of the publisher.

Pan Macmillan does not have any control over, or any responsibility for,
any author or third-party websites referred to in or on this book.

3 5 7 9 8 6 4 2

A CIP catalogue record for this book is available from the British Library.

Typeset by Palimpsest Book Production Ltd, Falkirk, Stirlingshire
Printed and bound by CPI Group (UK) Ltd, Croydon, CR0 4YY

MIX
Paper | Supporting
responsible forestry
FSC® C116313

This book is sold subject to the condition that it shall not, by way of
trade or otherwise, be lent, hired out, or otherwise circulated without
the publisher's prior consent in any form of binding or cover other than
that in which it is published and without a similar condition including
this condition being imposed on the subsequent purchaser.

Visit **www.panmacmillan.com** to read more about all our books
and to buy them. You will also find features, author interviews and
news of any author events, and you can sign up for e-newsletters
so that you're always first to hear about our new releases.

This is the last book Elaine wrote and I would like to thank all the lovely readers and followers who I hope have enjoyed her writing. There are so many people involved in the production of a book, from her agent, Caroline Sheldon, to all the staff at Pan Macmillan. I thank you, too.

Most of all, I thank Elaine for her love throughout the years and I therefore dedicate this book to her memory.

Michael Everest

*The untold want by life and land ne'er granted,
Now voyager sail thou forth to seek and find.*

Walt Whitman

1

February 1940

'I can't drive that.' Annie Brookes stood hands on hips, an indignant look on her sweat-covered face. 'Besides, we can't afford such a thing.' She glared at the two men. 'If you'll excuse me, I need to get back to work.' She turned towards the side of the house and the path that led to the outhouse, no more than a corrugated-iron shack, where steam could be seen wafting from the open-ended building. She stopped by a tap attached to a wooden post, cupping her hands under the icy water and scooping it up, sighing as the sudden coldness soothed her hot face and neck. It might be February but where they worked was extremely hot. Retying the colourful scarf that kept her unruly blonde curls from her face, she entered the room where they earned their money as laundresses and joined her mother.

'What did your Uncle Pete want?' Violet Brookes asked as she continued to put her weight against the handle of a large iron mangle that stood next to one of four steaming coppers, and pushed it slowly round. Annie grabbed the end of a linen sheet that appeared from between the rollers, guiding it into a wicker basket that lay underneath the mangle. Once the heavy sheet had gone through the process, they put it through the wringers one more time then each took a basket handle and heaved it outside to where a row of washing lines stood at the edge of a small orchard.

'He reckons we could improve the laundry business by having a van to deliver and collect the bag wash from our customers,' Annie said as between them they pinned the large sheet to the line using wooden pegs kept in the pockets of their aprons.

Once they had put a long wooden prop under the washing line to hold it up, Violet wiped her hands, pursing her lips as she did so. 'Does he now? I'll be having a word with him as he has nothing to do with this business and I don't want him poking his nose in,' she huffed, picking up the empty laundry basket and heading back through the outhouse towards the path that wove its way around their cottage and onto the dirt track road beyond. This then led to the marshes and the farm from which Blossom Cottage took its name.

'What's this all about, Pete?' she asked of the man who was still standing in the road talking to his and Violet's father. 'We haven't got the money for your hairbrained schemes. We don't see you from one month to the next and then you turn up telling our Annie she needs to be driving a van rather than using the horse and cart that's been good enough for the business since I was a girl. And her not even nineteen yet.' She turned and gave her father a waspish look. 'I take it you've had a hand in this idea?'

Jasper James raised his hand to shield himself from his

daughter's eyes. 'Don't you go blaming me! I just came out here to say hello to our Pete. I'll go back inside; I know when I'm not welcome,' he said, shuffling back towards the house.

'Check on Mum and see if she needs helping out of bed; her legs were playing her up yesterday. You could make her a brew and a slice of toast as well,' Violet called after him before turning to her younger brother. 'I thought you'd have signed up to fight for your country by now. It's been months since war was declared and what have you done?'

Pete shrugged his shoulders. 'They don't want me 'cos of my dodgy lungs; it runs in the family,' he said, glancing at the departing figure of their father. 'That's why he only fought for a little while in the first shout.'

'Laziness runs in this family,' Violet muttered as she looked at the van Pete was leaning against. 'Where has this come from?'

Pete, sensing Violet's interest, started to show her the vehicle. 'It might not look much, but with a tidy up and a lick of paint it would suit you down to the ground. I could add your name to the side – it might bring in a bit more business. Think of the extra work it would mean with our Annie being able to travel further to collect the bag wash. It wouldn't need much looking after, not like that old horse of yours that pulls the cart.'

'How old is it?' Violet asked as she walked slowly around the vehicle, poking her finger into a patch of rust and peering through the windows set in the rear doors.

Pete rushed forward and wrenched one of the doors open, ignoring the squeaks from the protesting hinges. 'Look how spacious it is,' he exclaimed with a sweep of his hand. 'Your Annie could get the round done in half the time.'

Annie's ears pricked up from where she'd been watching the scene unfold. Seeing her mother was holding court, she joined her, adding her two penn'orth. 'You're forgetting something, I can't drive. And don't we all need a licence to drive vehicles these days? Why doesn't Grandad drive it?' she asked in all seriousness as Jasper poked his nose out of the door not wishing to miss what was going on. She knew what the answer would be.

'If I could, I would, but my old war wounds mean I can do little these days without being in pain,' he sighed, holding his back for effect. 'I could teach you, though . . .'

Annie walked to the front of the van. 'It's seen better days,' she said.

'It would give you the freedom you crave,' her uncle said, nudging her arm and giving a wink before taking a handkerchief from his waistcoat pocket and wiping his brow. He gave her a knowing smile. 'You're like a small bird fluttering against a windowpane trying to spread its wings and fly.'

Annie vehemently shook her head. 'Stop with your flowery words. I'm happy here with my family and working with Mum.'

'I beg to differ. You're too much like your dad. You have a wanderlust, just as his family have . . .'

Annie looked over to where Violet was deep in conversation with her father, waving her arms and pointing into the van. 'You'd best not mention Dad's name here or Mum will go berserk. As much as I love him, he has a wayward soul,' she replied, thinking of her father and how he disappeared to be with his family's travelling fairground whenever the urge took him, even though he was needed here at home, especially now that war had been declared. 'We need all the help we can get to keep the laundry afloat,' she said, feeling selfish as she thought of her red-haired dad with a twinkle in his eye, who was always ready to share a tale or two with her and her younger brother, Albie – when he was home at least. That was until Mum had found out he'd been overfriendly with a woman he'd met down The Corner Pin. He'd soon scarpered with his tail between his legs and Violet's harsh words following close behind.

'The fair's going to be travelling once Easter's here; they're wintering over in Belvedere. If you could drive the van, you could go and see him. I'll keep your secret . . .'

Annie sighed as her eyes strayed to the van. It could certainly help her spread her wings. 'All right, but I'd rather you taught me to drive than Grandad as he's not the best of teachers. Besides, he's supposed to be keeping an eye on Nan while she's poorly. Mum can't do everything around here. You know you could drop by and help more than you do,' she said, wagging a finger at her wayward uncle. 'You're always off doing something or other.'

'It's called ducking and diving,' he chuckled, throwing an arm around Annie's shoulders and giving her a gentle squeeze. 'I promise to be here more to help out just so you can have some more fun.'

There's a fat chance of that, she thought to herself as she went to prepare to take out the horse and cart for the first of that day's collections and deliveries.

2

September 1940

Annie sucked in her breath as the van juddered once again. She must take more care when manoeuvring around corners, she thought. It was her first time out on her own visiting customers, and, on Violet's suggestion, seeking out new ones. It had been a long day and she still had to drop off two bags of towels at the outdoor swimming pool in Erith before heading up to Northumberland Heath and a private guest house where the owner was waiting for clean bedding. She'd been up until the early hours ironing and could hardly think straight, let alone watch the road ahead. It would have been so much easier with the horse and cart as Old Ned knew the roads almost blindfold. Perhaps she should have waited another day before trying out the van, but she had an ulterior motive for wanting to drive: Uncle Pete had tipped her the wink that Brookes Fair was up at Blackheath, and she longed to see her dad.

'Hello, Annie, what's all this?' Dora at the swimming pool asked when she came out to give her a hand.

Annie grinned at the young woman, who only ever wore

a robe belted over her swimsuit along with a rubber cap with the sides rolled up so she could hear when not in the pool. 'We're going upmarket,' she joshed. 'Uncle Pete found the van and did it up for us. What do you think?' she asked as Dora walked around the vehicle, giving a nod of approval at the family name painted in bright letters on the side.

'Don't let them work you too hard; you never seem to get any time to yourself as it is. I've not seen you in the pool all this summer. Why not come in and have a dip now? We're still open. I can lend you a swimsuit . . .'

Annie was sorely tempted, but with her mind firmly set on seeking out her dad she had to refuse. 'I can't today, but I'll put my costume in the van and see you on my next visit later this week. Speaking of which, is there anything for me to take?'

'Hang on a tick, I've got one bag tied up ready to go. I'll fetch it for you,' Dora said, hurrying through the doors to the pool.

Annie leant against the side of the van, feeling the warmth of the sun on the body of the vehicle. Not far from where she was workers were going about their day by the side of the River Thames. This part of the river was always busy and even in wartime there were ships and smaller boats heading up towards the East End of London and the docks while others headed down towards the estuary. She dreamt of what it would be like to sail away down the river and feel free of her family responsibilities. Perhaps if the *Kentish Queen* paddle steamer was still running off Erith Pier, she could talk her mum into having a day trip to Margate. She sighed. There was more than a little of her father's wanderlust in her blood. As she stood dreaming, the dreaded sound of an air-raid siren cut through the air and people started to run for cover.

Dora, who was halfway out of the door hauling a white linen sack over one shoulder, dropped it to the ground and called out to Annie, 'Quick, come with me! It's definitely a raid rather than a false alarm.' She pointed to where dark specks could be seen in the sky further downriver. As Annie watched, the flecks became larger and were joined by many more. In the seconds she stood paralysed, the drone of the planes' engines grew louder and louder.

'For heaven's sake, Annie, get your backside into gear!' Dora screamed.

Annie grabbed her bag and gas mask and followed Dora down an alley that ran beside the swimming pool building to where an Anderson shelter stood. 'Will there be room for me?' she asked, seeing two other staff members rush down the steps ahead of them.

'There are only four of us on duty today and all the customers have gone home so there's more than enough room for you. Hurry yourself,' Dora said, grabbing Annie's arm and pulling her to safety down the steps as the roar of planes could be heard overhead.

'I've never seen anything like it,' an older man said as he followed them into the shelter. 'There are hundreds of the buggers up there. London doesn't stand a chance.'

They all fell silent until the sound of ack-ack guns made them jump.

'Come on, boys,' the older man shouted, raising his fist in the air. 'Let's blow them out of the sky!'

Annie shuddered, thinking of her beloved country and

the hell it had become. How many people would perish today? 'There go my plans for the day. I wonder how long we'll be down here. I was hoping to see my dad; he's setting up the fair at Blackheath. Gosh, what if the fair gets bombed?'

Dora, who knew the family well, put an arm around Annie's shoulders. 'Don't worry, your dad knows how to take care of himself. There are public shelters all over the place,' she sympathized.

Annie shuddered again, thinking of what could happen to everybody. 'I hope so.'

'Your mum would have heard the sirens and will probably be down your shelter. I take it you've got one?'

Annie laughed with more than a little sarcasm. 'It's still a pile of corrugated iron and a half-dug hole as the men haven't got round to finishing it, not that Mum will leave the hot water coppers while there's a wash in them.'

'They'll be all right,' Dora reassured her. 'It must be safer out on the Crayford Marshes. Come and help me make a cuppa; we've got everything here to make our time down here as cosy as possible.'

Annie looked around the cramped confines of the shelter. There was a bunk bed along one side and crates covered in rugs opposite, with another that seemed to be used for teamaking holding a paraffin stove and a small tin kettle. She could see enamel mugs stored underneath, along with tins that must contain tea and biscuits. 'What can I do to help?' she asked, trying to pull herself together despite starting to feel claustrophobic, which she could do little about unless she wished to be outside while the enemy wreaked death and destruction. There was nothing she could do until the air raid was over apart from help make a cup of tea and wait . . .

Annie stretched her limbs and yawned as the all-clear sounded. 'I thought we'd be down here until tomorrow,' she said as Dora pulled back the sacking cover over the entrance of the shelter, letting in the daylight. She climbed three steps out into the open air. 'Oh, my goodness,' she exclaimed as the others joined her. 'I've never seen anything like it.'

The group stood in awe looking upriver to the port of London, before making their way to the front of the swimming pool building to get a clearer view.

Dora dashed tears from her eyes before swearing out loud. 'It's as if London has sunk into the bowels of hell.' She raised her fist skywards to a lone enemy plane that was heading away from the capital, followed by the sound of ack-ack guns.

'He won't get away! Our lads are after him!' one of her fellow workers exclaimed excitedly.

'But how many Londoners have perished? And think of the damage to the docks,' Annie said, unable to take her eyes from where smoke rose a mere few miles from where they stood. 'I hate this war. What can be done to stop it?'

'We all do, love.' Dora patted her on the arm. 'And a fine bunch we are with not one of us serving our country. I've been thinking of going to work in munitions up the Arsenal,' she said with a determined look in her eye. 'I just need someone to look after my old man and the kids. Mind you, I'm sending them off to live with my sister down in the Kent countryside; it'll be safer than it is here. Mark my words, it's going to get a lot worse.'

'Perhaps I should be doing some war work? I feel rather helpless watching this and knowing I'm not doing my bit,' Annie said, chewing her lip thoughtfully.

'Darling, you more than do your bit, working at your family's laundry. Don't you supply the local council? And I heard tell your uncle has offered your services at the cottage hospital.'

Annie frowned. What was Uncle Pete up to? Why, he didn't even work for the business and only seemed to turn up when he was after some beer money from Mum. 'That's interesting,' was all she could think to say. It was best she kept family matters to herself as Uncle Pete must be up to something. He called it ducking and diving, but they all knew he sailed close to the wind with his goings-on. 'I wonder if it's safe to be on my way?' she said, peering at the sky, black with smoke from the London docks. 'I still have work to finish before I can head home . . .'

Dora's colleague pulled a cloth from his pocket and went over to Annie's van, where he started to clean the windscreen. 'If you keep away from the river and listen out for air-raid warnings, you should be fine.'

Dora agreed. 'He's right, but can I add that you're to look out for public shelters and if you hear as much as a squeak from a siren, you stop the van and dash to safety. I don't trust the buggers not to come back. Now hurry,' she said, giving Annie a hug.

'But what about collecting the rest of your bag wash?'

'It can wait until next time. Come on, hurry.'

Annie did as she was told and after loading the one sack into the back of the van, she climbed into the driver's seat, picking up a sheet of paper with her delivery and collection route. It had been her idea to make a detailed daily worksheet along with the time she should be with each client. Today's timetable was now completely messed up, but she was sure customers would understand. There were four more stops on her route between Erith and Bexleyheath, meaning she would be home late and wouldn't have time to track down and speak to her father. Part of her wished she knew if he was safe, but then word would get to the family if he'd been injured – or worse. If only he didn't have a wanderlust and stayed at home with her mum. 'That's what comes of marrying a showman and not wishing to follow the fairs,' her mum had once told her when she questioned why Dad was always missing from home. 'It is what it is,' Violet had said with a touch of sadness in her eyes.

'If you were home now, at least I'd know you were safe,' Annie muttered out loud as she drove slowly through the town of Erith, carefully avoiding the many people standing out in the roads looking towards London. Fear was etched on their faces. This war would not be over any time soon.

She headed towards Northumberland Heath, making deliveries to two private houses. It used to irk her that she'd have to go to the service entrance of the grand properties, but these days it didn't worry her as it was all work and added money to the family's coffers. At one drop-off she was given a large bag of linen bedsheets along with an envelope. Handing back a receipt for the items being taken away, she pocketed the envelope knowing it would be payment for last month's washing. Humping the bag onto her back, she carried it to the van, grateful that she wasn't using the horse and cart. Old Ned would not have liked the sounds of the bombs and would likely have bolted if left outside the Anderson shelter.

Next, she pointed the vehicle towards Bexleyheath. It was the affluent end of the long Broadway, where her mum had told her to drop off the neatly written letters at the larger properties in the hope of drumming up more trade, now they had transport more suitable for a growing laundry business. Stopping to allow a mother to push her pram over the road, she ran her fingers through her hair. 'I must look a sight,' she said out loud before pulling over to the kerb. It wouldn't do to represent the family business looking like a down-and-out. She reached for the handbag she kept in the seat well, along with her gas mask.

'Drat,' she muttered, tipping the contents of the bag onto the seat beside her and rummaging through the items for a comb. It was at that moment she recalled using it before she left home; it must still be on the kitchen table where she'd stopped to talk to Albie. Opening a powder compact that had been a gift for her birthday, she peered into the mirror. 'I look a right state, and not even a scarf to tie around my hair to make me more presentable.' She dabbed her nose with the powder before wrinkling her face, knowing it didn't improve her appearance. 'I need to purchase a new comb; it's about time as mine is missing a few teeth,' she announced to the thin air before setting off towards the Broadway. 'I know the very place.'

Parking the van, she dashed across the road into a branch of Woolworths. Never having been into the store before, she stopped and looked about her. She'd shopped in the Erith branch a few times and always admired the smartly dressed assistants, the high counters and shining wooden floors; in another lifetime she could easily have worked there.

'May I help you?' a blonde assistant asked from where she stood behind a counter containing haberdashery items. 'You look lost,' she said with a smile.

Annie grinned. 'If you could direct me to where I could purchase a comb, I'd be so grateful. I have an appointment to keep and look and feel a frightful mess.'

The girl chuckled. 'You don't look that bad, but I shouldn't turn away a sale or I'll get the sack. If you go to the far end of this counter, you'll find a selection of brushes and combs along with kirby grips and hairnets.'

'Did I hear you have an appointment?' An older woman walked over from where she'd been standing just inside the door holding a clipboard and a pencil. 'May I have your name?'

'I'm Annie Brookes, but you won't find my name on your list unless you'd like me to collect your washing,' she replied, hoping she didn't sound facetious.

'My apologies. I thought you were here for an interview to be a sales assistant.' The woman sighed. 'I'm still short of three interviewees.'

'I wish,' Annie said, as she'd been hankering after earning a proper living which didn't rely on her family. At the end of the long counter the blonde assistant was now serving someone with a length of ribbon. Annie was busy choosing a comb and admiring other items when the woman with the clipboard walked over to her.

'If you change your mind about working here, please fill this in and drop it in to the staff supervisor's office,' she said, handing over a folded sheet of paper. 'There's an interview and a test, but you look the kind of girl who can add up and be polite to customers.'

'Oh, Muriel, you sound desperate,' the blonde girl said after bidding good day to her customer. 'Not that you wouldn't fit the bill to work for Woolies,' she quickly assured Annie.

'I am rather desperate. We've had a few women leave to work in munitions, and I'd really like to fill the vacancies before even more leave,' the older woman admitted.

Annie watched the exchange, thinking these people would be fun to work with. Pocketing the folded form and picking up a black comb, she handed it over to the sales assistant and then gave her a couple of coins. 'I'll think about it,' she said to the older woman, knowing in her heart of hearts she would adore to be a Woolworths girl. But what would happen if she was to disappoint her family?

3

'Put me down,' Annie squealed as Paddy Brookes lifted her in his strong arms and spun her around until she felt dizzy. She'd raced through her deliveries and decided to head to find her dad. After all, who knew what was around the corner?

'I'm so pleased you're here to see me and fighting fit. I've been that worried you were caught up in the bombing on the river a couple of days back,' he said, hugging her one more time before releasing her and keeping his hands on her shoulders until she was steady.

Annie bit her tongue against reminding him that if he came home more, he would know how the family were keeping. She could never be angry with her dad; no one including her mum could be annoyed with him for long. Paddy Brookes was a bear of a man. With his broad, strong body, he could carry a carousel galloper on one shoulder without breaking out in a sweat. Everyone who met him would smile at his sunny disposition. It was his wanderlust that was the bane of Violet Brookes' life. As she explained to Annie, she loved him enough to let him spread his wings when the fairground called and then welcome him back when he was in need of home comforts. He stood out a mile, not just for his build, but also because of his head of auburn red hair. Annie was pleased to have inherited his colouring. Although her hair was blonde, in the right light and if you looked closely enough, several auburn strands shone through. Like Paddy, she also had a scattering of freckles across her face and arms that came out when the sun shone.

'I see you've come up in the world,' he said, eyeing the van parked nearby.

Annie huffed. 'It's not as comfortable as the cart, and more temperamental than Old Ned. Uncle Pete reckons he can get us the petrol as we are a business offering a service that people and the government need, but I'm not so sure,' she said worriedly.

Paddy was thoughtful as he walked over to the vehicle, circling round it as he kicked the tyres and tapped on the bodywork. He opened the back doors and peered inside, checking their hinges then going to sit in the driver's seat and turning on the engine to listen before turning it off once more.

'What do you think?' Annie asked, wondering if he'd found a fault.

Paddy didn't speak as he climbed back out of the vehicle and then lifted the bonnet. At that point he was joined by a couple of other showmen, who muttered and peered closely at the engine before going on their way. Paddy wiped his greasy hands down his overall and stretched his back.

Annie grew impatient. 'Well?'

'As you know, I've not got much time for your mother's

brother, but he seems to have found you a decent enough vehicle. There's a bit of wear and tear, which is to be expected, but all in all it'll suit you well for your work.'

Annie sighed and leant against the van. 'I was hoping you'd say to get rid of it; I'm not cut out for all this driving about. I already miss not being able to gaze around and dream while Old Ned pulls the cart.'

Paddy joined her and put an arm around her shoulders. 'You're too much like me: a dreamer who is always looking towards the horizon.'

She stiffened at his words. 'I always pull my weight in the family business; no one can say I don't,' she threw back at him. 'I don't run away from my responsibilities.' Her hand went to her pocket for her handkerchief as she felt tears start to prick her eyes. It was always the same when she saw her dad as she wanted him home and for everyone to be happy. Her hand found the application for the Woolworths position, still there from her visit to the store. She pulled it out and waved it at her dad. 'I have dreams, but I know I can't follow them,' she sniffed as she watched him read the form. 'Family has to come first.'

Paddy frowned as he scanned the application form. 'It doesn't say what the job is. What are you going after?'

'Going after? I thought it was to be a counter assistant and wear a burgundy-coloured uniform,' she replied, thinking how it would suit her hair colouring.

'They could be advertising for cleaners, or stockroom staff,' he suggested, watching her reaction.

'Everyone's got to start somewhere, and it will be my goal to get behind a counter even if it isn't something glamorous.'

Paddy guffawed in evident surprise. 'I've never thought Woolworths was glamorous work. If you want glamour, come and work here at the fair. There'll be plenty of lads hanging around the stalls, even if you're on the roll a penny, or fishing for ducks,' he continued.

Annie blushed. Fancy her dad encouraging her to chase after the lads. 'There's plenty of time for courting when I'm older. I want to have a job and earn my own money – and before I get called to do war work in a factory. There's rumours of it happening.'

'Don't listen to gossip. It's probably the Germans trying to frighten us.'

'I'm not so sure about that, but don't think I'm against war work. It's just that first I want to taste life and see the world,' she sighed.

'Bexleyheath Woolworths is not seeing the world,' he said, taking her hand and giving it a squeeze. He realized Annie was serious and now wasn't the time to jest. 'Why don't I help you fill out this form and we can wait and see what happens?'

'Thanks, Dad. You wouldn't come home with me while I tell Mum what I intend to do?'

Paddy raised his hands in shock. 'That's a step too far, but if she kicks you out, I'll find you a berth here,' he said before taking a pencil from his pocket and licking the stub end. 'Now, get writing while I find us a mug of tea.'

'Cheers, Dad,' she called after him before straightening the single piece of paper flat on the van's warm bonnet, running her fingers over the creases. There were questions about her previous employment, which were easy as she'd only ever worked for the family laundry, and she spelt that out with care. Her education came next and details about her numeracy and spelling. Annie felt confident she was adept at these skills and sped through the other questions quickly so that by the time Paddy appeared with two large white china mugs of steaming tea she'd completed her task and was folding the page into a neat square.

'How's it going?' he asked, putting her mug down on the grass beside her.

'That part was easy, but I need to post it to the personnel manager and hope I'm called for an interview. I'll send it first thing tomorrow,' she said. Already feeling like she'd accomplished something, she reached for her tea and took a sip. 'Crikey, how much sugar is in this? Don't they know about rationing?' she spluttered.

Paddy gave a wink. 'Not if you know the right people.'

'Oh, Dad, you've got to be careful. It might have been all right to do the odd dodgy deal before the war, but not any more. Promise me you'll behave.'

'Who's the parent around here?' he laughed at her stern face.

'It's not a joke, you have to be careful,' she hissed, looking around to see if anyone was watching. All around the fair was taking shape, although due to the blackout they couldn't light up the amusements, which as a rule were linked to the mighty steam engine, named Goliath, which generated power for the lighting and rides, along with the fairground organ which entertained the crowds. At that moment the organ struck up a familiar melody. Annie stopped berating her dad to listen to Tchaikovsky's 'Waltz of the Flowers'; it had always been her favourite of the many regular tunes and as a child she had been allowed to help feed the perforated paper roll through the organ that produced each one. 'Is there something wrong as it doesn't sound as loud?' she asked.

'It's to do with the blackout. We've been issued with a list of regulations and must comply, or we could be shut down. Already some of the smaller travelling fairs have closed for the duration due to staff being called up, and it's going to get even harder.'

Annie felt like saying he should come home to the family if there wouldn't be so many travelling fairs but bit her tongue. 'In what way?'

'We must keep the noise down, so air-raid warnings are heard. We've sorted out a system where we have several people on the outskirts of the fairground listening out for the sirens and they ring handbells to alert stallholders and people running the rides who then direct the public to shelters. Oh, and we've closed the coconut shies as we can't get the coconuts any more and the punters don't want to win wooden coconuts.'

Annie was surprised. 'Gosh, I had no idea.'

'Then we need to close earlier to observe the blackout regulations, that's if we have somewhere to set up the fair. So many parks and open areas are already being turned over to growing vegetables.'

'Mum's trying to expand our veggie patch, but there's never enough hours in the day to get it done.'

'Let her know I'll be down next weekend to dig it over for her, but don't tell your Uncle Pete or you won't see him for dust. I've never known such a work-shy bugger,' he muttered, causing Annie to giggle at his words. Never had truer words been said.

'I'd best be on my way. Mum will be getting worried,' she sighed.

'Hang on a minute, you can make use of this,' he said, pulling a crumpled envelope from his pocket. 'Now you can deliver your application to the Woolworths store on your way home.'

Annie took the envelope and did her best to straighten it out before placing her application inside. 'Thanks,' she said as excitement gripped her. This could be the start of her new life, as long as her mum agreed.

4

Three days later, Annie was washing down the van when she spotted the postman cycling down the long dirt track road that led to their cottage. She'd wiped the paintwork with an old rag and was polishing the windscreen before he arrived, perspiring heavily. He climbed from his bike and mopped his brow with a large white handkerchief.

Calling out to her brother, Albie, to fetch the postman a cool drink, she walked over to greet him. 'It's good of you to deliver our post, but I could have collected it from the post office on Monday morning when I go into Erith.'

He downed the enamel mug of freshly drawn cold water before answering. 'My, that hit the spot. Thank you, young Albie,' he said as he reached into the canvas bag sitting in a basket at the front of his bike. 'I was over this way, and as these looked official, I thought as how you'd like them sooner rather than later.' He handed over three envelopes after looking at the names on each one. 'I take it this is still Paddy's abode?' he asked, raising his eyebrows. 'And this is for your uncle . . .'

'Dad will be here later today, I'll give this to him then,' she said with a bright smile. Her mum didn't like nosy people poking into their business and the postman, as pleasant as he was, was prone to sharing tidbits of gossip as he went about his round. She pushed the envelopes into the pocket of the brown overall she was wearing and picked up her cleaning materials. 'No peace for the wicked,' she said, hoping he would be on his way for the third envelope bore the emblem of F. W. Woolworths and Co. Ltd and she prayed it was good news.

He was soon cycling away after refusing another drink from Albie.

'Who are the letters for?' Albie asked.

'None of your business and don't go saying anything to Mum, you know how she worries about bad news.'

He cuffed his nose and shrugged his shoulders. 'No one tells me anything,' he huffed before going back to the stable to finish his chores.

Annie looked up as another vehicle came down the lane at such a speed that a cloud of dust and gravel made it indistinguishable until the driver honked the horn.

'It's Dad,' Albie shouted as he raced down the lane to meet the oncoming truck.

'Be careful, we don't want you knocked down and ending up in the cottage hospital,' she shouted after him.

As Paddy slowed down for his son to jump onto the running board Violet came out from the kitchen wiping her hands on a tea towel. 'I had a feeling you'd turn up today, so I'm making a larger steak and kidney pudding,' she said, having known full well he was coming as Annie had mentioned he'd be there to help with their vegetable plot.

Paddy rubbed his hands together. 'That'll do me nicely. I'll start on the garden now and perhaps Annie and Albie can join me when they've completed their chores. I take it the gardening equipment is still in the shed?' he asked, looking towards his son.

'Yes, Dad, and I've cleaned everything off like you taught me. I'll just finish off in the stable then I'll be with you,' he called over his shoulder as he raced back to his work.

'I'm finished here so I'll come with you now,' Annie said, wanting to show her dad his letter and read her own before Albie arrived and started asking questions.

They crossed the lane and pushed through a small gap in the hawthorn hedging. Before them was a roughly dug plot and a wooden shed that tilted to one side.

Paddy stood rubbing the red whiskers on his chin as he surveyed the plot. 'I should have come back before now; the shed is about to collapse, and no one has done much work here,' he said, kicking the sun-dried earth with his steel-toed work boots. He'd noticed Annie grimace at his mention of not being by for a while and averted his eye; he knew she was right, but the lure of the fairground was hard to fight. It was best to get stuck in straight away. Tugging at the padlock, it fell apart in his hand. 'I'll get a better lock than this once I've patched up the shed and given it a lick of paint,' he said before pulling open the door and passing out two forks and a spade to Annie. 'Your brother's made a good job of looking after the tools,' he continued, admiring the shining equipment.

Annie shoved one of the forks into the dry ground, showing her anger at her dad's words. 'Albie thinks the world of you, and he misses you. Can't you see that by doing things that would please you, he's hoping you'll appreciate him and want to see him?' she exclaimed before sinking to her knees and sobbing as the fork clattered to the ground beside her. 'Don't you realize we want you home with us, not just to keep you safe, but to have you care for us in these scary times? Mum will never say anything, but she misses you so much. Why don't you understand what you're doing to this family?'

Paddy went over to Annie and helped her to her feet before enfolding her in his strong arms and whispering soft words in her hair until she calmed down. 'I don't deserve any of you. I've been a waster and a wanderer all my life and that's not going to change any time soon. You may even see less of me than you do now,' he added as an afterthought.

Annie wiped her eyes on the sleeve of her overall and reached into the pocket. 'Would this letter have anything to do with you leaving us?' she asked as she handed him the envelope. Across the top was the name of a Kent regiment, just the same as the letter for her uncle.

She couldn't hate him any more than she did at present, even if she tried, she thought, as she watched him sit on an upturned box and rip open the envelope. She was about to ask what the letter was about when she saw his face crumple as he bowed his head into his hands; the letter fell onto the bare earth at his feet. Was he crying? she wondered as she stepped closer and heard a stifled angry growl of anguish. Perhaps he had been called up to serve his country, even though he was beyond the age group, she thought to herself. That'll curb your wanderlust, she almost blurted out loud as she bent to pick up the letter. His hand reached out and snatched it back.

'That's private.' He tucked it away in his jacket pocket.

'Let's get on with our work.' He kept his back to her as he started to dig the plot, putting his weight behind the fork each time he plunged it into the hard ground. She watched him for a few minutes. Something wasn't right. Her anger started to dissipate as she wondered about the contents of his letter. He'd often spoken of his time fighting in the closing year of the last war and she'd thought he'd enjoyed that even though he'd been injured. Why then was he upset at being called up again?

She tugged on his sleeve to gain his attention. 'Dad, speak to me. Why are you so upset?'

He threw down the fork and passed her the letter. 'They don't want me . . .'

Puzzled, Annie read the few lines. 'You mean, you applied to join up?'

He nodded his head. 'I thought I could make a difference and help bring the war to a close so my kids could sleep safe in their beds.'

'Oh, Dad.' She hugged him close, burying her head in his chest. 'That was a brave thing to do considering your injury. Perhaps you can do as much at home? You have a lot to give . . .'

'You mean march about with those old fools pretending to defend our shores with pitchforks and broom handles?' he scoffed.

'They would listen to you; you could teach them so much. After all, you were in the trenches in the last war, and you survived.'

'I'm damaged goods,' he said, reaching to touch an ugly scar on his stomach where he'd tackled an enemy soldier who was wielding a bayonet.

'Think about it, please . . .' she begged.

'I'll think about it, if only for you.' He smiled, holding her by the shoulders and looking into her sad eyes.

'Do it for Mum too,' she said, standing on tiptoe to kiss his cheek. As she did so, the other two envelopes rustled in her pocket. She pulled them out. 'I wonder if Uncle Pete has been rejected as well?' She showed Paddy the envelope which made a smile cross his face and she gave a sigh of relief.

'Make sure I'm here when you give him the letter,' he laughed. 'I don't think for one minute he's been rejected; he is the right age to be called up, although he likes to pretend he's got dodgy lungs. This will give the skiver the shock of his life.'

Annie had to agree that her Uncle Pete wouldn't be happy, but then a thought crossed her mind. 'Not that he's a great help, but it will mean one less person to lend a hand in the laundry.' She started to open her own letter, not sure if she would be disappointed if she hadn't been called for an interview, or relieved as her mum would need her help more than ever.

Noticing the Woolworths logo on the envelope, Paddy watched Annie's face. 'They must be keen to get back this quickly.'

'Or they've dismissed my application as soon as they looked at what I'd written.'

'We won't know unless you read it,' he replied impatiently.

She passed it to Paddy. 'I can't read it. You'll have to tell me what they've said.' She turned away and closed her eyes.

Her thoughts were so mixed she couldn't think straight. She could hear Paddy take a deep breath before clearing his throat.

'They want you to attend an interview on Tuesday at three in the afternoon. I reckon they'll take you on, my girl,' he grinned.

Annie was suddenly full of doubt. 'How can I leave Mum in the lurch, especially if Uncle Pete is to be called up? She'll be so angry. No, I'll tell them I've changed my mind. I was a fool to think I could follow my dream of doing something with my life.'

Paddy took her hand. 'Take a few deep breaths, calm yourself down and listen to me.'

Annie did as she was told as he led her to where they could sit down on a patch of grass. She drew in several deep breaths before giving him a weak smile. 'I'm listening. What have you got to tell me?'

'I know I've been a selfish man. Going off and working with the fair isn't what sensible fathers do, just as believing I could sign up to fight the Germans wasn't realistic either. The time has come when I must knuckle down and take on responsibility for my family. You will go for this interview, and if you're offered a job, you will accept it. Don't worry about the business, or your mum, let me do the worrying. It's time for you to spread your wings and fly. Promise me you'll attend the interview and I promise you I will play my part in our family.'

Annie knew Paddy was giving up a lot to do this for her. Never for one moment did she think he'd do such a thing and she was grateful for his sacrifice. He would find it hard to tie himself down to working in the family business alongside her mum and living in one place rather than travelling with the fair.

She flung her arms around him. 'I promise I'll do my best and make you proud of me, Dad.'

He hugged her tightly. 'I've always been proud of you, my love.'

5

Annie had never felt so nervous. Thankfully she'd been shown to a row of seats in an upstairs corridor to wait to be called by the personnel supervisor as her legs felt like jelly and she was sure she'd have crumpled to the floor. There was one other young woman sitting a few seats away who seemed to be calm and poised as she sat with a smart handbag on her lap. Annie grinned when the girl looked her way and was rewarded with a smile. 'I'm Annie Brookes,' she ventured.

'Emily Davenport,' the girl replied. 'Have you worked for Woolworths before?'

'No. In fact, it would be my first proper job,' she answered as she moved to sit next to her and shook her hand at the same time, thinking they must be about the same age. 'My family have a laundry business and I've worked for them for as long as I can remember. Now I'm ready to spread my wings,' she added, thinking of her dad's words as he dropped her off in front of the store in Bexleyheath before setting off to do the deliveries. He'd been as good as his word since his promise to show more interest in the business and had already started to help out.

Emily looked interested. 'My mother is against me working as she thinks I'll meet some ne'er-do-well who will lead me astray rather than up the aisle,' she giggled. 'I pray I get this position just to prove her wrong. She only agreed to me applying when I mentioned I could be called up to work as a Land Girl or go into a factory to work in munitions.'

Annie laughed, thinking how alike they were with their arguments with their parents, even though Emily spoke with no trace of a local accent. A question crossed her mind. 'Do you know how many vacancies there are? I'd hate to think we were both after the same job.'

'The sign I spotted in the shop window made it appear they were looking for a few staff members,' Emily said. 'Gosh, it would be awful to think they would choose only one of us.'

'Perhaps we will both fail,' Annie said. She thought how friendly the dark-haired girl was; it would be nice to work alongside her as she'd worried about not knowing anyone.

'I'd not considered that,' Emily said seriously before they started to giggle at the thought of them both being unsuitable as Woolworths girls.

It was at that point the door to the office opened and a middle-aged woman looked out. 'Oh good, you are both here. Would you like to come in together as you seem to know each other?'

Annie opened her mouth to explain, until Emily nudged her to stay quiet. It would be less worrying to be interviewed alongside this affable girl. She followed Emily, thinking how smart the girl looked in a navy-blue two-piece suit and matching felt hat. Annie felt uncomfortably shabby in a floral frock and a jacket she'd borrowed from her mum. It was clean and tidy, but she still felt like the poor cousin beside Emily. If the personnel supervisor was going to choose her staff based on how they looked, then she may as well turn round and go home right now. With her thoughts all over the place they were ushered into a large office that held two desks along with a row of old wooden seats and filing cupboards against every wall. She thought how a lot of work must take place in this room. A file on the desk labelled *applicants* caught her eye; were there many people after these jobs? she wondered.

'Now, ladies, I am Mrs Armitage, the personnel supervisor for the Bexleyheath store. I am looking for extra counter staff and if you get through this interview and pass the arithmetic test, then you will soon be wearing the overall of a counter assistant.' She nodded to where a smart burgundy uniform was hanging behind the closed door.

Annie felt a thrill of excitement run through her as Mrs Armitage explained about the shifts and what was expected of them.

'Do you have any questions?' she asked, looking between the two girls. Emily raised her hand.

'I wondered when we'll know which counters we will work on?'

'We have a little way to go before I make that decision,' Mrs Armitage smiled. 'Let's have you complete the arithmetic test first and then I'll have a little chat with each of you alone. Now, Annie, will you sit at the other desk and take this with you?' She passed her a pencil and a sheet of paper. 'Emily, you can sit at the end of my desk while I get on with some paperwork. You have half an hour. Please don't worry,' she added, noticing Annie chew the edge of her lip. 'The arithmetic is straightforward and remember, I wouldn't have invited you for an interview if I hadn't seen potential in your application form.'

Much relieved, Annie went over to the other desk and read through the paper and checked the time on the large clock on the wall. She nodded to herself as she answered the first question, which asked how much change she should give a customer if they'd spent four shillings and thruppence and handed over a ten-shilling note. Annie found herself counting on her fingers until she was sure of the answer, which was five shillings and ninepence. Breathing a sigh of relief, she moved on to the next question, which required her to add up four sums of money. Knowing she would have to do this as part of her job working on a counter and having just a small notepad and pencil at her disposal, she took time to add up the money until she was confident she was right. The next question was how many half-crowns were there in ten shillings, followed by another adding-up question. By the time she had finished, there were five minutes left. She used the time to double-check her answers and was happy with her work when Mrs Armitage informed the girls their time was up.

'I will take you through to our staff canteen and fetch you each a cup of tea while I mark your papers,' she said, ushering them out of the room and leading them down the corridor to a large room where staff members were enjoying their afternoon break. A few of the women gave them sympathetic looks as they passed by on their way to a small table for two close to the counter where two women were serving.

'Marge, would you send over two teas, please?' Mrs Armitage called to the older of the women. 'I'll come back for you shortly,' she said to Annie and Emily before returning to her office.

'This is pleasant,' Emily said as she gazed around at the rows of tables and chattering staff. The room was very light as the windows along one side were tall and wide. 'It would be so nice to work here. I hope I did enough to pass the test; I'm not that great at adding up.'

'I'm sure you did all right. You don't seem the sort of person to get flustered. Being calm and collected helps a lot in these circumstances.'

'It sounds as though you talk from experience,' Emily said as she thanked the woman who brought over their tea.

Annie thought of the times she'd had to deliver to grumpy customers who complained deliveries were late, while checking the money they handed over was correct, or if they needed change to settle their bills. 'I've had to think on my feet a few times when we've had unpleasant customers. It's something I would think we'll have to do here as well.'

'Gosh, I never gave a thought to unpleasant customers. Everyone always looks so happy when I pop in to purchase things; I'm not sure I could cope with one of those. Perhaps I should tell Mrs Armitage I'm not cut out to be a sales assistant?'

Annie was about to advise Emily not to be so silly and that she would make a very good sales assistant when Marge came over carrying a plate.

'Why the glum faces?' she asked as she sat down and placed the plate in front of them. 'Anyone would think you didn't want to work for this wonderful company. These will cheer you up.' She pushed the plate forward. 'I made a batch of rock cakes earlier; it's not often I have all the ingredients, but a supplier came by with some extras, so I decided to treat the staff.'

Annie's mouth watered as she looked at the cakes. She'd missed her midday meal as she was too nervous to eat and now her stomach was starting to grumble. 'This is so generous of you when we don't even work here.' She smiled as she took one of the cakes and bit into it. 'This is delicious.'

'There's more where that came from once you work here; we like to look after our staff.' The older woman winked. 'Now, tell me why you both look unhappy?'

'I was worried about unpleasant customers. I'm not sure I could cope with someone who isn't very nice. I thought perhaps I wasn't cut out for the job,' Emily explained before taking a bite from her cake.

'It'll just be your nerves playing up. Why, when I worked on the counters, we never really had a nasty customer, but that is where the supervisors and floor walkers come in handy. They're there to keep an eye on things and would quickly come to your rescue. Now, stop your worrying and eat up before Mrs Armitage comes back. You'll have plenty of training before they let you loose on your own downstairs,' she chuckled, going back to her duties.

'She's nice,' Emily said as she licked her fingers and picked a few crumbs from the front of her jacket.

'It just shows how a few words from the right person can put our minds at ease,' Annie said.

They'd just finished their tea when Mrs Armitage

appeared. 'I was going to interview you separately, but as you have both passed the arithmetic test with flying colours, I've decided to speak to you together. Come, let's go back to my office and I will explain what happens next. I'll also sort out your uniforms and give you a contract and starting date.'

As the girls followed Mrs Armitage from the staff canteen, they spotted Marge giving them the thumbs up. Annie gave a discreet wave back and mouthed 'thank you'.

'Did everything go well?' Paddy asked as he opened the door of the van for Annie to climb aboard.

'More than well. Your daughter is officially a member of the Bexleyheath branch of Woolworths! I start work next week.'

'If that smile on your face is anything to go by, you must have made a good impression,' he observed as he pulled out onto the busy road and headed the van back the couple of miles to Erith.

'How was your afternoon?' Despite her joy of succeeding in her interview, she couldn't help worrying that her dad had not enjoyed delivering the laundry and collecting fresh orders.

Paddy grimaced. 'I won't lie as I'd much prefer to be lifting gallopers and assembling the swinging boats, but needs must.' Seeing Annie's disappointed face, he quickly added, 'I found us another customer today and dropped off more of those leaflets. We're going to do just fine; you aren't to worry. Your mum will come round in the end if we both show her our plans will work. Now, tell me about your interview; did you meet any of the counter staff?'

Annie spent the rest of the journey talking about Emily and how they both passed the arithmetic test. Mrs Armitage was going to place them both on the haberdashery counter once they'd learnt about the stock and how to work with the ration cards. 'There's so much to learn; you'd have enjoyed completing the test as it was about adding up money and giving the right change.'

Paddy laughed as he drove the van down the long lane on the marshes. 'All my learning has been from the fairground and when I was a bookies' runner. We have to be quick, or the punters think we're diddling them.'

Annie shook her head. She was never surprised by what her dad told her. He was a good man, but the stories he came out with took her breath away at times. She wasn't surprised her mum was so exasperated by him, but she knew there was love between the couple regardless of his wanderlust. She just prayed he'd not get itchy feet and want to be on the move after a couple of months.

'Here we are,' he said as they pulled up in the yard at the front of the house. 'You go in and tell your mum your news while I take this lot into the laundry.'

Annie, who was climbing out of the van, froze. 'No, I'll help you first and we can go indoors together.'

'Not on yer nelly. It's your news to tell, and you should be proud you passed. Get yourself indoors. I'll only be a few minutes.'

'All right, but please don't dawdle or stop for a fag,' she begged. Her mum was a good and fair woman when things went her way, but she didn't believe Paddy's promises of staying around to help so Annie could take a job at Woolworths. As she walked up the short path towards the kitchen past her mum's carefully tended flower bed, she heard raised voices through the open window.

'You'll stay here and do your duty,' her mother shouted. 'No member of my family deserts their country.'

Annie flinched as she recognized who Violet was talking to.

'It's nothing to do with you what I get up to so you can mind your own business. If anyone comes asking questions, you'll say you've not seen me for a while,' her Uncle Pete snarled back.

'Look here, son . . .'

'Dad, keep out of it. Go and tend to Mum, I can hear her crying. I'll send you a postcard when I find somewhere to stay.'

'Don't take another step or you'll never be welcome in this house again,' Violet called out.

'Cheers, sis,' he shouted back. 'I'll not stop where I'm not welcome.'

Annie hurried towards the door. She had to do something before her family fell apart. It was too late as her uncle came barging out. 'Uncle Pete, where are you going?'

'Best you don't know, kid,' he said, kissing her cheek while pulling a rucksack onto his back and hurrying towards his motorbike.

She watched as he fired up the bike and disappeared up the lane, leaving a cloud of dust behind him.

'I had a feeling this would happen,' Paddy said as he appeared behind her and put a hand on her shoulder.

'What do you mean?' she asked, feeling herself shivering despite the warm day.

'It was that letter that arrived the other day. They were his call-up papers.'

Annie turned to face him. 'You mean . . .'

'I mean your uncle is a coward and is running away from fighting for his country,' he said with bitterness in his voice. 'What I wouldn't do to be fighting in his place. I'd swap places with him in a second.'

6

The family sat around the scrubbed pine kitchen table looking glum. Annie had poured more tea from a large Brown Betty teapot; it was the third round since her Uncle Pete had stormed out and her mother had fallen into a chair crying into her faded wraparound apron.

'We are a law-abiding family,' she cried, ignoring Paddy's broad smile. 'What if the police come here looking to arrest Pete? What will people think? This could affect our business, for God's sake. I always thought he was a wrong'un, but to run away from fighting for his country . . .'

Violet's mother, Ivy, walked stiffly to where her daughter sat. 'I'm to blame. I shouldn't have been so soft with him when he was a youngster,' she sniffed. She was a small woman dressed from head to toe in black, and Annie always thought her nan resembled the late Queen Victoria.

'Aw, Nan, you can't go saying that. I doubt you and Grandad are to blame.'

'There's often one bad apple in the box,' Paddy said as he patted his mother-in-law's shoulder, receiving a glare in return.

'You can keep your trap shut, Paddy Brookes,' Ivy snarled. 'Our family are respectable, not like you travelling types.'

Annie was quick to defend Paddy. 'Dad comes from a respectable showman's family that goes back generations,' she started to argue until Paddy hushed her from saying more. 'I'll make some more tea,' she said, moving to the sink to fill the kettle so no one could see her tears.

'By rights we should be living with the fair with our dad,' her brother chipped in, before a look from Violet shut him up. 'I'll go and see to Old Ned,' he said, knowing when he'd put his foot in it.

'Annie, tell us about your day,' her nan said as she turned away from her son-in-law. 'Did they offer you the job at Woolworths?'

'They did,' she replied, knowing she would be unlikely to accept the offer of work now that the family didn't have Uncle Pete around to help out; she'd been counting on him to take on some of the work, even though he was unreliable. Better an unreliable pair of hands than none at all, she'd thought. Aiming to change the subject, she described to her nan what it was like in the staff canteen and how well they looked after the workers with the delicious food. 'I heard they had liver and onions for lunch with mashed potato.'

Her nan licked her lips. Even in her advancing years she enjoyed her food and ate heartily. 'Do you think they'd take on an old maid like me?' she chuckled, lightening the heavy atmosphere in the kitchen as Annie pulled her leg about wearing a staff uniform and not being able to answer back to the customers.

So it was that her family were still sitting around the

table some two hours later. They were none the wiser about what to do about Violet's miscreant brother when there was a knock on the door.

Violet jumped up, causing her chair to scrape backwards across the floor. 'It'll be the police come to find Pete,' she said fearfully.

'I doubt it,' Paddy said as he took her arm, encouraging her to sit down. 'I'll go. You all relax and stop looking so worried.'

Annie quickly scanned the room to see if there was anything on show that shouldn't be there. Her mum would say they were law-abiding people, but with Paddy bringing home extra rations from God knows where, it was likely a policeman would notice. She quickly put the bowl of sugar in the pantry out of view and sat back down, trying to ease her fast-beating heart. Why was Paddy taking so long at the door? Going by the faces of the rest of her family, they were all wondering the same. The tension in the room was palpable as they heard footsteps approaching.

Paddy entered first. 'This is Pete's lady friend,' he said as he held the door open for a young woman to enter.

'I'm sorry to bother you all when you're having your tea,' she said, looking fearful. 'Pete was supposed to meet me and it's unlike him to be late. I was worried something had happened to him, what with there being so many raids these past days.'

Annie had no idea her Uncle Pete was walking out with a young lady, and young she certainly was as she couldn't be much older than herself. She had a heart-shaped face and generous waves of dark hair fell about her shoulders.

'Hello, I'm Annie, Uncle Pete's niece,' she said before introducing her to the rest of the family.

'My name is Ruth,' the newcomer replied, not volunteering a surname.

'How long have you been courting my son?' Grandad asked, giving her a gentle smile. The poor girl was terrified.

'Well, he came into the pub where I work early in the year and we hit it off at once; he can be so funny,' she said, her eyes shining as she thought of him. 'Mr Brookes said he wasn't home. When are you expecting him?' she asked, looking around at the faces watching her.

'Your guess is as good as ours,' Violet sniffed.

'So he isn't here? But I thought . . .' Ruth grabbed the back of an empty chair and swayed a little as her breath quickened. 'I . . . I . . .' was all she could say as she collapsed. She would have hit the stone floor if Paddy hadn't caught her and assisted her to an armchair by the hearth.

'Steady there, girl,' he said as Annie hurried to his side to help loosen her coat and flap her hands in front of the girl's red face. Violet passed her a cup of cool water, which Annie held to Ruth's lips.

'Sip it slowly or you'll be sick,' Annie said as Ruth grabbed at the cup. 'You must have overheated walking down the lane. I take it you walked in to Slades Green?'

Ruth nodded. 'I couldn't understand why Pete hadn't come to meet me; we had important things to discuss.' A blush covered her already hot face.

Nan, who was watching closely with a frown, spoke. 'I take it you are with child?'

Ruth put her hands protectively over her stomach. 'Yes, and he knows I'm having his baby. That's why I need to speak to him as soon as possible. We were going to rent rooms and get married, and I needed the money from him to put down a deposit.'

Violet looked to where her husband and father were shifting uncomfortably in their seats. 'You men get about your chores. This talk is for women,' she snapped, shooing them from the room. 'Annie, make this girl a hot drink while I fry her an egg. She looks all in.'

'I'll sort out the food and drink,' Nan said. 'You two sit and chat with her before she nods off. I could wring that son of mine's neck,' she muttered as she got cracking with the frying pan while the kettle was refilled and set on the hob.

'Let me take your coat,' Annie offered as Ruth shrugged it off her shoulders. 'Why you are shivering?' she said. 'Do you feel cold?'

'No, it took a lot out of me just to come to find Pete. He'd been avoiding me for days until I put my foot down and said we had to talk,' she said as an air of misery enveloped her.

Violet looked at Annie and raised her eyebrows as she reached for a woollen shawl she kept over the back of a chair and draped it around the girl's shoulders. 'That'll soon warm you up.'

Ruth stroked the green crocheted shawl. 'It's so soft. Did you make it?'

'I did, a while ago now when Annie was a baby, and I had a lot of time on my hands between feeds.'

'She means when her Paddy sodded off and left her to bring up Annie on her own.'

'Nan, please,' Annie begged, hoping she'd not make a

scene in front of a stranger. 'Ruth doesn't want to hear about all our family's woes. Besides, Dad is home now, and we are all one happy family,' she said without thinking.

'Apart from our Pete,' her nan sniffed. 'Gawd knows when we'll see him again.'

'So, he's already gone to join the army?' Ruth asked. 'I'd have thought he'd have come to see me before he left, but I suppose the army's need is greater than mine. I just wish . . .' A small sob caught in her throat. 'I just wish we could have been settled before he left as . . . as I don't know what I'm going to do . . .'

Annie knelt beside the girl and hugged her close, allowing her time to stop crying. 'Do you not have any family you can stay with?'

Ruth sniffed and tried to compose herself. 'I'm an orphan. I lost my family in the last war when I was only little; I can't remember them. That's why, when I met Pete, I knew he was the one for me. He was so loving and really cared. He promised me the moon and the stars . . . Now the army has taken him from me.'

Nan put a mug of tea in her hands before she started weeping again. 'Get that down you and pull yourself together. We've got something to tell you.'

Ruth looked between the three women as the penny dropped. 'He's legged it, hasn't he? I was warned he'd leave me in the lurch, but I scoffed at the idea. I'm right, aren't I?'

Nan nodded her head in agreement. 'It pains me to say so, but my son's a bad lot. You look like a nice girl; it's best you forget about him and move on to a better life.'

'I agree,' Violet said. 'Bad luck follows my brother like a bad smell. You're young enough to make a fresh start.'

Ruth shook her head. 'I can't move on. I don't have a penny to my name and the baby is his. I'm not someone who chases the lads. Pete was my first, if you get my drift.'

It was Annie's turn to blush as she realized what Ruth was intimating. 'We can't let Ruth leave, she's part of the family now she's carrying Uncle Pete's baby. That's my cousin in there,' she said, nodding towards Ruth's stomach. 'And it's your grandchild.' She turned to her nan. 'We must do something. Why, Uncle Pete may well come back, and he'd thank us for taking care of Ruth and his child.'

'She can stay with us until Pete returns, then he can make an honest woman of her,' Violet said.

'I'd not hold your breath,' Nan added as she put a plate of eggs and fried bread in front of the girl. 'We won't see him this side of the end of the war. He'll know where to hide away.'

Ruth was aghast. 'You mean he won't fight for King and country? Not at all?' she gasped as she lifted her knife and fork.

'The letter came last week,' Annie explained. 'It was the same day I heard from Woolworths and Dad heard from his old regiment.'

'What's this all about?' Violet asked furiously. 'He's too old and still suffering from the last war to join up. Or is he going to leg it as well?'

Annie looked towards the kitchen door hoping Paddy didn't appear as she felt she'd spoken out of turn, and he'd not be happy about it. 'You aren't to say anything. He applied to rejoin his regiment, but they turned him down. He's very upset about it as he thought he could play his part in this war.'

Violet shook her head. 'The bloody fool! Why do men want to be so full of themselves and then get killed or injured so they are no use to their families? With Pete gone, if Paddy had left, where would we be?'

Annie was wide-eyed with shock as her nan swore out loud and continued. 'Paddy's gone up in my estimation, not like that lazy son of mine. Mark my words, we'll have the coppers on our doorstep in a few days looking for him.'

Ruth looked down at her plate, which she'd almost cleared. 'I'm sorry, I had no idea he was like that. He was always warm and charming to me. I'll finish this and be gone.'

'Not so quick,' Ivy said. 'None of this is your fault and I won't be done out of another grandchild. Better you are under our roof and cared for than God knows where. We will find you a bed and when you're strong enough you can give us a hand around the house and in the laundry until the baby's due.'

Violet raised her eyebrows at her mother's words then nodded her head as she thought of what she'd said. 'Mum's right, you're as good as family and as long as you are honest and hardworking, you're welcome here.'

Ruth glowed with pleasure. 'I'll be no trouble to you, I promise. I'm as honest as the day is long. The vicar at St Augustine's will vouch for me. He'll be pleased I'm no longer working as a barmaid down at The Crown.'

'Where do you live?' Annie asked, fascinated that a girl who couldn't be much older than she had been making her own way in the world, even though she had no choice.

'I have a very small room at the pub. The landlord's family are nice enough, the only problem being I'm at their beck and call all hours of the day. Not that I don't like hard work,' she added quickly.

Annie gave her a smile to calm the girl's jitters. 'If you've finished, I'll give you a tour of the house and the laundry. I take it we can give Ruth Uncle Pete's room now he has no need of it?'

'That's a good idea. I'll call Paddy and your grandad in. They can clear it out and then we can make the bed with fresh linen. You'll not want to go in there until the room's been given a good airing; with the windows open that won't take long,' she said. 'It looks as though you have a new home in which to bring up our latest family member. If you behave, you're welcome here,' she called after Ruth as she followed Annie from the kitchen.

'Mum's not as hard as she appears. She's just had a gutful what with my dad, and also Uncle Pete, coming and going as they please, but Dad's back now and has promised he'll stay,' Annie explained.

'That's a strange set-up,' Ruth said, 'but no different to my Pete now he's upped and left. Do you think he'll get in trouble?'

'They've got to find him first. As long as we all stick to the same story and say we thought he'd gone to join his regiment, then we've done everything we can. We'd best discuss it when we're all together in case the police arrive.'

Ruth looked worried. 'We won't have to lie to them, will we?'

'Goodness, no. We can just say as far as we're concerned, he received a letter about being called up and left this afternoon. Granted, he argued with Mum, but I really didn't hear what it was about.'

'Oh, I see,' Ruth replied with a grin. 'Best not to know.'

'You're catching on quick. Come on, I'll show you the laundry. I'll miss not working here every day, but I'm excited to be joining Woolworths,' she said as she breathed in the clean smell of boiled sheets and fresh air from the gaps between the corrugated sheets of iron. Annie felt a weight had lifted off her shoulders with Ruth's arrival, knowing that the extra pair of hands meant she could now accept her job offer. 'I'll warn you now, it can be freezing out here in the winter and stifling in the summer.'

Ruth peered into the empty coppers. 'Everything is so clean, even though . . .' She came to a halt.

'Even though it's an old iron shed in our yard that's seen better days? Don't worry, me and Mum feel the same. We were hoping to have a better work shed built but then the war came along and something else needed to be built – and quicker,' she said, swinging open a back door of the building to show off the almost completed Anderson shelter. 'It's a good idea to know where the shelter is, but if you are at the front of the house, it would be better to head into our cellar; there's an entrance under the bay window and you can also access it from the cupboard under the stairs. I much prefer the cellar to the Anderson shelter, but beggars can't be choosers when the sirens start to wail. Come, we've got time for me to show you the outside entrance to the cellar, then we can go over to our vegetable patch.'

Ruth trotted dutifully behind Annie as they headed to the front of the property and she exclaimed at the size of the grounds. 'Pete never told me anything about his home.'

Annie refrained from saying her uncle didn't take much

interest and led his own life away from here. 'Nan's family have owned this for generations. It's a bit run-down, but I love living out here on the marshes.'

'There's so much sky,' Ruth exclaimed before pointing towards the river. 'What are those black specks?' she asked as the air-raid sirens started to scream for them to take cover.

7

October 1940

Annie stood to attention as the personnel manageress looked over the new intake. Apart from her and Emily there were three other women starting that day. She was pleased when Mrs Armitage, whose appearance was immaculate, nodded her approval at how clean and tidy Annie looked after an older woman, Nora, was told to go to the female lavatories and scrub her dirty nails until they were clean. She noticed Emily gave a sigh of relief as well.

'I needn't have bothered,' Nora huffed as she returned to the supervisor's office to be informed that she was working on the fresh vegetable counter. 'I came here to get away from greengrocery work, not to have to sell spuds for Woolies.'

'My thoughts in placing you on the greengrocery counter were that you could bring all your expertise to the store. At the moment we only have younger staff, so you would soon be in a supervisory position,' Mrs Armitage placated her.

'As long as I'm paid more,' the woman sniffed as she

looked down her nose at her fellow new employees, who were considerably younger.

'We do have a pay scale; we can talk about that when you've served your probationary period. Now, let me go over how we work with ration books and then I'll take you down to your workstations.'

Nora sniffed. 'It'll be a pittance. Only men do well in business.' She looked up to the clock on the office wall. 'It'll be time for our tea break soon,' she informed the others.

'She's a barrel of laughs,' Annie whispered to Emily before blushing when she realized Mrs Armitage had overheard her and rewarded her with a gentle smile.

'Perhaps, if we get cracking, we can have that tea break before you all go downstairs to start work,' she said, causing Nora to give a cheer.

'I'm told the first tea break is best as the food hasn't run out,' Nora declared.

'I can assure you all three tea breaks are allocated the same foods, just as the lunch breaks are,' Mrs Armitage said. She'd heard that comment a hundred times or more and it was becoming a little wearing. As she was pondering on the tittle-tattle that came from the store's staff, along with gossip about the war, her telephone rang.

'Store three hundred and ninety, Mrs Armitage speaking. Oh, hello, Betty. How are you today?' She listened as the person on the other end of the telephone spoke before making notes in her desk diary. 'I'll see you tomorrow. Why not have lunch before the meeting, and that includes your assistant? See you then,' she smiled as she replaced the receiver. 'That was Betty Billington from the Erith store. She is an example of how women can do well working for F. W. Woolworths. Work hard and you too could be in management one day,' she assured them, not looking towards Nora. 'Now, let's crack on.'

'Until the men come back from the war and want their jobs back,' Nora muttered.

The girls were introduced to an older colleague, Joan, by Mrs Armitage as they arrived at their counter. 'I know you're due for your tea break, but would you show Annie and Emily around? It won't take long.'

'Of course,' the older woman said as she showed the girls the till and the stock of brown paper bags. 'Haberdashery is a pleasant workstation as we don't really have a rush like some of the other counters. I do hope you like working here.'

'I know I will,' Annie smiled as she glanced around the counter. 'I enjoy knitting and sewing.'

'I'm keen to learn,' Emily added, happy she wasn't serving muddy potatoes with miserable Nora.

'This is the book where we make a note of wool that has been put by for our customers, and this,' Joan said, kneeling down to a shelf below the wool, 'is where we keep duplicate knitting patterns. As soon as one is sold, we replace it on the counter. I'll only be ten minutes. If you have a problem, ring the bell on top of the till and a supervisor will come over to help you.'

The girls both thanked her and watched as Joan walked towards the staff door.

'This looks like a nice place to work,' Annie said as she straightened a row of sewing implements and patterns.

They both stood behind a two-sided glass-fronted long mahogany counter. There was a gap at either end for staff to exit the serving space. Similar counters stood all around them, each with its own special items for sale. The big shop floor was abuzz with customers making their purchases, browsing the goods on display and passing the time of day. Before Annie had been able to look at what was being sold at their nearest counter Emily spoke.

'Oh, my goodness, there's a customer approaching me,' Emily gasped as she grabbed Annie's arm. 'Please help me.'

Annie tried not to laugh. 'I'll stand with you, and we can serve her together,' she reassured her new friend as she gave the customer a welcoming smile. 'How may I help you?'

'You're going to think me very daft, but I have no idea how to darn my husband's socks and his big toe has worn out every woollen sock he owns. I really don't want to ask my new mother-in-law how to do it and feel such a fool,' the woman said, blushing with embarrassment.

Annie gave her a bright smile. 'Of course I can help you. Would you happen to have a sock with you so we can match up the darning wool?'

'He only wears black socks,' the customer said, pulling one from her shopping bag. 'His mum made these for him before we were married as she reckoned I'd never be able to knit him any. I feel such a failure and we've only been wed six weeks. I was dead nervous coming in here and hung about until I spotted you younger girls.'

'Please don't upset yourself,' Annie said as she noticed the young woman getting tearful. 'We all need to learn. I was darning socks when I was ten years old as Mum was busy working in our laundry business. First you need one of these,' she went on, picking up a wooden item shaped like a mushroom.

'Whatever is it?' Emily asked as she joined the conversation. The young housewife looked just as puzzled.

'It's a darning mushroom and it will help you with the task ahead,' Annie explained as she slipped the large sock over the mushroom and showed both girls how to weave stitches across the offending hole until the sock looked as good as new.

'You could try to knit your husband a pair of socks,' Emily suggested as she took a knitting pattern from the counter and read the details before picking the right size needles and a ball of navy-blue wool. 'What do you think? If you get stuck, you can come into the store and we can sort you out. I've knitted many socks as my mum runs a knitting circle to provide items for the services. If you would like, I could have her invite you; you'd learn a lot. That's if you don't think I'm too forward making such suggestions,' she added, seeing Mrs Armitage heading towards their counter.

'I'm more than grateful for your help,' the young woman said as she handed over the coins to pay for the items while Emily placed them into a brown paper bag, returning her goods with a thankful smile. Turning towards the double doors which led to the street outside, criss-crossed with brown paper tape to protect pedestrians if the glass should shatter in a raid, the customer spotted the personnel supervisor who was now close to the counter. 'I must say, your staff members are very helpful. They completely put my mind at ease and showed me how to darn a sock.'

Mrs Armitage thanked the customer for her kind words and watched as she left the store before turning to Annie and Emily. 'Good work, ladies,' she said before moving on.

'Gosh, that was fun,' Emily tittered. 'I'll serve the next customer. I'm pretty sure I've got the hang of it now.'

'Remember to use your notepad to add up your sales or Mrs Armitage will be after you,' Annie reminded her as two more customers appeared through the double doors, both walking towards the bottom end of their long counter, with the younger of the two looking decidedly embarrassed.

'After you,' the younger woman said to the older woman as Annie walked towards them enquiring how she could help them.

'Honestly, I've got plenty of time and want to pay for some wool I had put by and choose a knitting pattern to make my husband a jumper. I've unravelled one I picked up at a jumble sale and just need a nice pattern.'

The young woman, who was standing slightly back, turned even redder if that was possible and went to turn away. 'I can come back another time.'

'No, there's no need,' Annie said, waving to Emily to serve the woman with her wool. 'Now, what can I help you with?'

The girl looked from left to right and did her best to lean over the high counter towards Annie. 'I wanted some . . . some ladies' things,' she whispered.

Annie was flummoxed. She would have thought there weren't many men who wanted to purchase haberdashery. 'I'm sorry, I don't understand,' she said, wishing she'd asked Emily to serve the younger customer. 'We have a good selection of sewing items if that is what you want?'

The girl shook her head. 'No . . . it's for my monthlies . . .'

Annie sucked in her breath as the penny dropped, just as the older customer butted in, calling from further up the counter where Emily was serving her, 'They keep them underneath the counter out of view, lovie,' causing people to stop and stare.

'It doesn't matter,' the girl said as she started to move away.

'It's not something you can go without,' the older customer called after her. 'Mind you, I still use rags and boil them.'

Annie wanted to curl up and die. Why, oh why, hadn't she understood what the young customer wanted? She quickly ran after the girl and caught her by the arm. 'I'm so frightfully sorry,' she said in a quiet voice so no one else overheard her. 'This is my first day working here and I had no idea what was kept under the counter. I hope you aren't offended by my lack of help?'

The girl smiled. 'I'll be fine. I was more embarrassed by the other lady. My mum usually collects them for me, but she's still lying in ... She's just had my baby sister,' she explained as Annie frowned.

'Goodness, I have so much to learn,' Annie said, feeling as embarrassed as the young girl who had started to laugh.

'What a pair we are.'

'Would you come back to the counter and let me serve you?' Annie begged, hoping Mrs Armitage hadn't witnessed the scene.

'Of course. But please don't forget to wrap the packet up before you place it on the counter.'

*

'Thank goodness she told me, or I'd have done it all wrong,' Annie said, feeling like a complete idiot when she told Emily all about it afterwards. 'There I was thinking it would be easy working on this counter.'

'Never think that working on any counter in this store is easy,' Mrs Armitage said, appearing from behind them. 'If the day arrives when I hear you say those words again, I will be moving you to work in the stockroom or the canteen. I require hardworking and diligent counter staff, not young ladies wishing to slack.'

Annie jumped almost out of her skin and turned to face the personnel supervisor. 'I'm sorry, Mrs Armitage. I appreciate we must always be hardworking, and on our toes. I shouldn't have said what I did.'

Mrs Armitage, seeing the look of fear on her new staff member's face, realized she had frightened the girl half to death. Her demeanour softened. 'Perhaps I was a little harsh with my words, but you must know that being a Woolworths counter assistant is a job that many aspire to but never reach. You will both do well, I am sure; I was watching as you served those two customers and couldn't have done better myself. It stands to reason that you will make mistakes along the way and that's why I and your fellow colleagues are here to guide you. Now, it looks as though you have several more customers so get cracking. When Joan comes back you may both go to your tea break together,' she smiled, seeing relief flood over both Annie and Emily's faces.

'Phew, I honestly thought we were both for the chop when Mrs Armitage started to speak,' Emily said as she placed a plate with two slices of bread pudding on the table.

'You can say that again,' Annie sighed as she slid a cup of tea across the table to where Emily sat. 'I do like bread pudding even though there isn't the usual sprinkling of sugar. Rations are such a nuisance,' she grumbled, biting into the pudding.

'I miss not having as much dried fruit in the mix, but this is tasty just the same. Don't laugh, but my mother doesn't allow us to eat this at home. It makes it more of a treat when I go out somewhere for tea, or when I did before the war interfered with our lives.'

Annie was aghast. 'Why would your mum do such a thing?'

Emily giggled. 'She comes from a different time when her family lived in a large house and had servants.'

'Crikey,' was all Annie could say, thinking of her family. 'We seem to have come from completely different walks of life,' she said, going on to explain about her mum's family laundry and how her dad was a showman from the fairground world.

'That sounds so romantic,' Emily sighed.

'I don't know about that. There have been times when my parents haven't seen each other for months on end when the fair's been travelling.' She didn't mention the arguments and the names her mum called Paddy when he arrived home out of the blue; she'd keep that information to herself until she knew Emily a lot better. It wasn't that she was ashamed of her family, but more that the unusual living arrangements would surprise some people and she found the scrutiny unnerving. What she did know was her parents loved each other very much.

Emily looked sad. 'At least you see your father. Mine

died many years ago and sometimes I find it hard to remember his face.'

Annie waited for Emily to tell her more, but just then the bell rang for staff to return to their workstations. She gave her new friend's hand a squeeze.

'He was lovely, I know that, but if only I could see his face in my mind's eye. I still miss him. Is that a silly thing to say?'

'Not at all,' Annie said as they started to return to the shop floor. 'I miss my dad terribly when he isn't at home. I'm grateful he's promised to stay home and help Mum so I can go out to work.'

'You must tell me more about life with the fairground. Have you never wished to travel with the fair?'

A faraway look came into Annie's eyes. 'I dream of seeing the world, if that's what you mean. Mum says I've inherited that from my dad.'

'That doesn't sound like a bad thing,' Emily said. 'But if we don't hurry up, we're going to get into trouble on our very first day, and may be sacked, then your dad might have given up the fairground life for no reason.'

Annie was soon serving customers, but couldn't stop thinking of Emily's words, wondering if Paddy really had turned his back on the life of a showman. After all, a showman's life was in his blood.

'Have you enjoyed your first day working for F. W. Woolworths?' Mrs Armitage asked as she met the two girls outside the staff room after they'd changed out of their uniforms ready to go home at the end of the day.

'It was interesting,' Annie replied, trying not to give away how much her feet ached and how sore her throat felt from talking to customers. 'Yes, I enjoyed it.'

'How about you, Emily?' Mrs Armitage asked.

'To be honest, I'm fit to drop, but that's because I've never had to be on my feet all day. I'll get used to it,' she added quickly, seeing the woman raise her eyebrows. 'Gosh, that won't go down on my personnel record, will it? I'd hate to blot my copy book so soon.'

Mrs Armitage's cheeks twitched as she tried her best not to laugh at the flustered girl. 'Were you planning on blotting your copy book?'

'Well, no, but my mother is always telling me I'm clumsy and act like a bull in a china shop at times . . . Oh dear, I'm making things worse, aren't I?' she exclaimed.

Mrs Armitage had the good grace to chuckle and was joined by Annie, who secretly agreed with what Emily had said.

'Time to go home, girls. I hope you have a restful evening. I will confide in you that after my first day's work I dreamt the till on my counter opened and tried to eat me, while all the bells instore kept ringing for my tea break.'

'Mrs Armitage is nice, isn't she?' Annie said as the two girls left the store, Emily to catch her bus to take her to the other end of Bexleyheath Broadway, and Annie to wait for her dad to collect her.

'All in all, it's been a good day, even though I wish I'd stopped rambling on like an idiot. I'm afraid it is something I do quite often. Can you do me a favour?'

'I'll try,' Annie said, waving to Paddy as she spotted the van coming down the road.

'If I let my tongue run away with me, would you elbow

me in the ribs to stop me talking? If I don't do something, I could talk myself out of a job.'

Annie gave her a hug and giggled. 'I promise,' she said as the van pulled into the kerb.

'Thank you.' Emily returned the hug. 'I'll see you tomorrow. I have a feeling it will be an interesting day.'

Annie waved back as she climbed into the van. Surely tomorrow couldn't be any more interesting than today? she thought.

8

'You look tired,' Violet said as she placed a glass of beer in front of Paddy.

'Thanks, love. It's been a busy day, what with dropping off and picking up the bag wash and stopping by the fairground.'

Violet watched her husband for clues that he missed working in his family's business, but he looked comfortable sitting in the armchair by the hearth, rather than twitchy as he often was when he'd rather be somewhere else.

'How is everyone?' she asked, trying to keep the peace even though she wasn't much interested in the showman's world.

'Fair to middling,' he said. 'Three more lads have joined up and we're short of workers to build the rides and take them down, but with fewer slots and staying local it hasn't really hit home yet. Time will tell if we close for the duration, or if we ever open again. This war will be the death of the smaller fairgrounds,' he predicted with a faraway look in his eyes. 'It could be the end of life as I know it.'

'Do you hate me for taking you away from all that?' she asked, holding her breath in case she didn't receive the answer she wanted to hear while continuing to knit from the armchair opposite where he sat. It was comfortable sitting in the kitchen of an evening with the kettle simmering on the warm hob, her parents in their bedroom and young Albie out with the Boy Scouts. Even Annie had decided to have an early night after her first day at work had tired her out.

'I'd never hate you, love. Not in a million years. There are times I wish you'd taken to the showman's life after we married, but I'd not force you,' he said before gulping down his ale.

'I did try, Paddy, but with Mum and Dad being poorly, even back then, I had no choice but to carry on my family's business.'

'There's no good done in chewing over old problems. You know I was torn between you and the kids and what was my way of life. I was torn whichever way I turned. There are still some in my family who won't have anything to do with me for marrying out of the fairground community, but it's water under the bridge now.'

'Next you'll be saying we've made our bed and now we've got to lie in it when we've been married for nigh on twenty-five years,' she huffed.

Paddy shifted in his chair, looking uncomfortable. 'I'm not saying I've been the best of husbands . . .'

Violet took a deep breath. There was no time like the present to speak her mind. 'Word gets around, Paddy, and I know there have been young women who've caught your eye from time to time.'

Paddy cleared his throat, not meeting his wife's eye. 'That was some time ago and only the once, whatever people have been telling you. I'd drunk more than I should have and regretted it soon after.'

'When she told you she was expecting your baby and wanted a ring on her finger?'

Paddy shook his head, not wishing to think of that time. 'It was all a big mistake; she soon came to her senses and knew she couldn't pull the wool over a member of the Brookes family's eyes. Anyways, I'm sorry you got to hear about that, I truly am,' he said, looking contrite.

Violet studied her knitting, counting stitches on the one needle before starting a new row. And so you should be, Paddy Brookes, she thought to herself. You may have a bit of the wanderlust about you, and be away from home months on end, but I love you enough to want to fight for you. 'Check the kettle on the hob, Paddy; it's time I made the cocoa as our Albie will be dropped off soon,' she said as she let her mind wander back ten years to when rumours had got back to her about Paddy straying. She'd left the children with her mother and set off to Erith recreation ground where the Whitsun fair was in full swing. It hadn't taken her long to spot the woman hanging around the flying boats with a gaggle of giggling girls and a couple of lads who oversaw the ride.

Checking Paddy wasn't about, she marched up to the girl and grabbed her long flowing locks. 'I want a word with you, missy,' she hissed, pulling her away from her friends and dragging her behind a nearby caravan. Pushing her against the side of the van, she went nose to nose with the startled woman. 'What's this I hear about you trying it on with my old man?'

The woman flinched. 'Word is Paddy Brookes is a free man and let's say he didn't push me away.'

Violet saw red and slapped her face, spitting out each word with another slap. 'He's my man and you'd best understand no trollop is taking him from me.'

Violet kept shaking her until her head ached as it repeatedly hit the side of the van and then the woman shrunk away from her. 'I get your message.'

'Now, what's this about a baby?' she asked, looking down at the woman's slim shape.

'There isn't one,' she said, trembling. 'I was having people on.'

'You mean, you was prepared to trick my Paddy into believing he was going to be a father for the third time? You needn't look like that, I have two of his kiddies at home who are very much loved and wanted. Both conceived once we were wed.'

The woman frowned. 'He said—'

'I don't want to hear what he said. You are to listen to me and listen well: you are never to set foot near this fairground again and if I hear you've as much as batted one eyelash in his direction, I'll find you and give you what for. Do you understand what I'm telling you?'

The woman nodded her head, fear showing in her eyes. 'I understand,' she whimpered before running away from the fairground.

Violet leant against the van trying to catch her breath. She wasn't a violent woman but she had no intention of allowing her Paddy to leave her and bring shame on her family, so fight she did. Straightening her hat and picking up her handbag where it had fallen to the ground during the struggle, she went to seek out her husband. It was now dusk, and the rides and stalls were lighting up powered by a large traction engine. She spotted Paddy feeding a concertina of cards into the old Gavioli organ that was powered by the engine he called Goliath, and carefully sidled up to him, so he didn't see her approaching. 'Fancy treating a girl to a toffee apple?' she asked.

Paddy spun round, surprised to see her standing there. 'Blow me down, you gave me a shock! Where are the kids?' he asked, looking around.

'Tucked up in bed. Mum and Dad are keeping an eye on them. I thought it was time I visited my husband rather than wait for him to visit me,' she said, giving him a saucy wink. 'Isn't it about time you clocked off and let someone else run this thing?'

Paddy got her drift. 'Give me a minute,' he said, feeding a new set into the organ before putting his fingers into his mouth and giving a shrill whistle to a man watching over another stall. 'Now I'm all yours,' he said, sweeping her up in his arms to the sound of the organ playing 'Waltz of the Flowers'. These days just hearing that tune sent shivers of delight down her spine.

'A penny for them,' Paddy said now, bringing her back to the present. 'What were you thinking of?'

Violet smiled to herself as she started a new row of her knitting. 'I was just thinking of the past when the children were younger; and now look at them. Our Albie enjoying the Boy Scouts and discovering the world, while our Annie has found herself a good job, and one that she seems to enjoy, although it's early days yet.'

Paddy checked the kettle on the hob then took the cocoa

powder from the cupboard. 'You've changed your tune. It was only days ago you were against her working at Woolworths and wanted her to remain here with the laundry business.'

'That was before you returned to the fold to help us out. If you stick around this time, all will be right in my world. I'm more than pleased with the way you've knuckled down and even brought in some new business. Who'd have thought it, eh? The way we're going, we'll turn into a right old Darby and Joan.' Violet couldn't help but chuckle.

Behind her Paddy clenched his hand around the handle of the kettle. Why, when everything was settled, was he starting to feel as though he was trapped? 'The thing is, love, I'll still have to help out occasionally at the fairground until we know how we stand with all these government rules. It's going to be hard for them to eke out a living.'

Violet spun round in her seat, a worried frown crossing her face. 'What do you mean, Paddy? You're not already thinking of letting me down, are you? I don't feel I could cope with you disappearing again.'

He patted her shoulder. 'I don't plan on disappearing. It's just that you've got to understand I have a loyalty to my family as well as this one. For one thing I'll be bringing Goliath down here; there's room at the back in the corner of the field where I can do some work on her.'

Violet gave a visible sigh of relief. 'Thank goodness. For a moment there I thought you'd be off on your travels again. By all means bring some of the machinery here and work on it in between the laundry deliveries.' She wasn't keen on the old traction engine; to her, it was big and threatening. But if it kept Paddy happy to have it here, then so be it.

Kept out in the back field it would be out of sight and, as far as she was concerned, that meant it would be out of mind and wouldn't remind her of the fairground and the memories it brought back. 'I hope our Albie isn't much longer. If you don't mind waiting up for him, I'll take my drink up to bed with me,' she said, putting her knitting into her bag and getting to her feet.

'I'm going to have to go out for a while later,' he said. 'I'll make sure he's home and in his bed before I do.'

'At this time of night? What in heaven's sake for?'

'I can't tell you the details, but it's to do with national security.'

Violet chuckled. Any fears she had of him going to meet a woman or back to the fairground dissipated. 'You're on patrol with the Home Guard. I'm glad you joined up; it'll make up for you being turned down by your old regiment.'

Paddy handed her a mug of cocoa and forced a smile. 'You could say that.'

He was saved by any further conversations by a loud hammering on the door.

Violet shook her head. 'I bet Albie's forgotten I told him the back door would be unlocked in case we all turned in early.'

Paddy went to let in their son ready to give him a piece of his mind. A minute later he returned to the kitchen followed by Sergeant Mike Jackson and a couple of men in army uniforms.

'Sorry to bother you at this time of night, Mrs Brookes,' Mike said. 'We wondered if your brother was home?'

'He's not here,' she said as a yawning Annie came downstairs and joined them, followed by Ruth.

'This is Ruth, Pete's young lady,' Violet said.

Paddy wished she'd kept quiet; at least then he could have made up something about him visiting a sick relative, which would have given him time to get further away. He envied Pete being called up and didn't understand why he'd run off. There again, perhaps it had more to do with the responsibility of soon becoming a father . . .

'What's going on?' Albie said as he arrived home to see a room full of people.

Sergeant Mike raised his hand to silence the excited chatter. 'May I suggest that only those directly involved stay here and the rest return to their beds?'

With many objections most of the family left the room, leaving Paddy, Violet and Ruth. Annie pulled the door to behind her and pushed her brother towards the stairs. 'Come on, Albie, hurry yourself; I have an early start in the morning. Goodness knows what state I'll be in after being woken. I doubt I'll get back to sleep anytime soon.'

'They should have let me speak to the army people,' Albie huffed. 'No one wants to listen to kids.'

Annie ruffled his hair and shooed him into his bedroom. 'Sleep tight and don't let the bed bugs bite,' she called as she closed his door.

9

'You look as though you need a couple of matchsticks to prop your eyes open,' Emily said as she peered at Annie's face. 'Did you have a bad night's sleep?'

'You could say that,' Annie said as she rubbed at her eyes with her fingers before going on to explain what had happened late last night. 'I'm going to be fit for nothing today and hope we don't have any air-raid warnings as I'd probably forget where to go.' She sighed, smoothing the collar of her new uniform as they hurried along the upstairs corridor.

'Your family lead such an exciting life. To think I went home to a Spam sandwich and a cup of cocoa before I sat with Mum listening to the radio.'

'That sounds like heaven to me,' Annie said as the two friends went down to their counter to face the day. 'What I'd not give for a Spam sandwich supper and a cup of cocoa, and perhaps a day without an air raid.'

'Or a night,' Emily added. 'The attacks on London haven't stopped. Surely it can't go on for ever like this?'

'I hope not. Heads up, we seem to have customers approaching,' Annie said, watching a middle-aged woman in a tweed suit approach followed by a dark-haired younger woman in what appeared to be her best coat.

'It doesn't look as if they have to make do and mend,' Emily whispered as she gave the ladies a bright smile. 'May I help you?'

'Thank you, my dear,' the older woman said. 'My name is Betty Billington, and this is Sarah Gilbert. We're here from store three hundred and seventy at Erith to see Mrs Armitage.'

'I'll run upstairs to her office and tell her you're here,' Emily said, not waiting for an answer.

Annie stood at her counter wishing a customer would ask to be served. She chewed her lip nervously, trying to think of something to say to this smart-looking woman. As it was, the younger woman spoke to her.

'Do you enjoy working here?' she asked, looking up and down the counter.

'Very much, although myself and Emily – that's the other girl who dashed off – have only just started here.'

'I've worked at the Erith store for nearly two years,' Sarah replied.

'I know that store very well as it's where me and my mum shop as we live down on the marshes.'

'Near the river? That must be delightful to go for long walks and breathe in the river air,' Betty Billington said.

'It is, but only in the summer days as in the blackout we can't see our hands in front of our faces. I fear falling into one of the ditches and never being found,' Annie giggled. 'Will you excuse me?' she added as a lady appeared asking for a short length of elastic at the same time as another appeared asking to collect the wool she'd put by.

'Sarah, perhaps you could help out until this young lady's

colleague comes back?' Betty Billington suggested before moving on to look at another counter.

Sarah gave Annie a grin and took off her coat, folding it neatly and putting it under the counter. 'Thank goodness I was wearing my overall,' she said, reaching for a roll of elastic. 'You'd best serve the lady who wants the wool as you will know the system.'

'I'll do my best, but Joan, whose counter this is, knows more. She's not in work today.'

'Then let us muddle through between us.' The dark-haired woman unrolled the elastic to begin to measure it.

'I'm sure we'll manage. I'm Annie, by the way.'

'Pleased to meet you. I'm Sarah . . . Oh, you already know that,' she laughed.

'Do you have a special job at the Erith store?' Annie asked after they'd served their customers.

'I do like to help in the office, but I jumped at the chance to visit another store. I must say, from the little I've seen of this one it is very nice and it's larger than the one at Erith.'

'I wonder if perhaps I should have applied to work in Erith as I could have cycled there rather than relying on my dad to drop me off in the van?' Annie sighed. 'There are buses, but it takes a while to get down to Slades Green and then walk towards the river.'

Sarah patted her hand. 'Look, it's early days. If you feel this store isn't right for you, then by all means explain your plight to Mrs Armitage and ask for a transfer.' As she spoke a bell rang. 'Is that your tea break?'

'No, I have the third tea and lunch breaks today. I don't mind as it means there's a shorter work period this afternoon.'

'I prefer that one as well. Would you mind if I joined you for the late lunch break? I don't know anyone else here and hate to eat on my own. Betty will be busy in her meeting with Mrs Armitage. That's if you don't have plans for your lunchtime?'

'Please do join me. We have a lovely staff canteen, and they provide a hot lunch. It's shepherd's pie today.'

'Ooh, yummy! I'm partial to shepherd's pie even if it will be more potato than shepherd,' Sarah grinned.

Annie liked the young woman and wanted to find out more about the Erith store. 'I'll see you up there. First one in the canteen saves a table.'

'Gosh, it's the same in our store; we all have our favourite tables. I must go and find Betty and ask if she needs me for anything. See you later,' Sarah said as she left the counter and headed towards the door to the next floor just as Emily returned.

'Sorry, I got caught up carrying a tea tray through to Mrs Armitage. Did I miss anything?'

'Sarah stayed to chat for a while and served someone. She's going to join me for lunch as she's on her own,' Annie said, noticing Emily looking a little put out. 'Of course, that includes you,' she added, which put a smile back on Emily's face.

'I must ask your cook for her recipe,' Sarah Gilbert said as she forked more of the delicious shepherd's pie into her mouth.

'It is tasty,' Annie agreed. 'Do you know the cook at the Erith store very well?'

Sarah took a sip of tea before replying. 'Yes, Maureen

is my mother-in-law. I met my Alan when I started work there not long before Christmas nineteen thirty-eight. He's in the RAF now,' she added, looking a little sad. 'I miss him terribly, but I have a few good friends at the store. You'll find lots of staff are related or meet their future husbands at work.'

'Gosh,' Annie said as she looked around the busy staff canteen wondering if her future husband was at this moment tucking into shepherd's pie. Perhaps only having worked in the store for two days was a little too soon for romance.

'Minced pigs' liver,' Marge said as she stopped at their table checking if there was any dirty crockery that needed taking away. 'That's my secret ingredient. By all means tell Maureen and give her my best wishes at the same time.'

Annie dropped her fork onto her plate while Emily's face turned green. She'd not seen Marge approaching.

'I was standing right behind you when you mentioned the shepherd's pie,' Marge laughed.

'My goodness, there was me thinking you were a mind reader,' Sarah said.

'I'll let you get on with your meal. There's more if you could squeeze in another spoonful?'

'I'm fine, thank you,' the girls replied in unison.

'If you change your mind, just shout,' Marge said, returning to her kitchen area.

Both girls looked at each other and grimaced. 'Liver?' Annie shuddered.

'It's very tasty all the same,' Sarah said as she poked at the meal with her fork before eating another mouthful. 'I'm not thinking about the liver.'

'I prefer mine with bacon, onions and a large serving of gravy, but waste not want not,' Annie said as once again she tucked in. 'Tell me more about your store? I've often shopped in Erith but not thought about the staff area.'

'It is very much like this store. The powers-that-be often design all stores on the same basis; what differs is the size and the counters that can be fitted in. Erith doesn't serve food to customers like you do here. Some stores are on several levels; Erith is a small friendly branch and I like that. I'm not sure I'd like working in a larger branch. My feeling is you just become a number when there are too many people in the workplace.'

As if on cue Betty Billington arrived at their table. 'Sarah, if you've finished your meal, I'd like you to come with me to look at the window displays; we may be able to take a few tips back with us. They are so patriotic,' she said, nodding to the two other girls and saying goodbye.

'Pop in and see us at the Erith store,' Sarah added as she made her goodbyes.

'We will,' Annie promised, thinking how pleasant the two women were and saying as much to Emily.

'I'd like to see the other store. Perhaps when we have a half-day we can go together? Erith is such a nice town. We can look around and perhaps have tea at Hedley Mitchell's?'

'That sounds like a grand idea,' Annie said as she pushed her empty plate away. 'My goodness, can't they even allow us time for a meal?' she groaned as the sound of air-raid sirens started to wail first in the distance and then closer as enemy planes advanced from the direction of the Thames Estuary.

'Perhaps we ought to hurry?' Emily said, worried now. 'I hope my mum will be all right at home. She didn't want me to go out to work in case something happened to one of us.'

Around them staff started to move, leaving their tables and heading downstairs to the cellar. Behind the serving counter Marge was switching off the oven, moving hot pans and a kettle of water from the stove top while calling out for everyone to hurry.

The girls picked up their gas masks. 'Lead the way,' Emily said as they hurried after their colleagues before ducking down as the building shook and plaster fell from the ceiling. 'They're closer than I thought. Are we far from the cellars? I didn't really check them out when we had our interviews.'

'We have to go back downstairs and then across the shop floor; there's an entrance over by the side wall of the store,' Annie replied as she moved slowly forward. 'Do you think it's safe to go down the stairs?'

'If you want to get out of here, it's the only way of escape and we need to hurry as I can smell burning.' Emily grabbed Annie's arm as the lights went out and the stairwell fell into darkness even though it was only early afternoon. The only light came from a small window at the end of the hall, which by now was obliterated by smoke. 'Can you remember if there was anyone else behind us?'

Annie started to cough from the smoke seeping through the damaged ceiling. 'Marge in the canteen, and Mrs Armitage was in her office. Well, she was in there when we came up for our lunch.'

'We have to go back for them,' Emily said as she turned.

'We're here,' Mrs Armitage called out. 'Keep going, we need to get away from the fire above us in the roof; it seems to be spreading.'

With Marge cursing the Luftwaffe they ran as fast as their feet would allow and were soon in a small hallway between the foot of the staircase and the door that opened out into the store. 'Be careful as we have no idea what's behind this door,' Mrs Armitage shouted.

It was too late as Marge flung open the door so that they could hurry to the cellar and safety. 'Oh my God,' the cook cried out as she was overcome by smoke and rubble raining down on her from all sides.

Mrs Armitage reached out and grabbed the back of her overall but fell on top of her. The two women were all but lost as Annie and Emily watched in horror. Then came another fall of rubble, causing the door to shut once more and blocking any attempt to open it. Now there was nothing they could do for them.

Annie looked up to the ceiling above them. All they needed was for that to come down. She tapped the walls and was relieved to find they were made of solid bricks. 'Let's stand in this corner out of the way,' she said as she put her hand to the door. 'It doesn't feel hot, which means we're safe for now and hopefully Mrs Armitage and Marge are at no risk from fire. I'm sure there will be help before too long. Let's sit away from the door and wait.'

'Can we really not help at all?' Emily asked, fearing that many staff would be injured.

They fell into silence as they sat on the bottom steps while time ticked by. 'It's been over half an hour,' Annie said, peering at her wristwatch through the gloom.

Emily reached into the pocket of her overall and pulled out a couple of toffees wrapped in a brown paper bag. 'I forgot I had these; they're a bit on the messy side but will taste just as good. My mum gave them to me this morning as a treat,' she said as she handed one to Annie. 'The sugar will be good for the shock,' she added, giving Annie a wink as she started to pick the paper off her sweet.

'Gosh, I won't say no, but wherever did your mum get these?' she asked.

Emily gave another wink. 'Ask no questions and you'll be told no lies.'

'You sound just like my dad,' she said, wondering if her family were safely in their Anderson shelter.

Emily chuckled as she put the sweet into her mouth. 'My mum knows someone who works in a sweetshop. Tell me more about your dad's fairground.'

Annie described the way it used to be, before the war changed everything, as it was a good way of not thinking about what was happening directly above them.

'I've been to a funfair on the Whitsun bank holiday; we live just down the road from the park,' Emily said as she licked her fingers, oblivious to the scattering of dust falling from the roof.

'Then no doubt Dad would have sold you tickets to some of the rides,' Annie said, feeling proud.

'I'm not one for fast rides, the swinging boats are enough for me. Mind you, I get dizzy watching the gallopers going round and round.' Emily paused, as she cocked an ear towards the door.

'Have you heard something?' Annie asked, thinking of Mrs Armitage and Marge and if they were injured. Surely if they'd been rescued, they'd have got someone to come through the door to rescue them?

'I thought I heard machinery and thought it might be a fire engine arriving.'

Annie went to the door and placed her hand against it again. It was considerably warmer, causing her to back away slowly, still trying to listen for the sound Emily had mentioned.

'The sound is coming from outside,' she said, standing on tiptoes, which made no difference as the small window was several feet above them. 'Shh, listen . . .'

The girls stood silently as they prayed the noise was coming from their rescuers.

'I know that sound.' Annie grinned. 'It's the traction engine, Goliath, from the fairground. Dad was collecting it to take back to our place as he wanted to do some repairs.' She cupped her hands around her mouth and shouted as loud as she could. 'We're trapped in here! Help!'

Emily joined in as they called out as one voice, over and over, until she sat down suddenly, starting to cough. 'Sorry, it's my chest, it always plays me up when it's smoky. That's the main reason Mum didn't want me going out to work because of coming home in the smoky evenings when people have lit their coal fires,' she explained, as they noticed smoke creeping under the door to the store. 'We're going to die in here,' she stuttered before a fresh bout of coughing overcame her.

'Give me your overall,' Annie said, knowing Emily had a frock underneath whereas she herself was only wearing a petticoat. A puzzled Emily did as she was told. Annie rolled it up and laid it along the bottom of the door. 'It helps a little,' she said before continuing to shout as loud as she could.

'It's no good, we can't be heard,' Annie said after a while. She looked behind her at the stairs to the upper floor. 'I'm going up to the room above us. I'm assuming it will have a larger window and I may be able to attract someone's attention.'

'Please, no, it's too dangerous,' Emily begged.

'It's our only chance and your chest is getting worse.'

'Then I'm coming with you,' Emily insisted.

10

'I'm not sure we should have done this,' Emily spluttered as they felt their way up the smoke-filled staircase.

'We're almost at the top, keep hold of my belt,' Annie called over her shoulder, feeling her throat constrict under the relentless acrid fumes. 'We're here,' she rasped as they reached the top. 'Don't let go.' She took a few steps to the right trying to recall how close they were to the staff canteen. She remembered noting that there were large windows in that room, and she prayed there'd be a chance they'd be seen and hopefully be able to tell rescuers that Mrs Armitage and Marge were trapped by the door on the shop floor. If only she'd taken more notice of the layout of the building as it would have put them in good stead right now, she thought as she blundered on, pushing aside chairs and stumbling at one point. Holding the lapel of her overall over her nose and mouth with one hand, she felt along the wall with the other until she stopped suddenly. 'Emily, where are you?' she shouted as she sensed her new friend lose her grip on the waistband of her Woolworths overall. There was silence for a moment before Emily cried out.

'Oh my God, the floor's giving way!' There was a

deafening sound then as a large section of the floor fell away, taking Emily with it.

Annie's heart pounded in her breast. 'Stay where you are . . . I'll find you.' She reached behind her not knowing how close she was to where her friend had disappeared. It wouldn't do for them both to crash to the floor below. 'Emily . . . ?' She held her breath, trying not to breathe as the thick smoke would make her cough and mask any sounds from the other young woman.

The few seconds she waited to hear Emily's voice felt like hours. Perhaps she had hurt herself . . . or worse? In the end, with visibility deteriorating, she couldn't wait any more and took a deep breath of air, trying hard to keep as much as possible of her nose and mouth covered by her Woolworths overall. 'Emily!' she shouted. 'Answer me!'

'Save yourself,' Emily called back, sounding as though she was far below Annie. 'I slid down a floorboard and fell onto the end of the haberdashery counter. I've got away with a few bruises. I'm going to look for Mrs Armitage; she can't be far away. I'll do what I can to get you help.'

Annie felt dizzy and knew she would have to save herself before she passed out. Stopping for a moment to work out her bearings, she held her breath before letting the front of her overall drop from her face. With both hands outstretched she gingerly reached out until she felt her way to the counter in the canteen. If she was correct, there was a stone sink and a tap to the right of the counter. She felt her way along the counter until she came to the end – just a couple of steps and she could bathe her eyes and take a drink before continuing. The water tasted like nectar and soothed her eyes. After drenching a tea towel that lay over the taps, she wrapped it around her face. Now to get to the window ledge and hopefully someone would spot her. She inched closer to where the two tall sash windows should be, trying to ignore the roar of fire nearby on what she assumed was the roof. Was this caused by oil bombs? she wondered. Not that it really mattered as at this very moment her life was in danger, along with the lives of her new colleagues. She gave a harsh laugh as she thought her days as a Woolworths girl were numbered.

'Now, come on, Annie, stop feeling sorry for yourself,' she said out loud before becoming consumed by a fit of coughing as her fingers touched the glass of one of the sash windows. 'Thank goodness,' she muttered, trying to push up the frame, but it refused to budge. In desperation she reached around her trying to find something with which to break the glass. As she turned, she all but tripped over a broom. 'That'll do,' she exclaimed before starting to cough again. Working her way back to the window, she raised the broom and hit at the glass over and over until there was a mighty cracking sound and large pieces of glass fell away from the building.

'Oi, that nearly cut my throat,' a familiar voice exclaimed from close by.

Annie peered through the large gap in the glass, being careful not to touch the jagged edges as black smoke billowed around her. 'Dad?'

She heard the juddering sound of Goliath move a few feet closer and then spotted Paddy scrambling onto the highest point of the engine.

'Be careful,' she called out as the metal canopy moved from side to side. 'I'm so pleased to see you, but how can you get me out of here before the floor caves in on top of the others trapped in the store below?'

Paddy judged the situation carefully before speaking. 'Can you jump if I catch you?'

She shook her head. 'Not likely. Besides, Goliath's canopy won't hold the pair of us,' she pointed out.

Paddy climbed down to where he sat when steering the engine and reached for a thick rope coiled up and hanging on a hook. Slinging it over his shoulder, he carefully climbed up the side of the steam engine until he was as close to Annie as he could get. 'Here, catch this,' he said, throwing one end towards her. Annie managed to catch it on the third attempt. 'I want you to knock out as much of the glass as you can; I'll keep clear and make sure no one else is close by. Then secure the end to something sturdy. Be quick,' he said, noticing flames above her coming from the roof of the store. He didn't want to worry her but knew she would need to be snappy.

'Dad, there are people trapped on the shop floor in front of you. My friend Emily fell from the first floor.'

Paddy winced. That didn't sound good. 'I'll see to that. You start breaking that glass or I'll have your mum to answer to if I don't get you out of there in one piece.'

While Annie used the broom handle to clear the glass Paddy looked across to where a fire engine had just arrived, thanking his lucky stars he'd decided to leave the fairground early as he had quite a journey to get Goliath back down to the marshes and home. She had seen better days and if she broke down, he wanted it to be in daylight where he could roll up his sleeves and get stuck in. Waving at the firemen and indicating he had one staff member at the window, he then nodded below, cupping his hands to his mouth. 'There are staff members trapped in there,' he said, giving a thumbs up as the firemen nodded back.

'All done,' Annie called. 'Shall I secure this end of the rope?'

'Yes, find something that will hold your weight as I want you to climb down the rope to me.'

'Will do,' she shouted. There was a metal stove close by. She wrapped the rope twice around the stove and gave it a good tug. It held well, as she used knots her dad had taught her when she was a Girl Guide patrol leader.

'Ready,' she called. 'I'm about to start climbing down to you.' She swung her legs over the window ledge and gripped the rope tightly.

Paddy held the other end of the rope after weaving it around a solid part of the steam engine. 'It's safe for you to climb down; I'll catch you when you're close enough,' he called out. Carefully, placing her hands one after the other, she lowered herself towards him. As soon as Annie was near enough, he held out his arms and caught her as she dropped. They hugged for ages before he lowered her to her feet. 'I always said you should have joined the circus,' he said with a gruff voice filled with emotion.

'I'm not good enough with heights,' she replied, giving him a weak smile. 'Have you heard how the others are?' She gazed around at the firemen attempting to put out the blaze. 'I can't see anything from here.'

'Let's concentrate on freeing you first, eh? Stay here and don't move,' Paddy said, guiding her to the small driver's seat before draping his old black work jacket around her shoulders. 'We don't want you getting cold, do we? I'll go and check what's happened before I get you home.'

'Find out about Emily and Sarah. Oh, and Miss Billington,' she begged as he made to go. 'You might also ask what will happen to my job . . . ?' she called after him before starting to chew at her fingernail, a childhood habit she reverted to at times of stress.

Paddy raised his hand to acknowledge her questions before turning. 'I wouldn't think you have a hope in hell of returning to work.' He nodded to the building where firemen were fighting to put out the fire that had taken hold. 'Don't move until I get back; I don't want you wandering off and getting lost among all the mayhem. You look just about all in.'

Annie nodded her head in agreement and watched him disappear into the crowd, now edging as close as they could to the front of the store. She shivered, pulling her dad's old jacket close around her shoulders.

'Here, love, drink this, it will perk you up,' a woman in a WVS uniform suggested, handing her a mug of hot tea. 'Would you like a sandwich?' she asked, holding out a doorstep-sized wedge of bread with what smelt like fish paste spread inside.

'No, thank you, I've not long had my lunch . . .' Annie started to explain before waves of nausea overcame her. She managed to pass the mug of tea to the woman and move to the side of the traction engine before she was sick.

'That's better, lovie, let it all out,' the woman said, rubbing her back until she was sick a second time. 'I bet you feel better for that, don't you?' she asked, passing back the enamel mug as Annie reached for a handkerchief she kept tucked up her sleeve.

'I do, thank you,' she sniffed as her eyes continued to water. 'I don't know what came over me.'

'It'll be the shock, but better out than in. I was the same when I first started volunteering. Why, the sights I've seen would make your blood turn cold. There was this time when . . .'

Annie had never been so grateful than to see her dad appear. The lady meant well, but she wasn't up to lurid descriptions of people's injuries.

'Is there any news, Dad?' she asked, praying he had good news as already she could see a blanket being laid over a body that had been carried from the building on a stretcher.

Paddy stood in front of Annie blocking her view. 'I've been told your friend Emily has a few scratches and bruises but is well considering her tumble through the ceiling. She's already on her way home with her mother.'

'Thank goodness.' Annie sighed, taking a sip from the mug and passing it to Paddy, who quenched his thirst. 'Does anyone know what exactly happened – what caused it? I never heard an explosion.'

'I've been told it was an oil bomb, whatever that is,' Paddy said.

The WVS woman explained. 'They cause fires like the incendiary bombs. Nasty buggers they are too. I've seen some damage they've done . . .'

Annie started to shake as she asked about Betty and Sarah. 'I only met them today, but they were so nice, they were visiting from the Erith store.'

The lady put an arm around her. 'No news is good news,

lovie, and as I was telling you, I've seen much worse than what happened here today . . .'

Annie looked to Paddy for help. 'When can I go home?'

Paddy scratched his head. 'Love, I said I'd stay here and help out with Goliath; she can help the fire brigade move heavy loads and beams so the building can be secured. I tell you what,' he added, seeing her face drop, 'I'll go over to the telephone box and put a call through to your mother. She can get someone to drive the van up and collect you.'

Annie gulped back her tears. 'Thanks, Dad.'

'Why don't you come along with me until your mum gets here?' the WVS woman suggested. 'You can help me hand out teas and sandwiches if you're up to it? It's not as if you can go back to work, is it?'

Annie gave a shrug. The woman was right. 'Of course I'll help you,' she said, giving her a grateful smile. She might be a gossip, but her intentions were good. 'Dad, will you keep an eye out for Mum, please, as I don't want to keep her waiting?' she said, wondering who Violet would get to drive her up to Bexleyheath.

For the next hour Annie helped the WVS unit by washing mugs and plates and brewing fresh pots of tea. She had to admit she enjoyed herself being able to help during a disaster. The women explained how they were called out a lot to bring food and comfort during bombings, although they did also appear at events where crowds gathered such as royal weddings and football finals.

'Why not consider joining us as a volunteer?' asked the lady who'd brought her tea.

'As soon as I know what's happening with my job, I'll

consider it. I do want to do my bit and I've enjoyed helping you all,' Annie said with a grin.

An older woman who seemed to be in charge tapped her arm. 'There's someone over there collecting names. Could it be something to do with the Woolworths staff?' she asked.

Annie hurried over to where she could see one of the staff members with a clipboard. 'I'm Annie Brookes, I started work here yesterday,' she said as the man ran his finger down a list of names.

'Here you are,' he said as he put a tick next to her name. 'Have you been injured?'

Annie explained how she'd escaped from the first floor with just a few scrapes and bruises. 'So I was quite lucky really. But have you heard if there's any news of Miss Betty Billington and Sarah Gilbert? Nobody seems to know, and they were so kind to me.'

The man checked his clipboard and sucked in his cheeks. 'Miss Billington's been taken away in an ambulance – I do not have any further information. Miss Gilbert has been driven back to Erith.'

Annie shook her head, hoping that the women who had impressed her so deeply would manage to recover. 'Will you write down my address being as I'm so new to Woolworths and my records could have been destroyed? I'd really like to continue working for the company if and when the opportunity arises.'

'We will be in touch. In the meantime, how will you get home?'

'My mother will be along to collect me soon. That's my dad helping out over there.' She pointed proudly as Paddy manoeuvred Goliath in position to drag away a pile of timber that had once been a large window frame at the front of the store.

'Good man.' He smiled before wishing Annie well.

'Here's my mum now,' she said as the family van pulled up. To Annie's astonishment, Violet was driving the vehicle.

'That took longer than I expected,' she said as she climbed from behind the steering wheel. 'It always looked easy to drive when you or your dad was doing it. Never mind, I'm here now.' She gave Annie a hug while checking her for injuries. 'Hitler's made a right mess of the store,' she added, hand on hips.

'Goodness knows when I'll be back to work,' Annie sighed as she took her mother's place behind the steering wheel.

'First thing tomorrow, I have laundry to deliver and new clients to collect from. You can say goodbye to Woolworths right now.'

Annie looked with sadness as she drove past the store. Her dreams to forge her own way in life were gone for good.

11

November 1940

'There's a letter on the table for you,' Violet called out as Annie entered the kitchen after a long day delivering freshly laundered washing to their clients.

Annie first went to the sink and filled a mug with cold water before going to the table and picking up the envelope. The past weeks had not been to her liking as Paddy had taken himself off to their dilapidated barn to work on Goliath; he had scarcely helped her with the laundry deliveries and was apologetic for letting her down, as he repeatedly told her. But she couldn't help thinking life had reverted to what it had been like before she had gone to work for Woolworths and before her father had come home. There'd not been any news from her Uncle Pete, although Ruth had settled in living with the family and was not far off her delivery date.

'Are you going to open it or stand there staring at it?' her mum asked. 'I see it's from Woolworths.'

Annie frowned. It had to be bad news; no doubt they were letting her go. 'When I met Emily the other day, she said workmen are busy in the building. She made a point of walking past to see what was happening as she lives close by. I can't see me returning to work anytime soon so this is probably my cards. Last in, first out, as they say.' She sighed, sitting down as she slit open the envelope. She fell silent as she read the single page in front of her.

'Come on, girl, tell us what it's all about?' her mum insisted as she moved closer to the table, wiping her hands on her pinny as she did so.

'Have they sacked you?' Ruth asked, joining them and sitting down carefully.

Annie shook her head in astonishment. 'No, they want me to go along to the Erith store to see about working there until such time as we can be moved back to Bexleyheath. There's even a reminder that we're not to talk about the attack on the Bexleyheath building.'

'That'll be to keep up national morale and to confuse Hitler into thinking his air force isn't as good as he thinks it is,' Paddy laughed as he came in wiping his oily hands on a piece of rag. 'Don't forget what the copper who was at Woolworths told us.'

'Careless talk costs lives,' Annie and Ruth chanted.

'Be like Dad and keep mum,' Paddy added.

'That's the telephone ringing,' Violet said, shaking her head at their mirth. 'Someone should answer it as we still need to bring in money to keep us, regardless of whether our Annie will be working or not.'

Annie hurried through to the front room where their black Bakelite telephone sat atop a crochet mat on the sideboard. She answered it politely, giving their number followed by 'Brookes Laundry'. She heard the mechanical sound as coins were put into the slot; it was someone using a public telephone box.

'Annie, it's me, Emily. Have you received a letter from Woolworths?' a voice asked excitedly.

'I have and don't mind telling you I'm so pleased as I thought they'd forgotten us.'

'I did ask when I walked past the store again this morning but the foreman in charge of the work there had no idea and said to ask head office.'

Annie sucked in her cheeks. 'I'd have been too frightened to ring London and ask about my job.'

'Me too. I thought perhaps we could meet tomorrow and go in together. What do you think?'

'I think that's a very good idea, we can support each other. Should we wear our uniforms? Mine still smells of smoke and there's a small rip where I caught it climbing out of the window.'

'I don't have mine. If you remember, you took it from me and stuffed it under the door to keep out the smoke,' Emily giggled. 'We can dress smartly as if we're going for an interview.'

'That's a good idea and perhaps afterwards we can go to Hedley Mitchell's for a cup of tea.'

After arranging when to meet, Annie bade her friend goodbye and replaced the receiver in the cradle. She felt quite upbeat as she went back to the kitchen to share her news. Life could turn on a sixpence and hers certainly had. As much as she liked to help with the family business, she knew it wasn't something she wished to do for the rest of her life. She yearned to do more. To some, working on the counter at Woolworths wasn't much, but to her, it was a step towards something more exciting; she could feel it in her bones.

The first thing she noticed when she walked into the kitchen from the front room was her father's pale face as he moved towards the back door. Before she could ask what was wrong her mum snapped a command at Paddy and then Annie.

'Paddy, wash your hands and get yourself out to the laundry. There are deliveries to sort for tomorrow and you'll not only be bagging up everything but taking out the orders. There's a list pinned to the wall telling you where you need to collect.'

He frowned. 'But what about you? That's your job.'

'There's a baby coming, as you've already noticed, and I'll have my hands full. Annie, go to my room and strip the bed. You'll find newspapers and old bedlinen in the closet. Put a thick layer of newspapers on top of the mattress before you remake the bed. You can also call your nan as she's birthed plenty of babies in her time and will be a welcome pair of hands.'

Without answering her mum, Annie nodded her head and hurried to get on with what she'd been instructed to do. Now it came in handy that Violet preferred a ground-floor room so she could start work early without waking the family. With her nan's assistance they made light work and were soon ready to help Ruth to the bed.

'Perhaps you could go back to the kitchen and keep an eye out for Albie. I don't want him wandering in and seeing things a young lad shouldn't see,' Ruth whispered falteringly.

'You can get a brew on the go as well,' her nan said. 'It's going to be a long night. And don't forget you'll be making our meal this evening, unless you want to change places with me?' she cackled, enjoying Annie's discomfort.

'I'll do that,' she said, determined to keep herself busy and away from the room where Ruth would be introducing their new baby cousin to the world in the next few hours. She had been too young when her brother, Albie, had been born to know much about what went on. In fact, all she recalled was her dad taking her mushrooming down on the marshes and coming home to a big fry-up and the sound of a baby's loud cries. Albie had been noisy ever since. She got busy making mugs of tea while scrubbing the kitchen ready to start preparing their meal. After carrying drinks through to the women, she took a mug out to her dad.

'Here, let me help you,' she said as she saw him struggling to put a sheet through the mangle. 'These aren't for tomorrow as they won't be dry in time and need ironing. Hang these over the inside line and that'll be that job done.'

They worked in companiable silence until the clean sheets were neatly pegged out. Tomorrow, with the boiler stoked up, they would gently steam dry while her mother got on with the other work.

'Drink your tea while I check the bags of clean washing are ready for the morning deliveries.' She took down a clipboard and started to go through the long list. 'I've decided not to go to Woolworths tomorrow as I'm needed here,' she said with a determination she didn't feel. 'Mum will be busy helping Ruth and can't be expected to work on her own out here.'

Paddy punched the mangle in anger. 'I'm not having my girl miss out on following her dreams. Your mum wouldn't want it either; she may be strict about family duty, but she is proud of you going to work at Woolworths. Look how she came to your rescue driving that van. I never thought I'd see that. It won't hurt me to pull my weight a little more around here until we get things under control. Your brother is old enough to help out and once Ruth is over the birth she will be helping us. She's a good'un. I'm not sure how she got caught up with your uncle and I hope he don't come back anytime soon, but she's family now. We'll get by and you aren't to make sacrifices for us, do you hear me?'

Annie stood on tiptoe, flinging her arms around her dad's neck. 'It's good to have you back, Dad. Now, we best get inside as I'm supposed to be making our supper.'

'If you don't mind, I'll be off out as I've got to see a few mates down The Lord Raglan pub. Don't look like that as I'm not boozing; this is about national security,' he said, giving a wink so she stopped asking questions.

Annie shook her head as she watched him walk off whistling a merry tune. Picking up the empty mug, she hurried indoors. It would be a long night.

Paddy Brookes slipped in through the side door of The Lord Raglan and walked through the long corridor to the back room. Looking round at the familiar faces, he sat at the top of the table accepting a glass of bitter from the landlord who had joined them. 'Thank you all for turning up tonight. I know you don't like leaving your families and have all got a lot on at the moment, especially you, Mike,' he said to the well-liked police sergeant sitting with them.

'I'm not agreeing to anything, Paddy, I just want to know what this is all about and hope it's nothing illegal.'

A few of the men agreed while others laughed at his discomfort.

'It's nothing illegal,' Paddy growled at the men and the laughter stopped dead. 'It came to my notice that down here near the river we see a lot of enemy action and I got to thinking how unprotected we are and how, if there was an invasion, our part of Kent could be infiltrated.'

'I don't know about that; the river's well protected by barrage balloons,' one man said.

'Come off it! It hasn't stopped the Blitz. What was it they called this stretch of Kent? Bomb Alley?' another said, thumping the table.

'If you've got any idea what we can do to protect our families, then let's be hearing it,' the landlord said as all the men agreed.

'I have,' Paddy said as he took a gulp of his beer, wiping his mouth with the back of his hand. 'We need to set up regular patrols down the marshes, especially during air raids in case the enemy are dropping their men behind the lines.'

Mike Jackson was thoughtful. 'I don't know, Paddy, aren't we stepping on the toes of the services?'

'They've all got their place in this war, but we men know the marshes and this part of the river. It's not something any outsiders would know about. All the paths, what leads where, and which places are safe and which aren't. None of us are likely to be called up due to age or injury in the last shout, so why don't we do something?'

12

'You look like death warmed up,' Emily declared when she met Annie at the corner of Pier Road in Erith just down from the Woolworths store. The street was lined with Victorian buildings, all with elegant facades, housing plenty of different businesses, and the pavements were teeming. People were keen to complete their shopping before the next siren sounded. 'Whatever has happened for you to look so pale?'

'Do I look that bad? I've only had a couple of hours' sleep. Ruth went into labour yesterday evening and she gave birth this morning to a beautiful little girl.'

Emily's eyes opened wide. 'Did you see the birth?'

'No, Mum and Nan wouldn't let me. They reckon it's not something for unmarried girls to watch. Mind you, if the yelling and screaming was anything to go by, she had a bad time of it. I put cotton wool in my ears so I couldn't hear.'

'I would have too, although I do wonder what happens. Mother hasn't told me much about that kind of thing. Now, you need a little rouge on your cheeks before we meet the manager or they will think you are sickening for something,' she said, stepping into a side alley and delving into her handbag. 'Here, let me do it,' she said, dabbing at Annie's cheeks. 'Does that look all right to you?' she asked, holding up a small mirror.

Annie rubbed in the red colouring, so it wasn't so blatant, and looked from side to side at the view of her face. 'Yes, thanks, that'll do. I just hope I don't yawn too much during the interview,' she said, wondering to herself how a mother couldn't explain the birds and the bees to a daughter but allowed her to use rouge on her cheeks. It was a strange world.

'Welcome to the Erith store,' Sarah Gilbert said as Annie and Emily were shown upstairs to the staff area. 'Did you have chance to look around downstairs?' she asked as she showed them to two seats set behind a desk in the personnel manager's office.

'We had a quick look before we were shown upstairs; I was surprised how similar the counters look to those at Bexleyheath. We only worked there a couple of days so I may be wrong, though,' Annie said, giving Sarah a broad smile.

'The layout is similar in most stores from what I've been told. Tell me, how have you both been since we last met? Have you been working?'

'I've been helping my mother with her charity work. I've knitted so many balaclava helmets I'll scream if I see another,' Emily declared.

'And I've been at home working in the family laundry business, although I've managed to do a little volunteering,' Annie said, going on to explain how she met the WVS woman at Bexleyheath after the oil bomb explosion and decided she'd like to volunteer. 'Mum is going to join as well as my uncle's wife, who lives with us, once she's got used to her baby.' She grinned at Sarah's surprised face. 'It only arrived earlier this morning and that's why I look an absolute fright.'

'You look very well, if a little pink-cheeked,' Sarah assured her, causing Annie to pull out her powder compact and peer at her reflection, which had changed somewhat since Emily added the rouge.

The girls laughed as Annie explained how Emily had helped brighten her pale cheeks.

Once the laughter had subsided Sarah looked serious. 'You may be wondering exactly why you've been invited here?'

The two girls looked at each other. 'The letter suggested we would be placed in another store until the Bexleyheath branch is rebuilt,' Annie said, sounding hopeful.

Emily looked as though she would burst into tears. 'Or are we going to get the sack?'

'My goodness, no,' Sarah exclaimed. 'In fact, we would very much like both of you to work here until such time as the Bexleyheath store is up and running again. We'd have been in touch sooner, but with Betty still being off work with her injuries we were in a bit of a two and eight trying to decide who would cover her work. I'm here part time at the moment, so I took on the hiring of staff. With Christmas on the horizon there's a lot to do. Are you happy with the decision to have you work here?'

'I'd love to work in this store. It's closer to home than Bexleyheath,' Annie beamed.

'I live further away, but it's not a problem as I can catch a bus. I may even cycle,' Emily added. 'When do we start?'

Sarah chuckled. 'Thank you for making that easy. I'd very much like you to start on Monday and you will both be on the Christmas counter with my friend Freda. I'm afraid the counter isn't as vibrant this year due to the war, but we've combined it with gifts and useful items, and it looks rather splendid if I say so myself. It's up to us to make the best of things, isn't it?'

Both girls agreed and after collecting clean uniforms they thanked Sarah and left the office. As they walked down the steep staircase to the store below, they couldn't help but grin. 'We are so lucky,' Annie said. 'I thought our two days at Woolworths would be our last.'

'My mother said I was wasting my time coming here today. I'll be able to tell her she was wrong.'

'Do you think she'll like being told that?' Annie wondered out loud.

Emily almost jumped for joy. 'For once I don't care. I'm going to enjoy working here and will make the most of it. Let's go and check out the Christmas counter before we have our tea at Hedley Mitchell's. I'll treat us to a cake, that's if they have any,' she said, looping her arm through Annie's and skipping down the rest of the stairs.

By the time Annie returned home she had a head full of gift ideas for her family all purchased from Woolworths. There was even a plentiful supply of calendars due to Woolworths doing a deal with the government; she had heard that from Freda, who was the young girl they would be working with. Her nan would love a calendar she'd spotted with a picture of a cottage with a flower-filled garden. Nan often said she'd like to turn their family vegetable patch into a proper English garden with every flower imaginable. Her dad was always a problem when it came to choosing gifts, but she'd spied a tool belt made from heavy canvas with plenty of pockets to hold his tools.

'I take it by that smile on your face you are still to be employed by Woolworths?' her mum asked when Annie sought her out where she was working in the laundry.

Annie checked the heat of the heavy iron before beginning on the first of a pile of cotton pillowcases. 'Yes, I'm starting at the Erith branch on Monday. I thought I'd check over my bicycle and use it to ride to work; there's a place where I can leave it out the back of the store. I'm going to be on the Christmas counter along with Emily and another girl,' she grinned. 'I'll be able to give you some money out of my pay packet every week for my keep.'

Violet nodded, not saying a word for a little while. 'A Christmas counter, you say? I wonder if there would be much need for one in the second year of the war. People have better things to spend their money on. I suppose some people have money to burn,' she added as she scrubbed at the collar of a man's shirt, rubbing it up and down a washboard until she was happy with the cleanliness. 'How long will you be there?'

'Sarah – that is, Mrs Gilbert – said we would be there until the Bexleyheath store has been rebuilt so I reckon at least until next summer.'

'As long as you are happy, that's all that matters.' Violet sighed. 'Why don't you leave that and go in and see Ruth? Your nan's been keeping her company most of the day while I get on with this work.'

Annie put down the iron and did as she was told. Her

mum didn't seem that pleased that there would be another wage coming into the house. Then again, perhaps she was also tired after being up most of the night. She checked the kettle was full of water and slid it onto the hob before going to the downstairs bedroom to see Ruth and the baby.

'Now you're here I'll go and see to our tea. Try to get Ruth to sleep for a while; she's done nothing but grizzle about our Pete being missing,' Nan moaned.

Annie perched on the edge of the bed. 'Don't take any notice of Nan. She's as worried about Uncle Pete as the rest of us,' she said, reaching out to stroke the soft downy hair on the baby's head.

Ruth sniffed and nodded. 'Take no notice of me, I'm told new mothers cry a lot. I am worried about Pete, but he can take care of himself, he's not daft. I just wish he was here to see his daughter and to help me support her.'

'Ruth, you are our family, and we will never turn you away, regardless of what Uncle Pete does,' Annie said, thinking back to the times her mum had had to rescue her younger brother from something or other he'd become mixed up in, whether it be petty crime or messing some poor girl about. Annie wondered whether if her uncle hadn't legged it rather than join the army, he'd have still left poor Ruth in the lurch, alone with a baby who would never have met her family. 'You need to rest and enjoy your baby. You have nothing to worry about.'

Ruth again looked tearful, but this time they were tears of joy. 'Thank you, that gives me such peace of mind. Would you like to hold her?'

'I would adore to if you don't think I'll drop her. I've never held anything so delicate in my life, not even a kitten, and there have been a few of them born in the outbuildings.'

'She's more demanding than a kitten,' Ruth laughed as she handed over the small bundle to Annie.

Annie felt an intense love wash over her as she held the baby close to her heart. 'Why, you sweet, sweet darling, I could eat you up,' she said before kissing her cheek.

'She likes you,' Ruth said. 'She almost yelled the place down when your nan held her.'

Annie giggled. 'That must have gone down well.'

'She said the baby needed a spoonful of gripe water,' Ruth explained as she wriggled up the pillows to make herself more comfortable. 'She also said I'm not producing enough milk, but your mum put her right and told her she'd forgotten about child rearing. There was a right ding-dong, I can tell you, and all I wanted to do was sleep.'

'Oh, you poor love,' Annie said, feeling sorry for the girl, who had had to go through the birth then put up with her mum and nan fighting over how to care for the baby. 'They probably thought they were doing what was right.'

'Yes, but I'm so tired I can't think straight. Your nan has sat here most of the day watching me in case I do something wrong, being young and a first-time mother. I was praying for the air-raid sirens to go off just so we could move to the Anderson shelter. It's very comfortable down there now your dad's finished it off, and it would have been good to be among the rest of the family even though it would have been uncomfortable to move out of this bed.'

Annie was thoughtful as she cradled the sleeping baby. 'I tell you what, why don't I take care of this little one? I can watch her in her cradle while she sleeps, and you can settle down and sleep yourself. I promise to sit in the corner and read my book and I won't wake you unless this little lady really needs her mummy.'

Ruth thanked Annie profusely. 'I don't want anyone to think I'm being ungrateful. After living on my own in a room over the pub it means the world to me to be part of a family, even if this little one's father has vanished off the face of the earth. I've never been part of a family before.'

Annie realized then how lucky she was to have her family around her even if they could infuriate her at times. 'I know what you mean, even though there are times I just want to shut myself in my bedroom to escape them all,' she smiled.

'Talking of bedrooms, it was so good of your mum to let me use her room to have the baby.'

'It made sense with this room being on the ground floor; you couldn't really get up to the top floor while having contractions.' Annie paused as an idea came to her. 'I wonder if you'd like to share my bedroom when you're ready? It's much bigger than the one you were in before. You'll need space now that there are two of you.'

'That's so kind of you, but I warn you, we could be in for some sleepless nights and with you starting back at Woolworths I'd hate us to be the cause of you not getting enough sleep.'

'Let's cross that bridge if we come to it. Now, you snuggle down and close your eyes and I'll settle this little madam,' Annie said, thinking how wonderful it must be to be a mother although she'd prefer to be married, otherwise her mum and nan would never let her hear the end of it. She cuddled the baby for a while longer before settling her in the wooden crib that Paddy had made for her and then her brother when they were born.

13

Annie's eyes started to droop, causing her book to slip into her lap; she'd only read a few pages. Coming to with a start, she looked towards the cradle where the baby was sleeping soundly after a nappy change. Annie was glad she'd watched how Ruth did this earlier and after one fail where the nappy slipped down the baby's legs and she'd had to start again, she'd soon got the hang of how it was done. Noticing Ruth was still sleeping, she decided to leave them both for a minute to go to the kitchen, see her mum and grab something to eat.

'They are both sound asleep,' she said as she entered the kitchen giving a long drawn-out yawn.

Violet looked up from where she was sitting by the hearth, a frown crossing her face. 'I thought it was your father. He's not home yet. Your tea's on top of the pan of water on the stove with a plate over the top. It should be all right as it's rabbit stew and dumplings, so it won't have dried out much.'

Annie grabbed a tea towel to protect her fingers and carefully lifted the plate onto the table, putting it on top of a copy of the *Erith Observer*. 'That looks tasty,' she said, licking her fingers where gravy had splashed them as she took a fork her mum held out to her. 'Has Dad eaten?'

'He wolfed his down and then went out. He told me he had to see a man about a dog,' her mother explained, sitting down opposite Annie. 'It seemed a strange time to go out. He's done the same a few times lately. I wondered . . .'

Annie looked up from her meal. 'What do you wonder?' she asked, seeing her worried face. 'The fair's not running at the moment if you think he's gone down there.'

Violet started to nervously pleat the edge of the tea towel Annie had left on the table. 'No, I'm just being silly. Ignore me.'

Annie lay down her fork. 'Mum, if there's something worrying you, please share it with me. You know what they say about a trouble shared.'

'I know it means the trouble is halved, but I don't want to burden you with my worries.'

Annie inwardly groaned. It had been the same since she was a youngster watching her parents bicker and fight. 'You know you'll tell me in the end, so why not spit it out now and I can help you before I go back to sit with Ruth and the baby?'

Violet thought for a moment before speaking. 'I believe your dad is carrying on with another woman and I don't have it in me to go and sort her out.'

Annie dropped her fork onto her plate, causing a clatter. Surely this couldn't be right after all he had told her about being here to help the family during the war? 'Are you sure, Mum? Could you be mistaken?'

Violet continued to fiddle with the tea towel until Annie

snatched it from her and looked her in the eye, willing her to speak. 'I have my suspicions.'

'But what if your suspicions are wrong? Just because he strayed in the past doesn't mean he has this time.'

'I hear him going out late at night when you've all gone to bed. Today it was earlier than usual and when I asked him what he was up to, he told me not to ask, which can only mean one thing. I'm going to wait up and confront him tonight, whatever time he comes home.'

'Promise me you won't do it tonight. We've all had a lack of sleep and perhaps tomorrow things will look a little different. Go to bed, and I'll get a rug and settle down in the armchair and watch the baby tonight. Use my bed as you've given yours to Ruth.'

'What will we do about your dad?'

'Next time he goes out late in the evening, I'll follow him and see what he's up to. Once we know, you can confront him.'

Violet got to her feet and kissed Annie's cheek. 'I knew I could rely on you,' she said before heading upstairs to bed.

Annie poked at her meal, having lost her appetite. Scraping the leftovers into the pig bin, she put the plate in the sink to soak and prepared for a night in the armchair. As she was turning out the lights and checking there was a bag of supplies along with their gas masks and torches by the door in case there was an air raid, she started as the back door opened and in walked Paddy.

'Sorry, love, I didn't mean to make you jump,' he said, putting the canvas bag he carried down on the floor. 'There's a couple of rabbits in there. I'll skin and get them ready for the pot first thing in the morning.'

'You'd best put them in the shed for tonight,' she said before going back to the baby. She couldn't trust herself not to ask him questions that could upset the whole household. No, she would do as she said and next time she would follow him to wherever he was going.

'Not another sleepless night with the baby?' Emily said, noticing the grey circles around Annie's eyes when the two girls met in the Erith store on Monday morning wearing their new burgundy uniforms.

Annie powdered her nose before checking her face in the mirror attached to the wall where their lockers were lined up in neat rows. 'I was on mother and baby watch duties and got so completely engrossed in my book I didn't notice the time.' She didn't like telling lies, but how could she tell Emily she'd been kept awake by thoughts of her dad carrying on with another woman? 'Come on, let's get in the festive spirit and go downstairs before the bell rings for the doors to open.'

The two girls enjoyed their morning working on the seasonal counter and really liked Freda, their colleague, who showed them the ropes. She was petite, and about the same age as they were, but she had an air of authority that made her seem far older than her years. In between serving customers and restocking the counter she told them about the social side of Woolworths and how they all took turns fire watching. Freda also helped with the Brownies and the Girl Guides at the local Baptist church and told them how she enjoyed tinkering with, and riding, Sarah's husband's motorbike now he was serving with the RAF.

'I wondered about Miss Billington . . . She was injured

when the oil bomb set fire to the Bexleyheath store?' Emily asked when there was a lull in customers, and they had time to take a breath before they became busy once more.

A cloud crossed Freda's face. 'You do realize we aren't supposed to talk about what happened to the store as the enemy may find out and claim a victory?'

'I'm sorry,' Emily stammered. 'I didn't mean any harm.'

'Careless talk costs lives,' Freda muttered as she looked around to see if anyone was nearby. 'I know you meant well but be careful in future as you have no idea who could be listening. For your information, Betty is taking a little time off work to get over what happened; it shook her up quite a bit. She'll be back at work before too long.'

'Thank you,' Emily said, looking downhearted. 'Gosh, we have a lot to learn, don't we?'

Annie agreed, feeling sorry for Emily and knowing she could easily have spoken out of turn and been reprimanded herself. 'Come on, let's tidy the calendars. It looks as though customers have rummaged through every row,' she said, picking up a pile to pass to Emily.

Freda joined them. 'They are looking for certain pictures; it's always the cottages with roses around the door. I suppose it's this blooming war making people wish for something they don't have and to hold on to a dream for when it's over.'

The girls agreed with her. 'I wanted one of those for my nan for Christmas,' Annie said, looking wistfully at the few that were left.

'Pick one now and put it under the counter. I'll show you how we make staff purchases when we clock off this evening. What about you, Emily? Would you like to buy one for your mother?'

'I think she'd like the one with the countryside scene, if you think it will be all right?'

'Of course it will.' Freda gave her a gentle smile, which made Emily feel the other woman was annoyed with her for her earlier gaff. 'We still have to pay for the items, but we get the perks of choosing when new items come in. It looks like we have customers, so hurry up and put your choices under the counter in case the next customer wishes to buy them.'

The two girls were quick to choose their calendars and Annie added four Chinese-style decorations to her purchases; they would cheer up the front room on Christmas Day.

A supervisor walked over to their counter at half past twelve and told the three girls they could go to lunch as two part-time assistants would take over. 'Freda can take you up to the canteen and show you the ropes,' she said as the bell for the lunch break started to ring.

'The morning went so quickly,' Emily said as they hurried up the staircase behind Freda. 'I was a little nervous going to the morning tea break on my own; it's nicer with you two. For a small store they seem to have plenty of people working here.'

'You'd be surprised what goes on behind the scenes,' Freda called back. 'Hurry up or we won't get a table for the three of us.'

'Over here, Freda,' a loud voice called across the canteen as they went through the two doors. Freda ushered Annie and Emily across the warm and spacious room to where a pretty blonde woman sat alone. 'I almost lost the table and had to tell two lads from the stockroom to sling their hook,' she said, laughing out loud.

'This is my friend Maisie,' Freda said, introducing the assistants to each other. Soon the girls were chatting like old friends as they compared notes on their counters and Maisie asked about working at the Bexleyheath store.

Emily looked at Freda when Maisie asked about the layout at Bexleyheath. 'Am I allowed to say it's just a pile of rubble?' she whispered.

Freda laughed so loud she started to choke on the cup of tea she'd been drinking.

Maisie thumped her on the back. 'Cough up, it might be a gold watch,' she guffawed. 'Come on, we have to get our food, or we'll be going without if the end-of-lunch bell starts to ring. Honestly, girls, you'll get sick to death of the bloody bells. Freda, I'll get yours; you stay here and save our table as those lads from the stockroom are giving us the eye.'

'It hasn't got anything to do with you flashing your legs,' Freda said as she managed to catch her breath.

'If yer got it, flaunt it.' Maisie winked as she led the two girls to the counter. "Ello, Maureen, me love, have you met Emily and Annie? They've moved here from you know where,' she said, giving another wink.

'Then you need feeding up,' the dark-haired woman said, with a warm smile. 'I've heard about the portions they dished up at you know where. Will sausage and mashed potato do you?'

Annie started to giggle thinking of the liver in their shepherd's pie. 'It looks delicious.'

They carried their food back to the table and were soon

tucking in, aware they didn't have long to eat before they had to be back on duty. Annie was surprised how popular Maisie was as people kept coming to the table giving her brown paper parcels or collecting clothing from a bag Maisie had placed under the table. There seemed to be a lot of money changing hands.

Maisie noticed Annie's puzzled expression. 'It's nothing illegal,' she said as she took a pile of coins from a woman and handed her what looked like a pair of men's overalls. 'I do a lot of make do and mend and my best customers work 'ere.'

'Maisie is a whizz on her sewing machine. She's been busy making us all siren suits to wear in the air-raid shelters.'

'I make them out of men's old suits I pick up at jumble sales or when women donate their 'usbands' clothing. There'll be many a man come 'ome after the war to find their wardrobes empty. If you ever want something run up, let me know.'

Annie was surprised but grateful. 'That does sound interesting. You're so clever,' she added as Freda shook out one of the siren suits made popular by Winston Churchill.

'Even Sarah's mum has one and she's ever so posh,' Maisie giggled.

Annie enjoyed chatting with her colleagues, thinking her time here in the Erith store would be most pleasant. When the bell rang for the end of their lunch break she returned to her counter feeling that whatever she was about to face that evening, at least she could look forward to her work with Woolworths.

14

The happiness Annie had felt all day slipped away as she cycled home through the dark night along the lane close to the River Thames, thinking of what lay ahead. Her bicycle had a dim, flickering lamp attached to the handlebars which pointed downwards so she was able to notice any uneven surfaces as she cycled, and thankfully she knew the journey almost as well as the back of her hand so she was soon pulling into the yard at the front of the house. Oh, for the days when lights from the house would have guided her home down the dark lane, she thought. As she pushed the bike down the front path, she rang the bell several times to let her family know she was home. Her brother, Albie, opened the door and ran up to her to take her bike to the shed as her dad bellowed for him not to let the light show or the Germans would find him, and to mind the blackout curtain at the door.

'At least he's still home,' she muttered to herself, not looking forward to what lay ahead.

'What was that?' her brother asked.

'Oh, nothing. I was wondering what was for tea. Come on, let's get inside, it's perishing cold out here.'

'It's bubble and squeak and a fried egg. The hens are laying again after that air raid frightened them half to death. I collected the eggs earlier for Mum,' he informed her before disappearing into the shed with her bike.

'Did you have a nice day at work?' Ruth, baby in her arms, asked as Annie joined them in the kitchen.

Annie bent over Ruth's shoulder to look at the baby. 'I swear she's filled out already; she looks so bonnie. Have you chosen a name yet?'

'She should wait until Pete can have a say in the choice,' Nan huffed. 'It doesn't seem right him not being part of the child's life.'

'Then he should have hung around longer rather than leg it,' Paddy snapped back.

'You're a fine one to talk,' she fired back at him. 'How often do you go off on your wandering and leave my daughter high and dry?'

'Now, now, Mum,' Violet said as Paddy stood up from the table, his chair scraping backwards on the linoleum floor. 'Please can we have a quiet evening for once? Look, you've woken the baby,' she sighed as the baby started to wail. 'Here, pass her to me while you get our Annie's meal on the table.'

'Mum, there's no need, I can do it,' Annie insisted, even though Ruth was on her feet and cracking an egg into the frying pan.

'I like to help out,' she said. 'You've all been so good to me and frying an egg won't tire me out,' she smiled, reaching into the oven where a dish of bubble and squeak was keeping warm.

'Not for me; I'm off out in a minute,' Paddy said as he went to where his coat was hanging from a hook behind the kitchen door.

'Wait, Dad. I wanted to tell you all about my day working in the Erith store,' Annie begged, hoping he didn't leave before she'd eaten. She couldn't really dash out of the house and waste precious food and it would look so strange to the others even though her mum knew what she was up to.

'Yes, Paddy, sit back down and listen to your daughter. I'll pour you another mug of tea,' Violet said, getting to her feet and reaching for the teapot before he could say no.

'I can spare ten minutes, but I really have to be somewhere,' he said, looking apologetically at Annie. 'How was your first day?' he asked, settling back in his chair with his tea.

Annie thanked Ruth as a plate was put in front of her and between mouthfuls of golden fried potato and cabbage and the perfectly fried egg, she described her new colleagues and working on the Christmas counter.

'I know Maisie,' Ruth said. 'She comes in the pub sometimes. She's wasted working in Woolies when her sewing is so good.'

Annie told Violet about the siren suits made from men's old suits and as she spoke, she decided to ask Maisie to make one for her mum as a Christmas present. It would keep her toasty warm while working in the laundry during the winter months. She noticed her dad drain the last of his tea and fold up his newspaper ready to leave.

'I must sort out my clothes for tomorrow,' she said, hoping no one would hear her leave the house to follow Paddy.

'Hold on a minute, I wanted to tell you all something,' Ruth said.

'Come back here, Paddy, Ruth has something she needs to share with us all,' Violet said.

Paddy groaned but stood in the doorway.

'I've decided on a name for the baby. If Pete was here, I'm sure he would agree. She will be called Ivy Rose after her grandmother and my late mother,' Ruth said, looking towards Annie's nan, who wiped her eyes but said nothing.

'That's lovely,' Annie gushed.

'I agree. Now, if you'll excuse me . . .' Paddy turned to go.

'There's something else . . .'

Paddy opened his mouth to complain but was silenced by his wife's glare and pursed lips.

'When baby Ivy Rose is christened, I would like Annie to be her godmother. I'm also going to ask the landlord and landlady of The Crown as they've been so good to me when I had nowhere to go. They gave me a room and a job, and I owe them a lot.'

'Perfect.' Violet smiled at the now sleeping baby and turned to her daughter. 'Just think, you will be part of this little girl's life from now on.'

Annie made her thanks, although a cold chill ran down her spine at what might happen later this evening.

'Now, Annie and Paddy, get on with what you were both going to do before we have more news to hold you back,' Violet insisted, shooing them from the room.

Annie hurried to her bedroom to collect her black coat along with a dark-coloured knitted hat and matching gloves; they would keep her warm and she'd be able to stay in the shadows without being spotted. Slipping a torch into her pocket, she crept back downstairs not far behind Paddy, who had just closed the door behind him. Praying her dad wasn't up to his old tricks, and she could report back to her mum that all was well, she stepped into her wellington boots and went out into the dark night.

Silently she prayed there would not be an air raid as then the rest of the family would notice she was missing, and her mum would have a problem explaining where she was. As she walked on for fifteen minutes or so, keeping Paddy in sight, she began to realize they were heading away from Slades Green, which meant they were even further from Erith. They were now deep in the Crayford Marshes, and it wouldn't be too long before they reached Dartford. It was then that she heard voices. Surely he wasn't meeting a lady friend out here on the marshes? Bending down behind some stumpy hedging, she thought it best just to listen to what he was up to. She may just recognize the woman's voice and could then report back to her mum.

It was cold bending down close to the damp ground and gradually her legs started to feel stiff, and one calf had cramp. She chewed on her lip then held her breath, but the pain would not go away. There was nothing for it but to try to move without drawing attention to herself. She reached out for a branch of the hedging hoping to be able to raise her leg a little and relax it. All the time she did this she could hear whispered voices nearby; at least her dad hadn't moved on. It was then that she wobbled and fell forward through the hedge.

'Blast,' she exclaimed before pulling herself up sharp. Had anyone heard her? She froze even though the cramp had her in a clamp-like grasp while sharp twigs were digging into her knees.

'Shh, did you hear that?' Paddy Brookes whispered loud enough for Annie to hear.

There was a harsh laugh from a man she didn't recognize. 'Don't say the German paratroopers are here already.'

'I heard it,' another man said. 'It came from behind you.'

Annie held her breath even though she wanted to scream as the cramp became progressively worse. Then there was a click that sounded very much like the gun her dad used for hunting, when he cocked it just before firing.

'Come out of there right now before you get hurt,' he snarled, the bush starting to shake as he worked his way towards her.

It was no use. If she didn't say something, her dad was likely to shoot her. Then what would her mum have to say?

'Please . . . please don't shoot,' she begged, hoping her dad heard her quivering voice.

'Annie, is that you? Blimey, girl, I was about to shoot you.' He swore again as he took her roughly by the elbow and pulled her to her feet.

'Ouch!' she sobbed as she brushed off the twigs embedded in her knees and hopped up and down trying to clear the cramp.

'What's she doing here, Paddy?' one of the four men standing with him asked. She couldn't recognize any of them as they were bundled up in dark coats and wearing knitted balaclavas to hide their faces. Annie recognized the helmets from the patterns her mum and nan used when they knitted for the WVS with many other women in the area. She was used to seeing the wool and half-made socks, gloves or balaclavas heaped on the table after they'd had a knitting session.

'It's my daughter, Annie. Why are you here, love?' he asked, his voice softening as he shone his torch into her face and saw how close she was to crying. 'Get her a drink, she's almost in shock,' he said, leading her to a tree stump to sit down.

Annie spotted a small billy can simmering over a fire built against a rock so the flames couldn't be seen from above. She took the drink gratefully and flinched as the hot coffee hit the back of her throat.

'Take it steady,' Paddy said, rubbing her back gently. 'Now, tell me what you're doing out here. I take it you followed me, or do you like wandering on the marshes alone at night?'

'I followed you . . . I wanted to know what you were up to as I'd heard you going out a few times late at night when I couldn't sleep.'

'Your mother didn't put you up to this, did she?'

How did he know? How could she say it was true and cause an argument between her parents? 'As I said, I heard you going out and was worried you were getting yourself into trouble. I'd better be getting back now as I have work tomorrow,' she said, handing back the tin mug knowing she was making lame excuses.

'You'll have to wait and come back with me. I'll be another hour at least.'

One of the men spoke harshly. 'Paddy, we can't have her seeing what we're up to.'

'I'm not letting her walk back alone, she could hurt

herself. Besides, she already knows something's going on. I trust her not to tell anyone.'

Annie became worried. What was it her dad was up to? 'I'll go home and forget I saw you all out here. I don't want to know what you're up to.'

'No! You're my daughter and I trust you. We're here working on unofficial national security,' he said, explaining how groups of local men were patrolling the marshes each night in case an enemy plane came down. 'We're the only ones who know the ins and outs of this place.'

'I want to help you,' she said. 'There must be something I can do.'

15

Late November 1940

As the weeks passed by there were times Annie didn't know if she was coming or going. She'd told her mother that as sure as she could be, Paddy wasn't carrying on with other women and that evening when she'd followed him, he had been out shooting rabbits with his friends to help local families eke out rations that were hitting them hard. He ensured he was home more in the evenings to allay Violet's fears and took her to the cinema several times. There were days when he helped in the laundry when not delivering to their customers. All in all, life had settled down, despite the incessant bombing along the Thames corridor.

What kept Annie's life on an even keel was working at the Erith store and she looked forward to cycling to work every day, although there was the odd occasion when her dad dropped her off when out delivering laundry. However, what lightened her days were the organized events at the store, not only for staff but also for the old soldiers and retired members of staff.

Coming home late one time after an evening out with

her friends to see *Went the Day Well?* at the cinema, she found her mum sitting alone in the kitchen, a cold cup of cocoa in front of her. Violet looked tense.

'Whatever's wrong?' Annie asked, pulling off her coat and hat. She hoped it wasn't something to do with her father as it disrupted the whole household.

'It's Ruth. She's informed me she's going back to work at The Crown three nights a week as they're short-staffed, and she says it will help her put some money by for the baby.'

'I thought we gave her something for helping in the laundry?' Annie said, sliding the kettle onto the hob.

'We do, but she insists on paying me for her and Ivy Rose's keep and that leaves her with very little. I could wring that brother of mine's neck leaving her in the lurch like that. She's a lovely girl and the baby is a little darling.'

'You don't have to tell me that.' Annie smiled, thinking back to the week before when she stood at the font in St Augustine's Church promising to look after the spiritual welfare of the little mite. 'Look, why don't we help her out so she can work her few hours as it'll make her feel more independent? We can care for Ivy Rose between us, and we have the van to pick her up after her shift. She can also borrow my bike.'

'What about the petrol? Only last week I overheard someone moaning that our van is seen about so much they wonder if it is just used for essential work; people can be so small-minded at times. I soon put her straight and told her to mind her own business. I may just have reminded her of the illegal pig club she has shares in!'

They both laughed together.

New Horizons for the Woolworths Girls

'I'm going to take my cocoa up to bed and if Ruth is awake, I'll have a word with her and say she has our support.' Annie turned towards the door. 'After all, it's only for a few weeks. I'll put my name down to help care for Ivy Rose as well. When is she due to start?'

'Tomorrow evening's shift.'

'Blimey, that soon?'

'It seems they're very short-staffed, and Ruth doesn't like to let the landlord and his wife down. They spoke to her at the christening last week and she's been plucking up the confidence to tell me.'

'Silly girl. Would you like another drink?'

'No, I'll warm this one up in a pan as the hob's still hot,' Violet assured her. 'Waste not want not.'

'I don't think another mug of cocoa will change the outcome of the war,' Annie chuckled as she kissed her mum's cheek and wished her goodnight.

Climbing the stairs, she heard Ruth talking to Ivy Rose. Now they both shared Annie's bedroom as it was the largest in the house, and Annie loved having the chance to care for the baby whenever she could. 'Not settled?' she asked, putting a mug of cocoa next to Ruth's bed.

'Thank you. A little bit of wind, that's all,' Ruth said as she patted the baby's back. 'There's a good girl,' she added as they were rewarded with a gentle burp.

'Here, let me take her while you drink your cocoa. Mum told me about you going back to work . . .'

Ruth's face dropped. 'Is she very angry?'

'Oh, of course not. We both feel it would do you good to get out and see your friends again rather than be cooped up with us all the time,' Annie said before outlining how they would help look after Ivy Rose, as well as pick Ruth up after her shifts at The Crown.

'I don't deserve all your kindness,' Ruth sniffed. 'To think I wasn't even married to Pete and have brought such shame on your family.'

Annie quickly put the baby in her crib and sat beside her friend. 'You have brought nothing but happiness to this family. Just because Uncle Pete is a bit of a rogue and has treated you badly does not make you a bad person. Do you think the vicar would have welcomed Ivy Rose into the church if he had any doubts about you? He's known our family for years and would have got a flea in his ear from Nan, I can tell you.'

They both chuckled at the thought and settled down to drink their cocoa.

'There is something else, if you don't mind me asking?'

'Ask away.' Annie tried not to yawn. 'If I can help, I will.'

Ruth turned to her bedside drawer and took out an envelope. 'All that talk in church last week about family and caring for Ivy Rose made me think. As much as I didn't want to, I knew I had to plan for Ivy Rose's future and if anything should happen to me . . .'

'Nothing's going to happen to you,' Annie protested as she started to climb into bed. 'I refuse to listen to what you have to say.'

'In that case, let me just tell you there are a couple of letters in this drawer . . .'

Annie turned her back on Ruth. She wasn't one for maudlin talk and refused to listen. 'Goodnight.'

'I never thought my working day at Woolworths would be spent in the cellar,' Emily grumbled, as for the second time that day they found themselves huddled underground with fellow colleagues and customers. The crowded space, humid despite the time of year, was lined with long benches but there were few other comforts.

'It could be worse,' Annie said, reminding her of what happened at the Bexleyheath branch. 'I still shudder when I think how I climbed out of that window. Thank goodness Dad and Goliath were there to help.'

'You're right, I shouldn't moan,' Emily said. 'I do hope my mother reached her cellar in time.'

Annie, who had met Mrs Davenport on several occasions and knew she never strayed far from the door to the cellar, consoled Emily. 'Your mum's not daft and can look after herself.'

'Let's 'ave a sing-song,' Maisie called out from the other end of the long cellar before launching straight into 'Down at the Old Bull and Bush'.

'I don't know this one,' Emily whispered to Annie.

'Once you've been down here more often, you'll know all the songs. Just hum along if you don't know the words,' she advised her before joining in with a 'la la la la la' while swaying from side to side.

'Are we 'aving fun?' Maisie asked as she stopped by the girls on her route around the dimly lit cellar to get everyone singing.

'I'd rather be doing something useful,' Annie said, thinking of her knitting in her locker. She'd planned to continue with the socks she was working on in her lunch break.

Maisie bent down to where they were sitting. 'My tip is to put it in a bag and keep it under your counter. The supervisors won't mind if you're doing your job and keeping an eye on the customers while we're down here. I've got some darning to do, and a hem to hand stitch on a frock I'm making for Freda for Christmas. Don't tell her, mind, as it's a surprise.'

'I could help you hem the dress, if you like?' Emily offered.

'Would you really? That'd help me a lot as I can't see me escaping this sing-song anytime soon.'

'And I'll help with your darning; it's something I do for my mum all the time. I'm handy at patching bed sheets as well, if you ever have anything like that. You'd be surprised how many torn sheets come into the laundry for repairs.'

'You'll wish you never asked,' Maisie guffawed before going to collect her bag.

'She's a laugh, isn't she?' a customer sitting next to them said. 'You'd not know what an awful start she had in life; her mother-in-law told me all about it.'

Annie nodded her head, knowing the woman expected her to ask what had happened. She didn't like talking about her new friends and was glad when Maisie reappeared with a bagful of work. 'Give me all of that,' she said, reaching out her hand as Maisie handed over a darning mushroom, a large needle threaded with wool and a pile of socks in random conditions.

'This one's going to have more darning than sock,' she laughed, holding up a navy-blue sock before getting stuck in.

They sat for another hour before the sirens started to announce the all-clear. 'There goes Moaning Minnie,' Annie said as she bundled up the socks, matching each pair to make it easier for Maisie.

'And I've finished hemming this frock,' Emily said, biting

the end of the white cotton thread between her teeth. 'I quite enjoyed doing that; it killed some time.'

'And no doubt the bombs raining down on us have killed a few poor souls,' the customer sitting next to Annie announced before raising her fist to the ceiling of the cellar. 'That bloody Hitler won't want to meet me up a dark alley, that's all I'm saying.' Annie's nan often said something similar, and she bit her cheek trying not to laugh. Emily wasn't so lucky and burst out laughing.

'You may laugh, my girl, but one day that Hitler will be walking up the High Street. What will we do then when there's no one to save us?'

Annie so wanted to contribute to the conversation and put the woman straight; if only she knew that every evening the men living in the area were out patrolling the marshes and planning for a possible invasion.

'Come on, let's get upstairs and see what damage has been done,' she said, stretching her legs as Emily held out a hand to pull her to her feet. 'It's only when you move you realize how uncomfortable those benches are,' she said, rubbing her behind. 'Perhaps we need to make some cushions if we're going to be down here a lot.'

Maisie, who was following the two girls up the steep stairs to the shop floor, simply groaned. 'Can't they fold up their coats and sit on them? I've far too much sewing and knitting work as it is.'

The rest of the afternoon went as smoothly as it could after a heavy air raid. Some of the girls helped sweep up dust that had fallen when the building shook, while others were sent outside along with stockroom staff to see if they could help shop owners who had fared worse that afternoon.

It was the late afternoon tea break by the time Annie and Emily sat down with Sarah.

'There's still a lot of clearing up to be done. Would you like us to stay after the store closes and help the cleaners? It seems unfair to put the burden of the enemy action on them,' Annie offered, surveying the Christmas counter. 'Even the Chinese lanterns look dusty; it wouldn't take long to brighten them up if we use our feather dusters.'

'That's so kind of you and I'll make sure the extra time is added to your pay packets,' Sarah assured her.

Emily looked uncomfortable. 'I'm sorry but I must clock off on time today. Mum has guests and I'm needed at home. I can work late tomorrow if that helps?'

Sarah gave her a smile. 'Please don't think you have to; there will be other opportunities.'

'And other air raids,' Annie said ruefully.

It only took an hour for the Christmas counter to look as good as new. Annie checked her watch as she left the store. Pushing her bicycle out to the road, she started to free wheel towards the High Street. As she reached the junction, she spotted a familiar vehicle and stopped to wave as it pulled over.

'You're late knocking off,' Paddy said as he leant out of the window.

Annie explained about working overtime. 'Can I put my bike in the back if you're going home?'

'I do have to see someone, but it can wait. I can't have my daughter cycling home in the dark now, can I?'

Annie looked at Paddy as she climbed in beside him once the bike was stowed away in the back of the van. 'You seem happy. Have you been drinking?'

'Just a pint when I dropped off Ruth. I was chatting to the landlord and let's say he's interested in helping us.'

Annie was alarmed. 'That's a bit quick. You need to be more careful who you confide in.'

He laughed at her concerns. 'He's a decent sort and in some ways he's family, what with him and his wife being Ivy Rose's other godparents.'

'I suppose you're right. I'm just a bit jittery . . . what the hell!' she shrieked as a loud explosion could be heard from the river, followed by the sound of sirens working their way up the Thames.

Paddy swore out loud. 'Hold on. A plane must have slipped through,' he said, swerving the van up Avenue Road. 'There's a public shelter on the corner. As soon as I stop run over there. Quick as you can.'

'What about you?' she asked, her hand already on the door handle.

'I'll park the van and join you as soon as I can,' he said before she fled towards the entrance of the shelter.

Inside she gave her name to a warden, telling him her dad wasn't far behind her, and found a seat, nodding to a few women she recognized from Woolworths. The benches here were just as hard. She chewed her fingernail nervously until he appeared minutes later as the shelter shook from the sound of more bombs dropping not far away.

'That was a close one,' she said, shifting along to make room for Paddy's large frame on the bench. He put his arm around her and felt her shaking.

'You're safe down here with me,' he said, holding her close.

Time seemed to stand still as they sat listening to the planes overhead, the ack-ack guns firing from the river, and people praying as they waited and hoped the townspeople of Erith escaped the onslaught from the enemy. Eventually it fell silent and still they waited; no one wanted to venture outside until it was safe and the all-clear had sounded. The warden at the entrance to the shelter peered out. They heard him call out to someone before he returned into the shelter.

'They've got The Running Horses and The Crown,' he said. 'Things are bad down by the river.'

Annie froze with shock before turning to Paddy. 'Dad, do you think Ruth got to safety?' she asked as a cold chill ran up her spine.

Paddy placed a hand on her shoulder to calm her fears. 'I'm going to find out. I want you to stay here and wait for me.'

'Oh no, I'm sticking to you like glue,' she said, standing up. 'Come on, let's get down there.'

They hurried over the road to where Paddy had left the van, which fortunately hadn't been damaged. After weaving through the crowds finding their way home Paddy drove down the High Street towards the river. What would they find when they reached the two pubs?

16

The van crept slowly past the shops in the High Street. Annie craned her neck to look up Pier Road towards Woolworths. Even in the dark night she could see enough to calm her worries. Thankfully the row of shops was in darkness and seemed to be in one piece with no sign of bomb damage or fires. It was little consolation when she looked up ahead and saw the thick black smoke and flames billowing into the sky over the Thames. They hadn't got as far as the police station when they were stopped by a policeman in the middle of the road waving his arms and using a torch to slow down the few vehicles trying to get through. Paddy stuck his head out of the window.

'Hello, Mike, what's it like up there? We're trying to get through to pick up Ruth. She's working a shift at The Crown pub this evening.'

Sergeant Mike Jackson rubbed his eyes, which were reddened by the smoke. 'It's bad, Paddy. I don't think much of the young girl's chances. The Crown is all but gone and we've yet to see any survivors. The Running Horses is still standing, but there are casualties; I could see drinkers sitting at their tables . . .'

'Do you mean . . . ?'

'Yes, the shock waves of the bomb killed every one of them by the look of it,' he said bleakly. 'I suggest you get your Annie home; it's not a sight for young eyes.'

'You need helping hands down there. I'm going to turn the van round and you're going to drive it home, Annie,' Paddy decided. 'Can you do that? I want to find Ruth.'

Annie nodded her head, unable to speak for a moment. Even her experience of the bomb at the Bexleyheath store bore no resemblance to what she could see ahead of her. 'I can do that, but how will you get home?'

'I'll manage, don't you worry about me.'

'Take the bike,' she suggested.

Afterwards she had no memory of how she navigated the dark roads driving through Slades Green and the marshes, her mind on Ruth and if she had survived.

Back at the house Annie sat with her mum and nan while they took turns to cuddle Ivy Rose. Her grandad and brother walked up and down the lane hoping Paddy would arrive with good news.

'I wish the bugger would ring,' her nan said, glaring at the telephone. 'There are days when it doesn't stop with people wanting their washing back or complaining about something. Now, because we want to hear what has happened it stays silent.'

Violet passed the baby to Annie and went to check the telephone. She held it out as if showing the others. 'It's not working. The raid must have knocked out the exchange.' She wiped it over with the edge of her apron and settled the receiver back in its cradle and patted it gently. 'I will say, they are handy when they work.'

'Shall I make us a drink, or perhaps a bite to eat?' Annie asked, glancing at the clock as the hands hit midnight.

'I'm awash with tea and if I eat anything, I'll be having nightmares,' her nan said as she looked towards the window. They were sitting in the dark with the curtains open hoping to see signs of Paddy's return. 'Why don't you put that baby down in her crib? Her routine is all out of kilter and there will be hell to pay tomorrow.'

Annie held the child closer. 'No, when Dad brings Ruth home, I want her to be able to see her baby and hold her. She would have been through hell and I'm sure cuddling Ivy Rose will give her comfort. The baby will soon get back into her routine.'

The women fell silent, all deep in their own thoughts.

'Dad's back,' young Albie exclaimed, rushing into the room full of excitement. 'He's outside talking to Grandad.'

'Time you were in bed, young man,' his mum said as she ushered him out of the room towards the stairs.

'But I want to hear about the pubs being destroyed,' he whined.

'Time enough for that tomorrow. Hurry up with you,' she said, tapping him playfully on the backside. 'Don't forget to wash behind your ears,' she called after him as Paddy walked through the door, putting a hand on her shoulder. She looked at his bleak expression and knew it wasn't good news. 'Come through to the kitchen and I'll put the kettle on, you must be parched.'

Paddy followed Violet and slumped down in a seat at the table.

'You've got to tell them, lad,' Grandad said as he joined them, heading for his seat by the fire. 'I've put the van away for the night. It doesn't seem right somehow . . .'

Annie looked between her dad and grandad. 'Please don't tell me she's . . .'

'It would have been quick, love,' Paddy said, unable to look her in the eye. 'I helped them remove her from what was left of the building. I said we'd be responsible for the funeral.'

'She's part of our family so it's only right,' Violet agreed.

'What about the landlord and his wife? Ruth told me they've been like family to her. Perhaps they might want to make the arrangements?'

'They died alongside her,' Paddy said, thinking of the sight he'd seen as he helped the recovery people.

Violet took the baby from Annie as she covered her face with her hands, leaning on the table and sobbing.

It was her nan who sat beside her and rubbed her back as she let out her anguish at the unfairness of Ruth's death. 'She had so much to live for,' she sniffed into a handkerchief her mum had given her. 'Ivy Rose will grow up not knowing her mother, how awful is that?'

'Who will have her?' Nan asked. 'With our Pete disappearing and him being next of kin, God knows who will take on the little mite.'

Violet shook her head. 'Ruth left our Pete's name off the birth certificate. She didn't want anything to do with him after he abandoned her.'

Nan looked at the expectant faces before turning to Annie. 'She confided in me not so long ago that she'd left the baby in the care of you and the pub landlords, in case anything should happen to her, and you're the only one left alive.'

Violet gasped. 'Mother! Just because they're godparents it doesn't mean they inherit the child. It is Ivy Rose's spiritual upbringing they must watch over.'

'Nan's right, though, Ruth wanted me to care for Ivy Rose. She was telling me last night about some letters she's written . . . and I didn't want to listen. I turned over and went to sleep . . .'

'There, there,' Nan said. 'It's no use blaming yourself. Save your venom for the enemy. This little sweetheart needs her family around her and for all intents and purposes that's us, and you are now her mother.' She passed the baby to Annie. 'Time to take her to her bed. From now on we keep a smile on our faces and only cry when the little lass is in bed. She may only be weeks old, but she will sense happiness and sadness. This little mite will only know love from this point onwards.'

Annie took the baby and started to head towards the stairs before turning to look at her family. 'I didn't know when I woke this morning that by this evening I'd be a mother,' she said, looking sad. 'But I'll do the best I can.'

Walking carefully up the stairs and into her bedroom, she first placed the sleeping baby in her crib which had been moved beside her bed. She checked the blackout curtains, trying hard not to look at the empty bed on the other side of the room. It was as Ruth had left it that morning, with her flannelette nightdress draped across the pillow and her slippers set neatly by the bedside cupboard. It was then that she remembered the letters and took them from the drawer. Leaving the others on top of the cupboard, she took the letter with her name written on the outside to her bed and sat down. Not wishing to turn on the light for fear of waking Ivy Rose, she held the single page close to her face and read by the light from the hall.

Dear Annie,

If you are reading this, then something has happened to me. I pray that Pete has come home and has met Ivy Rose, but then perhaps I am praying for too much as he is a wanderer, and we may not see him again. If the day comes when he returns to the marshes, please tell him of my life here and all about our baby since the day that she was born. However, I don't wish him to have a claim on Ivy Rose as I want her to grow up in a close family and be loved. For this to happen I turn to you, dear Annie, and entrust my girl into your care. Her godparents will always be there to help you. In fact, if you look in the small wooden box under my bed, you will find a few personal effects along with some money given to me when Ivy Rose was christened. Perhaps I would have added to it as I have high hopes of doing so with my job. At the time of writing, I have yet to start work.

I know you will be a good mother to my daughter. Tell her I will always look over her as she grows into a beautiful woman.

Your good friend,
Ruth

Annie held the page to her breast as scalding tears coursed down her cheeks and she thought of the way her life was about to change.

*

Sarah rushed to help Annie as she carried baby Ivy Rose up the stairs to the offices of Erith Woolworths. It was a fortnight since Ruth's death and the first time she had visited the store.

'Here, let me take the poor little mite,' Sarah said, lifting the baby from Annie's arms, leaving her to carry a bag of essential items for the child. Behind her two storemen were bringing the pram up the steep stairs.

Once settled in the office belonging to Betty Billington, Annie started to make her thanks until Sarah raised her hand to silence her. 'Annie, there's no need to thank us as we should be thanking you. Even to be considering returning to work when you have the responsibility for this child's upbringing is to be commended. Looking after a baby is a full-time job. I will say we all thought of you on the day of the funeral. December can be such a bleak month for such things.'

Annie could only nod her head in agreement. So many people had turned out to pay their respects to those who died that night at the pub. Brook Street Cemetery, on a hill looking out over Erith and the River Thames, was the resting place of many local people, but to say goodbye to a young girl who had left behind a baby and whose intended had vanished off the face of the earth was unbearably sad.

Annie was embarrassed by Sarah's words and wriggled uncomfortably in her seat. 'It's not as if I volunteered. I am Ivy Rose's godmother and along with the other two godparents we promised to look out for the child. I didn't expect that only weeks later I would be the only remaining person that Ruth had wished to care for her baby if anything should happen to her. My parents and grandparents will be helping, so I'm not on my own; that's why I wrote to you to ask if I could return to work. With all the family mucking in I can do just that.'

Sarah was thoughtful for a little while. 'Betty is returning to work next week, and this should really be her decision. However, I'm pretty certain she would welcome you back with open arms, on one condition . . .'

'What would that be?' Annie asked, feeling relieved on one hand and worried on the other.

'You come back part time until your life settles down. Let's revisit this at the end of January. By then you'll be used to being a mother to this little darling,' she said, kissing the tip of Ivy Rose's button nose. 'Now, why don't you take your daughter into the canteen? I do believe some of the staff are waiting to meet her.'

Annie placed Ivy Rose into her pram, covering her with the patchwork quilt her nan had made. She had stitched late into the night, while her mum had knitted a complete layette for their little princess, as they'd started to call her. 'Come along, sweetheart, you have people to meet.'

As her colleagues congregated around the pram, some out of a morbid curiosity and some out of maternal feelings for the baby, Annie wondered what it would be like to show off a baby she had conceived and given birth to; a child she had wanted and not been left like something in a will. She at once felt guilty for her thought and, trying to shake off how she felt, she chatted exuberantly about feeding times and nappies.

All too soon it was time for her to be leaving her workplace to return to their home on the marshes. It had been decided she would push the pram down to the front of

Erith Odeon where Paddy would have the van ready to collect them. As she started to leave by the double front doors of the store Maisie hurried over to her holding out something in her hand.

'Put this on yer finger,' she urged her, standing in such a way that no one else could see what they were doing.

Annie was puzzled. 'What is it?'

'It's a ring, only a cheap brass one, but it'll stop people gossiping when you're going out and about with the baby. Believe me, love, they'll be looking, and tongues will be wagging.'

'But I can tell them what happened with Ruth,' Annie said, looking at the ring in the palm of Maisie's outstretched hand.

'Perhaps around here with people who know you and what happened, but in the outside world you'll be seen as a scarlet woman. Take it from one who's had the finger pointed at her, you'd be better off wearing it,' she urged, pushing the ring closer to her.

Annie took the ring and slipped it on her finger. 'Thank you for thinking of me,' she whispered, suddenly finding this whole new world she had stepped into rather daunting. 'I'd best be going as Dad will be waiting for me.'

'Tell anyone who asks your husband's away in the army,' Maisie called after her.

As she hurriedly pushed the pram down the High Street, Annie kept her gaze in front of her, not making eye contact with anyone. Were they watching her? What were these people thinking? She felt as though she stood out like a sore thumb and was relieved when she reached the Odeon cinema and spotted Paddy waiting for her.

'How did it go?' he asked as he handed the sleeping baby to Annie before lifting the pram into the back of the van.

'Very well, considering. Everyone adored Ivy Rose and I'm to return part time. My hours will be reviewed in the new year.'

'That seems fair to me,' he said as he started up the engine.

'There was something else . . .'

'If they've upset you, I'll go in and have a word,' he said, sounding agitated.

Annie couldn't help but laugh at his words. 'It's nothing like that.' She raised her left hand. 'I'm a respectable woman now. I've gone and got myself married.'

Paddy had to work hard not to steer the van into the pavement such was his shock.

17

April 1941

'Thanks for letting me come out with you this evening,' Annie said as she buttoned up her coat. 'I just needed to get out for a while and clear my head.' She looked towards her dad, who was wearing a heavy duffle coat and a black hat on his head that she'd knitted for him. He had a rifle over one shoulder and was pulling on a canvas backpack. 'You won't get in trouble for having me with you, will you?'

'Don't worry yourself about that. I'm on a patrol duty with Fred Linton; it's not official Local Defence Volunteer duties tonight.'

Annie tried not to giggle as Paddy took his unofficial war work very seriously. 'You mean, it's your private group of defence workers?'

He looked sideways at her and smiled. He knew she liked to josh him. 'That's right. We're patrolling down past the football ground and on towards the railway station.'

'And ending up in The Lord Raglan, perhaps?'

'Depending on what we have to report,' he smiled, putting an arm around her. 'Now, tell me what's on your mind before we meet Fred and he dominates the conversation with the state of his bunions and his nagging wife.'

'I hope you don't think I'm moaning, it's just that I don't want to worry Mum and Nan all the time.'

'If I knew what it was you were trying to say, then I could make the right comment . . .' he said, turning from the slight wind to light a cigarette.

'I'm not sure I'm a good enough mother to Ivy Rose. After all, what do I know about bringing up children and she is so tiny,' Annie confessed. 'I'm so frightened I'm going to do something to endanger her life because of my ignorance.'

Paddy started to laugh.

'Dad, it's not funny, stop laughing,' she said, getting more annoyed with him the more he chuckled.

'Sorry, love. I'm not laughing at you. I was thinking back to my mum telling me how she dropped me on my head when I was a baby, and did your mum tell you how she left you outside the butcher's in Erith and came home without you? Don't even get me started on your nan, but then perhaps I shouldn't say considering how your Uncle Pete turned out. Honestly, love, it will take a while, but you'll get the hang of things. I know it was a shock us losing Ruth like we did, but she had faith in you enough that she chose you to care for Ivy Rose if anything should happen to her. Besides, it's not as if you're caring for the little one on your own. That's if you can trust us after what I've just told you.'

It was Annie's turn to laugh. 'I don't know why I was worrying.'

'Paddy, is that you?' a gruff voice called out from behind a nearby hedgerow.

'Yes, it is, Fred, and you can come out from behind there as I'm not talking to the enemy. This is my eldest, Annie.'

'Hello, Mr Linton,' Annie called out as she heard the rustle of leaves before he appeared. 'How is Mrs Linton?'

Paddy groaned as Fred started to go on about his wife until the wail of an air-raid siren sounded from further down river. 'Fred, you know the streets around here, where can we take shelter?'

'There's one down the railway sheds, come on,' he said, hurrying towards the sidings as they followed, barely able to see in the fading light. They dived down six steps and found themselves in a semi submerged cellar where two men were seated.

Fred introduced them as he seemed to know everyone, and they settled down to wait.

'That was close,' Paddy said as the ground shook and dust fell on them all.

Annie was worried. 'Can you smell burning?'

'I bet the bastards have hit some of the rolling stock,' one of the rail workers exclaimed, getting to his feet. 'We can't wait for the all-clear in case they blow. Who's coming to help me?'

Paddy was on his feet in a second and following him to the door. 'What do you mean, blow?'

'There are six wagons in the sidings loaded with bombs. We need to check they aren't on fire or the whole area will be obliterated,' the man called back. 'Keep the girl in the shelter as this is no place for her.'

Annie bristled with indignation; she could put out a fire as good as the next person. Hadn't she been trained for fire watching and putting out incendiary bombs on the roof of

Woolworths with buckets of sand? 'Where's the sand?' she called out as she followed them out into the night air.

Fred waved his hand towards a pile she could just distinguish as it was illuminated by the burning incendiary bombs. 'You'll find buckets and a shovel close to the sand but stay away from the sidings,' he yelled as he ran after the other men. She could see there were other rail workers already using hosepipes aimed at railway carriages a few hundred yards down the track; every person she could see was working at speed and with purpose to get the situation under control.

'Let me take those,' a man said, reaching for the two metal buckets Annie had just filled with sand.

'Please bring them straight back to me,' she called after him, noticing there were only another six buckets stacked by the sand pile. As she worked filling the next ones, she could hear whistling sounds and close by a small fire started next to a shed filled with track equipment. 'You can't fool me, Adolf, I'm an expert at this,' she called out, although no one was nearby to hear her. Picking up a shovelful of the damp sand, she expertly covered the small incendiary bomb. As she did so she thought of the night she worked alongside Freda and several other colleagues on the roof of the Erith Woolworths store doing the same thing. She'd also learnt how to use a stirrup pump but found it rather slow, what with having to pump up and down and make sure the other end of the attached hosepipe was in a full bucket of water; she much preferred a bucket of sand and a shovel.

Once the buckets were full, she looked about her to see where she could use them and spotted a small fire on the top of a passenger carriage. Seeing a ladder nearby, she dragged it beside the carriage, carefully balancing the bucket as she scaled the steps. Next time, she would only half fill the bucket, she thought to herself as she struggled with its weight. Once there she scooped up the sand with her hands and covered the fire as best she could until she was confident it had been put out. Climbing back down the ladder, she peered through the window of the carriage and was shocked by what she saw: the burning oil from the bomb had ripped through the roof and the plush seats were now ablaze. 'I need help here!' she called out to the man who had returned to the pile for more sand. Between them they forced the door of the carriage open and attempted to put out the fire before it took hold.

'That was scary the way the bomb ate through the roof,' she said, shivering a little. 'I'm going to walk the length of this train and check we haven't missed another as it could spread so quickly.'

'I'll do the same with the other train over there, then we need to refill the buckets.' He removed his cap to wipe his brow.

Annie had reached the very front of the train before she spotted another fire. She called for help then opened the carriage door to tackle the flames with her half bucket of sand. She was soon joined by several of the rail workers and together they extinguished the blaze. 'No one will be travelling in this carriage anytime soon,' she said sadly.

'Don't you be so sure, love,' grinned one of the workers. 'We've got all the equipment here to be able to work on these trains even if it means making one new carriage out of two damaged ones. We can't let 'itler stop our railway.'

They'd hardly stopped to reflect on the glory of what they'd managed to do when there was a shout from the other side of the yard. 'Big trouble over here, mates,' Annie heard her father call out. As she ran with the other men towards the wagons in the sidings, she could see a blaze had taken hold in a row of sheds close by.

'Bugger me, if those wagons catch hold, they could blow up all of Slades Green,' bellowed the man who'd been helping her fill the sand bucket. 'Get the hosepipes aimed on those barns alongside the railway sheds,' he shouted out.

'I can help with that,' Annie said, thinking that a few of the men would be better getting close to the sidings where fires were still burning.

'No, Paddy would never forgive me if something happened to you. You stay here and keep an eye on these carriages in case we missed something.'

'But where is my dad?' she asked anxiously, trying to make out the sidings through the smoke that still hung in the air. No one answered her as they were all busy with their own tasks to save the yard. Annie peered through the smoke more closely. She spotted him at the front of the row of wagons as he climbed onto the engine. Whatever was he going to do?

'Get back,' he yelled at her as she approached. 'Your mum will be none too pleased if two of us failed to get home tonight.'

Annie did as she was told and stood watching, chewing the finger of one of her gloves as Paddy started to move the steam engine slowly forward, taking the bomb-laden wagons away from the burning sheds.

It felt as if it took for ever until finally she could run to

New Horizons for the Woolworths Girls

him and hug him as he climbed down. 'I've never seen anything so brave or so foolish,' she scolded him. 'How did you know how to drive the train?'

'A steam engine's workings aren't much different from those of Goliath,' he shrugged. 'We were lucky she'd been stoked up ready to move out otherwise it could have been a different story.'

'And all this was going on while people were fast asleep in their beds,' she added as the all-clear started to sound.

'Perhaps make that asleep in their shelters,' Paddy said. He tried to clear his throat, rough from the smoke. 'I don't know about you, but I'm gasping for a cup of tea.'

Along with the other workers and Fred they went to the railway canteen that was inside the main brick-built sheds, all the time checking around them in case they'd missed an incendiary bomb. Soon they were tucking into doorstep-sized bacon sandwiches and drinking strong tea from pint-sized mugs.

'Anytime you want a job down here we can put in a good word for you, Paddy,' one of the men said. 'I reckon you saved our bacon this evening.'

'In more ways than one,' Fred said, taking another bite of his sandwich. 'Young Annie here more than did her stuff as well. We owe a debt of gratitude to the Brookes family.'

18

December 1941

'Take a seat,' Betty Billington said with a gentle smile as Annie entered her office at the Erith store. 'How are you keeping? Is everything well at home?'

'Very well, thank you for asking. It's been a year since . . . since Ivy Rose lost her mummy, and I took on her care. Things are ticking over nicely,' Annie replied, smoothing the skirt of her burgundy-coloured overall.

'I hope what I'm about to say doesn't upset the apple cart too much.'

Annie frowned and wondered if Miss Billington was unhappy with her work in any way. The last year had seen so many changes in the store with male staff leaving to join up and older women returning to work. Stock had been low on certain counters, and she had heard that management worked hard to bring in enough for their customers to purchase. Unlike the larger stores, they didn't have a cafe bar, although there were some biscuits and vegetables on sale. She'd been informed that Betty had made a deal with a local farmer to sell them produce direct; goodness knows how she worked her way through all the loopholes the government had created. Annie was miles away and jumped as Betty spoke again.

'With the Bexleyheath store due to open before Christmas I'm having to say goodbye to some of my best staff.'

'Goodbye?'

'Don't look so worried; your job is safe. I value your work here and I'm sad to see you leave this store, but you are required back at Bexleyheath,' Betty said, placing her elbows on her desk and leaning forward. 'It will mean promotion for you.'

Annie felt as though a lump had formed in her stomach. She was happy at the Erith branch; it was easier to reach than Bexleyheath and she had made so many friends in the past year. 'Are you certain I have to move back to Bexleyheath?'

Betty sighed. She liked Annie, who had fitted in very easily with her team of workers and was so well liked. Everybody had shown sympathy for the plight of Ivy Rose, but Annie had stood up to the challenge with fortitude and hadn't ducked her responsibilities.

'I'm afraid my hands are tied. Head office and the new manager at Bexleyheath have observed your employment file and want you there as a supervisor and to be trained in personnel. You get on well with everyone and we like to reward hard work.'

Annie couldn't believe her ears. This would mean an increase in her wages and as she was putting as much by as she possibly could for Ivy Rose's future, she would be an idiot to turn down the opportunity. 'I'm grateful to management for thinking of me. I did wonder if, having a child, people would think I was a . . . an unmarried mother,' she said as she twisted the ring on her left hand that had remained there since Maisie gave it to her.

Betty knew the story behind the ring and although Maisie meant well, she couldn't help thinking it would stop any suitable young man from courting her. In her mind nothing would be better than to see Annie settle down with a nice young man and produce a few siblings for Ivy Rose. 'Annie, you must remember you are not an unmarried mother and have taken on a beautiful baby when her mother perished at the hands of the enemy. Could you perhaps only wear the ring when you are out and about with the child? I'd rather see you not wear it when at work.'

Annie slipped off the ring and put it into her pocket. 'I'll do that,' she said. 'Can you tell me more about my move to Bexleyheath, please?'

'That's better. Now, the store is opening in ten days, in time for the Christmas period. There's a team already in there stocking the counters and getting everything ready. There's an advertisement in tomorrow's local newspaper with open interviews for staff starting the day after. We will not be asking for postal applications as potential staff can walk in off the street to be interviewed. I will be there, and I'd like you to accompany me.' She waited for Annie's reaction.

Annie's face glowed. 'I'd really like to work with you to choose the staff.'

'Then tomorrow we will go up to the store together and prepare. There's no need to wear your Woolworths uniform. I wonder, will you be all right? I know you had quite an experience escaping from the building.'

'No worse than yours,' Annie replied, knowing how it had taken Betty a while to recover from her own ordeal.

'I don't expect to encounter any ghosts of what happened last year, but if we do find it harder than expected, we can prop each other up.'

'That seems like a good idea,' Annie said before leaving Betty's office to head downstairs. She was again working on the seasonal Christmas counter, but unlike last year, she was teaching two newer staff members. Emily sidled up to her as she stepped behind the counter.

'Why did Miss Billington want to see you?'

Annie looked around her to check no one was listening. 'I'm to be moved back to the Bexleyheath store as it's opening soon.'

Emily frowned. 'I wonder why I've not been told?'

'I would think Miss Billington will speak to you soon,' Annie placated her, hoping her friend would also be working with her, especially as she lived so close to the store.

As if on cue a supervisor walked by and informed Emily that she was wanted upstairs in Miss Billington's office. 'I'll see you at tea break,' Emily grinned as she hurried away.

She had changed her tune by the time Annie arrived in the canteen.

'It's just not fair,' Emily huffed as soon as Annie joined her carrying two cups of tea.

'What isn't?' she asked, feeling in her bones it would be about her promotion.

'I'm being sent back to Bexleyheath store when it opens, which I don't mind. However, I've been told some staff are being promoted to supervisors and I'm not,' she pouted.

'That's a shame as you would make a good supervisor,' Annie sympathized as she stirred her tea too much until it slopped into the saucer. How was she going to explain about her own promotion to Emily? Although she was proud Betty felt she was ready for a better job, she felt sorry for Emily and knew she would be hurt. 'Look, Emily . . .' she started to say.

Emily glared at her. 'There's no need to keep your little secret, I saw the list on Miss Billington's desk. Supervisor and trainee personnel officer; why couldn't you tell me?' she sniffed, obviously upset. 'I thought you were my friend.'

Annie sighed. At times Emily acted young for her age; perhaps that was why she had not been offered promotion. 'Why not speak to Miss Billington? Perhaps there's a long list and you'll be invited soon?'

'I just wish you'd told me as it was horrid finding out that way. Why didn't you?'

'There wasn't time as I'd come straight from the office to our counter, then you were called upstairs. I would have told you, honest I would,' she said, looking her friend squarely in the eye. 'I don't want us to fall out.'

'And neither do I,' Emily replied, giving an embarrassed smile. 'It was a shock, that's all, what with us starting work on the same day and everything.'

'I understand how you feel, and I'd probably be upset if the boot was on the other foot. Look, once I'm in my new job I'll be able to put a word in for you and before you know it, you'll be wearing a supervisor badge and bossing all the new kids about.'

'I'd like that . . . I mean I'd like to be a supervisor. It would please my mum as well,' Emily replied, her face determined. 'She's always said I'd amount to nothing working here and I'd like to show her. Is that bad of me?'

'No, we all want to get on in life, and I'll help you all I can,' Annie promised. 'Now, we'd best drink up or the bell's going to ring for us to get downstairs and we'll not have finished our tea.'

The next day Annie accompanied Betty, who drove in her little car up to the Bexleyheath store.

'There's no sign the store was damaged so badly. The builders have done a marvellous job on the exterior of the building,' Annie said, looking up and down its length while Betty locked up her car after reaching in for a pile of papers.

'I agree. I just hope the interior is as good. Here, take some of these and we'll go up to the office. These are what we need to fill out for each new employee.'

'Crikey, that's a lot of paperwork,' Annie said.

'We won't be using all of it. I brought enough along for future use,' Betty explained as they entered the building. 'Doesn't this look wonderful? Although the smell of fresh paint is still a little overpowering.'

Annie looked around the shop floor. 'They've done a good job. The counters look the same as before, just newer,' she said, going over to run a hand over the mahogany woodwork and glass edges. 'I can't wait to be working here again. Not that I won't miss the Erith store,' she added quickly in case Betty thought she was being ungrateful.

'I know what you mean. I've worked in a few different branches since starting as a youngster. I was a cleaner to begin with at the Woolwich branch towards the end of the last war. Every branch I worked in I adored, then I felt unfaithful to the previous one,' she chuckled.

'You don't look old enough to have been working for so long,' Annie said, trying to count the years.

'Don't look too closely at my grey hairs,' Betty smiled, raising a hand to the brown hair neatly folded into a bun at the nape of her neck. 'Come on, let's go upstairs and get started on our long list of jobs.'

Annie felt a shudder run through her as they climbed the stairs to the first floor of the building that held the staff canteen and the offices. This was where she could have lost her life after the oil bomb set fire to the roof. She stopped at the top of the stairs and gazed around. It was hard to see the blackened walls and smoke-filled corridor now, but she could still picture it all in her mind's eye and imagine the smoke and the fear.

Betty placed a hand on her shoulder. 'It's all right to feel the fear of that day all over again. It happened to me for a long time. Just give me the word and we'll leave. You can continue to work with me in Erith if you prefer?'

Annie took a deep, shuddering breath. 'No, I'll be fine. I can overcome this. Lead the way,' she said, letting go of the banister and placing one foot in front of the other as she followed Betty to a small office with a view out over the main road. 'I've not been in here before,' she said, looking at the small desk and two chairs set in the middle of the floor.

'There will be some more office furniture arriving tomorrow, then the room will feel much smaller, but it will do for now. Put the papers down on the desk and we can make a start once we've had a cup of tea. Shall I go?' Betty asked, knowing the canteen was the room Annie had escaped from. Marge is in there.'

'No, I've got to do this and knowing Marge is there will help. I won't be long,' Annie said as she walked briskly to the staff canteen, staring straight ahead of her until she pushed open the doors.

'Hello, ducks, I'm that pleased to see you,' Marge said, enveloping her in a bear hug. 'I don't mind telling you it took a lot for me to come into this building. My old man said to give up the job, but I was climbing the walls at home with only him to talk to. I even thought about getting a dog for the company,' she chuckled. 'Are you back here to work?'

'Yes, I'm working with Betty Billington. We're going to be interviewing new staff tomorrow when the advert comes out in the paper.' Annie paused and blinked hard. 'It was difficult for me to come back into the building too. I almost ran away when I reached the top of the stairs just now. Betty felt the same.'

Marge shook her head. 'That's not good enough. If we don't learn to live with this, then the enemy have won.'

'I never thought of it like that. You're right, we can't let this ruin our lives. We're stronger than this. Thank you for pointing that out.' Annie turned to go. 'Oh, silly me, I came in for two cups of tea before we make a start.'

'Get back to your work and I'll brew a fresh pot and bring it in to you. I'm here a few days early to sort out the kitchen area and do some baking, and I may just have something to keep you going until your lunchtime.'

Annie hurried back to the office to tell Betty what Marge had said about not letting the enemy win. By the time they'd made neat piles of the different forms and notes for the interviews Marge arrived with a tea tray.

'Tea for two and slices of seed cake,' she announced. 'Good old Woolworths always come up trumps with provisions.'

'Come and join us,' Betty offered.

'Another time. I have meat and potato pies in the oven, and I'd hate them to burn. If you like, I can put two by for you for later?'

'They sound delicious. Shall we say one o'clock? We will have accomplished a lot by then and will be ready for a meal.' Betty smiled as she adjusted the glasses she wore when reading.

'I'll have it ready for one. There are some staff downstairs who will also be here at that time, but I'll save the pies for you,' Marge promised, leaving them to get on with their work.

'We need more help if applicants are expected to wait around while we interview each one. We can't be in here and downstairs at the same time,' Betty said as she scanned the notes they'd made.

'I suppose I could move a table down into the store and work there; that way I can see anyone who comes in and give them an application form at the same time as doing interviews,' Annie suggested.

Betty gave her a nod of approval then added, 'A commendable idea, but you have forgotten that interviews should be undertaken in private, and you would be continually interrupted. Believe me, it can get very busy when we have open interviews. No, we need a third person here for the days we're interviewing.'

'I have the ideal person; Emily would be perfect to welcome the potential employees. She looks good in her Woolworths overall, has perfect manners and lives close to the store. I happen to know she wants to be considered for promotion when an opening occurs, so this would be a perfect way for you to see her doing something rather than working behind a counter.'

'And a suggestion like yours shows me you would be perfect working in personnel,' Betty beamed as she reached for the telephone to place a call through to the Erith store to give instructions to Emily to report to the refurbished store the very next morning.

Annie breathed a sigh of relief knowing Emily would be pleased to be given a new challenge.

19

'They've done a good job refurbishing the store,' Emily said as she looked around, taking in the polished floor, the new lighting and the stocked counters. 'I'm going to enjoy working back here, are you?'

'I am,' Annie agreed. 'I did have a slight wobble yesterday when I came in and walked up the stairs where we were trapped, but I'm fine now and I've run up and down them so many times I've completely forgotten what happened last year.'

'I can understand that. Now, what do you and Betty want me to do?'

Annie explained that they wanted Emily to greet the applicants as they came in through the doors. She was also to check that no shoppers thought they were open as so many people missed the signs of when the grand opening would be. 'If the applicants sat on this row of seats, you could give each one a form and a pencil. Once completed, you could cast your eye over them quickly to make sure they haven't missed anything and then add their name to the list. Betty and I will come down to see out the person we've just interviewed, and you can point out the next person for us to see. Do you think that will work?'

Emily thought for a moment before agreeing. 'I can't see there's any problem but if one becomes apparent, we can change what we're doing as the day progresses. There is just one thing: what if I wish to visit the ladies' or take a tea break? And what's going to happen about lunch?'

'Gosh, I'd not given that a thought. I can ask Marge to bring tea down. In fact, Betty mentioned providing tea and biscuits for the applicants so I must get that arranged. Perhaps when one of us comes downstairs we can stand in for you while you dash to the ladies'?'

'That's a relief,' Emily said, grinning at her joke. 'Perhaps the same could be done for a short lunch break as we can't put a sign on the door asking applicants to come back later.'

'I think that's it, apart from me sorting out a tea table. I'll do that as soon as I go upstairs.'

'There is something else. I want to thank you and Betty for choosing me for this job. I'll do my very best to make you both proud of me.' Emily gave Annie a quick hug.

'Think nothing of it. You were the first person we thought of when it became apparent we couldn't do it between us. Now, why not come upstairs and leave your coat in the office? We have ten minutes before we must open the door. Our new manager isn't starting until next week, so we have full use of it. Oh, and best call Betty Miss Billington in front of the ladies who come in for interviews as it's much more professional.'

'Say no more,' Emily said as she followed Annie upstairs.

Betty welcomed her into the office and told her more about the staff they were looking for. 'We have ten who worked here before. The rest have either stayed where they were placed or have moved on to new jobs or joined the services.'

'This doesn't really affect what I'm doing downstairs, does it?' Emily asked, looking worried. 'I'd hate to pick the wrong person.'

'No, it doesn't, but I like to keep you in the picture as we will be working together as a team for the next three days.'

Emily looked at Annie and gave a small grimace. They were both thinking how important it was to do a good job and not let Betty down.

Annie helped Marge and her assistant carry the teapot, crockery and biscuit tin downstairs while Marge told her assistant to pop down every half hour with fresh tea and clean crocks. 'We have to make a good impression,' she admonished her.

'We all seem to be on our best behaviour,' Annie smiled.

Betty unlocked the door dead on ten o'clock and let in six women who were already queuing outside before retiring to her office. Emily handed out application forms and answered questions while Annie served tea before showing the first two ladies upstairs to the two offices they were using for interviews. She'd been a little wary of taking on the responsibility of choosing staff, but Betty assured her she would soon get the hang of things and she was to trust her gut feelings if she was unsure. If someone was not suitable, they would be told a letter would be in the post to them, saving Annie the worry of turning down an applicant. As it was, Annie soon got into the swing of welcoming the person and chatting about the store while she checked through their form. She found it easy to ask questions and could tell early on if the person seated across the desk from her would make a good Woolworths employee, and at that point the applicant was given an arithmetic test. It was almost lunchtime before Annie came across one young girl fresh out of school who had got almost all the arithmetic questions wrong. Annie could see she was very nervous and decided to give her another chance.

'Why don't you try it again? I need to pop out for a couple of minutes, so I'll put this in front of you so you're able to think clearly without me sitting nearby.'

'Thank you,' the girl said anxiously as Annie left the room. Outside in the corridor she bumped into Betty, who was just showing another applicant into her office. She pulled the door to so she couldn't be overheard.

'How's it going?' Betty asked.

Annie explained about the young girl retaking the test. 'I have a feeling it's just nerves as she is so personable that I think she'll make a good counter assistant.'

'You are probably right. There was one time when I didn't put forward a person for a vacancy but fortunately for me another became available, and I called her back. She has been one of my best employees to date.'

Annie frowned. 'Would I know her?' she asked before thinking perhaps she was being too nosy.

'It was the first time I'd undertaken a group interview on my own and the person I almost lost was Maisie. My gut told me I'd made a mistake and thankfully I acted on it.'

Annie was astonished as she had seen how good Maisie was at her job, as well as being a helpful colleague to all new employees at the Erith store. 'I just hope I listen to my gut feelings too,' she said as they both returned to their offices.

As it was, the young girl had completed the second test without making one mistake. 'Being alone, I was able to use my fingers to count on,' she explained before slapping her hand to her mouth as if she had spoken out of turn. 'Gosh, it won't look good if I use my fingers to count on when I serve a customer . . . That is, if I get the job.' Her cheeks turned bright red.

Annie reached for a pile of small notebooks that were tied to a pencil with a length of string. 'You will be given one of these to attach to the waistband of your overall. I find this a great help as I list each item and then add them up as I did when I was at school.'

'So, I won't need to count on my fingers?' The girl breathed a sigh of relief.

'Just be careful not to stick your tongue out as you do the sums. I was reminded I did just that,' Annie laughed. 'Now, tell me, will you be able to start work on Monday?'

'You mean, I've got the job?' the girl asked before bursting into tears of joy.

Annie then remembered Betty's warning to always have a stock of freshly laundered handkerchiefs in her desk drawer.

After seeing the young girl to the door downstairs, she turned to Emily to ask who was next.

'This gentleman is next, but he asked to see Miss Billington . . . He hasn't completed a form,' she replied, raising her eyebrows.

Annie held out her hand to the man. He was tall and slim with dark hair slicked back with Brylcreem, and his blue eyes sparkled as he looked at her. As he was dressed in a suit and navy-blue tie, his shoes polished to a high sheen, she thought he couldn't be there for a storeman vacancy. 'How do you do. May I ask why you are here if you do not wish to fill out one of our forms?'

He took her hand and shook it firmly. 'I was passing and spotted the signs with Betty's name. I popped in on the off chance she was available.'

Annie pulled her hand from his, even though it felt comfortable in his grasp. 'I'm sorry, but as you can see, we are rather busy conducting interviews for the imminent opening of the store.'

'In that case I will complete the form and await my turn,' he said, giving her a warm smile before returning to his seat with an application form he'd picked up from the table on the way.

'Who's next?' Annie asked Emily.

'Mrs Downes. She's applying for the position of part-time cleaner,' she said, handing Annie the woman's completed form. 'Would you follow my colleague, please, Mrs Downes,' she called out to a stout woman in what looked like her Sunday best coat and hat. As they reached the staff door that led upstairs to the office Betty appeared, seeing out her latest interviewee. They both stepped back to let them pass. Betty had only taken a few steps when she shrieked, 'Simon, is it really you?' as he got to his feet and hurried towards her, lifting her in his arms and swinging her round.

'Good grief, put me down, man! Whatever must these people think?' she declared, straightening her suit jacket and checking her hair with her hand. She looked up at his smiling face. 'Wherever did you come from? The last I heard you were . . .' She looked around at the faces all pointed in their direction avidly listening. 'Come up to my office, we have a lot to discuss. Are you able to carry on alone for now, Annie?'

'Of course,' she replied. 'Take as long as you like.' She watched them head towards the staircase. Simon looked back at her and mouthed his thanks.

'You've made a conquest there. Such a shame you're married,' said Mrs Downes, giving her a nudge. 'Come on, let's get this over with; my Percy will be wanting his meal sometime today and I've not even been to the fishmonger's yet.'

Annie looked down at her hand. She'd forgotten to remove the pretend wedding band and swore under her breath. It was time to remove it once and for all. She conducted the interview in a haze, trying to pick up odd words from the next room along with Simon's warm laughter and Betty's higher pitched giggles.

'Is that it then?' Mrs Downes asked as she got to her feet.

'Thank you for coming and I look forward to seeing you at work,' Annie replied, thankful the lady had an excellent record and two very good letters of recommendation from her previous employment.

'You'll only see me if you start work at the crack of dawn,' she chuckled as she got up to leave the room. 'I'll wish you good luck as well with . . .' She nodded her head towards the sound of Simon's voice.

'Oh, be off with you,' Annie laughed as she showed Mrs Downes downstairs.

'Only two more and they came in together: mother and daughter,' Emily said as she checked the paperwork before handing it over. 'Mum worked for the company a few years back, and the daughter is still at school and was interested in working Saturdays as well as the holidays.'

Annie looked across at the two women. 'Lock the door. I'll see these two together then we can close for lunch. I know it's not what we planned, but with Betty busy with her friend we may as well lunch together.' She turned to the two women and smiled. 'Follow me, ladies.'

Afterwards, when sitting with Emily in the staff canteen tucking into Marge's pies, she commented how the women were a pleasure to employ and wished more interviews had been as easy. 'They came across as nice people from what I could see as I watched them when they entered the store. I'm looking forward to working with them.'

Emily agreed. 'It will be interesting working with a whole new team and us all starting at the same time. It's as if we're starting out in a new store.'

They were still enjoying Marge's food when Betty appeared, followed by Simon.

'He's still here then,' Emily whispered. 'I wonder how Betty knows him?'

'We may get the opportunity to find out,' Annie replied as the pair approached their table.

'May we join you?' Betty asked. 'The food looks good.'

'Of course. We closed the front door and put a sign up to say we would be back in an hour, as it was impossible for me to interview on my own,' Annie explained.

Simon apologized. 'That's my fault taking up Betty's time. I promise to not monopolize her any more once we've eaten.'

'I can recommend the pie,' Annie said as plates of piping hot food were put in front of the pair by Marge's assistant. 'How do you know each other?' she asked.

Simon looked towards Betty, but when she didn't speak, he told the girls, 'Betty trained me when I first joined the company. I was fortunate to be placed in her store as she is extremely thorough.'

Emily frowned. 'Why did you leave?'

Betty cleared her throat. 'There's a rule that trainee managers move on to other stores until they are given their first branch management position. Simon, although in reserved employment, decided to join the RAF.'

'I received an injury when I was shot down and rather than take a desk job I decided to return to F. W. Woolworths.'

The girls made sympathetic noises while continuing to eat.

Betty gently scolded him. 'If you aren't going to tell them, then I suppose I must. Simon, Mr Greyson, is to be the manager of this store. Though I didn't expect to see him today.'

'You could say I was keen to get stuck in,' he grinned.

Emily and Annie were almost dumbstruck. 'But you seem rather . . .' Emily started to say before turning pink in the cheeks.

'Young?' He chuckled. 'I can assure you I am old enough to manage this store and have survived my strict training.'

Emily wanted to know more. 'What does your wife say about you taking on this store?'

Betty raised her eyebrows at Emily's blatant interest in his love life.

'I'm free and single,' he said, giving her a wink.

Emily blushed even more. 'Just as I am.' She glanced at him coyly.

Annie's stomach sank. Was this what it was going to be like now she had responsibility for Ivy Rose? While her best friend made an instant play for their new boss? That was so unfair. She was deep in thought as one of the men stocking the storeroom ran into the canteen waving a newspaper in the air.

'The Japs have bombed Pearl Harbor,' he called out excitedly before joining his mates at a nearby table where they pored over the newspaper.

'Excuse my ignorance, but where is Pearl Harbor, and why is he so excited?' Emily asked to no one in particular.

Simon's face showed no sign of his earlier humour. 'Pearl Harbor is a major American port in Honolulu, and Japan bombing them can mean only one thing . . . America will join the war within days.'

20

June 1942

'You are such a clever girl,' Annie said to Ivy Rose, kissing her cheek as the child held up a piece of paper with crayon marks across the page.

'Mummy and Nanny,' she said seriously, pointing a chubby finger at each of the scrawls.

Annie's heart lurched. It was always the same when Ivy Rose said the word 'Mummy'. The child had no idea Annie wasn't her mother and it worried her what her reaction would be when she found out later. Her instinct was to forget about it for now, but then the thought would drift back into her mind, often keeping her awake.

'She's growing up fast,' Violet said as she watched the child toddle off waving the crumpled piece of paper to Nan, who was snoozing in the armchair closest to the kitchen stove. 'What are you planning for today?' she asked. 'It's not often you have a day off from your work.'

'I'm going out in the van this morning to make the deliveries and then this afternoon I'm helping you in the laundry. You and Dad have been a godsend keeping an eye on Ivy Rose so I can work full time at Bexleyheath, and I want to try to pay you back by helping out with the business whenever I can.'

Violet smiled. 'There's no need. We have a good routine these days, which works well around Ivy Rose. She's a joy to care for. Mind you, your dad is off out most evenings so sometimes he's not fit to drive that van the next morning. You might have a word with him if you can?'

Annie could tell Violet was worrying about something. 'Mum, you've got nothing to worry about with Dad; you know he's with his friends either catching food for the pot or with the volunteers. He's with Sergeant Mike, so nothing untoward will be going on,' she said, hurrying to stop Ivy Rose tugging at Nan's cardigan and waking her.

Annie took the delivery list from where her mum had placed it on the kitchen table and went out to the laundry to retrieve the bags of clean washing. She double-checked she had everything before going out to the back field to look for her father. As she expected, he was in the barn tinkering with Goliath, the steam engine. Due to the many restrictions now imposed on the showmen's business the equipment was stowed away, much of it in the Brookes' back field, while the men in the family undertook different work. Two of Annie's showman uncles were now chimney sweeps for the duration.

'I'm ready to go now,' she called out to Paddy above the sound of the engine running.

He appeared, wiping his hands on a piece of rag. 'Give me ten minutes to wash and put a clean shirt on. Can you start loading?'

'All done and dusted, and I've planned our route. I

thought, if there aren't any air raids, we could drop off a few leaflets around the end of Bexleyheath Broadway in those big houses. What do you think?'

'That's a good plan. We could also leave some in the big houses close to the railway line in Erith,' he suggested before hurrying back to the house. He was as good as his word and joined Annie ten minutes later looking spick and span. 'Your mum made these sandwiches for us,' he said, passing her a small parcel wrapped in brown paper.

Paddy got behind the wheel promising Annie she could drive the van when they'd covered half the round and they set off towards Bexleyheath. 'You must be sick of travelling this route?' he laughed.

'No, I love working at the Bexleyheath branch. I only wish it was as close as the Erith store.'

'I've been thinking about that; it's time we had a second vehicle for the laundry business.' He kept his eyes on the road ahead as two army lorries sped by. 'They look like Americans,' he said with interest. 'I heard there were some up near Woolwich.'

Annie didn't take any notice as she was puzzled by his previous comment. 'What do you mean by a second vehicle?'

'One you could use to get to and from your work, and it could be used at other times for collecting and delivering washing. If we keep a bag or two in the back, you won't be stopped and questioned about why you're using petrol when you aren't on business.'

Annie thought about his suggestion. 'I like the idea, but I'm not going to break the law. Why don't you change the delivery and collection schedule so I can drop off and collect either side of work? If anyone else needs the van when you're busy, they can drop me off. It would help if we had a few more contracts in Bexleyheath or even Crayford as we can cut through that way from Slades Green.'

Paddy roared with laughter. 'I'm beginning to wonder if you are my daughter: you never break the law and want to work long hours. I'd have to get up early not to get caught out by you, love.'

'Which reminds me, Mum is worried you aren't getting enough sleep with you out so late with your mates.'

'Not so much of the mates. I'll have you know we are all members of the Local Defence Volunteers. But perhaps I'll get home a little earlier, just to please your mum, as I don't like knowing she worries about me.'

Annie gave a satisfied smile. 'You are happy being at home, aren't you?'

'I am, love, I am. My wandering days are over.'

'That's good to hear. Now, can you pull over here and I'll put a few leaflets through these doors before we drop off the next bag wash at the doctor's house? Mum's pleased as he hasn't used our services before.'

She placed the heavy bag of clean laundry at her feet while she lifted the door knocker, but before she could begin knocking the door opened, causing her to step back in surprise. She was even more surprised when she saw it was Simon, the manager from work.

'Why, Annie, whatever are you doing here?' he asked.

'I could ask you the same question,' she said, hating him to know her business.

'I live here. It's my father's practice.' He peered past her to the van where Paddy raised his hand in greeting. 'Isn't that your surname on the side of that vehicle?'

Annie squirmed, expecting him to pull her leg, although she wasn't sure why he would. 'My family own a laundry service and I help out when I can,' she explained. This was awkward, as she realized Simon must be the son of their family doctor. How could they not have known?

'You are a busy bee, what with caring for your daughter as well.'

She stumbled over her words. 'How do you know . . . ? I mean who told you . . . ?' she asked as very few people knew about Ivy Rose at the Bexleyheath store.

'Your friend, Emily, mentioned it when you refused to join us on a staff trip to the theatre. I've not been snooping in staff records I can assure you.'

It fleetingly crossed her mind that Emily was keen on their manager and would stop at nothing to get his attention, but would she tell tales on her friend? 'Please do check my records as you may learn something,' she sniffed as she raised her left hand. 'Please note there is a reason I do not wear a wedding ring. If you will excuse me, I have work to do,' she said, not listening as he called after her.

'Hurry up and start the engine,' she insisted as Paddy looked out of the window at Simon.

'He seems to want to speak to you.'

'I don't wish to speak to him. Please, Dad, just hurry,' she begged.

Paddy sighed and did as she requested. 'I take it you know this chap, or do you treat all prospective customers in the same way?'

'He's my manager at Bexleyheath, and he asked one too many impertinent questions about my life.' She sniffed back tears. 'He said Emily told him I was an unmarried mother.'

He shook his head. 'It's not like you to get upset; as a rule, you stand your ground. I take it you like this person?'

Annie pulled out a handkerchief from the cuff of her cardigan and wiped her eyes. 'Don't be daft, I hardly know him. Although now I realize who his father is.'

'I'd have thought your store has social get-togethers as you used to attend a few when you worked at Erith.'

'There are, but I prefer to come home and see Ivy Rose before she goes to bed. I see very little of her as it is, and she is my responsibility. I see her as my daughter even if that is being used against me by Emily, which hurts a lot.'

Paddy pulled over to the side of the road and switched off the engine. He turned to Annie. 'There are going to be times when you find out people aren't as sincere as you thought they were, and by the time you realize, you may have told them your personal details and shared secrets. I've experienced this a few times as a lad due to coming from a showman family. We are called all kinds of things which I won't repeat here. You learn to be hard and protect yourself. Mix with these people but grow a hard shell. I know you can do it,' he said, leaning over and giving her a hug. 'Now, where is our next stop?'

It was with some trepidation that Annie went to work the next day. Thinking over the words she had exchanged with Simon on his doorstep, she felt embarrassed. There had been no need for her to have snapped at him like she did, especially as when she returned home later that day her mum informed her that the doctor's surgery had placed a regular order for their laundry services.

Today was her day for pulling together numbers for head office to pay the weekly wage bill. It was when she was collecting the clocking in cards that she bumped into Simon.

'Miss Brookes, could you spare me a few moments, please?' Annie nodded her head in agreement and followed him into his office. He indicated that she should sit down as he sat in his chair opposite her.

'About yesterday, I'm very sorry for my rudeness,' she said as at the same time he said, 'I must apologize for my rudeness . . .'

They both laughed together.

'After you,' he said.

'No, after you,' she giggled. 'After all, you are the boss.'

'I want to make it up to you for my rudeness. Have you seen the poster in the staff room? There are a group of us going up to London on the next half-day to see *Blossom Time* at the Lyric Theatre. I wonder, would you join us? I appreciate you like to work in your family business and that you have a daughter to care for, but if you could make it, I would be very pleased. And I did check your personal record and again apologize for my thoughts,' he said, looking embarrassed.

Annie smiled. She felt sorry for his embarrassment and knowing that she was partly to blame, how could she refuse? 'I would very much like to join you and thank you for thinking of me. Who do I see about buying a ticket?'

'It's my treat, and we may have time to go dancing afterwards so wear some comfortable shoes.'

She got up to leave the room. 'Thank you,' she smiled. 'No, thank you.'

She was so glad she had listened to her dad yesterday. She needed to find time to enjoy herself and be Annie again, rather than Annie with a child. The trip to London would be, she hoped, the first of many such times.

21

Annie looked up from where she was checking through her handbag as she sat in the staff canteen. For the life of her she couldn't find her purse. How could she go out with her colleagues and not have any money with her? A sudden memory came to her. She had taken it out of her bag to leave ten shillings on the kitchen table for her mother just before she left that morning; she'd been in a rush sorting out a dress for the outing along with her last decent pair of stockings. She knew there wasn't time to go back home to collect it. Whatever could she do?

Marge noticed her unhappy face and came over from behind the counter. 'Is there something wrong, dear? I couldn't help seeing you were flustered.'

Annie started to explain her dilemma when the door to the canteen opened, and a little voice shrieked, 'Mummy!' as Ivy Rose toddled into the room carrying Annie's purse in her chubby hands.

'You little sweetheart,' she exclaimed as Violet followed Ivy Rose into the room. Annie jumped up to hug her mum. 'Don't say you drove up here just to drop off my purse?'

'I knew you'd need it,' Violet said, taking Ivy Rose's hand

to stop her running around the canteen and bothering people. 'There were a few deliveries to make, so we did those at the same time to save your dad coming out as he's busy looking at another vehicle.'

'I can't believe he's doing this; it'll make life so much easier. Sit down, Mum, I'll get you a cup of tea.'

'There's no need, dear, I don't want to trouble anybody. I'm not even sure we should be up here.' Violet gazed around nervously.

'Of course you should,' a voice said from the counter as Simon walked over to join them. He bent down until he was face to face with Ivy Rose. 'Who is this beautiful young lady?' he asked, tweaking her nose.

'Ibee,' the child giggled.

'This is my daughter, Ivy Rose, and my mum, Violet.'

'Welcome to the store, Mrs Brookes,' he said, shaking her hand and then shaking Ivy Rose's as she held it out. 'You have impeccable manners for a young lady,' he added seriously.

'She can't quite say her name yet,' Violet explained with a smile.

Marge brought over tea for Violet and milk for Ivy Rose, while Simon sat with them chatting to Violet about her business.

Emily entered the canteen and made a beeline for their table, giving Simon a sweet smile and sitting next to him. 'I see you've met Annie's daughter,' she said pointedly, causing Annie to gasp at the blatant cheek.

'I'm very proud of my daughter and how she's holding down a good job as a supervisor, as well as providing for Ivy Rose,' Violet said, squeezing her daughter's hand.

'I think we can all agree with that, Mrs Brookes,' Simon said, leaning over to lift the little girl up onto his lap. 'You have a very clever mummy.'

Emily frowned, looking around the cosy circle. 'I'd have thought F. W. Woolworths would have frowned upon someone whose mind is unlikely to be fully on her job?'

'The company think very highly of Miss Brookes and I second their decision.'

Emily visibly shrivelled in her seat. 'My apologies, I must have missed something,' she almost whispered as she got up, and went to sit with another table of counter assistants who had been watching what was going on.

Annie was mortified. She'd always thought of Emily as a good friend until the green-eyed monster appeared. 'I'm sorry, I don't know what all that was about,' she said miserably.

'We must be on our way, I don't want to hold you up. Enjoy your trip to London,' her mum said, taking Ivy Rose from Simon. 'It was a pleasure to meet you,' she added.

'Likewise,' he said, shaking her hand then watching them leave the canteen.

'There are a few things I need to do before we leave for the train station,' he said to Annie. 'I'll say just one thing, you have a wonderful family, and it is others who are wrong about you. Don't listen to them.'

Annie nodded as he left her alone at the table. Emily came over to join her, looking contrite.

'I'm sorry for what I said. I had no idea you'd set your cap at Simon.'

Annie drew herself up in her seat. 'You couldn't be more wrong; I haven't set my cap at anyone. If Simon chooses to talk to me or my daughter, that is his choice and no one else's. I have too much going on in my life for romance,' she said seriously.

Emily took a moment to absorb this comment. 'Thank you for explaining to me as I'm rather keen on him myself. I hope I haven't offended you?'

Annie assured her she was not offended but deep down inside felt that their friendship could never be the same again. 'Nothing has changed,' she lied rather than cause a scene.

'Then we can sit together on the journey to London?'

Annie forced a smile on her face. 'Of course, I can't think of anything I'd like more.'

Annie was in raptures as she watched the musical *Blossom Time* at the Lyric Theatre in London, the cherry on the icing being that there wasn't an air raid during the matinee.

'What did you think of the show?' Simon asked, helping her into her coat before stepping out of the theatre into the busy street; with Daylight Saving Time the sky was still bright.

'I thoroughly enjoyed it. Thank you for arranging the trip,' she said and she meant it. Her family weren't ones for visiting the theatre although they liked a pantomime at Christmas, so this was a real treat.

For a moment it seemed as if he would hold out his arm for her to take it. But, she realized, that would be to single her out and he had to be careful of his position as manager. 'The hotel where the dancing is held is just a couple of streets away. I've reserved two tables for us otherwise we may not be able to get in, let alone sit down. Keep up,' he called to the rest of the Woolworths group.

'This is nice,' Emily said as they entered the foyer of the hotel, with its plush maroon carpets and gilt-edged lampshades. She pushed in between Annie and Simon as she spoke, aiming her comment towards him. Annie let her actions wash over her; what did it matter? If Emily wanted to stand with Simon, then she could.

'The dance is held in the basement ballroom. Follow me,' he said, counting the heads as the colleagues hurried downstairs, leaving their coats with a hat check girl and putting the numbered ticket she gave each of them away safely.

'Hang on to your gas masks,' Annie called out, noticing several of the girls handing them in with their coats and hats. 'They may not look very smart but they could be lifesavers if we're attacked.'

'I'm thinking of covering mine to make it look smarter; I noticed Maisie at the Erith store had done just that,' Emily confided.

'She's a clever seamstress. Mum was delighted with the siren suit I gave her at Christmas. Nan has requested one for her birthday. She reckons if it's good enough for Winston Churchill, then it's good enough for her,' Annie chuckled.

'Bless her, she'll look so sweet.' Emily had a soft spot for Annie's grandparents. 'Perhaps we should have a Woolworths version of a siren suit as we spend so much time in the cellars at the moment and it can get quite chilly down there.'

'Now that's a thought,' Simon said. 'Annie, you asked me about the staff keeping a cardigan or hats and gloves under their counters to be grabbed if the sirens go off. I can't see that would be a problem if they were kept to hand with their gas masks. Well done for the suggestion,' he added as he pulled out two velvet-covered chairs for the girls to sit at the table.

Emily raised her eyebrows, but Annie pretended not to notice.

Soon waiting staff were bringing a selection of sandwiches and cakes to their tables. 'Did we pay for this?' Annie whispered to Emily. She was worried she might not have enough money in her purse for such treats. It was clearly a classy place: the white tablecloths were starched, the napkins neatly folded.

'No, we don't have to pay. Simon had a word with head office, and they have covered the meal with the hotel. This all looks rather scrummy, don't you think?'

Annie agreed, wondering if she could slip one of the small cakes into her bag to take home for Ivy Rose. She didn't notice Simon speaking to the waiter hovering by the table until he returned with a small cardboard box tied with a ribbon and placed it in front of her.

'Compliments of the management, madam,' Simon said with a bow. 'A treat for my favourite girl.'

For all her apologies and promises Emily looked daggers at Annie.

Annie burst out laughing as the penny dropped. 'Thank you, Simon, Ivy Rose will be so delighted with the cakes,' she said as she peered into the box. 'What a treat!' She decided to ask her daughter to draw a special picture for Simon as a way of saying thank you.

'We are close to head office and use this hotel for entertaining, which means we can usually arrange a special event here,' he explained. 'The staff are very kind and look after us.'

'I'm thoroughly enjoying myself and know I've already said so, but thank you for our treat. If you will excuse me, I need to visit the ladies' room,' she said, reaching for her handbag that was by her feet.

'I'll come with you,' Emily said.

As they followed the corridor towards the stairs that went up to the next level, they were alerted to the sound of many voices coming down the stairs.

'Wow, American servicemen. I'd heard they were over here helping with the war,' Emily said, holding back to see them more closely.

'Don't be so obvious,' Annie hissed, pulling Emily through the door of the ladies' room by the sleeve of her best frock. 'I would think they'll be here for the dancing, so you won't miss seeing them,' she said. 'I've heard they do some very strange dances. That will be interesting to watch.'

The girls touched up their make-up and returned to their table, noticing at once how the atmosphere in the ballroom had changed. With the band warming up and the American soldiers at the bar the place felt as though it was buzzing. 'Things are going to get lively, not just here but all over England with these lads in town,' Emily grinned.

Annie was worried. In the time she'd known Emily she'd learnt that the girl had led a sheltered life and hadn't mixed with lads very much. 'Be careful,' she warned her friend as Emily smiled in the direction of the men.

The band struck up and the servicemen fanned out across the ballroom inviting young ladies to dance. Emily was soon swept away by a blond-haired soldier.

'Would you care to dance?' Simon asked Annie as he

stood up. 'I'm not very good, even worse since my injury, but I'll give it a go if you will?'

Annie, who was worried about being asked to dance by the bold Americans, quickly agreed. 'I'd love to, and you have no need to worry as I'm not very good either.'

They shuffled around the floor for a couple of foxtrots then retired to their table as the tempo picked up. 'I enjoyed that, thank you,' she said. 'I hope your injury didn't play up too much?'

'I'm fine,' he assured her. 'It's my knee. It took a bullet early on in the war and was enough to invalid me out, more's the pity.'

'Oh, you men! My dad had the same attitude. He wanted to fight but an injury in the first war put paid to that. He sulked for ages until Mum had a word with him,' she smiled, thinking of the memory.

'Would you like a drink?' he asked, getting to his feet.

'A lemonade would be nice, thank you. It is getting rather hot in here.'

She watched the crowded dance floor, trying to seek out the girls from Woolworths. Thankfully their dance partners seemed polite and courteous, although she couldn't say the same for some of the other men. She looked to where Simon was at the busy bar purchasing their drinks and didn't notice the soldier standing behind her until he reached out and took her hand. 'Dance?' he said, pulling her out of her chair and towards him. It was a command, not a request.

'No, sorry, I can't do this,' she said, waving her other hand to the dance floor where men were almost throwing the women about, up in the air and swinging them around.

The band had sped up; she didn't recognize the music at all. It was as if she was in another land she didn't know. She felt herself swung around and tried to hold the skirt of her frock down to protect her modesty as the soldier ignored her refusal.

'Leave the lady alone,' a familiar voice insisted.

'Man, we're having a good time, aren't we, doll?'

'I said leave the lady alone,' Simon growled.

Annie heard a loud thump and found herself free of the soldier's grasp as she staggered away from him. He'd swung his fist straight at Simon, and she struggled to maintain her balance.

Screams and shouts alerted her to where Simon was now brawling with the soldier. She started to scream as more soldiers joined in with the fight. The few men in the Woolworths party ploughed in trying to help Simon who was underneath the scrum. They were joined by other men in British uniforms and some in suits.

Whistles started to sound as military police charged down the stairs waving truncheons above their heads. The women stood in front of the stage trying to get away from the affray.

'You caused this,' Emily spat at Annie. 'I was having a good time until this happened.' She turned her back on Annie and walked away. Thankfully the other Woolworths counter assistants came to her rescue and comforted her as the military police arrested each of the American soldiers, carting them away until all that was left were exhausted guests and worried staff who started to put right the tables and chairs and check the men who seemed to be injured. The ballroom manager was running around waving his hands about, bemoaning the state of the ballroom, shouting at people to leave.

'We need to get our party together outside,' Annie said to the women, all the while wondering where Simon was and hoping he wasn't hurt. 'Get your bags, coats and gas masks. Let's see if we can find the men.'

The women agreed and started to pull their colleagues to their feet before heading to the staircase. Annie was relieved to notice one familiar figure leaning against the banister.

'Simon, come on, we're getting out of here,' she said as she checked him over. 'Are you badly hurt?'

'A few bruised ribs,' he said, wiping blood from the corner of his mouth. 'More importantly, how are you?'

'I'm fine, thanks to you. It was the drink making them brave.'

'They had no right to act as they did. They're an embarrassment to their country.'

'Forget it, they're gone now. Let's get back home, shall we? I just need to get my coat and handbag,' she said, walking over to where their table had been turned up the right way by a waiter who handed Annie her bag.

'I believe this is yours, madam,' he said, passing her the small cardboard box.

'That's very kind of you,' she said, thinking how excited Ivy Rose would be even though the trip had been tarnished by what happened in the ballroom.

'Your party are all outside, sir,' he said as Simon joined them.

Simon reached into his pocket and took out a few notes. 'This should recompense you for any damages. If not, you can contact me here,' he said, passing over a business card.

The man thanked Simon before helping him up the stairs to the foyer where they joined their colleagues. After checking everyone was no worse for their ordeal, he asked who wanted to head home and who wanted to carry on with their evening.

Annie was relieved when over half the group said they wanted to go home. Simon called a couple of taxi cabs, and they piled in. The last Annie saw of Emily was her walking down the road with two other girls from Woolworths, clearly with no intention of going home just yet; their heads were close together and they were laughing at something Emily had told them. Annie raised her hand to wave goodbye, but Emily stared at her before looking away. Whatever she said to the other two girls had them glare back at Annie with hatred in their eyes.

22

September 1942

Since the unfortunate events in London the staff of the Bexleyheath store seemed to have fallen into two camps. Annie did her best to keep herself to herself but working as a supervisor in between training for the personnel side of office work, she found she was mixing with many of the girls who had decided it was fun to socialize with the American soldiers. Often, she would walk into the canteen and silence would fall on the room and she wondered if she'd been the subject of the conversation. As the mother of Ivy Rose, she would mix with the married women and grandmothers at tea breaks and felt more comfortable doing so. One day, as she'd just completed a morning working in the office, she decided to go for a walk to get some fresh air. She had pulled on her coat and hat and slung her gas mask over her shoulder when Simon called her into his office.

'I'm sorry, were you going somewhere?' he asked, noticing her outdoor clothes.

'Just to clear my head. I've had a morning of checking figures,' she said, wondering what he wanted.

'This won't take long. Have you seen these?' he asked, passing a small booklet across the desk and nodding for her to sit down. 'Woolworths had a hand in the information, and I wondered if you thought there should be something else added?'

Annie flicked through the booklet. 'It seems to be a guide for American servicemen who are visiting England to help them get used to our ways.' She frowned as she read some of the instructions. 'It's true what they say about England and America being divided by the same language. Is it possible to add something about them being more polite when in the company of our women? They aren't used to the Americans' loud ways.'

'That might have something to do with the drink that was involved,' Simon said generously.

'Then there should be something added about controlling the amount of drink they consume when out enjoying themselves. I don't want to be a killjoy but what happened that time in London was uncalled for.'

Simon had to agree with her. 'I was informed that some of the American soldiers were charged,' he said, which she seemed to accept. 'However, I'll write down your points and send it back to head office. As Woolworths has contributed to the production of these booklets it's only right that we have a say in what's included in the next edition.'

Annie was thoughtful. 'We do have to remember that these lads are far away from home and for many of them it will be the first time they've left their families. I wonder if we can go some way to welcoming them to our country? They've heard of Woolworths, as there are many stores back in their hometowns. Do you think perhaps we could invite them for a meal in our canteen, so they get to meet some real English people?'

'That's an excellent idea!' Simon exclaimed. 'Can I leave you to arrange the meal with Marge? Give them some proper English fare they can write home about? I'll have a word with head office and sort out a guest list; they should be able to contribute to the meal.'

'That's it then, we reach out our hands across the water with steak and kidney pudding and spotted dick and custard, if our resident cook agrees.'

Simon warmed to the plans. 'A few bottles of brown ale will hit the spot and perhaps a sing-song afterwards.'

'I can't see anything wrong with that,' Annie said, thinking how many people in England would be glad of such a meal, but then she brought herself up short. These young men may be brash and loud, but they were here to fight the same enemy and for that they should be grateful.

'Annie, may I have a word, please?' Emily stood at the entrance to the office where Annie was working on a list of staff who would be invited to the special welcome meal.

'Of course. Don't stand in the doorway, come in and sit down,' Annie said, doing her best to pin a smile to her face. Since that evening in London the two girls had steered clear of each other, Emily preferring to go out with a group of younger staff to dances with the American soldiers. 'We've not seen a lot of each other lately,' she said as Emily settled in the only other seat in the room. Since all the filing cabinets had been installed the place seemed smaller than ever.

Emily seemed embarrassed and stared down into her

lap. 'I've wanted to come and talk to you, but you're always so busy with Simon and work, and in the evenings, I've been going out with some of the other girls.'

Annie tried to laugh and make light of the situation but found it hard: it had hurt when Emily had chosen other friends. She cleared her throat. 'Just because we started work on the same day it doesn't mean we're joined at the hip. Our lives have changed so much in a few short years. Perhaps we should make more of an effort to meet up sometimes and go to the cinema?'

'You may not want to when you know what I have to tell you.'

Annie frowned. 'Whatever do you mean by that?' she asked as she twiddled a pencil that had been lying on the desk.

'I think I'm pregnant. I'm the sort of girl my mother would cross the road to avoid.'

Annie threw down the pencil and rushed round to the other side of the desk, kneeling beside Emily and putting her arms around the girl as she dissolved into tears.

'Hush,' she said as she soothed her friend. 'I don't like to ask, but are you sure?'

Emily wiped her nose on the handkerchief she pulled from the cuff of her uniform. 'Yes, I'm certain as I've not had a period for two months and it's getting close to three now. I've heard that you can tell, and I do have sore breasts and feel sick of a morning and can't face breakfast. Mother is getting suspicious and I'm more worried about that than I am of having a baby,' she sniffed.

'What a pickle,' Annie said. 'However, your mother will probably come round to the idea once you've told her, and I can assure you, having a little one in your life is a joy.'

Emily nodded her head as she thought of Annie's words. 'Would you come with me when I tell Mother? She likes you and adores Ivy Rose. It would soften the blow.'

'I'll support you all I can, but would it not be best if your young man went with you?'

Emily fell silent before saying, 'I've not told him.'

'Then before he hears this from someone else you need to break the news to him. After all, it will be his baby as well as yours. Is it someone who works here?' Annie asked, trying to think of the single young men who were employed in the store.

'He's in the army . . . the American army,' Emily said with a defiant look in her eyes.

Annie sucked in her breath. She knew Emily had been going out with the girls quite a lot and she liked dancing, but surely it wasn't one of the lads from that visit to London? At once she thought of the booklet being produced for the American visitors and wondered if it was too late to add another line. *Do not get the English girls pregnant.*

'Whoever he is, he does have a duty of care towards you. Have the pair of you spoken of the future at all?'

Emily gave a sarcastic laugh. 'After the war he'll be going back home to Seattle . . . Please don't look at me like that,' she begged. 'I know I was a fool, but we spoke about love, and he was so charismatic. What am I going to do, Annie?' she asked as she started to sob once again.

Annie's knees were beginning to ache, so she stood up and returned to her seat. 'You need to make a plan. If I were you, I'd write a list and try to plan ahead,' she said, pulling a sheet of paper from her drawer and placing a pencil on top. 'Would you like to do that now?' She slid the paper across the desk towards her friend.

Emily backed away, a horrified look crossing her face. 'I wouldn't know where to start. Could you do it for me?'

Annie shrugged her shoulders. 'I can write down your list but only you can decide what that is,' she said, trying to appear sympathetic although she was exasperated by Emily's attitude. 'This baby is going to be born whether you like it or not, and the sooner you start to plan, the better. Now, my suggestion is that you first see your doctor and have everything confirmed. After that you tell the baby's father, then you speak to your mother,' she said as she briefly wrote down those points: see doctor for confirmation; tell father and mother. 'Do you agree?'

'Perhaps you should add where I will be living, how I'm going to survive when I can't work, and how I can have the baby adopted?'

Annie was shocked by what Emily said. She bit her tongue; what if she'd had the same attitude when Ivy Rose was left without her real mother? She took a deep breath before speaking. 'My suggestion is that we won't note down what you said, as these things may never happen. Instead, we start on what we already have and add to the list as and when we need to.'

'If you say so,' Emily sighed. 'Do you think I could go off sick for the afternoon? I really don't feel like working.'

'Get yourself a strong cup of tea and something to eat and then go for a short walk. I'll expect you back at your counter in half an hour.'

Emily blinked her eyes but said nothing.

'Did you understand what I said? You can't afford to lose part of your wages just because you're expecting a baby;

you need to save every penny you can. Do you have any savings?'

Emily became more alert with Annie's words ringing in her ears. 'I have a post office savings account, but I've withdrawn quite a lot lately. There's also my piggy bank at home. Mum puts money into it for me; she says it's for a rainy day.'

Annie thought how Emily's mother had cossetted her daughter far too much. 'You may find that rainy day has arrived,' she said, placing the list in the top drawer of her desk. 'Now, be off with you so I can get some work done, but I will accompany you to see your doctor after work. We can't leave any earlier as I'm in the middle of organizing a meal for some of the American soldiers, to welcome them to our country.' Annie watched Emily leave the room and wondered how many other English girls had been overly welcoming to the American soldiers.

Annie checked the clock on the wall. The store was about to close, and she wanted to be ready when Emily left her counter. Picking up some paperwork that she needed to leave with Simon, she quickly tidied her desk and headed down the corridor to his office before knocking on the door. When he called out, 'Enter,' she walked into the room refusing the seat he offered her. 'I need to leave on time as I have an appointment. Here is what you've been waiting for. I checked with Marge, and she's agreeable to the changes you suggested. She's a little worried that she may not have enough sugar for the gypsy tart and asked if you could have a word with head office?'

'I can do that first thing in the morning. I don't think it

will be a problem. I'll let you know as soon as I hear something,' he said, skimming the pages. 'There's nothing here about the beers we were going to leave on the table so the American soldiers could experience drinks produced in this country.'

'Sorry, I did make a list but I must have left it in the folder in my desk drawer. I'll finish it for you right now.' She glanced quickly at the clock on his wall.

'No, you get off, I don't want to make you late for your appointment. I can find the folder.' He followed Annie into the corridor where Emily was waiting. Such was her nervousness that she didn't see Simon following her friend.

'Thank goodness you're ready. Do you know what we should ask the doctor?'

'Yes, I'm a little nervous but I know what we should say,' Annie said, slipping on her coat that she'd held over her arm. 'Come on, let's get going.'

Wondering if Annie was ill, he went into her office to fetch the information on the British beers. Pulling open the top drawer, he was faced with a sheet of handwritten notes and picked it up to check it was what he was looking for. He was confused by what he read. For what reason would Annie need to see a doctor? She looked so healthy. And then to have to tell her parents . . . A horrible suspicion formed in his mind, though he didn't want to imagine she could be pregnant, as he thought better of her. Deeply troubled, he replaced the page into the drawer and rummaged until he found what he'd actually been looking for. For a while now he'd realized he had grown fond of Annie and was much impressed by how she had become a stand-in mother to little Ivy Rose. 'That would teach me to become interested in the staff,' he muttered to himself as he made his way back to his office.

Annie sat upright on a hard wooden chair in the waiting room of the doctor's surgery. It wasn't a building that she'd visited before as her doctor was in Erith, closer to her home. Of course, she now knew that he was also Simon's father. All the more reason to visit Emily's doctor, whose rooms were situated in part of a large Victorian house just off the Broadway.

Behind a heavy oak door, she could hear mumbled voices but could not make out what the doctor was saying to Emily; she prayed he was being kind to her as the girl was not strong. In fact, Annie had no idea how Emily was going to cope. She would just have to be the best friend that she could and support her through the months ahead. She jumped in her seat as the door suddenly opened and Emily appeared red-eyed and teary.

'I want to leave now,' she said, not waiting for Annie to get to her feet, and she was out of the front door before Annie could utter a word. Out on the pavement she rushed to catch Emily by the arm. 'For heaven's sake, wait for me and tell me what happened in there,' she said, gasping for breath.

Emily turned to face her, tears streaming down her cheeks. 'He called me names I will never repeat and told me he will be making a phone call to my mother to inform her what a . . . what a . . . what a whore I'd been if I did not return to the surgery with her by my side in three days' time.'

'What a horrid thing to say! He should not have spoken to you like that. If you like, I'll take you to see my doctor as he has more of a caring nature in his little finger than that despicable man.' Annie thought it best not to mention the connection to Simon. After all, Greyson was a common surname and besides, she was sure doctors had to maintain confidentiality.

'I'd like that, thank you,' Emily whispered. 'He did confirm I was expecting, and he was quite rough when he examined me.' She collapsed against the wall. Annie did her best to support her, fearing she was going to faint.

'There's a cafe down the road. Let's go in there and have a cup of tea and plan what's going to happen next,' Annie said, taking her friend's arm and leading her slowly into the busy cafe. Helping Emily to a seat by the steamed-up window, she went to the counter to order, assuring the woman serving that they only wanted tea when she pointed out that they would be closing soon.

'Here, drink this up,' she said to Emily as they contemplated the light colour of the tea. 'It'll be wet and warm if nothing else.'

'What can I do now?' Emily distractedly stirred the tea. 'I know I don't want to tell Mother until I've seen a sympathetic doctor.'

'He won't tell you anything more,' Annie pointed out.

'But he will probably be more sympathetic to my plight,' she said. 'When can I see your doctor?'

'We can go there tomorrow; it's half-day shopping so I can drive us both down there from work. I'll make the appointment in my name, and we can explain once we're in his surgery; that way, we won't have to sit in the waiting room waiting to be seen.' She paused a moment trying to form the words she really wanted to say to Emily. 'Don't be annoyed with me but I feel you should speak to the father of the baby and do it now before you're showing and gossip starts to spread, and he hears second hand about your situation. Where are you meeting him?'

'We'd not made any concrete plans as I'd blown him out a few times, but the gang usually meet at the Prince of Wales pub in Erith. They're due there this evening at eight o'clock. I'm not sure I can face him. Would you go?' she asked. Yet again the tears started to flow.

'Look, Emily, I'm happy to hold your hand while you visit the doctor and possibly while you speak to your mother, but I can't do everything for you. I can't have the baby for you.'

Emily gripped the mug of tea tightly as her hands shook. 'I know I'm going to have to do more for myself and I intend to. It's just that I'm frightened. Once he knows then things will get better, and I'll be able to cope . . . but I can't face him yet. Can you . . . ?' She looked at Annie with imploring eyes.

Annie sighed. 'It looks as though I'll be giving good news to the father of the baby this evening . . .'

23

Annie took a deep breath before pushing open the door to the public bar of the Prince of Wales pub. She'd driven home first and changed, not wishing to meet the American soldier in her work clothes. Even though she wasn't wearing her burgundy-coloured overall she felt she should at least have a wash and wear a clean frock. Promising her mum she'd not be late and managing to wriggle out of answering questions as to where she was going, she hurried out of the house after kissing Ivy Rose goodnight. Earlier she'd dropped Emily off in Pier Road, Erith, as they both agreed that if she'd gone home with Annie her family would have asked too many questions. She pulled up alongside her in front of the now closed Woolworths store. 'Jump in and we can have a quick chat about what I'm going to say. First tell me his name and what he looks like, or I'll end up talking to the wrong man.'

Emily looked around the small vehicle Paddy had bought for Annie. 'Are you working?' she asked, noticing the sacks of bag wash in the rear of the van.

Annie chuckled. 'They're there in case I'm stopped by the police; we aren't allowed to use petrol for private use.

Dad has the name of the laundry painted on the sides as well.'

Emily didn't approve and made her feelings known.

Annie raised her hand to stop her friend's objections. 'I'm not going to argue, but you know why we're here...'

Emily shut up, but looked out of the window pouting until Annie reminded her she needed to answer her questions. 'What's his name?'

'Dirk... Dirk Wolenski. His family originally came from Poland.'

'And apart from being in uniform, what does he look like?'

'Tall, sandy-coloured hair and blue eyes,' she said with a sigh.

'That's enough information. If I can't see him, I've got a tongue in my head and will ask. Now, I'm going to drive a little closer to the pub and will park the van and leave you here for a while. I'll do my best not to be too long.'

The interior of the pub was smoky, and the sound of jovial drinkers made her reel back for a moment. She'd not expected as many people, but then she heard darts hitting a board and scores being called out. There was a tournament in progress and no man would miss such an event. She glanced around worried her dad would be there, but then his allegiance was to The Lord Raglan in Slades Green, so unless he was playing an away game he was unlikely to be here. Darts was a serious business. So where were the Americans?

'Are you lost, love?' an elderly man called out to her from behind the bar. 'This isn't the right place for a young lady as it can get quite rowdy once the games start in earnest. You need to go round to the snug where the ladies are sitting; you'll be safer there.'

'I wonder if you could tell me where the American soldiers are as I need to pass on a message?' she asked.

He frowned and an unpleasant look came over his face. 'We don't want none of that in this pub. We are a respectable establishment. Be off with you.'

'Gosh, you've got me all wrong! I'm not a . . . a lady of the night,' she said, leaning over the bar so no one else could hear. 'I truly do have a message to pass on. I work for Bexleyheath Woolworths,' she said, hoping that gave her an air of respectability.

He roared with laughter. 'No self-respecting lady of the night would use that excuse. I believe you. You need to go through the bar to the hall at the back. We allow them to drink in there as they tend to get rowdy.'

She blushed a little at the way he mocked her before thanking him and walking towards the hall. She did know this room as she'd attended wedding receptions in there a few times as well as a retirement party. If she thought the public bar in the pub was loud, then this sound coming from the hall was even worse. A cheer broke out as she entered.

'Lookee what we've got here, lads,' a young soldier said, circling round her with a cigarette hanging from the side of his mouth and his cap at an angle. His tie was loose around his neck, and he stank of beer. 'Come and dance,' he said, pulling her forward to the middle of the floor. A man sitting at a piano struck up a tune and before she knew what was happening, he was swinging her around the floor. Her stomach lurched as memories of the London ballroom came flooding back.

'No, no, no, you've got me all wrong.' She pulled away from him and stamped her foot on the wooden floor in anger. 'I want to speak with Dirk Wolenski . . . It's about my friend Emily who he's been stepping out with.'

Some of the men roared with laughter. 'You Brits sure have a novel way of talking. Hey, Dirk, you're wanted over here,' he called to the back of the hall where a fair-haired man was deep in conversation with a woman sitting on his lap. He kissed her lips and stood up, taking no notice that she had slid to the ground.

'Come into my office,' he said to Annie as he tapped his foot at the woman to make her move away.

Annie had no idea what he was talking about – there was no office, just a circle of chairs around him that were empty since his lady friend had slunk away. Preferring not to sit down, she stood in front of him, keeping a chair between them as she didn't like the way he freely dismissed the woman so casually. 'Are you Dirk Wolenski?' she asked, in no doubt that he was as he seemed to fit Emily's description.

'And who wants to know?' he asked, looking her up and down.

'My name is of no consequence to you,' she said, wondering how Emily was so attracted to the man. 'I'm here on behalf of my friend, Emily Davenport. I believe you know her?'

In his defence he did look worried as he sat up straight in his chair at her question. 'I am acquainted with the young lady. Has she been injured? You guys seem to have so many air raids.'

'That's because we're at war, if you hadn't noticed. And to answer your question, Emily has not been injured in an air raid. However, she does have a health problem at the moment to which you have contributed.'

His eyes opened wide. 'I can assure you, ma'am, I have passed nothing on to your friend.'

Annie almost choked; he had misconstrued her words. 'It's not so much what you've passed on as what you've left her with. Do you get my drift now or should I explain more, Daddy?'

His eyes opened wider as the penny dropped. 'You mean . . . ?'

'I mean she is expecting your baby and because she is so distraught I am here to see what you're going to do about it.' Annie stared him out, placing her hands on her hips. 'I'm sure your senior officers would like to know how you're treating the women of England as your personal entertainment . . .'

'Now, you look here,' he snarled, checking around him that none of his friends were listening. 'What went on between me and Emily was consensual. She's as much to blame for her condition as I am.'

'I disagree with you as you pounced on a young innocent woman who had her head turned by someone in uniform who showered her with attention.' She felt as though she was poking him with a very big stick as she added, 'Are you going to offer to marry her and make an honest woman of her before she is ostracized in her own community?'

He baulked at the suggestion. 'Ma'am, I'll have you know I'm already happily married with four lovely children back in the States.' He reached into his pocket and pulled out a wallet, opening it to show her a photograph. A proud look passed across his face.

'I cannot believe that you're cheating on your wife and these lovely children,' she said, unable to take her eyes from the photograph of the five faces beaming into the camera lens.

'What my wife doesn't know won't hurt her. Besides, we need some form of entertainment as there's very little in this country to keep us amused before we go off to war.'

'Emily is a little more than entertainment! Does she mean nothing more than that to you?' Annie was appalled at his attitude.

He shrugged his shoulders, dismissing her words. 'She'll be latched on to another guy before too long and give him the same news. Hey, how do I not know that the father of the baby was the guy before me and the pair of you are just trying to fleece me?'

Annie was shocked beyond words and knew then that Emily would not be receiving any kind of support from this despicable man. Yes, she'd been foolish, but if an innocent girl being lured into a man's web made her a bad girl, then there was something wrong with the world. Emily was going to have to live with her mistake and Annie did not envy her. She herself had received some unpleasant comments concerning Ivy Rose when people found out she wasn't married and were unaware of the situation; she wouldn't wish that on Emily. 'Don't think this is the last of it,' she spat at him before walking away, followed by some rather rude comments from his fellow soldiers. She wasn't sure what could be done but from now on she would have to concentrate on supporting Emily.

Returning to the van, she was met by Emily's expectant gaze. 'Did you see him? What did he say?' she asked, checking over Annie's shoulder to see if he was coming out of the pub to speak to her. She looked disappointed when there was no one there.

Annie settled herself behind the steering wheel before she spoke. 'There's no easy way to say this, but he's not interested. He even insinuated that he was not the first . . .'

'But he was the first! Honestly, Annie, you've got to believe me when I say I'm not the kind of girl to throw myself at any man I meet.'

Annie took Emily's hand and gave it a squeeze. 'I know you're not; you weren't brought up that way. He was an older man who fooled you as he knew you were smitten,' she said, feeling angry all over again.

'I'm more than smitten. I love him and want to spend the rest of my life with him, perhaps even going to live in America and having more children with him,' she said as a faraway look came into her eyes.

'Oh, Emily, you've got to realize that's never going to happen. He has a life far away from this town and the war is just a small interlude in his life.'

'You're wrong!' she cried, pulling her hand away. 'I need to speak to him!' She went to open the door to get out of the van just as the door to the pub swung open and a group of the American soldiers appeared. 'Look, I can see him . . .' she said before gasping, 'No, I don't believe it.'

Dirk appeared with his arm around the woman Annie had seen earlier. He kissed her soundly as she clung to him provocatively, before following the group towards the town, walking close to where the van was parked. Emily called out his name from inside the vehicle and Annie held her breath, hoping he hadn't seen or heard her.

Too late he glanced sideways and, noticing a distraught Emily, he raised the bottle of beer he was drinking from and carried on walking away.

'Can you see now that he doesn't care?'

'Perhaps he didn't understand what you told him about the baby.'

'He understood all right,' Annie said between gritted teeth. 'Emily, you aren't going to like what I tell you. I was going to keep it to myself, but as you need convincing, I've no choice but to say he has a wife and four children. He carries their photograph in his wallet – he showed me,' she added as Emily opened her mouth to protest.

'He told me I was the only one . . .' she whimpered before burying her head in her hands, sobbing uncontrollably. Annie could only put her arm around her and wait for the tears to subside.

Eventually Emily lifted her head and, staring ahead, she whispered, 'I was supposed to be the love of his life.'

Annie's heart broke for her friend. She'd led such a sheltered life alone with her demanding mother so no doubt when Dirk came along, she was susceptible to falling in love, even if he was the wrong person. 'Look, I know all you feel is pain right now, but things will get better and as soon as we sort out the little problems, you'll be able to see the way ahead more clearly.'

'It's no use, I can't think straight. All I can see is Dirk with that woman and how I've been such a bloody fool,' she sniffed.

'That's good as you're accepting what has happened,' Annie said, giving her a quick hug.

'What do I do next?'

'I suggest, as I mentioned before, that we visit my doctor

tomorrow. He knows all my family and is a nice person. We can explain your predicament and ask him to add you to his list. He'll be able to guide you forward. Do you remember Daphne who worked with us for a while until she left to have her son? She told me how nice everyone was at the Hainault Maternity Hospital. Perhaps the doctor will be able to book you in there?'

Emily frowned. 'Isn't there a home for unmarried mothers next door to the Hainault? I don't want to go there as they aren't very nice to the mums, and I've heard they take their babies away from them . . .'

'You do want to keep the baby then, regardless of what your mum says?'

A determined look passed over Emily's face. 'At first, I didn't want the child but knowing how horrid the father is, I can't give it away and have it think no one wanted it in years to come. I'll do my best for the baby.'

'That's the spirit.'

'You will come with me, won't you?'

Annie agreed she would help all she could, as she realized she would have her work cut out helping her friend until she was brave enough to stand on her own two feet.

24

Annie was checking the staff work schedule pinned to the wall the next morning before she went onto the shop floor to cover for a supervisor who was poorly when Simon entered her office.

'I don't know why we bother with these things as a week doesn't go by when they don't have to be changed,' he said.

'We'd be lost without them. At least I know where some of your trainee managers should be,' she spat back at him, irritable after a sleepless night worrying about Emily.

Simon took a step back. 'There were just the two who'd sneaked off for a smoke. It's not exactly a hanging offence,' he pointed out, trying to raise a smile from Annie. It didn't work.

'Did you come in for something? It's just that I have to go and cover for a supervisor, and we also have Emily off sick. I hope to have her back in work tomorrow.'

'Nothing too serious then?'

Annie just sniffed at his words and went to leave the office.

'Before you go, I wanted an update on the meal for the American soldiers,' he asked but was met by a glare.

'To be honest, Simon, I don't feel I'm the right person to work on this project. Can you find someone else to take over?'

Before he could ask why, she had left the room and was walking down the corridor at a brisk pace, and he didn't like to call after her in case she bit his head off. It must be something to do with the list he'd seen in her desk, he thought. If she was indeed pregnant . . . perhaps the father was an American soldier? That would explain her change of heart, and in that case maybe he should ask another member of staff to organize the meal.

Downstairs Annie started to walk between the counters checking all was well with the staff and stopping to answer questions from customers. She was just approaching the fresh vegetable counter when a young child ran into her. Bending down, she tried to find out why the child was fretting.

'I think she's lost, lovie. She's been kicking up quite a stink running up and down,' an elderly woman said before asking for two pounds of spuds at the counter.

Annie picked the little girl up and tried to get her to say her name. The child was having none of it and shook her head violently before trying to get back down to the floor.

Annie held on to her as the child started to scream. 'Enid, would you grab a couple of girls and walk the floor looking to see if anyone has lost this charming child?' she asked as she received a hefty kick in the shin. Lifting her higher in her arms before she slipped any more, Annie started to talk quietly to the child to try to calm her down. It was too late as the child heaved and was sick down the front of her overall, just as a harassed-looking woman approached her.

'There you are, Christine! Has the lady upset you?' she asked, taking her child and walking away without a backward glance or a thank you.

Enid returned to her counter and grimaced at the state of Annie's uniform. Handing her a piece of newspaper to wipe off the vomit, she bent down beneath the counter and pulled out an overall. 'Here, miss, we keep a spare here as sometimes we can get mucky from the muddy spuds.' She shook it out and they could both see it was a small sizing. 'It'll do to get you back upstairs as you can't walk through the store in your petticoat.'

Annie thanked her and quickly changed overalls while Enid and another assistant stood in front of her. It was a tight fit even though she breathed in as she did up the buttons. 'Phew, thank you both very much. It's a bit small but will do for now.' She grinned at them as Enid passed back the soiled overall now wrapped in one of the sheets of newspaper they used when serving potatoes and other muddy veg to help keep the customers' shopping bags clean.

Thanking them once again, Annie hurried back upstairs holding the parcel at arm's length. In the women's toilets she ran cold water over the overall before leaving it to soak. Heading back to her office across the corridor, she spotted Simon coming out of his. He raised his hand to get her attention. 'Not now, Simon, I have a lot to get done, and I must leave on time as I have an appointment I can't wriggle out of. Can it wait until tomorrow?' she asked, not waiting for an answer as she closed the door on him while he muttered, 'Another one?'

'It'll have to wait,' he told the closed door. 'I happen to be leaving on time myself . . .' After waiting a moment to see if she would reply, he wandered to the staff canteen. There was time for a quick drink before he finished work for the half-day. His reason for knocking off on time was to see his sister who was visiting with her new baby. He was especially eager to see the young lad as he had been invited to be a godparent. Taking a cup of tea from Marge, he stood stirring in a teaspoon of sugar that her assistant had slipped into his cup.

'Marge, can you call the cleaners?' one of the older staff called out as she entered the staff room. 'It smells like someone's been sick. I hope we haven't got another pregnant staff member on our hands as I can't keep knitting bootees,' she grinned.

Simon shook his head. He couldn't keep up with these women. It all added up now, though, how off colour Annie had seemed today. And come to think of it, her overall seemed a tad on the tight side. There was no denying it, he suddenly felt downright dejected.

'I'm sorry I'm late meeting you. I had no choice but to go home to wash and change my clothes,' Annie apologized, explaining what had happened.

Emily could not help but giggle at Annie's eventful morning. 'I'm sorry, I shouldn't laugh, it sounds awful. And then to have to change your overall on the shop floor by the vegetable counter . . .'

'I'm so glad I was wearing my best cotton petticoat and not an old off-coloured one; that wouldn't have looked good for a supervisor.'

'Crikey, I've gone without a petticoat when it's been too hot and in the winter worn a larger size uniform so I can fit a jumper underneath,' Emily said before looking up the steep steps that led to the doctor's surgery in Erith. 'I suppose we'd better go in. I've never felt so nervous in my life. Tell me it'll be all right?' she pleaded.

Annie assured her she would be looked after very well. 'All my family use Doctor Greyson and even Ivy Rose is happy when she sees him, although he does give her a sweetie that he keeps in a special tin. Perhaps if you're good, you too will get one,' she said, trying to cheer up her friend.

Annie gave her name to the lady sitting behind a desk and they both took a seat. Emily had just had time to look around the room with its cosy armchairs and a row of dark-wood upright chairs when they were called into the surgery. She glanced with longing at the magazines scattered on a side table. It would have been lovely to curl up in one of the armchairs and read the latest *People's Friend* and block out the outside world.

'It's this way,' Annie told her as Emily followed her through a short corridor, past an open staircase and in through an oak door which Annie closed after them.

What the girls did not notice was Simon coming down the staircase. He stopped as he thought he recognized Annie's voice and couldn't help wondering if she was there for the reason he suspected. But then perhaps it wasn't her. After all, she'd only spoken a couple of words. Curiosity got the better of him and he went to the waiting room to chat to Miss Milthorpe, his father's faithful secretary. He knew she would scold him if he asked directly about a patient, so he casually chatted about her cats and her elderly parents and did his best to look at the open appointment diary. Yes, he was right as there in black and white was Annie's name . . .

'Come in, Miss Brookes. How is young Ivy Rose? I've not seen her in a while,' the doctor asked as the two girls sat down in front of him.

'She's keeping well and growing quickly,' Annie replied as he gave a questioning look towards Emily. 'I hope you don't mind, Doctor, but I brought my friend Emily Davenport along as she has a problem that she wasn't able to speak to her own doctor about as he knows her mother.' She thought it was best to tell a little white lie rather than explain that Emily's doctor wasn't at all sympathetic to her plight.

Doctor Greyson nodded in agreement and looked at Emily. 'I promise what we talk about in this room will go no further. Are you happy for your friend to remain here?'

'Oh yes, and she has been such a help to me I don't know what I'd have done without her,' Emily said as she went on to explain her predicament. 'You must think I'm such a bad person?' she added once she'd given all her details and answered his questions.

'I think nothing of the sort,' he corrected her. 'No one is perfect in this world, and we all make mistakes. What we need to do now is to prepare you for the birth and to work out what is best for you. I'm not saying I can solve all your problems but I have contacts and can point you in the right direction. Now, I need to examine you. Annie, can you ask Miss Milthorpe to come in to assist me? You may wait in reception for your friend.'

Miss Milthorpe looked up as Annie entered the reception.

Hearing her voice, Simon slipped out the back door and into the garden. Although deeply worried about Annie he knew now wasn't the time for him to speak to her or for her to know he was aware she'd had an appointment with her doctor.

Annie sat down nervously. What was the doctor doing? She was unsure of what happened during these examinations and hoped it wasn't too harrowing for Emily. She picked up a magazine by way of a distraction and was engrossed in an article about the making of Woolton Pie to entice young children to eat when a pink-cheeked Emily followed Miss Milthorpe into the waiting area.

'How are you?' Annie asked, placing the magazine back onto the side table.

'A little wobbly, but I'll be fine.'

'Nothing a strong cup of tea won't fix,' Miss Milthorpe beamed. 'You will go through worse when the baby comes into the world, but afterwards all the pain will be forgotten. There's a cafe up the road towards the station,' she added helpfully.

Emily gave her a weak smile and followed Annie outside. 'I need something stronger than a cup of tea, but that will have to do for now.'

Simon entered the waiting room through the door from the garden. 'Has the patient gone, Miss Milthorpe?'

'Yes, and your father is alone if you wish to speak with him,' she said, having known him long enough to be able to tell when he was loitering for a reason.

'Thank you. I hope the patient wasn't ailing too much and will recover?' he asked, chancing his luck that he'd find something out about Annie's visit to the surgery.

Miss Milthorpe sighed. 'I'm afraid it is a growing illness

among young women, and we don't seem to be able to stop it spreading.'

He felt the blood pounding in his ears and tried not to let Miss Milthorpe see how he was affected by her words. This sounded as if he might have misunderstood everything and there was something far worse going on than he had imagined. He must not reveal his fears that Annie, whom he had grown so fond of, might be unwell. 'How long?' he asked, not really wishing to know the answer and trying nonchalantly to relax in one of the armchairs and flick through a magazine.

'No more than six months. She was in shock after your dad explained everything. I just hope her friend can support her to get through this.'

Simon had nothing to say and got up to leave.

'I thought you wanted to see your father?'

'I've changed my mind,' he replied hoarsely, thinking the offer he'd received to go back into the RAF would have to wait. Besides that, he had other thoughts about his future. However, for now he wanted to be here for Annie for as long as she had left to live. There was no need to discuss this with his father as what he'd just heard had made his mind up for him.

'Gosh, I'm hungry,' Annie said as they sat down in the cafe in Station Parade. It was only a short walk from the surgery, so she'd left her van parked close to the doctor's. 'You must be hungry too as we both missed lunch at work?'

'I was, but with everything I've been told I don't know if I can keep anything down.'

Annie reached across the table and squeezed Emily's hand. 'That's understandable and added to that you've got the disappointment of Dirk's attitude. I don't blame you for feeling sick. Why, I could have wrung his neck then you'd have had to come to rescue me from the police station,' she said, trying to make Emily laugh.

Although she smiled, Annie could see it was an effort. Thankfully a lady who'd been wiping down the oil-cloth-covered tables came over to see what they would like. 'Two mugs of tea, please, and what do you have to eat?'

'I could do you some Spam fritters, or perhaps bubble and squeak and a fried egg? The eggs were fresh this morning. I also have some vegetable soup . . .'

Emily looked even paler at the thought of food and started to decline what was on offer.

'Come on, you'll feel better with something in your stomach,' Annie urged her.

Emily quickly got to her feet with one hand clapped to her mouth and dashed to the door marked 'toilets'.

'Oh dear, I take it she's in the family way?'

'It's early days but yes,' Annie replied, not wishing to give too much detail away apart from agreeing on what was obvious.

'In that case I'll rustle up some scrambled egg and a dry piece of toast. It used to work wonders for me. What would you like, love?'

'I'd like the bubble and squeak and a Spam fritter, please. It's so nice not to have to cook for once. Can I help carry the tea over?'

'Thank you, love, and I'll get on with your food. Do you have a big family to cook for? You don't look old enough,' she said as they both went to the counter with the kitchen behind it.

'I still live with my parents, my grandparents and my adopted daughter, but we all muck in with the household duties and the family laundry.'

'That's where I know you from,' the woman replied. 'You're Paddy Brookes' daughter. Is he back working on the fairground yet?'

Annie was explaining how it was difficult to travel with the fair during the war so many of the men who hadn't been called up had taken on other work. 'Dad is full time with the laundry these days,' she explained, glad to see Emily returning. 'I'll take this tea over.' She hurried to where Emily had sat down. 'Do you feel any better?'

'I think so but can't understand why I always feel sick in the afternoons now. I thought it was supposed to be morning sickness.'

'It gets us all differently,' the woman called from behind the counter.

Annie grinned. 'She means well, bless her. She suggested scrambled egg and dry toast. Do you think you could try a little?'

'I'll do my best, thank you. I also want to thank you for all you've done for me, I really do appreciate it. I don't know what I would have done without you.' Emily was a little teary.

'No more tears,' Annie scolded her light-heartedly. 'I want you to do your best to get some food inside you. I want you to be as strong as possible and having an empty stomach will not help you one little bit.'

Emily was puzzled. 'I will try, honest, but what are we going to do next?'

'We are going to see your mum to tell her everything. We might as well get all the nasty stuff out of the way, then it should be plain sailing, and you won't feel sick for ever,' she said, seeing Emily grimace.

'No, it's not the sickness I'm worried about. It's giving birth . . . I'm petrified.'

Annie couldn't help her in that respect and was relieved when their food arrived. She should have guessed the cafe owner had overheard them.

'Don't worry about that. You'll forget all the pain once you have a bonnie baby in your arms. Why, I can just about remember my two coming into the world and they have families of their own now,' she said with a smile before leaving them to eat their meal.

Annie was worried for Emily as she saw her flinch at the woman's words. She just hoped Emily's mother would be able to support her daughter through the months and years ahead.

25

Annie always thought Mrs Davenport's home was like a relic from the Victorian era. There was even an aspidistra in a large copper pot in the front room. She could be gracious and kind, but still Annie felt uncomfortable, almost intimidated, on the occasional times she had visited. This time, as Emily ushered her into the less formal sitting room, she felt her stomach lurch at what was to come. Perhaps it was the bubble and squeak she'd not long eaten, but it was more likely to be nerves. Emily looked extremely sick, but it couldn't have been the food she was served as she'd hardly touched it.

'It isn't often we see you here, Annie. Welcome to my home just the same.' Mrs Davenport was friendly but reserved.

Annie thanked her and sat next to Emily on an overstuffed sofa. They fell into silence with Mrs Davenport watching them until Annie nudged Emily for her to say something.

'Mother, I have something to tell you,' she said, after clearing her throat. 'I'm not sure where to start or how you'll take my news.'

They both watched Mrs Davenport as she put down her knitting, placing her hands on her lap. 'Start at the important place; I can ask questions afterwards. But please do hurry as I have guests arriving in half an hour.'

'It is Mother's afternoon to entertain the bible group,' Emily said to Annie.

Annie could only hope the dust would have settled before the group arrived as this was not going to go well.

'Mother . . .' Emily took a deep breath. 'Mother, I am expecting a baby,' she said, the last words coming out in a rush.

Silence fell in the room, with Annie frightened to breathe as she watched Mrs Davenport's face turn white and then puce. She counted down silently, waiting for her to explode.

'You are with child?'

'That's what I said, Mother.'

'Have I missed something? When was the wedding?'

'There hasn't been a wedding, Mother.'

Silence fell again as the clock over the mantle slowly ticked while Mrs Davenport considered Emily's words.

'When is this child due to be born?'

'Another six months, from what the doctor has calculated,' Emily said, raising her chin defiantly until one look from her mother had her staring into her lap once more.

'You mean to say you visited Doctor Beckley? How dare you draw my family friends into your sordid little affair; I'll not be able to face any of them. Goodness knows what's being said behind my back, and as for the church, I'll never be able to set foot over the threshold again.'

Annie bristled with indignation. 'If I may say something, Mrs Davenport. Emily attended my doctor's surgery as she was aware of the gossips . . . I mean someone mentioning something out of turn.'

Mrs Davenport turned to look at Annie, who felt as though the woman was looking at something she'd trodden in. 'How do I know that this doctor is suitable for my daughter?'

'He has looked after my family for many years and still treats my grandparents for any ailments they may have. He is very good with children; my daughter Ivy Rose adores him. I can also confirm that he is extremely discreet and would never disclose a confidence.'

'I should hope not indeed,' the woman exclaimed, forgetting that only moments ago she'd been mentioning her own doctor and circle of friends who'd gossip about Emily's predicament. She took a moment to gather herself, staring down at the faded Turkey rug. Then she stood up and shouted at Annie. 'So, you are the bad influence on my daughter! I knew nothing good would come of her working as a shopgirl. You will resign at once, Emily. I need to think about this . . . this situation, but for now you will remain in your bedroom when I have visitors, and once I have written to your Aunt Elizabeth you will stay with her in Somerset until after your confinement, when arrangements will be made for the child to be placed in a home.'

Annie couldn't stand any more of the woman's interference and stood to face her almost eye to eye. 'You cannot talk to Emily in this way! Why, you've shown no compassion and not stopped to ask how she got herself into this situation. She may well have plans of her own for all you know.'

Mrs Davenport backed away as if Annie had slapped her in the face. She sat down as abruptly as she had stood, but there was no softening in her attitude.

'What about the father of your child?' she fired at Emily. 'Can I expect to meet him and ask what his intentions are, or should I continue with our plans for you to travel to Somerset?'

'I do know who he is, but I have no plans for a future with him, just as I don't intend to agree to your plans to send me away.'

Her mother fluttered her handkerchief in front of her face. 'You mean he's married, don't you?'

'That's of no consequence as I don't plan to see him again. If you allow it, I will stay here for a couple of nights until I find suitable accommodation, then I will be out of your hair for ever.' Emily was no longer afraid of her mother. 'I expected something like this to happen, and in the short while since seeing my new doctor I started to think about my future. I've never been happy here living with you, and I get the feeling you are of a similar mind. Therefore, after a few days you need not see me ever again.'

Annie was astonished at Emily's bravery and felt she had to say something. 'You can come home with me until you've made your plans, and you're welcome to stay as long as you like. Let's go and collect your things now; there's plenty of room in my van for your possessions.'

She was rewarded with a smile and a hug from her friend and a look of hatred from Mrs Davenport. With luck, Emily would have a decent future without her controlling mother and would learn from her mistakes.

26

October 1942

'I'm not looking forward to this one little bit,' Emily said as they stood to the side of the staff canteen door welcoming their guests, the American army personnel.

'Me neither and I've not had much to do with the organizing side of things since I told Simon I wished to step down. I couldn't have faced doing anything related to those Yanks.'

'I'm sorry to have caused you this problem,' Emily sighed. 'Has Simon said anything to you since then?'

Annie looked around to check they weren't being overheard. 'It's funny you should ask as he hasn't said a word to me. I'd almost say he's avoided me and the odd time he's bumped into me on the shop floor he's hardly been able to look at me. It's not like him to act so strangely because as a rule he's very friendly.'

'You're quite keen on him, aren't you?'

'I like him, and we do get along quite well when at work, or we did until recently. But even if he showed an interest in me, it would never work as I have Ivy Rose to consider,' she sighed. 'It would take somebody very special to accept my unusual circumstances. Look, our guests seem to be arriving. Let's help Marge with the tray of drinks.' Emily followed her into the big, bright canteen, deep in thought.

'It seems to be going well,' Annie said as she helped clear empty plates from the tables. 'The soldiers certainly enjoyed your steak and kidney pudding.'

'And the Kentish brewed beer is going down very well,' Simon said as he arrived with a tray of dirty glasses and placed them on the draining board before running hot water into the sink. 'I need to wash these and get them filled again.'

'Here, let me help you,' Annie said, picking up a tea towel. 'You wash and I'll wipe.'

'Would you like to sit down while you're doing that?' he asked. 'I'd not like you to tire yourself.'

'I know it's been a long day, Simon, but I'm no more tired than you are, although it was very nice of you to offer.' She gazed up at him, noticing frown lines on his forehead. 'We don't seem to have spoken much lately. No doubt you've been very busy, but I have missed our meetings. I wonder, have I offended you in some way?'

Simon, clearly uncomfortable, turned to the sink, furiously scrubbing at a few of the beer tankards. 'I'm not sure what you mean,' he blustered, unable to look her in the eyes.

In for a penny, she thought to herself before blurting out, 'I thought you liked me, and that in time . . .' She couldn't finish her words as nerves got the better of her.

'I do . . . I mean I did,' he said, still not looking at her.

'So, what changed things?' she asked, reaching out and placing her hand on the sleeve of his jacket.

'Your illness. If you had been honest with me and confided in me, I may have been able to accept things, but as it is I could lose you soon and not have had the nerve to tell you how I feel. What time is left should be for your family, not a romance.'

Annie was flabbergasted. 'What are you talking about, Simon? I'm not ill! Whatever made you think I was?' But as she went to ask him to explain himself further there was a shout from the other side of the room followed by chairs and tables being scraped back along with raised voices. A couple of women screamed before the pair could get to where the rumpus was occurring.

'Oh my God, no! Emily, put down the knife,' Annie shouted across the room to where Dirk Wolenski was cowered. Emily stood over him holding a large carving knife Marge had been using to slice up a cake, as if she was going to stab him. Annie started to walk slowly towards Emily but found herself being held back by Simon.

'No, this is something I should deal with,' he insisted.

'But you have no idea what's caused this situation,' she said, jerking her arm away from him. 'Emily is expecting his child, and he didn't want to know her. She's a good girl and this shouldn't have happened to her.'

Simon kept his eyes on the situation while whispering to Annie. 'Wait, it's Emily who's pregnant? Not you who's ill?'

'For goodness' sake, Simon, there's nothing wrong with me! If you don't believe me, speak to your father as he's my doctor.'

'I know and you were there recently – I spoke to Miss Milthorpe. She said you have six months . . .'

'Oh, you idiot! It's Emily who saw your dad, and she now has five months before her baby is due.'

Simon groaned. 'I've got so much wrong. Is there anything else I should know?'

'Only that Emily is currently living with my family, and she is also currently waving a knife at the baby's father.'

They were pushing their way through the crowd of staff and guests as another scream filled the room and people backed away, causing Annie and Simon even more difficulties as they tried to reach the fracas. As the staff closest to the couple stepped aside, they could see Emily crumple to the floor on top of Dirk, who was doing his utmost to crawl away from her as a large pool of blood seeped onto the floor.

Simon immediately took control, barking out orders to a couple of trainee managers. The first was told to clear the room of people but not to let anyone leave the building. To the second he said to ring for the ambulance and the police. Marge hurried forward with a first aid box that was kept in the kitchen along with a bundle of clean tea towels.

'Can you do anything with these before the ambulance arrives? I can't see who has been wounded as there's too much blood.'

Annie watched, not believing what had happened. She could see Dirk had blood all over his torso and legs and was leaning against two of his mates, who were bending down beside him. Both were white with shock as they gazed towards Emily, who lay completely motionless.

Simon and Marge were holding a wad of tea towels to her stomach. Around her the staff who'd been having a good time only minutes earlier singing around the piano were sobbing uncontrollably; some were saying Emily had died. Annie tried to give herself a talking-to: standing here observing the room was not doing any good whatsoever. 'Brenda, take Nina and Pam into my office and do your best to calm them down as these hysterics are not helping anybody. Doreen, make a big pot of tea and hand out as many cups as you can – and get some help as there are people downstairs who can hopefully give statements once the police arrive. Oh, and Julie, can you go into Simon's office and tell the manager who is calling the police that he should contact the American military police as well? The rest of us can sort out the washing-up until we're told to vacate the room.'

She was looking around to see what else could be done when Simon tried to call her over. Annie couldn't hear what he was saying amid all the noise and chaos until one of the girls who had started the washing-up tugged at her sleeve. 'Annie, you're wanted over there.' She nodded before averting her gaze from the pool of blood around Emily.

Annie walked slowly across the room scared of what she would see and what Simon had to say. She straightened chairs and upturned tables as she went, putting off the moment of truth as long as she could. 'How is she?' she asked Simon, desperately wanting to avert her eyes from Emily's injuries.

He reached up from where he was kneeling and took her hand. 'The ambulance will be here soon, but until then we've got to try to keep her with us, do you understand?'

Annie nodded. Was he saying she was going to die? 'What do you want me to do?'

'Sit on the other side of Emily and hold her hand. Talk

to her about anything that will keep her awake. Can you do that?'

'Yes, I can,' she said as she moved around Simon and Marge, who were holding more blood-soaked tea towels against Emily's stomach. She sat down on the tiled floor next to her friend, ignoring the blood soaking into her frock, and took her hand. It felt cold and lifeless. 'Emily, it's me, Annie, can you hear me?' she asked, stroking her hand and lifting it to her lips to kiss her palm. 'Come on, Emily, you've got to talk to me. Remember how we spoke about taking Ivy Rose and your baby to the seaside once the war is over? We're going to paddle in the sea and have fish and chips. I think we decided on Margate, didn't we? Someone told me there's a lovely Lyons tea shop where we can have a meal; they do jelly and custard for the children . . . What was that, love?' she asked as Emily fluttered her eyelids and mumbled a few words.

'Tea . . . a nice cup of tea . . . and a paddle in the sea . . .' A fleeting smile crossed her lips.

'I don't know about a paddle in the sea, but you can have that cup of tea right now.' She waved to the girls who were taking tea to the people outside the canteen. 'Can I have one here for Emily, please?'

'Here you go, I've made it milky ready for her to drink,' one of the girls said, passing the cup to Annie while blinking back tears. 'Get well soon, Emily. We're all rooting for you,' she added as she backed away.

Simon helped Annie support Emily's head and shoulders as she put the china cup to her lips. 'Just a small sip,' she said as Emily tried to take more before coughing. 'Nice?'

'Mmm,' was all she replied as she opened her eyes wider

and gave Annie a smile. 'I've loved being . . . Woolworths girl,' she said as her head rolled sideways and the look in her eyes turned into a vacant stare.

'Emily?' Annie cried out as she gave her friend a small shake. 'Come on, the ambulance people are almost here, and they're going to make you better. Don't give up now.'

Helping hands lifted her to her feet as the ambulance workers finally arrived. She stood back to enable them to do their best, staunching Emily's wounds and lifting her onto a stretcher, before expertly transporting her out to their waiting vehicle. Annie followed them as far as the corridor, sure that all hope was lost, but then she looked back to see Dirk loitering outside the door to the staff room. She turned and flew at him, pounding his chest with her fists. 'You deserve to die for what you've done to Emily! You stole her innocence and now her life and that of her baby – and your baby!' she cried, unable to contain her anger and grief. 'I hope you die a long and horrid death for what you did!'

He cowered away from Annie's blows as a man pulled her from him. 'Please, ma'am, we've got this now,' a compassionate American voice said as a military policeman put handcuffs on Dirk and led him away, followed by his comrades, all of whom looked horrified by what had happened.

Simon joined her and took her into his office. 'Such a waste of life,' he said as he enveloped Annie in his arms and let her cry until no tears were left.

27

Annie opened her eyes to see her mum sitting in a chair by her bed. 'What time is it?' she asked as she rubbed her eyes and gazed about her, noticing the empty bed in her room. That was where Emily had been sleeping since she'd had to leave her own home. Looking again at her mum, she frowned for a moment until reality hit her like a sledgehammer. 'Oh my God,' she cried out, remembering the events of the day before. 'Did it really happen?'

Violet leant over the bed and held Annie in her arms, rocking her back and forth and murmuring words of comfort until her panicked breathing calmed down. She reached for a glass of water from the bedside table. 'Here, take a sip of this and I'll settle you down again,' she said as she started to straighten the crumpled bed covers. 'Ivy Rose is with your nan feeding the chickens and your dad is out doing the deliveries. He should be home soon.'

Annie handed back the glass as a thought came to her. 'What time is it? I must get up for work; there will be a hundred and one things to do today. I can't leave Simon to cope on his own. We have a new batch of trainee managers in, and they won't be much help.' She went to swing her legs out from under the covers.

'Stay where you are,' Violet commanded. 'You had a big shock. Doctor Greyson has left some pills to help you sleep.'

Annie felt so frustrated. 'I don't need pills, I just need to get to work.'

'Darling, listen to me. It has been a day and a half since Emily was stabbed. You needed to sleep as you were close to collapse. Simon visited yesterday; he accompanied his father and left those flowers for you. They came from their family's garden,' she said, nodding to where she'd displayed them in her best china vase.

'That's kind of him,' Annie smiled, leaning back onto her pillows.

'He said he would visit again this evening, if you're up to it?'

'I will be. I can't lie in bed all day when this awful thing has happened.' A thought hit her. 'Emily's mother . . . has anyone given her the terrible news? I know she fell out with Emily, but she is still her mother and will need to know how Emily died. And her wishes need to be considered for the funeral—'

Violet held her hand up for Annie to stop talking. 'Darling, we were going to wait until you were properly awake. Emily is still alive. She lost a terrible amount of blood, and is so poorly, but she is still with us.'

'No . . . no . . . that can't be right, I saw her . . .' she cried out.

'From what Simon told us there was so much going on that none of them realized or were told there was a chance Emily could pull through. Now, I want you to take another of these pills and try to sleep for a couple of hours. After that I'll bring up a bowl of water and help you wash and put on a fresh nightdress, then if you're up to it, you can come downstairs for a bowl of soup and to see Ivy Rose. She's been asking after you non-stop.'

Annie nodded in agreement and swallowed the pill to please her mum. And after settling down under the covers she fell into a deep sleep within minutes.

Violet sat with her for a while thinking of what Annie must have experienced. From what Simon had explained when he visited yesterday, the store had been closed and would remain so for the next couple of days until the police and the American military police had completed their investigations. Paddy had promised to stop off at the cottage hospital at the end of his delivery round to enquire after Emily. She couldn't stop thinking about Simon and what a fine man he'd grown up to be. Being on the books of his father's practice, she had seen him on numerous occasions as he grew up. She'd always thought it a shame that he was just that bit too old to be friends with Annie – and then of course he'd gone to grammar school and their paths would not have crossed that way. However, it was the way he cared for her daughter that was on her mind now. It was obvious he loved Annie, but were his feelings reciprocated?

Paddy entered Erith cottage hospital, marvelling at how quiet the building was. Just inside the doors there was a waiting room with a window built into the wall. He could see a brass bell on the ledge and went to ring it before there was a polite cough on the other side of the window. 'How may I help you?'

He noticed a woman in a nurse's uniform and gave her a polite nod. 'I'm here to enquire after Emily Davenport. She was brought in the night before last from Woolworths Bexleyheath with a stab wound.'

'Are you a relative?'

'No, but my daughter is her best friend and Emily lives with us. My name is Paddy . . . Patrick Brookes.'

'If you take a seat, I'll see if there's any news,' she said before closing the little window between them.

As he sat down on one of the hard wooden seats, he could hear her footsteps fading away down a long corridor. Hospitals made him nervous. Whether it was the smell of the antiseptic or all the stern nurses he wasn't sure, but he fought the urge to get up and walk out. If he went home without any news, Violet would have his guts for garters.

After five minutes of waiting, he heard footsteps approaching down the linoleum floor of the corridor and stood up.

The nurse smiled reassuringly, immediately putting him at ease. 'Mr Brookes? I can tell you Miss Davenport is doing as well as expected.'

'Thank you. I will take that news home to my family.' He wanted to ask about Emily's baby, and if it had survived, but feared he'd not be told. He turned to leave the small hospital but paused as he heard his name being called.

'Mr Brookes! May I have a word?'

He turned to see an impeccably dressed woman hurrying towards him. 'Of course,' he replied, wondering if he knew her. Perhaps she was one of his customers, he thought, trying to think back over the routes he took when making deliveries and collecting dirty washing. He remained standing until she had taken a seat. 'How may I help you?' he asked. He knew how to speak properly when circumstances dictated, keeping his rougher language for when he was with his mates and family on the fairground. He smiled inwardly, remembering how early in their marriage Violet had taught him there was a time and a place for talking common and it had put him in good stead over the years. His wife was a clever woman; he just wished he'd been a good husband to her.

The woman took an embroidered handkerchief from a well-worn black leather handbag and delicately dabbed at her nose. 'I wanted to thank you and your family for all you've done.'

Paddy frowned. Was she talking about her laundry or something else? 'I beg your pardon?'

'For Emily . . . She's my daughter.'

'Ah,' Paddy said as the penny dropped. 'I'm pleased someone contacted you. I'd have done so myself but wasn't sure where you lived in Bexleyheath. Our Annie has been in bed since Simon, the store manager, brought her home that night. Our doctor thought it prudent she was given a sleeping pill to help settle her after what happened, so I've not yet questioned her.'

'It was a Mr Simon Greyson who came to tell me what had happened. Annie's a good girl and was a true friend to my Emily at a time when I was not being a good mother and was more concerned with what my neighbours and friends might say about . . . well, about the situation,' she said, wiping her eyes. 'I just wanted to convey my thanks. Sitting here for almost two days has given me time to think. I almost lost my daughter, and I don't intend for that to happen again.'

Paddy took a closer look at the woman. Her navy-blue dress and black jacket were creased where she must have sat waiting for news over the past forty-eight hours and there were dark shadows around her eyes. He wondered if she'd eaten properly in that time. If it had been his daughter lying there, inches from death, he doubted a crumb would have passed his lips. 'She's a lovely girl, and in the time that she's been staying with us she's been a good help around the house and with the laundry business. Our Annie doesn't have many friends so it's good to see them together. We value Emily and think of her as part of our family. We aren't a family for praying, but we've certainly been communicating with Him upstairs, and putting in our requests since Emily was injured.'

'She's a lucky girl to have your family look after her,' Mrs Davenport said with gratitude in her eyes.

Paddy had a thought. 'I wonder, what are you going to do now?' he asked.

'I'm told there will be no change overnight so plan to go home and sleep in my own bed tonight. I'll be refreshed ready to return tomorrow as Emily needs clean nightwear.'

'In that case, can I invite you to visit my home this evening? We have clean clothing belonging to Emily and my wife, Violet, always prepares enough hot food to feed an army.'

'That is very kind of you, and I will confess to not having much in my larder due to not shopping, but I don't wish to be a burden.'

'My family will tell me off if I don't extend a welcome to our home. Simon is popping by this evening, as is our local policeman, who will be giving us more news on developments about what happened. Annie still has to be interviewed and will like another friendly face to support her,' he said, hoping Violet had been able to speak to Annie and encourage her downstairs.

She faltered. 'I'm sorely tempted, but can't visit empty-handed, it wouldn't be polite.'

'Just bring yourself, that is more than enough. Why not give Emily a kiss goodnight and I'll leave our telephone number in case someone here wants to contact you?' He didn't add in case Emily took a turn for the worse.

'Then I will be delighted to accept your invitation, thank you,' she smiled.

Paddy thought how much Mrs Davenport looked like her daughter when she had a smile on her face.

28

'Come along in,' Paddy said as he guided Mrs Davenport indoors.

'Are you sure this is all right?' she asked nervously. 'I don't wish to impose on your family's evening.'

Paddy gave her a wink as he closed the door behind them. 'The more the merrier,' he said as he helped her out of her coat and hung it on the mahogany coat stand in the hall. 'Come this way,' he said, pushing open a door into the front room where Annie had just been settled in an armchair by the fire and Violet was tucking a rug around her.

'So good to have you downstairs. You even have a little colour in your cheeks,' Violet said, turning to where Paddy stood with a strange woman by his side. Annie just looked surprised.

'This is Emily's mother, Mrs Davenport. I bumped into her at the cottage hospital. Mrs Davenport, please let me introduce you to my wife, Violet, my son, Albie, and my wife's parents, Jasper and Ivy James. And of course, you've met Annie.'

The men got to their feet to shake hands while Mrs Davenport stepped forward to say hello to the women.

'I hope you're feeling brighter today, Annie,' she said, leaning down to kiss her cheek. 'I want to apologize to you for being so unpleasant when you accompanied Emily to tell me about her baby. I was a silly, silly woman and I hope you will forgive me. It has taken two days' sitting in the hospital watching Emily fight to stay alive to make me realize I needed to change my ways. Please say you'll forgive me?'

'There's nothing to forgive, as I would have been the same if my own daughter had come home and given me the same news.'

'Talking of which,' Paddy said, lifting the child from where she sat on his mother-in-law's lap, 'here's our gorgeous Ivy Rose.'

'It's lovely to see you again, Ivy Rose,' Emily's mother said, tickling her under the chin. 'You are a very lucky young lady to have such a loving family around you.'

'Would you like a cup of tea?' Violet asked.

'That would be very nice, thank you,' she replied as Paddy showed her to an empty armchair close to where Annie was sitting.

Violet's mum followed her out to the kitchen and started getting their best cups from the dresser. 'She's nothing like what our Annie said,' she whispered.

Violet got closer so no one could hear. 'I reckon she's in shock after what happened. Do you think I should invite her to join us for a meal?' she asked, thankful the chicken soup she'd made earlier had thickened and she'd added a few dumplings.

'I would. The poor cow's probably going back to an empty house. A hot meal will do her good, she looks all skin and bones.'

'I'll invite her when we take the tea in,' she said, putting boiling water into the teapot to warm it before throwing the water away and adding tea leaves and more hot water. 'There, we're all ready to go,' she said, lifting the tray and following her mum back into the front room.

'We wondered if you'd like to stay and join us for a meal, Mrs Davenport?'

'I'd be delighted, but please do call me Jocelyn. Here, let me help you with that,' she said.

Annie watched, shaking her head in disbelief and expecting the old battleaxe to resurface at any moment. 'Can you tell us how Emily is?' she asked as Jocelyn passed her a cup of tea.

'We'd all like to know,' Violet said as there was a loud knock on the front door.

'They must have smelt the teapot,' Paddy chuckled as he went to answer, returning minutes later with Simon and Sergeant Mike Jackson. 'Two for the price of one.'

'We arrived at the same time,' Simon said. 'I'm here for social reasons but I believe Mike needs to speak to Annie. How are you?' he asked, going to her side and handing her a pretty posy of flowers.

'They are beautiful, you really shouldn't do such a thing.' She smiled, thinking how attentive he was being. 'I'm much better, especially now I know that Emily hasn't . . . I mean she's going to get better,' she said, trying to be careful what she said in front of Mrs Davenport. Then she turned to their family friend. 'It's nice to see you, Sergeant Mike,' she said. 'I understand you wish to speak to me?'

Mike removed his helmet and sat down on the chair Paddy had carried in from the kitchen. 'I just need to take some notes on what you saw that night, and how you acted.'

'Is it really necessary, Sergeant?' Jocelyn asked. 'Poor Annie has been through such a lot and now Emily is on the mend it doesn't really matter.'

'I promise not to tire Annie, and it shouldn't take long, but you'd be surprised what small details can be missed by one witness while another is more observant.'

'I understand,' Annie said. 'Where shall we start?'

Violet interjected. 'We were just about to have a bite to eat. Why don't you join us and then interview Annie afterwards? That includes you,' she said to Simon. 'We can eat around the kitchen table as there's more room. Come through in ten minutes,' she said, thinking it would give her time to add a few more dumplings to the pot and cut up some bread to make the meal spread further.

'Your mother's a good cook,' Sergeant Mike said as he followed Annie and Simon back into the front room and waited while Simon settled Annie in her armchair before he went to leave.

'You can stay as I have your statement, but please don't be tempted to prompt Miss Brookes,' he said, taking out his notebook and sitting on the chair next to Annie. 'Can you tell me how Emily met Dirk Wolenski?'

Annie drew in a deep breath before explaining about the trip to London and the punch-up in the ballroom caused by the American soldiers. 'I'm not sure if Dirk was one of them, but that's the evening Emily realized she wanted to have more fun and I didn't see her for a while as she would go dancing with other girls from Woolworths.'

'You weren't invited to join them?'

Annie gave a sarcastic laugh. 'Sergeant Mike, once you have a child, even if you didn't give birth to her, you are no longer thought of as free and single. If anything, I was included with the married women with children. Don't get me wrong, I enjoyed the other women's company', she added, quickly seeing the horrified look on the two men's faces. 'But for me and Emily, it meant we didn't see much of each other for a while, until she came to me for help . . .'

She explained how she confronted Dirk when it was obvious he wasn't interested in supporting Emily or providing for the child. 'He was a despicable man, as were his comrades. Emily had fallen in love with him, so finding out he didn't care for her, and then . . .' – she looked towards the closed door – 'and then her mother not supporting her made Emily very bitter.'

Mike nodded his head as he wrote quickly. 'Can you give me the names of the women she socialized with when she was meeting the American servicemen? They may be able to shine more light on the way Dirk Wolenski acted towards her.'

Annie reeled off the names of the younger women who all worked at Woolworths. 'I'm not at liberty to give you their addresses, but Simon would be able to help you,' she said, looking towards him for guidance.

'Perhaps if we make an appointment for you to come to the store, that way you could speak to the women concerned and anyone else who comes to mind?'

'That would help greatly,' Mike said. 'Now, Annie, do you know if Emily had any contact with Dirk Wolenski after she moved in here with you?'

Annie thought for a minute. 'No doubt she'd have said something if she had. No, I reckon him turning up at the meal Woolworths organized for our American friends was a complete surprise. I think he had a blooming cheek knowing Emily would most likely be there. Thankfully he wasn't noticed until after the meal had finished and the first I knew was when the altercation started. I wish I'd known what was said.'

Mike apologized. 'Sorry, I'm not at liberty to tell you.'

'I can update you later,' Simon said. 'I've heard several versions from staff – even some who weren't there.'

Annie turned to Simon and gave him a grateful smile. 'It won't go any further. I just want to know the complete story. One minute everyone was having a nice time, and the next Emily was fighting for her life . . .'

Mike turned a page in his notebook and gave a small cough. 'Can you tell me if Emily was holding a knife and, if so, where did it come from?'

Annie had been dreading this question as it could incriminate her friend, but what confused her was if Emily was holding the knife, how come she was the one who was injured? It was best she told Sergeant Mike the truth and let him work it out. 'I was talking to Simon on the other side of the canteen when a cry went up and furniture was knocked over. That was when I saw Emily holding the knife. I didn't go to that side of the room until Simon called me for my help. What I saw will stay with me for the rest of my life. To be honest, Sergeant Mike, I thought Emily had died. I was only informed today that she was poorly but alive.'

Mike could see she was getting upset. 'Just one more question and I'll be finished for this evening. What did you say to Dirk Wolenski outside in the corridor before he was taken away by the military police?'

Annie placed her head in her hands. 'I can't recall my exact words, but I was so angry with him. Don't forget I thought Emily had died.'

He snapped his notebook closed and stood up. 'I've got enough so I'll not bother you any more and I'm sorry to interrupt your evening. I'll say my goodbyes to your family and go out the back way.'

Simon stood up and shook his hand. 'Thanks for coming over, Mike, rather than asking Annie to go to the police station. She still needs to rest up a little more before she's fighting fit again.'

Mike turned to Annie and tousled her hair, very much as he had when she was a child. 'You'll be fine,' he said before leaving.

'You look exhausted. Would you like me to call your mother to help you up to your bedroom?' Simon asked as the door shut behind the policeman.

'No, I'd just like to sit here for a while and think about everything. Having slept through yesterday I feel as though I've missed out on so much. For one thing, I should have been at the store helping you. Tell me everything that happened so that I'm up to speed when I return.'

He sat down opposite her. 'I was in early, long before staff arrived. I decided to keep only essential staff on the premises and sent the rest home until next Monday. There was no use in having counter staff standing about when there wouldn't be any customers to serve. I kept on the trainee managers, supervisors, canteen staff and the cleaners.'

'That seems to be a good plan,' Annie acknowledged. 'What have head office said about all this?'

'They're sending us some specialist people who usually step in when stores have been bombed as they know how to get things moving towards opening again.'

'It seems so heartless in so many ways, but I can appreciate we need to keep the store open as customers rely on us. Have you heard much from the American army's military police?'

Simon stopped to listen if anyone was about to come into the room. 'If I change the subject, don't look surprised. The Yanks are saying Emily caused this as she was about to stab Dirk until he fought her off and that's when he had to defend himself. They are baying for her blood.'

Annie couldn't believe what she was hearing. 'No, Emily's not like that! She couldn't kill someone. She may have been angry with him, but she would never have tried to kill him as she would have known how strong he was, and that he'd have overpowered her.'

'I'm not sure how we can prove this,' he replied before they both fell silent.

'I've got it,' Annie exclaimed, sitting bolt upright in her armchair. 'We need to draw a map of the canteen and pinpoint where everyone was at the time of the stabbing. Then we need to have them say what they saw.'

'It's a good plan.'

Annie pointed Simon to a bureau in the corner of the room where he found a large exercise book and wax crayons. They first made a list of all the invited guests, as well as members of staff. They numbered each person before starting to place their positions in the room.

'Thank goodness many were still sitting at their tables eating Marge's cake and drinking tea while singing along to the tunes being played on the piano,' Annie sighed, studying the diagram they had produced.

'I'll have to check some of the table placings with Marge and the chart in my office, but this is a very good start,' Simon replied.

'I'm so sorry I refused to help further with the organization of the meal. I couldn't face being nice to the American soldiers when they had shown such disrespect to an innocent girl. It would be too soon if I never met another of them.'

Simon took her hand. 'I do understand, but remember they're over here to help finish this war. Besides that, not everyone is a bad apple. I'm here to protect you.' He leant in closer to her as if to kiss her when the telephone rang in the hall.

Only a moment later, Paddy burst into the room. 'That was the hospital. Emily has taken a turn for the worse and they want her loved ones there as soon as possible.'

29

Within minutes they were either in the van or Simon's car and heading from the marshes towards Erith cottage hospital. Jocelyn travelled with Simon and Annie, who had only stopped long enough to pull her coat over the lightweight frock she'd changed into when she'd come downstairs late that day.

There was silence in the car until Jocelyn spoke. 'What do you think has happened to Emily? I do wish they'd said more.'

Annie agreed. 'I supposed it's so we don't worry or think the worst.'

'It hasn't worked, has it?' Simon added as he gripped the steering wheel, following close behind Paddy's van.

'I promised to use the telephone to let Nan and Grandad both know when we've heard something, although she's frightened of using the telephone. She jumps and backs away every time it rings.'

'It may be best to update them with the news once you're back home,' Simon suggested.

'You're right, and I don't want to be waking Ivy Rose in the middle of the night. It was good of them to stay behind and care for her. They love Emily and are so worried.'

Jocelyn sniffed into her handkerchief from where she sat on the back seat. 'Your family have been so kind to my daughter.'

Annie looked over her shoulder wishing she'd sat with Jocelyn. 'She's a lovely girl who just met with an unpleasant person. One day she'll look back on this and be able to smile,' she said, hoping that would be so. The more she thought about what had happened, the more she hated what she thought of as the American invaders. There was a popular saying doing the rounds about them – 'overpaid, oversexed and over here' – and she couldn't agree more. She was still ruing the day that Emily had fallen for one of them as they arrived at the hospital and hurried to the entrance.

A nurse put her finger to her lips and beckoned for them to follow her to a nearby office. 'The doctor will see you soon. Would you like a drink while you wait?'

They all thanked her and said no; they were too nervous to drink tea.

Jocelyn raised a hand to get the nurse's attention. 'I wondered what happens if there should be an air raid?'

The nurse pointed to signs on the wall. 'Just follow the arrows and you will find yourself in our cellars where it is completely safe.'

Violet kicked Paddy's ankle as he opened his mouth. One of his favourite jokes was to mention Red Indians when told to follow the arrows. 'Not now, Paddy,' she hissed, although she smiled thinking of how he had a joke for most occasions.

'Sorry, I didn't mean our safety. I was thinking more of my daughter and the other patients,' Jocelyn said apologetically.

'There's no need to apologize,' the nurse said. 'Our operating theatre is underground. Thank goodness this is an old building with deep cellars. All the able-bodied patients are led there, and every staff member is assigned a patient to take care of.'

'That's put my mind at rest. One never thinks of these things until . . .'

Violet put her arm around Emily's mother and let her weep. She knew she'd act the same if it were Annie in this situation. 'She's in very good hands,' she murmured.

Dawn had started to appear in the sky before a surgeon appeared looking world-weary, his pale blue operating gown rumpled and spotted with blood. 'Mrs Davenport?' he asked before sitting down opposite her as a nurse stood nearby. All eyes were on him as he rubbed his eyes. 'We did our best and fought for most of the night. I want to make it clear Emily was very poorly and had lost so much blood when she was stabbed.'

'Oh no,' Annie gasped, hiding her face against Simon's chest while Paddy reached over to put an arm around Violet and Jocelyn.

'The good news is Emily is stable for now, although sadly she lost her child.'

Jocelyn visibly brightened. 'If my daughter is still with us, that is all that matters. She's young and will have more children in the future.'

The surgeon shook his head. 'I'm afraid there was too much damage. She will never be able to conceive, let alone carry a baby.'

Silence fell across the room as they digested the surgeon's words. 'May I see her?' Jocelyn asked.

'In a little while. She's just being brought back up to the ward and is sleeping soundly. I doubt she will awake for hours but if she does, I'd like you to be with me when the news is broken to her.' The doctor nodded meaningfully at Jocelyn.

'We'll wait with you,' Violet said. 'Simon, I suggest you take Annie home. You can come and see her another day,' she added as her daughter started to object.

'You are not to go to work,' Paddy instructed. 'We don't want you collapsing.'

Annie was too tired to argue with them as Simon helped her to her feet. After kissing her mother and father and hugging Jocelyn tightly she headed to the car with Simon holding on to her arm. 'Life is just too bloody unfair,' she said as he settled her into the passenger seat. 'Emily does not deserve to be denied having children just because of that man.'

Simon was thoughtful as he got behind the wheel of his vehicle and started the engine. 'As hard as it may feel, don't do or say anything at this time. We started to plan last night and now even more so we should get on with this before Wolenski is sent home and evades possible arrest. I promised your parents you would not be going into the store today and I intend to stick by that. However, if you agree, I'll bring all the information to you, and we can work on it together until you're up to coming back into Woolworths. What do you say?'

'I'd like that very much and thank you for allowing me to help,' she said, knowing she would do her best to get to the bottom of what really happened. 'May I be cheeky and make some notes of what I would like to see? I'll throw in breakfast while I do it.'

'It's a deal. Emily is your friend, and you deserve to be part of our investigation.'

Annie was as good as her word and while frying eggs and bread she jotted down ideas in a notepad. 'You need to speak with Marge as she oversaw the staff room and would know of any seating changes. Also, her girls who carried out the food. I'm particularly interested in the area where Dirk and his mates were seated. Did anyone leave early and what were the temperaments of the Americans like when they arrived and during their stay?'

'Why do you ask about their temperaments?'

'There was a ruckus on their side of the room, and it may be that Emily was caught up in it.'

Simon rubbed his chin. 'I'm not so sure, I think you're clutching at straws. Didn't she go rushing over there?'

'That's what we need to verify,' she said, tearing off the sheet of paper. 'If I think of anything else, may I call you during the morning?'

'Please do, although I think you're in the wrong job, Miss Marple,' he laughed, leaning over to kiss her cheek very gently.

Annie chuckled. 'Sit down and eat your breakfast then I suggest you go home for a shave.' She rubbed her cheek where his stubbly chin had grazed her skin.

After she'd waved off Simon, she went back to clear up the kitchen before going to her bed. Expecting not to sleep, she took the notebook with her but as soon as she entered her bedroom Ivy Rose clambered out of her own little bed and ran to her demanding a cuddle. Annie lifted her into her own bed, tucking the covers around her where the child snuggled up to her and, sucking her thumb, fell into a deep sleep. Annie thought how lucky she was to have this little one in her life, and then she remembered Emily's child who had died in the night. Would it have been a boy or a girl? Would it have looked like Emily or Dirk? Would it have grown up to be a happy child? Would it later have had brothers and sisters? The world could be a cruel place, she thought as she finally closed her eyes and slept.

Once she was up and dressed later that morning, she wanted to crack on with what she had chatted about with Simon. She did her best to note down everything that had been on the pages she'd given to Simon to take with him. Paddy found her sitting in the front room with paper spread out around her on the dining table.

'Can I look?' he asked, already peering over her shoulder.

'Of course you can,' she said and began to explain what she and Simon planned. 'You weren't there, Dad, so looking at this as an outsider, what questions would you ask?'

Paddy thought long and hard as he turned the pages back and forth. 'You say here that you were on the other side of the canteen to where Emily and the American soldiers were. Did she say anything to you earlier in the meal, and did you watch her all the time? I only ask as there seems to be a gap between when you heard the shrieks and when she was injured. I would also like to know how she came to be holding the knife. Some may say she was trying to stab Dirk – don't look at me like that, we must look at all possibilities. Perhaps she was taking it from him and somehow was stabbed, or perhaps he stabbed her and what you saw was her holding the knife after she pulled it from her stomach.'

Annie frantically scribbled down his questions. 'These are great questions, Dad, thank you. It's amazing what a fresh pair of eyes can see.'

Paddy looked embarrassed, not being one to accept praise. 'I'm afraid I've been in fights, or helped break them up at the fairground, so I've seen this type of thing in the past. It's quite surprising how onlookers who have only seen part of a fight then come up with their own versions of what happened. Get the police involved and someone could end up in prison even though they're innocent.'

Shocked by his words, Annie put a hand to her chest and took a deep breath. 'You don't think the police believe Emily was trying to murder Dirk, do you?'

'I'm not going to second guess what the police think. What I do know is that Sergeant Mike Jackson is one of the fairest policemen we have and if he is faced with every piece of evidence, he will act accordingly. I'm not saying that just because he's been a family friend for many years, but only as you couldn't find a straighter copper if you looked from here to kingdom come.'

'I know I'd trust him with my life, but we mustn't forget the American military police are involved as well.' Annie paused to ponder the situation. 'Do you think Jocelyn should consider finding a solicitor for Emily?'

'No, let's leave things for now. There's no point in distressing the woman unless we have to.' He turned back to the notes. 'If you like, I could drop these off to Simon while I'm out on my deliveries.'

'Thanks, Dad, this is all a great help. You have a brilliant mind.'

'No, love, I've just been around a lot of criminals and know how to duck and dive. It comes in handy sometimes. I'll give you a shout when I'm ready,' he said as he started to leave. 'You like this lad, don't you?'

'Who, Simon? Yes, he's a good friend,' she said, turning away for a moment.

Paddy grinned to himself as he left the room. He looked forward to having a son-in-law.

'Are you ready?' Simon asked the next day as they sat in his office each at a different desk.

'Very much so. This is one step closer to clearing Emily's name. It's going to be a long day with thirty people to interview; we must make it clear this is just a chat to put our minds straight over what happened and it's not an official enquiry.'

'I suggest after we've each spoken to three staff members, we take ten minutes to update each other on what we've learnt,' he said.

'I agree. Let's get this show on the road,' she grinned, happy to be feeling better and raring to get to the bottom of what happened.

'I'll call in the first two staff members,' Simon said, going to open the door. They'd already had a long chat with Marge, and she'd been able to furnish them with lots of information which Annie had noted down. Each had a plan of the staff canteen and were going to ask the staff members they spoke to to point to where they were and what they saw or did.

Annie was a little nervous as one of the older counter assistants sat in front of her. She made it clear this wasn't an official interview and how much she valued the woman's feedback. 'Where were you sitting, Nellie?'

'I didn't have a seat as such as I was one of the waitresses; it used to be my job years ago and I volunteered to help, especially as my eldest daughter is married to an American lad and lives in Idaho. I thought it would be a friendly way to show them how we're linked across the sea.'

Annie agreed that it was and moved the neatly drawn diagram of the room closer for the woman to see. 'Can you point out where you were working?'

'Apart from going to the counter to reload my tray I was mainly around this area.' Nellie pointed to where the American soldiers were seated.

Annie couldn't believe that she was about to get to the truth so early on. A shiver of excitement ran through her. 'Did you see what happened when your colleague was injured?'

'That's the thing, I should have seen it all, but someone had knocked my elbow and I'd spilt a jug of custard on the table. In fact, when people shouted out in alarm and some chairs were turned over, I thought it was because of what I'd done. You've got to laugh, haven't you?'

Annie replied through thin lips that yes, you had to laugh.

The morning shot by with varying degrees of success, although Annie despaired at times of her colleagues' memories of something that only happened days before. Some women said they'd been told by their family members not to get involved, even though she explained that once this became a police enquiry, they would have no choice but to say what they saw, despite what their families told them.

'I know it's exasperating but we can only do our best,' Simon told her. 'Once we've completed our interviews, then we pass everything over to Sergeant Mike and offer our support. Hopefully it will speed up the investigation process.'

Annie sighed. 'I suppose you're right. After all, the police have so much to do these days and Dad was telling me they're short-staffed.'

They collated their plans of where staff were onto the main layout.

'There's a gap I'd like to fill,' Simon said, pointing to tables behind where the American soldiers were sitting. 'Someone must have seen something from there.'

Annie reached for the table arrangement Marge had given them. 'There are four staff members sitting on this table and two people who were waitressing that area. 'Shall we call them in next, before we stop for lunch?'

'That sounds like a plan,' he agreed, studying the drawing in front of him.

'I'll pop downstairs to the shop floor and ask the ladies to come up two at a time and warn them not to speak to each other, not that they've all not already huddled together surmising what has happened.' She shook her head as she spoke, praying the women would see sense and tell them what they knew.

'I don't want to get the boys in trouble,' a belligerent staff member pouted, tossing her wavy chestnut hair. 'They've always been great fun when we've gone out with them. Why, they could be sent back to America because of this.'

Annie decided it was time to get tough. 'Linda, you do know that a crime has been committed and if it's found that you've covered up for anybody, you too could be sent to prison.'

The girl's mouth dropped open. 'But I've not done nothing . . .'

'You must tell the truth about what you saw. Put it this way, if it was one of the lads who stabbed Emily, what's to stop them stabbing you?' she asked, her voice rising enough that Simon heard from the other desk and raised his eyebrows.

The girl looked shocked. 'But they like me . . .'

'They liked Emily,' Annie pointed out, knowing that she was losing this fight. 'You may return to your work but expect to be interviewed by the police next and they won't be as easy-going as me.'

'The police? My parents won't like that.'

'Then please, why not make it easy on yourself and just tell me what you saw?'

'All right, as long as the police aren't involved.'

'Linda, I can't promise that, but as you're only a witness, it's not as if you're breaking the law, is it? Now, can you point to the chart and tell me where you were sitting when it happened and who you were with?'

After getting through to Linda the importance of her help Annie was able to place where people were sitting at a table next to the soldiers. 'Now, think carefully, who was holding the knife?'

'Dirk ended up with knife. Joanne was carrying a tray with the cake and a knife on it and as she approached him, he started to joke with her about her carrying a lethal weapon. She's only a kid and went a bit silly because they were joshing her. One of the other soldiers took the knife and she tried to grab it back and dropped some of the cake. At that point Emily appeared and snatched the knife. She seemed so angry and really laid into him. I don't know why . . .'

'Go on,' Annie urged her. 'You're doing really well.'

Linda started to cry. 'It's so horrible to think about. Dirk managed to take the knife away from her but then Emily slipped on some of the cake that had fallen from the tray, and she reached out to grab something to save herself, but it was too late. She fell against the knife and that's when people started screaming and trying to run away . . . There was blood everywhere and then I felt faint, and my friends took me outside. I'm sorry, I don't remember much more than that.'

'Sit and compose yourself for a little while,' Annie said, pushing her cup of tea towards her. 'Drink that, it will help calm you,' she said, absorbing what the young woman had just said. Linda had witnessed it all close up, and it was an accident – a tragic, terrible accident.

30

November 1942

'Are you ready?' Annie asked as she gripped Emily's hand.

'As I'll ever be. I just want to get this over with.'

They both climbed the steps to Bexleyheath police station, a short walk from the Woolworths store, and were directed through the building and upstairs to a large, bright room full of rows of chairs, where Simon stepped forward to join them.

'We're to be seated over here,' he said, pointing to where three seats had *reserved* cards on them.

Emily looked around her with fear in her eyes. 'Is he here?' she asked. 'I don't think I could face him, not after all that's happened.'

'Dirk and his comrades will be seated further up the room, so you have no need to walk past them or to see them,' Simon said, which calmed her at once. 'Come, settle yourself here.'

Annie continued to hold her hand. 'You know, Emily, there is nothing to fear as you're completely innocent. The police have proof it was an unfortunate accident.'

Emily started to shake uncontrollably. 'An accident that killed my child,' she sobbed, placing her hand on her stomach.

Annie turned to whisper to Simon. 'I don't think she's strong enough to face this. I wonder if she can be excused?'

Simon looked to where Emily was huddled in her chair shaking uncontrollably. 'I'll have a word with Mike, he'll know what can be done,' he said, going to where Sergeant Mike stood in his full dress uniform chatting to a colleague. He quickly pointed out that Emily, as was clear to all, was in no fit state to attend the enquiry.

'There's a waiting room just down the hall on the left. Can someone sit with her?' Simon returned and spoke quietly.

'I will,' Annie offered. 'Mrs Davenport is joining us shortly and she can be with Emily while I return here in case I'm needed.'

'You'd best move her now, before the proceedings start,' Sergeant Mike said, approaching them as the room grew noticeably busier. 'I'll let them know.' He nodded to where dignitaries from the police and the American army were taking their seats at a table set upon a raised platform at the top end of the room.

'It's almost like a court,' Annie said nervously.

'A crime hasn't been committed; it's just an enquiry due to the delicate nature of our visitors being involved,' Mike explained. 'God knows what would have happened if someone had been murdered.'

Annie shuddered at the thought. 'I'm relieved that our staff told the truth, and their statements were accepted. Even now, six weeks later, customers are still coming into the store to ask what happened.'

'At least the takings are up,' Simon grinned. 'Now, let's get Emily settled before we interrupt anything.' He stood to let Annie and Emily get to the aisle.

'This is cosy,' Annie said as the pair sat in the smaller room where a fire was burning in the grate. She pulled off her gloves and held her hands out to warm them. 'It's such a miserable day,' she added, peering through the window criss-crossed with blast tape out to where mist was drifting along the street. 'It's been a cold autumn,' she said, turning back to her friend. 'You haven't told me much about Somerset. What is it like living with your aunt? When will your mum be living there with you?'

Emily shrugged her shoulders. 'It's somewhere to live. I couldn't stay here as there are too many memories.'

'That's a shame as given time your life would have settled down and you could have returned to work in the store. So many people miss you,' Annie assured her.

Emily gave a harsh laugh. 'And have everyone watch me and talk about me behind my back? No thank you. I know it's not been long, but life will never change for me. My aunt fusses around me too much and once Mother's joined us it will be twice as bad. It's like living in a prison where everyone is pitying me. There again, staying here it would be no different.'

'You know, you could always come back and live with us on the marshes.'

'Don't you understand? It will be the same as living in Somerset. Even though your parents mean well they too would cosset me. Ivy Rose is a sweetheart, but she would be a reminder of the child I lost and the children I could never have all because of my anger and stupidity.'

Annie had found it hard to get through to Emily ever since she'd left the cottage hospital. Jocelyn doted on her daughter and the pair of them had stayed with the Brookes family rather than rattle around in their house in Bexleyheath. Emily had spent long periods alone wandering through the marshes in all weathers in clothes she'd borrowed from Annie. Violet had told her daughter to leave Emily alone as she was the only one who could work through her demons.

Once she was deemed fit enough to be interviewed about what happened at the store, she seemed strangely to come to life a little and that's when she decided it was time to go to Somerset. Jocelyn suggested she wait while the house was packed up or possibly rented out and then they could travel there together. Emily didn't listen and once she'd packed a suitcase and had a travel pass, she left the area, only returning after much insistence from everyone involved in the investigation. Sergeant Mike had offered to arrange for somebody to collect her, but she decided she wanted to travel alone and had stayed with Annie for the past two days.

'I don't know what to suggest to make life better for you again,' Annie said through blurred eyes. It was so painful to see her friend like this, so distant and alone.

Emily gave another harsh laugh. 'It will all come out in the wash, isn't that what your nan says?'

They sat in silence, apart from coals settling in the fire and the occasional footsteps in the hall outside the door.

'I thought it was really clever of you the way you pieced together everything that happened that day,' Emily said after a while, reaching into her handbag for a cigarette, her hands shaking so much she could hardly light it. This was another side of Emily that Annie had never seen before.

'I wanted to do everything possible to prove your innocence; there was talk that you had intended to stab Dirk and it had all gone wrong. Who in their right mind could believe it? All the same, it had to be proved that you were innocent, and just the victim of a nasty accident. Goodness knows what would have happened if it was proved you tried to murder him. I was so relieved to get Linda's statement.'

Emily stubbed out the partially smoked cigarette into a glass ashtray on a side table. 'The girl's an idiot.'

'What do you mean?'

'I mean that she really wanted to be part of my circle of friends and mix with the American soldiers. Of course she wasn't going to say anything negative about what happened . . . Just the opposite. She'll say whatever it takes, that one, to stay part of the gang.'

For a moment Annie couldn't say a word. She must have misheard. Surely her friend wasn't telling her that she'd got it all wrong, not after all that painstaking work? 'You . . . you mean?'

'I mean I went over there in a rage to kill him. I could only see red and, after the way he treated me, I wanted him out of my life. Correction: I wanted him dead. He'd ruined my life and I planned to ruin his.' Emily spoke quite matter-of-factly, as if the truth was the most obvious thing in the world.

Annie couldn't believe what she was hearing. 'Why are you telling me this now when you could have kept quiet? After today it would have made no difference.'

'I wanted you to know the truth and how my hatred of him was eating me up inside. I would have been left a single mother and was already ostracized by my own mother. That wasn't the life I'd planned for myself, but I could see no other way out.'

Puzzled, Annie tried to think over what Emily was saying. 'Let me get this right, you planned to stab Dirk and then . . . ?'

'And then this,' Emily said, raising her hands from beneath her handbag where she was holding a pair of scissors. Before Annie could react Emily had plunged them into her own stomach and bright red blood gushed across her lap.

'I'm so sorry, Annie.' Simon had taken on the sad task of following the ambulance workers to their vehicle, even though they could all guess the result of their efforts. 'They did as much as they possibly could for her, but she was still weak after losing so much blood when she was stabbed,' Simon went on, trying to pull her into his arms to comfort her. She pulled away.

Annie was in a state of shock. 'None of this makes sense. I had the evidence in that statement that said it was an accident.'

'Linda lied in the statement she gave to you, and you told me Emily said as much.'

'But then how . . . ?'

'The counter assistants I interviewed at the same time you were interviewing Linda told me what really happened. But even though we had statements to say that she intended to kill Dirk it's only now with her talking to you that she confirmed it.'

'You mean, someone was listening to our conversation in the waiting room just now?' Annie was almost shaking at the betrayal.

'We had no choice but to do so,' Sergeant Mike said as he joined them.

'And you couldn't trust me enough to tell me? Think how I feel! You've kept information from me and allowed me to believe it was a terrible accident and all the time you had the evidence that Emily had planned to kill Dirk? I've just seen my friend bleed to death. Please, just leave me alone. I really don't want to speak to anyone right now.'

'But Annie, you must see that we had to find the truth and telling you that Linda lied might have got in the way of that . . .' Simon's protests fell on deaf ears as Annie strode away, unable to take any more from the man she had begun to think of as so much more than a good friend. She couldn't bear to pass the door to the little waiting room and hastened away in the opposite direction, halting only when she was far enough away not to overhear any more conversation between the two men who had let her down so badly.

She jumped as a familiar voice could be heard behind her. 'Jocelyn? I didn't expect to see you here?' she said, thinking Mrs Davenport would have followed Emily to the hospital, even though there was no hope by the time the ambulance arrived.

Jocelyn shook her head before putting her arms around Annie. 'Emily was a lost soul from the moment she laid eyes on that man. Whatever you or I said or did, it wouldn't have changed the course of events. I'm of the belief that the path we follow in life has been designed for us long before we are born. Emily, for all her good points, was set on one of destruction. I shall mourn my daughter for what she could have been, not what she turned into in these past months.'

'I'm sorry, I should have done more,' Annie said, gripping the older woman's hand.

'There is nothing any of us could have done. I don't want you going through life blaming yourself. Chart your course and step out bravely,' she said, kissing each of Annie's cheeks.

'What are you going to do now?' Annie asked, worried that Jocelyn would be lonely.

'First there is a funeral to arrange. It will be a quiet one with just a few friends. Perhaps you would help me, my dear? After that my plans will not change, and I will join my sister in Somerset as before. We've always had a fancy to open a tea room, so if ever you are down our way, please seek us out. Of course I will keep in touch, as you are my only link to my daughter.' Her voice wavered for a moment. 'We mustn't forget what caused this to happen,' she said before turning to leave.

Annie watched her disappear down the bleak corridor, leaving her standing alone and unsure what to do. She had planned to return to the store, but with fifteen minutes before closing it seemed pointless. Her van was parked behind the police station, so she decided to drive home. Her family knew nothing of what had happened to Emily, and she had that upsetting news to impart. Deep in thought, she headed towards the main staircase until she was pulled up by a group of people leaving the big meeting room. American voices had her step back into an alcove as the group of soldiers who had been with Dirk walked by. She froze as she could hear them congratulating him that the case was closed. Peering out, she observed him being slapped on the back and being told he had got off lightly by being sent back to the States.

She stepped out in front of them, not being able to stop herself if she tried. 'So, you got off lightly?' she asked, staring Dirk in the face.

'Ma'am,' he said politely, trying to walk past her. She stepped sideways to stop him.

'Have you no shame for what you did?'

He stopped and removed his cap. 'Ma'am, there was no case to be found against me or against any party, and I'm being sent home to prepare for a new mission.'

'And to see your family?'

'I hope so, ma'am, as it has been a while.' He started to look around him nervously to see who was watching. 'Hey, do I know you?'

'We've met, but it was my friend you knew particularly well. In fact, you knew her very well indeed.'

'I do know you, you're that fruitcake Emily's friend. Where is she?' he asked, looking past Annie. 'Waiting to jump out at me with a knife?' He laughed out loud, his friends joining in. 'You Brits sure are a strange bunch.'

Annie tried hard to remind herself she was only there to speak to the man, not to lash out as she so badly wanted to. If her feelings got out of control, she could end up being arrested and that wouldn't do at all.

She took a deep breath, holding back the urge to scream. 'For your information Emily has died. She never really got over what you did to her. The way you treat women, what do you expect?'

He looked ashen-faced as around him his friends backed away. 'Dead?'

'Yes, so perhaps think twice in future before you use vulnerable young women as your playthings. Go home to your wife and never forget that she could find out about this . . .'

'Ma'am, are you threatening me?'

'No, she isn't, she's simply pointing out that next time you may not be so lucky,' Simon said as he suddenly appeared at her side. The two men glared at each other.

'Wolenski, come with me,' his commanding officer bellowed.

'Sir,' he said, turning to follow the man, looking back just once at Annie as she returned the stare while he walked away.

'We need to get out of here and talk.' Simon took her elbow to lead her away.

'But I don't want—'

'Just do as I ask for once,' he pleaded.

She nodded but didn't speak and they left the building and crossed the road to a cafe.

'Anything to eat?' a woman asked when he ordered two teas.

He looked questioningly at Annie who shook her head. She could not face trying to eat in the presence of Simon, she was too hurt. 'No, just the tea, please.' He took the cups and looked around for a quiet place to sit but they were out of luck. With no other choice, they sat in the middle of the crowded cafe with people all around them. 'So much for my quiet goodbye,' he muttered.

'Goodbye? What do you mean?'

'I'm leaving the Bexleyheath store,' he sighed as he started to stir the stewed liquid in his cup.

'What do you mean, you're leaving? Have you been transferred to another store?' She knew management could be moved from store to store during their careers.

'No, I'm leaving the company. I've thought for a long time that I should return to my studies, especially after I was invalided out of the army. Before I was Betty's trainee, I'd been studying medicine, as it was what my father wanted. Then I gave it up to try something else. It was easier for me to work at Woolworths while I recuperated, then I fell into the habit of not thinking about the future and stayed.'

'I thought you were happy at the store,' she said, startled by how upset she was at his news.

'I was . . . I am . . . but it's not the future I had planned before the war. I'm going back to studying to be a doctor, just as my father and my grandfather did. For a while I resisted following in their footsteps and thought that my life lay in a career at Woolworths, but with everything that has happened, well, I'll be more needed as a doctor, I can see that now.' He stared at her as if willing her to believe him. How important it was to him that she did.

She had to concede that his father was an exceptional doctor. 'I hope you enjoy your new career,' she said, rigid with dignity. 'Thank you for the tea. I really must be getting back to Jocelyn as she needs my help right now. I'll see you at work tomorrow.'

Simon watched her walk away looking as though she had the worries of the world on her shoulders.

31

Easter 1944

'My goodness, she is such a cutie pie,' Betty Billington exclaimed as Annie walked into the staff room at the Erith store holding Ivy Rose's hand. 'How old is she now?' she asked, bending down so she was face to face with the child.

'Thank you so much for inviting her to the Easter party for the staff's children; she's never attended anything like this before. Ivy Rose is three and a half and growing so fast,' Annie smiled. Even though she knew Betty Billington very well she always felt intimidated by the older woman and some of her staff, who all seemed to be such good friends.

'You're wearing such a pretty party dress,' Betty said. 'I wonder who made it for you?'

Ivy Rose put her thumb in her mouth and looked around the room before pointing to where Maisie was standing talking to Sarah. 'Fweeda,' she said without removing her thumb.

Annie laughed. 'She gets everyone's names mixed up. Maisie passed on the dress from one of her stepdaughters.

My mum knitted her cardigan, and the wool came from one of my old ones that had gone at the elbows. It's amazing how resourceful we've become.'

'We have,' Betty said, getting to her feet. 'I must have a sort out myself. I too have stepdaughters and they're shooting up.'

Maisie joined them and they stood chatting. Annie, not having much idea about the Erith store women's home life, found it all very interesting. 'Are Sarah and Freda here today?' she asked as she looked around the staff canteen. It was like the Bexleyheath store's layout albeit it on a smaller scale.

'Sarah's helping Maureen in the kitchen. She's made an Easter cake, and Freda is about somewhere. She has a special surprise for the children; it's something we've never done before.'

'That sounds intriguing,' Annie chuckled. 'I heard Freda is involved with the Brownies and Girl Guides. It's something I'd like to have Ivy Rose join, when she's old enough. She sees too few children where we live.'

'Then we'll have to all get together with our children,' Betty suggested.

'We have plenty of them between us,' Maisie said. 'My girls are wearing bunny ears and fluffy bobtails to help Freda. Look, here they come now.' A gaggle of small children dancing around Freda entered the room followed by a group of American soldiers. Freda, dressed just like the children, was carrying a straw basket full of homemade fluffy chicks and bunny rabbits. She stood in the middle of the room and the children sat at her feet. Ivy Rose looked up at Annie for her approval before running over to join the other children.

Some soldiers went to the side of the room where a couple of them started to help Maureen as she sliced up the cake to hand out to the guests.

All at once Annie felt dizzy as the room began to spin. She couldn't believe what she was seeing.

'Attention, everyone,' Freda said as she clapped her hands. 'We're going on an egg hunt, and it has all been laid on by our friends the American soldiers from Hall Place. Many of us, me included, had never heard of this before, but it seems it is very popular with children in America. As a rule, chocolate eggs are hidden, and all the children run around trying to find them. Unfortunately, even with Woolworths resources, we do not have enough chocolate eggs to hide.'

Everyone in the room groaned, especially the children.

Freda raised her hands for silence. 'Instead, we have hidden . . . tennis balls!' she said, raising one in the air that she took from her pocket.

'When I blow my Girl Guide whistle each child in the room will accompany an adult to go searching for their special Easter tennis ball. Every adult will have a map of where they can go in the building.'

'That was a clever idea otherwise the kids will be running all over the place,' Maisie whispered to Annie, who could only nod her head as it still hadn't stopped spinning.

'When the child brings back their special tennis ball, which I borrowed from the church hall so I must remember to return them, the child may exchange it for one of these fluffy chicks or bunnies in my basket.'

'Wait!' Maureen bellowed. 'First, we should eat our cake as these lovely soldiers donated most of the ingredients. Then you can start your egg hunt.'

New Horizons for the Woolworths Girls

Annie was grateful she had a few moments to compose herself before she collected Ivy Rose to go hunting for their tennis ball. She took a couple of deep breaths, but it made her feel worse.

'Are you all right? You look a little pale,' Betty observed.

'I just feel a bit warm. I'll be fine in a moment,' Annie replied, not wishing to cause a scene.

Betty led her to a seat nearby and fetched her a glass of water. 'Sip this slowly and relax. I'll keep an eye on Ivy Rose for you,' she promised, turning towards the group of children as two of the soldiers approached, one carrying the cake on a tray while the second held a pile of plates.

'Cake, ma'am?' he asked.

Annie went to say no thank you, but Betty at the same time said, 'Two pieces, please.'

He raised the knife to slice two portions, at which point Annie let out a cry and crumpled in a faint on the floor.

The soldier carrying the plates passed them to Maureen who was standing nearby and lifted Annie into his arms. 'Where can we take her?' he asked Betty.

'Follow me, we can use my office. It'll be cooler in there. I have some sal volatile in my first aid tin.'

Annie came to with a start and pushed the soldier's hand away as the ghastly smell started to make her eyes smart. 'I'm fine,' she began to say until she noticed the soldier and tried to back away from where he had placed her down gently in Betty's office chair. 'Why have you come back? Emily's dead!' she exclaimed in her confused state.

He looked towards Betty for assistance. 'I have no idea what she's talking about. Has she mistaken me for somebody else, do you think?'

Betty had an inkling of what Annie was referring to. 'My friend had a terrible experience and I think in her confused state it has come to the forefront of her mind. Would you mind going back out and asking Maisie to join me, please? She's the tall, striking blonde woman.'

'I know who you mean, ma'am,' he said. 'I hope your friend will be fine.'

'Thank you for your help,' she replied, thinking what a polite young man he was. Even in her current state she realized he was good-looking in a clean-cut kind of way: hair very short in the military style, of course, but a deep shade of brown, with nut-brown eyes that twinkled with intelligence.

'What 'appened?' Maisie asked as she hurried into the room carrying a glass of water to see Betty bending over Annie in concern.

'Annie's had a shock,' she said, indicating to Maisie to close the door. 'I don't wish anyone else to hear this.'

Maisie bent down beside Annie, who seemed to be coming round a little more. 'What's up, love?'

'I feel so silly,' Annie said. 'Thank you for your care. I'd best get back to Ivy Rose as she'll be fretting.'

'You stay where you are.' Maisie poked her with a manicured finger. 'Here, drink this, and tell your Auntie Maisie all about it,' she said, perching herself on the edge of Betty's desk.

'I think I can guess what has happened,' Betty said in concern. 'Does it have something to do with the incident at the Bexleyheath store which led to the eventual death of your friend Emily?'

'It does,' Annie said.

'Gawd, I'm so sorry, I should have realized.' Maisie clapped her hand to her mouth.

'It was watching the American soldiers handing out the cake that caused me to have a flashback to the scene from then. You must think I'm so foolish,' she added as she sipped the cool water and shuddered. 'Emily was an innocent young woman, she wasn't worldly-wise, and in fact, she thought that horrible man loved her. He preyed on her vulnerability. I still can't help thinking I could have done more.'

'You handled it the best way you could,' Betty told her.

'I'd have killed him,' Maisie exploded before apologizing. 'You know what I mean.'

Annie gave her a weak smile. Maisie was a kind-hearted woman.

'I'm surprised it's taken this long for you to collapse with the shock of it all,' Betty consoled her.

'Yeah, considering how many Yanks there are over here now, a day doesn't go by when we don't see them round and about,' Maisie said, shaking her head.

'We must remember that these men are a long way from home and here helping us fight the enemy, and there are bound to be a few rotten apples in the barrel.' Betty shrugged sadly.

'And one maggot as near as damn it killed Emily,' Maisie snorted in anger.

'Do we know what happened to the man? Was he reprimanded in any way?' Betty asked.

'Emily's mother was told that he and the soldiers in his circle were sent back to America, but we did wonder if that was true.' Annie shut her eyes in despair.

Betty thought to herself how finding out what had happened to this man would help Annie to, in some way, draw a line under what had gone on, even though it wouldn't bring her friend back. She decided there and then she would make some telephone calls to see what she could find out. 'Can you excuse me for a moment?' she asked as she picked up the receiver and rang Erith police station, asking to speak to Sergeant Mike Jackson.

'Sergeant Mike is a lovely bloke,' Maisie whispered to Annie.

Annie agreed. 'My dad knows him very well. We're lucky to have such a decent copper in the town.'

Betty put a finger to her lips and the two girls fell silent before Maisie asked in a stage whisper what the current manager was like at Bexleyheath, and did she miss Simon? The second part of her question accompanied the suggestive raising of Maisie's eyebrows.

'I miss his enthusiasm for new innovations in the store,' Annie replied seriously.

'If you say so,' Maisie snorted, causing Betty to point at the door. Putting her hand over the mouthpiece, she said, 'I'll see you both in the canteen in five minutes.'

Annie followed Maisie outside and ignored her prying about Simon. If truth be known, she did miss him, but she wasn't about to say that to Maisie. 'We have a lovely manager. He's been transferred in from a store in Essex and has been with the company for over thirty years,' she said, hoping that would put paid to Maisie's cheeky questions.

Maisie grinned. 'Is he married?'

Annie smiled politely.

Back in the canteen the children were now on their egg hunt, and the upper floor of the building resounded to their excited shrieks.

'This sounds like a lot of fun,' Betty said as she joined them.

'Ivy Rose is in her element,' Annie smiled as the young child jumped around excitedly clutching Sarah's hand as she collected her prize.

'I've managed to obtain some information from Sergeant Mike Jackson,' Betty said, turning her back to the room and speaking quietly. 'I've been assured the man in question is no longer in this country, although he couldn't tell me more than that. But I felt he was probably fighting rather than sitting at home.'

'It's quite sobering when you think about it,' Annie said, before jumping as an American voice spoke from behind them.

'I hope you're feeling better, ma'am? I was informed by a colleague of your experience and the loss of your friend and would like to extend my condolences.'

Annie knew then she should put what happened behind her; it was time to move on. 'Thank you, I feel a lot better,' she smiled at the man. 'I'm grateful for your help.'

'Anytime, ma'am,' he said. 'I like to help a damsel in distress.'

'He can help me anytime,' Maisie said as she watched him go back to his colleagues.

'Honestly, Maisie, you're incorrigible,' Betty groaned. 'I hope Annie knows you're simply jesting?'

'I do,' Annie laughed, thinking what a hoot Maisie could be. 'Thank you both for looking after me. With your news,

Betty, and the American serviceman being so understanding I feel as though I may have turned a corner and can get on with my life without feeling so bitter.'

Betty patted Annie on the shoulder. 'I'm pleased to hear that. Now, shall we have some of that cake before it's all gone?'

32

June 1944

'I'm going to buy two copies of every newspaper so we can put some away as souvenirs and for Paddy and your mum to read so they don't miss out. This is real history.'

Annie, who had her nose in the newspaper marvelling at how the day before Allied troops had invaded mainland occupied Europe, looked up at her nan. 'It's a good idea to put copies by as Ivy Rose will want to read them when she's older, but don't waste your money buying extra copies. They do have newsagents in Somerset. Besides, Mum and Dad watch the Pathé News when they go to the pictures. But it was lovely of you to think of them.'

'I never thought of that. Would you like me to top up your cup?' Ivy asked, holding up the large Brown Betty teapot. 'I feel we should celebrate as this could be the end of the war.'

'No, ta, I must get cracking with the laundry round, or I'll never get home before blackout. I wanted to do so much with my day off.' Annie sighed – there were never enough hours in the day.

'I've made you a sandwich to take with you. I know what you're like when you're working and never stop to eat. Mind you, it doesn't look very appetizing. I'll be glad when we can buy decent bread and not this National muck.'

'I don't mind what I eat, Nan,' Annie said, reaching across the kitchen table to help wrap the food in a piece of paper that had covered the loaf. She wrinkled her nose. 'Is that fish?'

'It's snoek. Erith Woolies have had a load come in. I spotted it in their window and thought it would make a change from what we usually eat; the cans will last for ever.'

Annie dared not tell her nan that the Erith store couldn't give it away as it was so awful. Another branch had run a competition for the best recipe using the product, with the prize being ten tins of the stuff. No one entered. 'Thanks, Nan, I'll try not to be too late.'

'Take your time. I've never liked to think of you driving that van on your own; it's not ladylike. Ivy Rose will be all right with me. Your grandad is taking her down to the riverbank to see all the ships, then later we're going to draw them and colour them in.'

'Oh, Ivy Rose will adore that. For her age she produces very good pictures. I wonder who she gets it from? We knew Ruth such a short while we never learnt much about her. Was Uncle Pete artistic as a child?'

'Not so you'd notice,' Ivy snorted. 'But your mum is, although her talents are in her needlework and knitting, and you're quite handy in that department. You should try more,' she added, warming to the subject.

'One day, when I have more time perhaps,' Annie replied,

picking up her sandwich and heading to the van. Once seated she again looked at the list of stops on today's rounds, wondering what it would be like inside Hall Place, the historic old house which sat in its own extensive grounds nearby. Her dad had visited and asked about their laundry requirements and had come home with a wide grin on his face and a hefty contract. All they knew was there were new people at the hall doing war work. Perhaps she would get to look around the building, as she'd never had the chance before. Paddy and Violet were away for a few days visiting Jocelyn, who was still staying with her sister in Somerset. With petrol being rationed, making it hard for personal trips, Paddy had gained permission to fuel their larger van to take Jocelyn's property to her new home. When Annie had asked how he'd managed this he had winked and told her not to ask.

Driving through Crayford, Annie first stopped off at the large Vickers factory and after showing her identity pass and answering a few questions she was allowed past the guards on the gate and headed round to the canteen where she dropped off clean table linen as well as towels for the boardroom.

'No Paddy today?' one of the female staff asked.

'He's away at the moment,' she replied politely, knowing how the ladies liked her dad and looked out for him. 'He'll be back next week.'

'Then take this. I made it for his lunch, but I don't want to see it go to waste.'

Annie looked inside the paper bag and grinned. Whatever was inside the golden pastry would be tastier than her snoek sandwich. 'Are you sure?'

'Of course. I made plenty and daren't eat many more or I'll ruin my figure. Paddy wouldn't like that,' she said, running her hands over the hips of her tight skirt.

'Get back to work, Deirdre. Paddy Brookes would no further look at you than he'd spy for Germany. Be off with you,' an older woman in a supervisor's uniform snapped. 'Honestly, we can't get the staff these days,' she apologized to Annie.

'Not to worry,' Annie said, waving the paper bag in the air. 'At least I have some lunch for today.'

'Give my love to your nan,' the woman called after her as she drove off.

Annie couldn't help but grin to herself. Wherever she went there was someone who knew her dad and at times she felt as though he was as famous as those Hollywood movie stars she drooled over when she went to the Odeon cinema.

Approaching the grounds of Hall Place, she marvelled at how the once-famous lawns were now vegetable plots. People were certainly digging for victory around here. She went to pull in where there had once been impressive-looking metal gates that had long since been sent away as a contribution for the war effort. She was thinking it was time their family had another sort out as there must be some more old saucepans and pieces of metal that Albie could take along to the Boy Scouts; they were trying to collect enough to have a Spitfire built in their pack's name.

Before she had time to think clearly there was a screech of brakes and she felt her van being lifted and spun around. She clung on to the steering wheel like grim death and closed her eyes, praying it would soon be over. Frightened to open her eyes, she sat there breathing deeply, hearing men's voices shouting out loud as they ran to her rescue.

'Are you all right, ma'am?' a familiar voice enquired as he forced open the driver's side door.

'I think so,' she said, wondering if she could still feel her arms and legs.

Somebody had climbed in on the passenger side while the person with the familiar voice gently took one of her arms to help her out of the van. Both men carefully checked she was able to stand unaided.

'Thank you both for helping me. I really don't know what happened.'

'Some jerk pulled in behind you too quickly and rammed you up the rear end,' the voice she didn't recognize informed her. 'We'll deal with him later, don't you worry.'

Quickly her memory came back and she turned to the other man. 'Aren't you the American soldier who helped me at the Easter party at Woolworths when I came over all peculiar?'

He held her shoulders gently and peered closely at her face. 'And you must be the damsel in distress I had the pleasure of carrying. Sergeant Dean Delaney at your service, ma'am,' he said, saluting her smartly. 'This reprobate here is Corporal Joe Garcia.'

'I'm pleased to make your acquaintance, both of you,' she said, giving them a wide smile.

'That smile is enough to make me forget home,' Corporal Garcia said, 'but I'm not so sure your vehicle is going to be so forgiving.'

'Go easy, Joe, you're talking to a lady, not one of those girls you pick up at the dance hall,' Dean said, giving her a compassionate look.

Bless him, she thought, he's remembered what he was told about Emily. Looking away from him, she gasped at the state of the van. 'My dad is going to kill me! However are we going to do our deliveries?' she almost cried out. As the other vehicle was with her dad in Somerset she had a vision of going back to using their horse and cart. She may well have objected to retiring Old Ned, but she'd soon got used to the luxury of driving a van.

'This is our fault, and we'll put right any damage, ain't that right, lads?' Dean said, turning to a group of soldiers who had joined them after hearing the crash.

'The American army is at your service,' one of them assured her as they all stood to attention and saluted.

Dean took her arm. 'Let me take you to our refectory and treat you to American hospitality while the lads look over your van and see what's to be done.'

'There is a bag wash in the back which I was to deliver here. All the details are on the label tied to the bag. Can one of you hand it over for me and get a signature?' Annie fretted.

'Soonest mentioned, soonest done,' one of the men said as he forced open the back doors. 'What about the other bags?'

'Oh gosh, I don't know what to do. The other deliveries must be with their customers today otherwise they could complain and cancel our business,' she replied worriedly.

'Consider it done,' Dean said. 'We put you in this jam and we're going to get you out of it.' He snapped his fingers.

'Leo and Carl, can you drop these off to the addresses on the labels, give them the compliments of the American army and perhaps a little gift.' He nodded knowingly. 'Tell them their bills will be covered due to us holding up the deliveries.' He looked at the side of the vehicle where Paddy had painted the name of the laundry. 'Tell them we are proud to be assisting the Brookes Family Laundry. Now, Miss Brookes, come with me while my comrades check over your vehicle.'

Annie looked around her in awe as they made their way towards the ancient hall. The walls were of an extraordinary checkerboard pattern made of flint, and she had never seen anything like it. As she stepped inside the entrance hall she caught her breath. To think she had been impressed by the theatre and hotel in London on that trip years ago – and something so much grander was just down the road all along. 'This is beautiful! There must be so much history within these walls,' she said, feeling ignorant of such a beautiful stately home nearly five hundred years old and only a few miles from her home.

'You should have seen the place before they put plywood shutters on the walls over the old mouldings and the main staircase, to protect against us uncouth Yanks,' he grinned. 'I was fortunate to see some of it when I first arrived.'

Annie caught a glimpse of activity going on through partially open doors. There were sights that seemed to be at odds with the historic building: rows of desks with soldiers busy at work on typewriters, or scribbling away intently as they sat at what looked like wireless sets to Annie's untrained eye. She had a feeling she shouldn't be seeing half of what she'd observed. There was a sense of exuberance in the air. 'This seems like a very pleasant place to work,' she said as Dean opened a door that led into a refectory with just a few soldiers either eating or sitting playing cards.

'We're all pretty excited after news of D-Day yesterday. The guys here just want to go home and what has happened has certainly shortened the war. Not that we don't love being here in your country,' he added with a grin in case she was offended.

'I'd be the same if I was working away from home,' she said as he held a chair out for her to sit down. There was a delicious aroma of bacon coming from somewhere and her stomach started to complain that she was hungry.

'I'll be back soon,' he said as he headed to a serving counter staffed by two women in white overalls. Annie sat thinking how her impression of American servicemen had been blackened by what had happened to Emily. There would always be a small corner of her heart that remembered her and the way Annie's attitude had changed when her friend met Dirk Wolenski. She fought against that memory and tried to replace it with the quiet girl she first met on that day they attended their interview at Woolworths.

Dean was soon back with a laden tray. Annie's eyes opened wide as he put before her a large plate filled with sausage, bacon, eggs and fried bread, which certainly wasn't the grey National Loaf they were used to at home. One of the serving women followed with a small brown teapot like their own Brown Betty one at home, although Dean, it seemed, preferred coffee. 'I hope this is to your satisfaction,' he said as he sat down opposite her.

'My goodness, what a spread,' Annie declared as she picked up her knife and fork. 'Are you always fed like this?' She didn't like to say that she'd heard the American servicemen lived a completely different life to that of the British soldiers.

'We are looked after rather well,' he said, sounding embarrassed. 'I've only been here in England a short while, and in that time I've learnt of the hardships of your countrymen, and women. That's why the news of the D-Day invasion is so important: we all want an end to this war so life can get back to normal as soon as possible.'

Annie agreed with him as she savoured the thick, juicy rasher of bacon, although in her heart of hearts she realized no matter when the war ended life wouldn't change overnight. However, today wasn't a day for dark thoughts.

'Forgive me for asking this question, but what exactly do you all do here?'

Dean shrugged his shoulders before taking a mouthful of coffee. 'Who knows? We're given orders, and we follow them. Joe, who you met earlier, is a Jack of all trades; if something needs doing, he can sort it out. While I spend the day hammering away on a typewriter. Just look at my beautiful nails worn down to the quick,' he said, putting on an over-exaggerated sad face.

Annie knew then she wouldn't be told any more than that and they finished the rest of the meal with him asking questions about the family laundry business and her working at Woolworths.

'You know, we have Woolworths stores over in the States. They're often called five and ten cent stores.'

'I've heard a song about a guy who meets his girl at a five and ten cent store,' Annie chuckled. 'Over here the saying is that we sell everything at thruppence or sixpence, although all that is changing due to prices increasing and not having the stock due to the war. Saying that, head office work wonders.'

He shook his head in wonderment. 'I'll never get used to the money over here. But something I do appreciate is walking into one of your stores and feeling like I'm back home with everything being so familiar. If you ever come over to the States, and you should, you'll be more than welcome in our Woolworths stores.'

Annie thought it highly unlikely she would ever leave these shores, but it was lovely to dream. 'Tell me, where do you come from and what did you do before the war?'

His face lit up as he told her about his life in a small town in Oregon and how he still lived with his parents, who were heavily involved in their church and all the social committees in the area, while he worked at the local newspaper as a journalist. 'I can never escape typewriters,' he chuckled.

'I don't understand why you aren't out reporting on the war for your country's newspapers. Surely your journalist skills are wasted?'

He laughed out loud. 'This hack from a little town who only reports on church socials, changes of mayors and news on local crops isn't what the big guys are looking for to report on news from Europe. I'm happy with my lot,' he said, although Annie sensed that perhaps he wasn't convinced by his own words.

'Perhaps you should write about your experiences of England for the readers back home?'

'Perhaps I will,' he said, not seeming that interested. 'Have you seen the grounds here? There's even a river. It sure is quaint.'

'I've never been here before. These kinds of properties are more for landed gentry than working-class girls like me,' Annie chuckled. 'It seems the war has opened doors for the likes of us to see what it's like for others.'

'Gee, I've never known a country so divided by class. Back home we're all equal,' he said confidently. He looked up as Joe joined them.

'Bad news, your vehicle is going to need some repairs to the bodywork,' Joe told her. 'The good news is the engine is fine and we can do the repairs here in our own body shop.'

'I can't ask you to do that,' she exclaimed.

'Annie, we caused the problem, and we're going to fix it,' Dean assured her. 'I'm going to borrow a truck and get you back to your home and I won't hear a word otherwise.'

'Well, if it's not taking you away from your work,' she answered gratefully. She had been wondering how she would get back to Slades Green and their house on the marshes without transport.

33

Albie's chin almost hit the ground as the army truck pulled up in the yard and Annie climbed down from the passenger seat assisted by a real live Yank. He sidled up to his sister lost for words for all of two minutes. 'Where's our van and why is the Yank here?'

Annie gasped. 'I'm sorry for my brother's bad manners, Dean. I can assure you if our parents were here, he'd be receiving a clip round the ears for being so impolite,' she said, giving Albie a stern look.

'What's our Albie been up to?' Nan appeared from the doorway wiping her hands on a tea towel.

'A Yank's brought our Annie home in a truck,' Albie said before Annie could explain how rude her little brother had been.

'Nan, this is Sergeant Dean Delaney. He's based at Hall Place. Our van was hit by another vehicle and Dean and his comrades are getting it fixed. In the meantime, he brought me home.'

'That's good of you. Come along in. Have a cup of tea and then we'll help you unload the truck.'

'A cup of tea would go down a treat,' Dean said, which

made Annie smile because while they were eating together, he mentioned how he could not get used to the English addiction to tea drinking.

'We'll go through to the kitchen as we spend most of our time there. Is that something you do in America? Tell me, why weren't you out helping with the D-Day landings?'

Annie's heart sank. Why were her family hell-bent on ruining her new friendship with all their questions? She was relieved Dean answered politely.

'Ma'am, just as in your country there are servicemen and women who are working on other important tasks to bring this war to an end. We all must play our part, just as you do, making a pot of tea for this thirsty Yank,' he replied, giving Albie a wink as he reached inside the cabin of the truck and pulled out a parcel that he tucked under his arm. The lad still looked at him suspiciously.

Annie led him into the kitchen, with her nan scurrying in ahead to slide the kettle onto the hob and quickly tidy away some underwear she'd been repairing which was draped over the back of one of the chairs by the table.

'Sit yourself down, lad, the tea won't be long,' she said as she went over to the stone pantry and opened the door, appearing to search for something. 'I can offer you a slice of bread pudding,' she said, bringing out a small plate covered with a muslin cloth. 'It's not the same without sugar sprinkled on the top, but it's just as tasty . . . Although there aren't as many currants inside due to—'

'Please don't go to any trouble on my account,' Dean said. 'A cup of your English tea will suffice. In fact, I have a gift for you and your family by way of recompense for causing such inconvenience to your business,' he said, placing the parcel onto the table.

Albie looked expectantly between his nan and Annie. 'Can I open it?'

'Go ahead, lad, but be careful with the string and paper as we can use it again. This is very kind of you,' Nan said to Dean even though she had no idea what he had given them.

Albie impatiently picked at the knot in the string which secured the parcel until he looked at Annie in despair and she took over the task.

'You've got yourself in a right muddle,' Annie muttered as she picked at the tight knot he'd formed. 'There you go.' She passed back the parcel for him to open as Nan took the string and wound it round her fingers to form a small ball which was put into the drawer of the kitchen dresser.

Albie gasped as he pulled back the brown paper. 'Chocolate, sugar, coffee and what's this?' he asked Annie as his attention went back to the chocolate.

'It's a bar of soap,' Annie laughed. 'No wonder you didn't know what it was.'

'You really shouldn't have,' Nan said as she gazed at the items, not sure she could believe her eyes.

'It's my honour. We're instructed never to visit a home empty-handed as you folk only have your rations.'

Through a mouthful of chocolate Albie declared, 'You can visit us anytime.'

Dean roared with laughter as Nan slapped the back of Albie's hand and took away the chocolate. 'You've got to make that last, and share it with Ivy Rose,' she scolded him. 'Now, come over to the sink and let me wipe your face. I've never known someone manage to wear their food as much as you do,' she complained as she took him by the sleeve and pulled him protesting over to the sink.

Annie poured the tea and placed a cup in front of Dean. 'I've made it a strong one as I know you're not keen and thought this would taste better. It's awfully good of you to bring the provisions, especially after all the help and the lovely meal I've received today.'

'It was all the fault of the American army, so we had to make recompense. Besides, it is as I explained, we never arrive without bearing gifts.' He paused for a moment and then smiled. 'I did wonder if you would accompany me to a dance? There's one this Saturday evening in Welling. I'm not much of a dancer but can shuffle around the floor when called to do so.'

Annie bit her lip as she thought of his invitation. She did like him, but memories of that night in London when Emily met Dirk came flooding back.

He noticed her thinking about his invitation. 'I can have someone vouch for me if you're worried? I'm clean-living, don't drink and can cook a little when called to do so.'

'Go on, say yes, sis, then he'll bring us more chocolate.' Albie appeared by her side with his face freshly scrubbed. 'We don't need no more soap, though,' he said, looking hopeful.

'I'd be delighted to join you on Saturday,' Annie said.

Dean grinned. 'Then it's a date,' he declared, standing up to leave.

Annie walked him to the truck as they discussed what time he would collect her and if he was meeting friends;

she wasn't keen on being part of a larger group but didn't like to say. He shook her hand before he left.

'He seems very nice,' her nan said as Annie went back inside. 'But perhaps don't get too fond of him after . . .'

Annie finished her sentence. 'After what happened to Emily?'

'Yes, although lightning doesn't usually strike twice in the same place. You deserve to have some fun as you work too hard, as well as looking after Ivy Rose.'

'Oh, Nan, you all chip in and care for her.'

'But you're legally her mother now, we have the certificate to prove it, and she only knows you as her mum. Why, she even calls you Mummy, and she knows no different.'

Annie felt a shiver of joy run through her. 'And I do think of her as my daughter.'

'Talk of the devil,' her nan said as Ivy Rose ran into the kitchen followed by a red-faced Jasper, who sat down unable to speak until he'd caught his breath.

'That child has run me ragged,' he gasped. He looked at the cups on the table and counted them. 'Have we had a visitor?'

'Our Annie's young man has just left,' Nan said as she collected the cups and placed them in the sink.

Albie, not one to get left behind when there was news to share, tugged on his grandad's sleeve. 'He's a Yank and he brought me a bar of chocolate.'

Ivy Rose gave Albie a hard stare. 'Where's mine?'

'You look very nice,' Dean said as he helped her out of her best coat and left it with the cloakroom girl. 'I'll take care of this,' he said, putting the numbered ticket into the breast pocket of his jacket.

'Thank you,' she said, feeling nervous and smoothing her hands over the skirt of the dress she'd only finished hemming the night before.

'If it's not wrong of me, may I ask if you made your dress?'

'I did,' Annie said, unable to resist giving a little twirl. 'You don't think it's too homely, do you?' she asked, noticing a group of women taking off their coats to reveal sophisticated cocktail dresses. She felt a little dowdy in her green flower-sprigged cotton dress with a white collar and covered buttons.

'You would never suit those kinds of outfits; your dress is perfect. My mother would approve,' Dean said, taking her arm to lead her through to the ballroom where they sat at a large table. The place was filled with similar tables, all showing signs of wartime wear and tear, but the atmosphere was full of energy after the D-Day triumphs.

'Are we the first?'

'Yes, Joe and the other guys will be here soon. They reserved the table. Would you like a drink?' he asked. 'I'll get us both lemonades.'

Annie was surprised he didn't ask her what she would like, but as she'd have no doubt requested lemonade, she let it pass, saying, 'That would be nice.' She had to admit he had impeccable manners and she felt special in his company.

'Tell me more about your family,' she said when he returned with the drinks.

'I'm an only child. Mother had a bad time when I was

born so they have lavished all their hopes and dreams on me. I still live with them, there's no point in moving out when the house is so large. Mother organizes much of the charity fundraising in our town and supports our church,' he said proudly.

'Does she not work?' Annie asked, thinking that as her son was grown-up she would be wanting to return to her job.

Dean frowned. 'Father wouldn't like that.'

Their conversation was halted as Joe and his colleagues arrived with their lady friends on their arms. Introductions were soon made, and Annie found herself sitting with the girlfriends as the men went to collect drinks from the bar. She was pleased to see that the women were very much like her, and she didn't feel intimidated at all.

'I have a feeling I've seen you before,' one of the women said. 'Do you work in Erith?'

Annie explained how she had for a while worked at the Woolworths store before moving back to Bexleyheath. She was careful not to mention the oil bombs.

'Then that's where I've seen you. I work in Hedley Mitchell's across the road from Woolies. I'm in the accounts department.' She introduced herself as Doreen and suggested they meet on their afternoon off.

'I would love to,' Annie answered. 'There are times I feel that if I'm not at Woolworths, I'm working in my family laundry and delivering orders. I also have my daughter, Ivy Rose, to care for.'

'Then bring her along. Some of us have children and with having lost our husbands we all need to stick together. And before you ask, none of us would be courting the

Yanks if we had husbands. We're different to others,' Doreen said, looking pointedly to where the women Annie had seen in cocktail dresses earlier were laughing raucously with some sitting on the laps of their men friends. She was relieved not to be with that group.

They watched as the band started to tune their instruments ready for the evening's dancing.

'What time does it finish?' Annie asked Doreen. 'I never thought to tell my nan and grandad and I'd hate for them to be sitting up late waiting for me; Mum and Dad are away visiting friends at the moment.'

'You've no need to worry, the lads will have us home by ten o'clock. They've never been late before,' Doreen assured her.

Another woman called Jean leant over and in a stage whisper said, 'They have important top-secret work to do and have to be at their workstations by seven in the morning.'

The other women hushed her up as the men returned with their drinks. Annie thought of the open doors she'd glanced through on the day she'd visited Hall Place. Gosh, to think that there was secret work going on in their part of Kent.

They were soon on the floor dancing to the tunes of the day and although Dean wasn't a dancer his friends gave her a turn around the dance floor. It was when Dean agreed to a slow waltz that she felt someone tap her on her shoulder. She turned and gave a gasp.

'Why, Simon, what a lovely surprise!' she exclaimed, letting go of Dean's hands and giving Simon a hug. Dean looked put out. 'I'm sorry, Dean, this is Simon Greyson.

He used to be my manager at the Bexleyheath branch. Why don't you join us? That's all right, isn't it, Dean?'

'Be our guest,' he answered brusquely.

'No, no, I'm here with friends,' he said, pointing over towards a corner table. 'We're here to celebrate me passing the last of my exams. I'm now officially a doctor.'

Annie couldn't help herself and leant up to kiss his cheek. 'Why, Simon, that is absolutely wonderful,' she declared, flinging her arms around him regardless of what it must look like to Dean and his army friends. She realized that she was being far friendlier than she had ever been when they worked together, but there was something about the air of celebrations after the Allied landings, combined with him passing his final exams, that made her briefly throw caution to the wind.

'I say, could I pinch your partner for a quick dance? Then I'll hand her back and get out of your hair.'

'Be my guest,' Dean said, leaving them alone as a foxtrot struck up.

'You look well,' he said as he spun her around.

'So do you,' she replied, her eyes sparkling as she looked up at him.

'I know it's an awful cheek when you're here with your . . .'

'Friend?' Annie finished his words.

'Yes, friend,' he said, glancing over to where Dean's table were looking their way. 'I wondered, could we meet up on your half-day? I have so much to tell you and to ask you.'

'Of course, I'd love to meet you. Shall we say the little cafe where you took me . . .' She faltered, realizing she was about to mention the day Emily killed herself.

'Yes, why not? We can chase away a few ghosts at the same time,' he said, bending over her to kiss her cheek. 'Until then.'

Annie was surprised how that one gentle kiss affected her for the rest of the evening, and how much she looked forward to seeing her dear friend after so long.

34

'Welcome home,' Annie greeted her parents when two days after her date with Dean, Paddy and Violet returned from Somerset.

'What's been going on while we've been away?' Violet asked as she looked around her kitchen for signs of change.

'Our Annie's been seeing a Yank, and he gave us chocolate,' Albie muttered as he tore the paper off the gift his dad had passed to him. 'Oh, great, a Spitfire!' he exclaimed as he at once went into battle, sweeping and soaring around the room and chasing Ivy Rose, whose present was a small peg dolly.

While Paddy digested what his son had said, Violet told off the children. 'Stand still or there will be an accident! You know not to run indoors.'

Paddy thanked his mother-in-law as she placed a tray of drinks on the table and then looked to Annie for an explanation. 'I noticed the van looked clean and a small dent that had always been there had disappeared. What's been going on, love?'

Annie explained what had happened to the van and how helpful the American servicemen had been even though one of them had caused the accident. 'You'll like Dean,' she assured her dad. 'He's nothing like the bloke Emily got tied up with.' She was thoughtful as she tried to explain her feelings. 'I got it wrong: very few American soldiers are bad. Dean has a loving family in Oregon. They're nothing like us, but then who else is?' she chuckled.

'You'll be seeing him again?'

'Yes, he's coming round this afternoon after his church parade.'

'So, he's religious?'

'From what I can work out, he is God-fearing, if that's what you mean, and he doesn't drink. But please don't think he's dull because of that,' she said, noticing Paddy lift his eyebrows and trying not to grin. 'He's a kind man. Anyway, you'll meet him today as he's calling by to take me and Ivy Rose out for the afternoon.'

'Then I'll reserve my judgement until then,' Paddy told her.

'I thought you were meeting your Home Guard colleagues?' she said, starting to worry he would say something to embarrass her, or worse still, scare Dean away. The more she thought about Dean, the more she thought how pleasant he was and how life with him would be enjoyable.

'I can go later,' he said, reaching into the pocket of his best jacket and handing her an envelope. 'It's from Jocelyn.'

'Oh golly, I meant to write to her but with everything that's been going on it slipped out of my mind,' she said, slitting open the envelope and sitting down to read it. By the time she reached the end of the page she was cuffing tears away. 'I don't believe what I've just read.'

'Aren't you going to tell us?' her nan asked.

Annie folded up the letter and put it into the pocket of her cardigan. 'She has set up a savings account in my name which she says will look after me if I'm ever in need of help. She'd started to do the same for Emily until she . . . until she took her own life, and as she thinks of me as the nearest thing she has to a daughter, and Ivy Rose a granddaughter, then she wishes to do the same for me.'

'What a kind gesture,' Violet exclaimed. 'She never said a thing to me when we were visiting.'

'I got the feeling she was up to something when she kept asking me about your future. However, we knew nothing of this boyfriend of yours. I wonder if she would be as generous if she knew?' Paddy raised his eyebrows.

Violet was horrified. 'Paddy, Annie must do what she thinks is best for her future. She can't be swayed by money that may come her way regardless of how much it is.'

'I'd spend it all on chocolate,' Albie announced, ducking as his nan flicked her tea towel at him.

'I'll write her a letter now and catch the midday post. I don't want there to be any secrets between us, as I do care for Jocelyn and would hate to fall out.'

'I agree you should, but as you've only known this man a little while please don't make too much of it in your letter,' Violet suggested.

'I won't. I do have other news for her, and for you. I bumped into Simon; he's now a fully fledged doctor.'

'That is good news! Is he going to work with his father in the Erith surgery?'

'I know little more than what I've just told you,' Annie replied hurriedly. 'I'm meeting him for a chat on my half-day. It's good to see him home again, but he's studying somewhere up north, so he might stay working up there, I suppose.'

Annie got up to fetch her envelope and paper, not noticing the smile that passed between her parents. 'Come and help me, Ivy Rose. You can draw a picture to send to your Auntie Jocelyn.'

'This is really kind of you,' Annie said as they were shown to a table in the posh Hedley Mitchell's tea room just across the road from the Erith branch of Woolworths. As ever, the wooden furniture was polished to within an inch of its life and there was an arrangement of flowers on the mantelpiece, even if not quite as ornate as those before the war.

'Next time I'll take you both up to London and we can have a meal in the famous Lyons Corner House,' Dean said as he waved to a waitress for her to take their order.

'Just tea and a slice of cake for me, thank you, and my daughter will have the same, but with milk.'

'Are you sure?' Dean looked disappointed. 'I suppose I'd best have the same but with coffee.'

'Nan's making a stew. She queued for ages to get the scrag end and Dad has dug up some veg to go with it, so you'll need to save some room for that,' she said as she tucked a napkin into the front of Ivy Rose's dress. Coming up to four years of age, she didn't like anyone helping her dress and that included wearing a napkin tucked in her neckline, and so she promptly pulled it loose.

'Do as your mother tells you, Ivy Rose,' Dean said. The little girl pouted and tucked the napkin back where it had been.

Annie felt a little uncomfortable until Dean smiled at her and reached for her hand under the table, giving it a tight squeeze.

'Explain more about this Simon. You say he's a manager at Woolworths?'

'He's a good friend and did so much to help when Emily had her problems. He left to finish his training as a doctor; his father is a general practitioner here in Erith. I had no idea he was back until we bumped into him the other evening.'

'And he's only a friend? Although a woman doesn't usually have male friends,' he pushed.

'Perhaps not where you come from, but here we do and there doesn't have to be anything between them,' she half-heartedly scolded him and was then surprised at the scowl that crossed his face.

She'd had very few male acquaintances but was flattered that he seemed to care there may have been another man in her life. 'What do you think of my parents?' she asked, knowing her dad had been on his best behaviour, no doubt having had a talking-to by her mum.

'An interesting couple. I've never met a couple with different occupations before.'

'It's quite simple. Mum took on the laundry business which had belonged to her parents, while Dad preferred the showman's life, although he's back home to help while the travelling fairs are grounded for the duration. There are a few fairs, but with so many restrictions it isn't as viable as a business. The younger showmen are serving their country so all in all it is harder work than usual.'

He was thoughtful as the waitress brought their orders to the table, only speaking when she had left. 'What life would you prefer?'

Annie's eyes shone as she placed her elbows on the table and cupped her chin with both hands. 'If you'd asked me a few years ago, I'd have told you I wanted to spread my wings. But now it's simple: I'd travel with the fairground and have my own stall or ride. Dad has always said I have the blood of a showman,' she said before biting into her slice of cake. Somehow Hedley Mitchell's never ran short of dried fruit or sugar and their cakes were delicious. 'Of course, it only feels like that because it's impossible these days. However, I can dream.'

'It doesn't worry you that people say you're gypsies?'

Annie shrugged her shoulders. 'Gypsies and show people are a world apart. Besides, I've been brought up with people looking down their noses at us. I take no notice as we're good people. These days people are more likely to sneer at me for working in a shop than anything else. You can't let these things eat you up,' she said, turning to wipe Ivy Rose's face with her napkin. 'Surely you've experienced people's prejudices being an American and over here?' She didn't quote the rest of the popular saying.

He gave her a blank look. 'Why would anyone say such a thing? We're here to save you from the Germans.'

She shook her head and bit her tongue from saying how blooming grateful they were. 'Oh, Dean, you've been locked away in your room at Hall Place for far too long. We may be grateful you've come into the war but too many people feel it is rather late and are bitter.'

Dean was about to bite back when Ivy Rose spilt her milk across the table and the conversation came to an end.

Later that night as Annie sat drinking her cocoa at the kitchen table with her dad, he asked her how her afternoon had been.

'Apart from squeezing milk from Ivy Rose's best dress do you mean? I shudder when I think that Dean had mentioned taking us to London for a meal at the Lyons Corner House; imagine the state she'd get into there,' she sighed.

Paddy laughed. 'That's all part of the joy of having children. She'll soon grow up and you'll be moaning how her early years flew by so quickly.'

'We had a very nice afternoon although it came home to me how different the Americans are to the British. Of course, that may just be Dean's way,' Annie replied thoughtfully. 'I get the impression he led a sheltered life as a child. How did you get on when you showed him around the property?'

'He seemed interested in what we did for a living,' Paddy said, not adding that he couldn't take to the man. If Annie was happy, then who was he to question her choice in boyfriends. He'd probably be shipped out before too long and they would lose contact. 'He never did tell me what he was doing over here.'

'Why, Dad, he's fighting a war,' she chuckled.

Paddy shook his head in despair. 'You know what I mean, what are they up to over at Hall Place?'

'You know we're not supposed to ask things like that, Dad. All I can tell you is the one time I went into part of the building I saw men sitting at what looked like wireless sets and others were typing. There seemed to be a lot of motorbike activity as well and the riders were in a hurry. I quickly got used to the sound of the motorbikes while I was in their refectory having my meal. Does that help you at all with your enquiries?'

'I'm just as much in the dark, but it does sound quite interesting. Let me know if you find out anything and I can add it to the material we keep in one of the dugouts over the marshes. You never know what will come in handy. When are you seeing Simon?'

'On my half-day,' she replied, still wondering why her dad wanted to know what was going on at Hall Place.

'Don't forget to give him my best wishes and tell him not to be a stranger. He's welcome here anytime.'

'I'll do that,' she said as she carried her empty cup over to the sink. Why did she get the feeling her dad preferred Simon to Dean? It wasn't as if she was linked to either of them romantically.

35

'Annie, I'd like you to work full time in the personnel office,' the Bexleyheath store manager, Mr Grant, said as he sat down opposite her in the small office she nowadays shared with the cashier. A rotund man, he gave a sigh as he relaxed in the creaking chair.

'Is there a reason for your decision?' she asked before realizing she was being rude. 'It's not that I'm ungrateful, but I've enjoyed my work schedule being split between a supervisor on the shop floor and then working here.'

'And you work well in both positions. May, who shares the job with you, as you know, has been off sick for some time. Her husband has decided they should move to the coast to live with their daughter. They feel the sea air will be good for May.'

'That's understandable, the poor woman has been so poorly with her chest,' Annie sympathized. 'In that case I will accept the promotion . . . I take it this is a promotion?' she asked cheekily. She liked Mr Grant. He fitted in well at the store and was like a father figure to the younger staff. He was so different from Simon who had been young for a manager.

'Of course. I will give you the figures so you can process the pay rise when you work on the payroll,' he said, getting to his feet. 'Can you promise me one thing?'

Annie frowned. 'Of course, if I'm able to.'

'Good. If you decide to leave the store, please give me as much advance notice as possible as it will be hell trying to replace you. And if you ever wish to return to work, speak to me first even if I've moved to another store.'

Annie was touched by his words. 'I don't plan to go anywhere, but if I do, I promise you will be one of the first to know.'

He thanked Annie, handing her details of her pay rise before getting back to his work. Annie stared at the figure on the piece of paper. She decided there and then to put the money aside in a post office savings account for Ivy Rose's future. What she'd never had she wouldn't miss, she thought as she opened a ledger on her desk. With it being her half-day she had a lot to get through before she left work and walked down the Broadway to meet Simon. As she worked, she couldn't help wondering what life held in store for her friend.

'I'm sorry I'm late,' Annie said as Simon stood up from his seat at a corner table and kissed her cheek. 'Head office rang asking for some figures just as I put my coat on.'

'Never mind, you're here now,' he smiled, looking at her flushed face. 'I take it you were in the office this morning? I don't know how you keep up with your work.'

She pulled off her coat and grinned. 'I have some exciting news to share with you and you're the first to hear about it,' she said, ignoring his question as he hung her coat over the back of her seat.

'I've already ordered; it's your favourite,' he told her, nodding to the waitress to bring it over.

'Not Spam fritters with bubble and squeak?' she sighed as a plate was placed in front of her.

'I know you too well,' he said as they tucked into their meal. 'However, it would be nice if you'd accompany me up to London for a show and a meal as it's been an age since we've enjoyed ourselves. In fact, it was . . .'

'While Emily was still alive,' she added, feeling sad all over again for the loss of her friend. 'Will this sadness ever go away?'

'It won't disappear, but we'll learn to live with it . . . Will you come out with me?' he asked, looking hopefully at her.

'I am in demand! Only the other day Ivy Rose and I were invited to dine in London.'

He raised his eyebrows, his fork poised over his plate. 'Are you telling me I have a rival for your heart?' he joshed.

'Oh, Simon, if only you meant it.' She laughed off his words while thinking if only he did mean she had a place in his heart. 'It was Dean. He took us for afternoon tea at Hedley Mitchell's and suggested next time we all went to the Lyons Corner House, but I fear he's changed his mind.' She pulled an over-exaggerated sad face.

'What happened? I'll sort out the blighter if he upset my girls,' he said, sounding offended. 'I don't know, these Yanks, they come over here—'

Annie raised her hand to stop him, trying not to laugh too loudly as other diners were looking their way. 'No need to say it,' she smiled. 'Ivy Rose spilt her glass of milk, and I don't think he knows how to react around little children.'

'Oh well, there's no use crying over spilt milk,' he said with a twinkle in his eye.

'If you don't stop cracking jokes, I'm going to walk out of here and leave you to eat my Spam fritters,' she said with a broad grin before turning serious. 'I think he's sweet on me.'

Simon felt his stomach plummet. 'Are you sweet on him?'

'I like him. He's good company.'

'That's a start, I suppose. Will you still come up town with me for one last celebration?'

'One last? What do you mean?'

'That's why I wanted to see you. Well, that, and to enjoy this fine meal. I'm going to be working in Edinburgh for the next two years. Dad's brother, my Uncle James, has invited me to work at his surgery. Dad thinks it's a good idea before I come home and prepare to take over when he retires. He thinks it will do me good to see medicine in action in another part of the world.'

Annie squeezed his hand. 'Your dad is right, it will broaden your knowledge. You will write to me, won't you?' she asked, feeling as though she was losing another friend. Edinburgh was so far away.

'Of course I will, and I'll be home to see Dad as much as I can.'

'That's good,' she said, feeling suddenly bereft that he was leaving. 'Oh, and I've had a lovely letter from Jocelyn,' she went on to explain, forcing herself to sound bright and cheery, although she'd given up eating her food.

'That's damned good of her. She's a decent woman who has lost so much.'

'I was keeping in touch with her anyway and always will, but I'm not sure about taking her money. I want to say no thank you, especially now I've been promoted at work. It means extra money which I want to put away for Ivy Rose's future.'

'Why, that's marvellous! Here's me bleating on about my career and you've sat there bottling this up. I'm so proud of you,' he said, standing up and giving her a hug. 'You're a Betty Billington in the making.'

'Steady on, Simon, I've only been moved to the personnel office full time,' she said, trying to shake off his suggestion. 'I'm not sure I'm management material like Betty.'

'Now we must celebrate. I'm off in three days, so can I drag you away before then? What about Sunday?'

'Oh, Simon, I can't as Mum has invited Dean to dinner. She wants to show him what a proper English Sunday dinner is like. Dad's been told to lean on his contacts so she has all the trimmings. It seems lots of families are doing this. Mum says it's a hand across the ocean thing that is gaining in popularity and seems only right when the lads are so far from their families. Two of Dean's comrades are joining us. Why don't you come along as well? I know the family would love to see you again; it's been a while since you visited.'

'I'll do that,' Simon agreed, although he felt as though it was the last place he wanted to be. If it was the last time he saw Annie for a while, he wanted to be alone with her and tell her of his feelings for her. However, he may get her alone long enough to speak his mind. Something inside his head was telling him to explain his feelings right now in case there wasn't the opportunity on Sunday, but a noisy cafe full of shoppers wasn't how he imagined professing his love to the woman he wanted to spend the rest of his life with. But would Annie worry about the setting being right? She may well tell him she had already lost her heart to the Yank. Imagine having to get up and walk out of the cafe on his own while not showing his emotions. Perhaps he should have found a table closer to the door . . .

'Simon?' He looked up to find her pulling on her coat. 'I need to make a move. I'll see you on Sunday?' He stood up as she passed him, kissing him briefly on his cheek. 'It's wonderful news about you working with your uncle in Edinburgh,' she said before walking away.

'But you haven't eaten your fritters,' he mumbled as the cafe door opened and she had gone.

'This is going rather well,' Violet said to her mum as she closed the door to the oven, her face flushed bright pink from the heat. She was determined to put on a Sunday dinner that her visitors would remember.

'Have you seen the gifts those Yanks brought with them? I've had to put the sweets at the back of the pantry before our Albie is sick through stuffing too many.'

'They have been too generous, but Mum, can you not call them Yanks as it seems a rude name to me? If you can't recall their names, then say Americans.'

'If you say so,' Ivy said, while poking the contents of a large pan with a fork. 'The greens are about done. Is everyone here?'

'The last I heard we were only waiting for Simon to arrive then we can sit down.' Violet turned as Annie entered the kitchen carrying empty cups and saucers. 'Leave them in the sink, love. Is Simon here?'

'No, not yet. I'll walk up the lane a little way to see if he's coming. I'll take Ivy Rose with me to calm her down. She's overexcited with so much attention.'

Annie called her daughter; they'd got as far as the gate when Dean caught them up. 'Hey, wait for me,' he shouted.

Annie sighed. It would have been nice to meet Simon without company. He could have had a few minutes with Ivy Rose before they went back to the house. 'I won't be long. We're only going to meet Simon. Why not go back to the front room and help Dad entertain your colleagues?'

'Your father is coping admirably. Besides, I'd like some time alone with my girl. Couldn't Ivy Rose go back inside?'

'Don't want to.' The child stamped her foot and glared at Dean.

He reached down to take her hand. 'You must try to control that temper, young lady,' he admonished her.

'Please, Dean, leave her to me. She became too excited and that's why I brought her with me to wait for Simon.'

He stopped in his tracks still holding Ivy Rose's hand tightly. 'I didn't realize he'd been invited,' he said through pursed lips.

'Simon is a good friend of the family and is moving away for his work so of course he's been invited,' Annie said, rather shocked by his attitude.

He could see he had upset her and was about to apologize when Ivy Rose tugged at his hand to get away from his hold. He pulled her back and she tripped, falling face first on the gravel road. At once she screamed in pain. Annie and Dean both bent down at the same time to lift her to her feet. With their faces inches apart Dean took the opportunity to kiss Annie.

At the bend of the road Simon was cycling towards them. He braked suddenly as he noticed them in an embrace. Turning his bicycle round, he pedalled as fast as he could before he was noticed. He could not bear for her to see him. It was as he feared, he was too late to declare his love to Annie.

'We must go back, Ivy Rose needs her knees bathed,' Annie said breathlessly.

He took her arm, and they strolled back slowly with a now subdued child by their side who had spotted Simon on his bicycle. 'Simon . . .' she said, tugging at Annie's skirt.

'No, darling, it doesn't look as though he's coming,' Annie said, leading her into the outhouse where she bathed her knees and checked her for scrapes before giving her a quick cuddle. All the while her mind was reeling at what Dean had done, trying to work out how she felt about it. She knew they had to go back into the house where Paddy was waiting for them, and there was little chance of any time to think. After consoling Ivy Rose, Paddy turned to Annie.

'Simon just rang. He apologized as it seems something last minute came up at his father's surgery. He said he would write to you once he's settled in his new job.'

36

Christmas 1945

There had been much celebration in the Brookes' home on the first Christmas in peacetime, with the family members doing their utmost to make it a special day. They'd all stood as the national anthem was played after King George VI finished his speech. Only Dean remained standing as he took Annie by the hand and, in front of her family, got down on one knee and asked her to marry him.

Annie didn't know what to say, while her family and friends were shocked. 'This is a surprise, Dean,' she said, encouraging him to stand, which he did while still holding a red velvet ring box.

'You can say that again,' Paddy huffed as he loosened the tie Violet insisted he wore for their special meal. 'I'm not sure if it's the case where you come from, lad, but over here it's customary to speak to the girl's father first.'

'Then he speaks to his wife,' Violet said, looking red in the face.

Dean looked around the table at Annie's family. Jocelyn and her sister had joined them for a few days as well, and both looked embarrassed to watch a family discussion. 'I'm sorry, I didn't wish to upset anyone. It's just with Annie being a mother and me being posted elsewhere before too long I thought it would be appropriate for me to ask today.'

Ivy Rose started to snivel. 'What about me?' she asked, looking towards Annie, who was getting more confused by the minute.

Jocelyn dabbed at her mouth with her napkin before nudging her sister, Della, who was sitting next to her. 'Ivy Rose, would you like to take a walk with us? I'd very much like to show my sister the marshes before it gets too dark.'

Ivy Rose brightened up as she left the room with the two sisters, although she called back towards Annie, 'Don't leave without me, will you?'

Annie assured her nothing had been decided as Dean gave her a questioning glance.

'Now the child is out of the way I feel we need to discuss this properly,' Paddy said. 'Violet, I know it's customary for the men to do the washing-up after our Christmas dinner, but on this occasion . . .'

'It's understandable under the circumstances,' Violet said, starting to collect the dishes. 'Mum and Annie can help me while you and Dad have that chat with Dean.'

'I'd rather take a nap if you don't mind,' her dad said, yawning as he loosened the belt of his best trousers. 'I'm not used to all this rich food.'

'You go and have your nap. We can call you later for a slice of Christmas cake.' Despite Dean's interruption of the celebration meal Violet was proud of the spread they'd managed to put on for the family and their friends. Paddy had come home with a chicken telling her not to ask any questions and her dad had laboured on their vegetable plot, meaning there was plenty of veg on everyone's plates to eke out the meat. Jocelyn and her sister had arrived with a basket containing bottled fruits and a Christmas pudding they said had been won in their community centre's draw, while Dean's box of tasty items had embarrassed her, not being used to such luxuries. She'd been frugal with their rations to the point they'd enough food to see them through into the new year. The Christmas cake, although small, was perfect and had been Annie's contribution. She explained that although she'd had to supply some of the ingredients the rest had been provided by Woolworths and the cake made in the kitchen of the Bexleyheath store. She had proudly carried it home the week before along with six mince pies, which Violet planned to cut into halves to accompany the cake. All in all, she expected it to be the perfect Christmas get-together, not imagining Dean would come up with his display of affection towards her daughter. As Ivy followed her to the kitchen similarly laden down with crockery, she gave Violet a knowing look.

'Did you have any inkling this would happen?'

'No, I didn't, and going by the look on our Annie's face neither did she. I had hoped that Simon would have been the one to ask for her hand, but we've not seen hide nor hair of him for far too long, so I think he's out of the running,' she sighed as she started to fill the large stone sink with hot water from the kettle that had been simmering on the hob.

'Men are fools. Our Annie is a good catch, and I'd have thought many a lad would have been after courting her.'

Violet sighed. 'Mum, you're forgetting she is for all

intents and purposes seen as a mother to Ivy Rose and some lads won't be interested in taking on someone else's child. There will be those who think she's spinning a line when she says she never gave birth to the baby and as time goes by locals will have forgotten about Ruth and her death, let alone my bloody brother doing a runner. It's over five years now and not a word from him. He could be dead for all we know,' she said, wondering if she'd crossed the line speaking of him like that. 'I'm sorry, Mum, I shouldn't be so rash with my thoughts, although I do wonder if Paddy and me should have adopted the child.'

'It's nothing me and your dad haven't said when we lay away at night thinking about our family. You must remember it was Ruth's wish that our Annie took on Ivy Rose and no one can say she hasn't made a good mother, even though it has most likely ruined her chances of making a good match for herself. Even Simon scarpered. If only . . .'

'Hindsight is a wonderful thing, but not much help in Annie's situation. Now, let's get on with this washing-up as it won't do itself.'

Outside the door, Annie stopped and listened to what her nan and mum were saying. She knew nothing good ever came out of eavesdropping, but she couldn't turn away. Placing the heaving tray on a side table in the hall, she tried not to make any noise as their conversation came to an end. What they said was true as not many lads had asked her out. When she'd met new people and mentioned Ivy Rose, they'd assumed she'd been born out of wedlock. In the end, as the years passed, she'd given up explaining, thinking there was no point. If people thought the worst of her, then so be it. However, of late she'd had a yearning to settle down and have her own family. She'd seen colleagues marry and been a guest at their weddings, wishing more than once she was walking down the aisle on her dad's arm as he gave her away to the man she loved. She liked Dean, but did she like him enough to walk into the sunset with him? And where would that sunset be?

Paddy leant against the wall by the vegetable garden and took out a packet of cigarettes, first offering them to Dean. They both lit up and gazed across the wall towards the marshes. It was late afternoon, the weak sun was low in the sky and there was a chill in the air – not usually an afternoon for wandering outside apart from to do chores.

'I'm not going to give you a hard time, lad, although you deserve it going off half-cocked like that. I'm surprised the old folk didn't have heart attacks.'

'I'm sorry, sir, I didn't mean to startle anyone. I'd built this idea up in my mind for so long I didn't stop to think how it would appear. I suppose you want me to leave?'

Paddy laughed out loud. 'And break my daughter's heart, let alone upset the women folk? Not on your nelly!'

'Nelly?'

Paddy brushed away his question. 'You have a lot to learn about our country and our language if you're to live here,' he chuckled.

'No, sir, you have it wrong,' he said confidently. 'When I return to my homeland it will be with my bride.'

Annie walked into the kitchen with the laden tray. 'I couldn't help hear what you were saying.'

'I'm sorry you had to hear that. We were only thinking of you, love,' Violet said as she took the tray.

'But I agree with you. I'm twenty-four and most girls my age have settled down and have started their families. Even with a war on and their husbands away so much they can manage to have babies and a family life of sorts. I'm grateful I was entrusted with Ivy Rose's care and whatever happens she'll be with me, come hell or high water. But you're right, I have limited choices as many men just want their own children. Dean seems to accept Ivy Rose, and I've decided that if he asks me again, I'll accept his hand in marriage.'

Violet stopped what she was doing and sat opposite her daughter. 'That's a big step, love. Are you sure your head hasn't been turned by the uniform? Those Yanks are generous with their money, throwing gifts about all over the place. Why, I could've been attracted to them myself. What about you, Mum?'

'I'd not say no either,' her nan said, giving Annie a hug. 'But mark my words, there's a lot of years after the wedding cake's been eaten and the flowers in your bouquet have faded and died. Will you love him enough to stick it out?'

Annie took only seconds to decide. 'I care for him enough to follow him to the ends of the earth,' she said as her mum hugged her and her nan burst into tears.

Albie ran into the room and laughed at the women hugging each other. 'Is it time for the Christmas cake yet?'

'You only ever think of your stomach, Albie Brookes! You've come in here at a beautiful moment when your sister has decided to get married and can only talk about cake,' his nan admonished him.

'There she was talking about following him to the ends of the earth and you go and spoil it! Even young men don't have an ounce of romance in their blood,' Violet said, giving him a kiss, which he scrubbed away with his hands.

'Yuck, get off me! Besides, you got it wrong. She's following him to America and that's not the end of the earth – it's further away. I heard Dean telling Dad when I followed them.'

37

Annie sat at the bottom of the stairs listening to Dean make his apology for messing up his proposal and smiled as he became more and more flustered. In the end she raised a finger to his lips to silence him. 'There's no need to apologize, so please can we start at the beginning and get it over with?' As soon as her words left her mouth, she realized she wasn't being romantic. In all the films she'd watched there were violins playing in the background while the man swept the woman off her feet with words of love.

Dean took the ring box from his pocket and went down on one knee again. He cleared his throat and looked at the closed door into the front room before asking beseechingly, 'Annie, would you do me the honour of becoming my wife?'

'Of course I will, Dean, and thank you for asking me,' she said as she helped him slip the solitaire ring onto her finger. She held her hand out to admire the sparkling stone. 'It's so pretty.'

'It was my grandmother's. She left it to me in her will.'

'And you carried it with you when you came over here

in case you met someone and fell in love with her?' She couldn't help but chuckle.

'No, I wrote to my mother and had it collected and sent over securely courtesy of the American army.'

'Fancy that,' she said as she held her hand up to the small ceiling light. 'Look how it sparkles. Was your mother happy that you had found your bride? I take it you told her all about me?'

He smiled. 'I gave her a glowing report so of course she approved.'

'What about your father?'

'Pa will do as my mother says, so we don't need to worry there.'

'I can't wait to meet them. Perhaps I should write a letter . . . I hope we can have them here for the wedding. My goodness, I'm so excited I don't know what I'm saying. A June wedding would be lovely! We'll have to speak to the vicar at St Augustine's. I wonder what paperwork you'll need to marry an English girl?'

Dean reached for her and pulled her close, silencing her questions with a long kiss. 'I've wanted to do that for so long,' he sighed as she nestled into his shoulder.

'There was nothing stopping you,' she giggled coyly.

'I'd not be so forward until I'd made my intentions clear.'

'My goodness, I had no idea you were so old-fashioned.'

'Are you complaining?'

'Not at all, I rather like it. Now, tell me what happens next. It's not every day a girl gets proposed to. Will we have a long engagement, and will we have a honeymoon? I need time to prepare,' she asked excitedly. 'Mum and

Nan will want to be involved and Ivy Rose will look adorable as a bridesmaid. I can't believe this is happening.'

Dean put his hands on her shoulders to calm her down. 'Annie, I need to explain to you that I'm being moved away from Hall Place and will be established somewhere else by February.'

Annie's face fell. 'I'll miss you, but we can write letters and talk on the telephone and you'll get leave to come home for the wedding, even if we have a short honeymoon.' She blushed, feeling embarrassed to mention what would be their first time alone together.

Dean ran his hand through his hair. 'You don't understand, the wedding will have to be soon because I won't be here come February.'

Annie gasped at that bombshell but just then her family came bursting through the door congratulating them and taking the couple back into the warmth of the front room, where Paddy managed to produce some whisky to toast the happy couple. 'It's not French champagne but it'll warm the cockles all the same,' he said as he raised his glass and gave a toast.

Annie joined her mum on the overstuffed sofa and showed her the ring, telling Violet what Dean had said.

'Oh no, we can't have that. You deserve your white wedding even if we have to beg, steal and borrow to make it happen. Paddy, have you heard this? I won't have any daughter of mine getting married in a registry office.'

He shot Dean a venomous look. 'You should have given us more notice.'

Dean bowed his head. 'I only heard myself two weeks ago.'

Violet shook her head. Thank goodness the laundry business was normally quiet after Christmas; she would need all the hours God gave to see Annie walk down the aisle.

'I'll speak to the vicar to see if he can speed up the banns. We can have the reception here, there's plenty of room. We just need to sort out your dress, and the flowers.'

'It sounds simple when you say it like that,' Paddy laughed before turning quiet when he saw the look on Violet's face. 'It'll be lovely, regardless of the weather.'

'Oh my God,' Violet said. 'It better not snow, or I'll be having a word with Him upstairs.'

Jocelyn, who until then had been sitting quietly with her sister taking in all that was happening, started to speak. 'If you don't think it's an imposition, I have a bridal gown that I'd be happy to donate. Fortunately, it's still at my Bexleyheath house as I wasn't sure what to do with it. I'd heard there was a charity where wedding dresses were loaned to brides and that was where I was going to send it. If you like the dress, you're more than welcome to use it.'

The women all looked at each other and burst out laughing. 'Crikey, Jocelyn, I'd never have expected that of you,' Violet laughed. 'My dress was cut up to make a christening gown, and was worn by Annie, Albie and our Ivy Rose. Perhaps one day I'll be passing it on to a grandchild to wear?'

'There's plenty of time for that, Mother,' Annie protested, feeling her cheeks turn pink. 'Jocelyn, I'd be honoured to borrow your gown if it fits. In a way it would make me feel as though Emily was with us on the day.'

The women all fell silent thinking of Jocelyn's daughter and the last year of her life. It was Paddy who spoke, saying aloud to Dean, 'Have you thought about where you're taking my daughter on her honeymoon?'

'I haven't, sir. I was going to ask around to see if anyone could recommend something.'

Jasper spoke out from where they all thought he'd been dozing off in his armchair. 'Speak to Sergeant Mike Jackson. His dad, Bob, was talking about a guest house he visited down in Ramsgate. He was saying how the owner was very nice, was a decent cook and the one room she still lets out was warm and comfortable.'

'Leave that to me to sort out. It can be my present to you. You can borrow one of the vans as well,' Paddy added.

'That's very good of you, sir, but I can arrange the transport. What do you think, Annie?'

'I can't thank you all enough. We only need to find a dress for Ivy Rose to wear, and everything will be sorted out.'

'If I may make another suggestion: there's a shop that's not long opened in Erith,' Jocelyn offered. 'It is mainly second-hand clothes, but the owner is amazing with a sewing machine and can make almost anything. She used to work at the Erith Woolworths, but now runs her shop, Maisie's Modes, full time. She's quite the businesswoman.'

'My goodness, I know her,' Annie exclaimed before going on to tell everyone what a lovely lady Maisie was, and how she'd looked after her when she'd been poorly at the Erith store's Easter party. 'I'll pop into the town on my half-day and see what she can do to help us. I can take Ivy Rose with me as well in case she needs measuring up. Now, as much as I hate to break up the party I really do need to get some sleep. Boxing Day is always stocktaking day, and my manager expects me in from midday onwards to help out.'

'And I must get back to Hall Place,' Dean said, standing up and shaking hands with everyone present.

'I'll see you out.' Annie followed Dean to the door and snuggled up against him, wondering why she'd had doubts only a few hours ago. Now, as she was enveloped in his strong arms, she felt safe and secure. 'I'm going to love being married to you and showing you off to all my friends as my husband.'

'I could say the same thing, and when we get to Oregon my friends and family will entertain you royally.'

'That will be something to look forward to in years to come.'

Dean moved away from her a little and even in the dim light Annie felt as though he had something to tell her. 'What is it, Dean?'

'The thing is, once my next job is completed, I could well be shipped home. We weren't meant to be here for ever. A ticket will be arranged for you on one of the ships going back home and I hope to be there to welcome you after you travel over.'

Annie felt sick and wasn't sure whether it was the small amount of whisky she'd sipped, or the thought of what was to come.

'Silly me, I never gave a thought to the idea that we might be living in America. I assumed you would be living here with me and my family . . .'

'My mother and the rest of the family will adore you.'
'And Ivy Rose?'
'Of course,' he said stiffly, kissing her cheek and wishing her a good night.

38

Annie gave a big yawn as she pulled a pile of loose pages towards her and gazed with bleary eyes at the rows of stock items that had to be added up. The sheets were coming in thick and fast to the office, and along with a colleague it was Annie's job to not only complete the calculations on each page but to check her colleague's workings as well. After that the paperwork went away to be double-checked before the powers-that-be would decide if the store was in profit or whether there was a problem. For store management it could be a worrying time and rumour had it that some managers could be demoted or moved to different stores in other parts of the country.

She'd been working solidly for three hours when Mr Grant popped his head around the door, giving her a beaming smile. 'I hear congratulations are in order?' he said, pointing to her left hand where Dean's ring shone brightly. 'You kept that quiet.'

Annie's colleague got up and left the room, leaving them able to speak privately. 'As did my fiancé,' she said, explaining how he proposed marriage after their family Christmas dinner.

He took the vacated seat and gave a sigh. 'You know what this means?'

'I'm getting married?'

'It means Woolworths are going to lose one of their best staff members when she sets sail for America, but thankfully it won't happen for a long time.'

Annie hated having to put him straight. 'Our wedding will be in just over a month if we can convince the vicar to hurry the banns through.'

'Oh,' he said, raising an eyebrow. 'Do I need to congratulate you on something else?'

Annie gave a cry of mock horror. 'Mr Grant, if you're implying I am with child, I can assure you that isn't the case. I'm not sure I should be telling you this, but Dean is leaving Hall Place and being posted elsewhere. I'll be accompanying him to America where we will live with his family in Oregon.'

'You do know this will take some time?' he pressed.

'I don't have many details yet but assume I shall have to book a passage on a ship for myself and Ivy Rose. It would be lovely if Dean could travel with us.'

He shook his head sadly. 'My wife's cousin married an American serviceman and had to travel alone with a young baby nine months after first applying. It took ages to get all her paperwork in order.'

Annie's face dropped. 'I have a lot to learn. I have to confess to being nervous about leaving England and my family, but at least I'll have Ivy Rose with me and it sounds as though I'll have time to prepare her for her new life,' she said as she thought how she had a lot to do before she headed across the sea to her new home. It was beginning to feel like an impossible task.

'At least it means we'll have you here for a little longer and don't forget, I'll make sure you have impeccable references for your new employers.' Mr Grant brightened. 'Who knows, you may even find work in a Woolworths store in America.'

Annie felt her spirits start to rise. To be able to work in a Woolies store in America would be like coming home.

'I'm not going, and you can't make me! I hate Dean and now I hate you too!' Ivy Rose screamed as Annie and Violet looked on. There were times the child could be difficult, but this went beyond any tantrum she'd had in the past.

Annie looked with pleading eyes towards her nan, who stood arms folded in the doorway between the kitchen and the living room where Ivy Rose had thrown herself onto a rug in front of the unmade fire and was currently waving her arms and legs about in anger.

'Leave the little madam to get on with it. She'll soon calm down when she doesn't have an audience,' Ivy predicted. 'Come out into the kitchen and we'll shut the door on her. Paddy will be home soon, and he can deal with her. He spoils the child rotten and he's to blame when she acts like this.'

Annie followed the women into the other room thinking her nan was being unfair on her dad, but there again, he did call Ivy Rose his little princess, treating her with sweeties when he could put his hand on them. There had been a short time when Albie resented the child and would pull her pigtails when he thought no one was looking.

'Perhaps once we're in America, she may shake off her tantrums and start to act a little more grown-up,' she said.

'I'd not count your chickens. Her dad was the same at that age. The apple hasn't fallen far from the tree with that one.'

Violet gave Annie a sympathetic look. 'I don't think she's as bad as her dad was; she's just been spoilt by Paddy. I'll have a word with him about it when he gets back.'

'Where's he gone?' Annie asked as she checked inside the biscuit tin and found half a broken gingerbread. It had been a while since her lunch break at work.

'He's taken Jocelyn and her sister up to the house in Bexleyheath to collect the wedding gown for you to try on,' her mum said. 'Please don't say anything if it isn't suitable, Mother. We can sort it out after Jocelyn has gone back to Somerset.'

'But if I don't wear the dress, she'll notice when she comes to see me getting married,' Annie objected, thinking how this wedding wasn't going to be straightforward.

Violet patted her hand. 'Don't you worry about a thing.'

'Why are you always so calm, Mum?' Annie sighed.

She gave a gentle laugh. 'I've had to learn to be, what with living with your dad.'

'Poor Dad, he can't do right for doing wrong, can he?'

'That sounds like them now,' Violet said as the van could be heard pulling up in the yard. 'Can you wave at them to come in through the back door, so they don't see Ivy Rose until I've had a word with Paddy, please, Mum?'

While they were alone Violet told Annie she had telephoned the vicarage to find out if she and Dean could be married at the end of January. 'I was told there wouldn't be a problem if Dean had the right documents; I've left the list by the telephone in the hall. Make sure you give it to him so he can get cracking. Apart from that the vicar would like to see you both together to discuss the marriage. Don't look alarmed, all couples have to sit through his talk.'

'Gosh, I hope I don't blush too much as I've known the vicar since I was a kid.' Annie did not like the sound of this one bit.

'What's this about our Ivy Rose being a little madam?' Paddy was in the kitchen before she had even realized.

'Dad, she doesn't want to go to America with me, I don't know what to do,' Annie wailed.

Violet put her hands on her hips. 'You're to blame for this, Paddy Brookes, as you spoil the girl. Get yourself in there and sort this out once and for all. We don't want one of her tantrums during the wedding.'

Without saying a word Paddy disappeared through the door where seconds later Ivy Rose could be heard crying her eyes out as Paddy started to pacify her.

Thankfully at that moment Jocelyn entered with a large box, placing it on the kitchen table, which took their minds off the little girl and her tantrum. 'This hasn't been opened for years and I was too afraid to open the box when Paddy lifted it down from the top of my wardrobe. I did dust it off,' she added as she nodded to Annie, encouraging her to lift the lid.

Annie held her breath as she slowly did so and placed it to one side. All she could see was faded tissue paper. Would the dress look as time-worn? she wondered.

'Oh, it's beautiful,' she gasped as she had her first glimpse of delicate white lace. Taking the dress by the shoulders, with help from Violet, she lifted it from the box. The gown was high-necked with long sleeves and a fitted bodice, and the skirt floated to the ground with a small train behind. 'I've never seen anything so beautiful in my life and it's so different to the wedding gowns I've seen in magazines.'

'It is nearly thirty years old,' Jocelyn said apologetically. 'If you don't think it's right for you, I will understand. I'd hate for you to wear it just to please me.'

Annie held the dress to her breast. 'You have no idea how much I want to wear this dress. It's perfect. I just hope it fits me.'

'There's no time like the present! Go and try it on,' her mum said. She again lifted the skirt of the dress and followed as Annie led the way upstairs to her bedroom.

'You forgot this,' Jocelyn called as she took a headband made from the same fabric from the box and hurried after them.

Later that evening as they settled down after a dinner made up of leftovers from their Christmas Day meal, Annie was in a dream thinking of the beautiful dress she'd be able to wear on her wedding day and how it would only need taking in a little at the waist. The fabric was as fresh and clean as the day it had been made for Jocelyn, and Violet had declared she would hang it in the laundry for a day to freshen it up.

Violet had collected Ivy Rose from where she was sitting quietly with Paddy while Annie had tried on the gown; she was calm and a little tired, but there was no sign of the tantrum. Paddy gave her the thumbs up to say all had been resolved. 'Come and see Mummy's wedding dress,' she'd said, taking her by the hand. 'We're going to have a dress made for you as well; would you like that?'

The child nodded her head as she looked at Annie in all her finery. 'I will go to America,' she said begrudgingly.

Violet wondered how Paddy had calmed down the girl and talked him round. She was about to ask him when there was a knock on the door. She followed her husband to the door and greeted Dean as he entered. Following him back to the front room, she tugged on Paddy's sleeve. 'What miracle did you perform to bring our Ivy Rose round?'

'The miracle of money,' he chuckled. 'I've promised to pay her half a crown for every month she stays in America.'

'Oh, Paddy, I'm not sure that's the right thing to do, but if it works, then it will be worth it, if only for our Annie's peace of mind.'

In the front room Annie had greeted Dean with a kiss and they'd sat down to look at the paperwork he'd brought with him.

'There's so much,' she sighed as she looked at the notes he'd written. 'Mum, look, I must go to the American embassy in London and the American army headquarters. It's almost as if I must be vetted to enter their country. I'm bound to get all my answers wrong and then they'll refuse me entry. Poor Dean will never see his bride in Oregon.'

'Then I'll come with you. No American is going to refuse my daughter,' she said before quickly apologizing to Dean for what she had said.

'My manager at Woolies, Mr Grant, is going to get me some information from a relative of his who has moved to America. He reckons when we have all of that at our fingertips it'll seem so much easier.' Annie bit her lip, trying not to think of all the potential hurdles ahead. 'I'd just like to know when Ivy Rose and I can set sail.'

39

January 1946

'Trust you to pick the coldest day of the year to get married. I've never known it to be so perishing cold as this before now,' Maisie said, checking Annie's lipstick as they stood at the entrance to St Augustine's Church.

'Oh, stop complaining,' Sarah said, and she straightened the veil while Freda giggled and handed Annie her bouquet.

'You look beautiful, and I wish you lots of luck with your American soldier. You're a very brave person.'

'I don't feel very brave at the moment,' Annie said as she shivered with nerves. 'Are you sure Dean is in there?'

'He most certainly is and looking very handsome,' Betty Billington said as she poked her head around the door. 'It looks as though most of your colleagues from the Erith and Bexleyheath stores are in there too, as well as a few American soldiers. It was good of you to have your wedding on our half-day so we could come along to see you marry.'

'Are you ready?' Paddy asked as he came from the side of the church where he'd been having a crafty sip of brandy from his hip flask. He too looked through the door to the church and waved at a few of his showmen family. 'We've a right motley crew in there.'

Betty, Freda, Sarah and Maisie kissed Annie's cheek and wished her good luck before entering the church to take their seats, while Ivy Rose, who had been sitting just inside the door to keep warm, came out to join them.

'Are my two girls ready?' Paddy asked, looking proudly at Annie and Ivy Rose. A tear pricked his eye as he thought that soon they'd be thousands of miles away and he may not see them again.

Just as they were about to step inside the church a high-pitched toot was heard from the road. Annie turned to see their steam engine, Goliath, decorated in ribbons stopping close by. She looked to her dad, who shrugged his shoulders.

'I couldn't leave her at home, could I? Besides, I thought you and Dean would like a ride back to the reception.'

Annie chuckled. 'I can't think of anything I'd like better, although Dean may not be so keen.'

'I don't know, he seems to be coming round to our way of life,' Paddy said as the organ struck up and he started to walk his daughter down the aisle. He didn't tell her he'd had a long chat with the American and made it clear he should treat Annie well, or he'd be there in a shot to sort him out.

The service seemed to be over in a flash, with Annie just remembering the outpouring of love from her family and friends as they stood outside while Dean's friends took photographs; every one of them seemed to have a camera. Everyone cheered as Paddy led the happy couple towards Goliath and helped his daughter climb onboard.

'We're only going as far as The Corner Pin as it would

take too long to journey down to the marshes,' he said, much to Annie's relief. As it was, she was worried about the smuts on her beautiful gown until he draped her in a large white sheet. She dared not ask if it came from someone's bag wash.

She snuggled up to Dean, feeling like the luckiest girl in the world, with people coming out of their houses to cheer on the bride and groom. At The Corner Pin pub, they climbed down from Goliath and were helped into the larger of the two laundry vans, again decked out with bunting just like Goliath.

'This has been such a wonderful day. Are you happy?' she asked him.

'It hasn't quite been what I expected,' he laughed, 'but at least I have my bride, and we'll soon be heading home.'

Annie felt a sharp stab of disappointment. He may be going home, but she was leaving hers. She tried to ignore that thought but as their departure time got closer, she couldn't ignore it any longer . . .

'This is a wonderful wedding reception, thank you all so much for making my day perfect,' Annie said, catching up with her parents, grandparents and Jocelyn as they were collecting more food to lay out on the trestle tables in the barn. Bales of hay and several small bonfires kept the area cosy and warm even though there were flecks of snow in the air. A wind-up gramophone gave them music to dance to. The front room and kitchen were taken over by the older guests who were enjoying a chat. Annie made sure to move around while talking to everyone. Checking the time, she thought she should change into her going-away outfit as it was a long drive to Ramsgate.

'Dad, have you seen Dean? We'll have to make a move soon,' she asked.

Paddy frowned. 'Hasn't he spoken to you?'

'What about?'

Paddy muttered an unrepeatable word under his breath. 'There was a telephone call for him and his mates. They're being called back to their barracks. Let me help you find him.'

They walked through the house and outside until they found the soldiers standing around a fire drinking beer from bottles. Annie went up to Dean. 'Darling, it's time we left,' she said, linking her arm through his.

He turned to look at her. 'Sorry, I was going to find you and got waylaid,' he smiled as his mates all cheered. 'Something's come up and we've all been recalled to barracks. We're shipping out in the morning.'

'But don't they know it's our wedding day and we're off on our honeymoon later tonight? It's only for two days.'

He looked contrite as well as slightly tipsy. 'I have to go where the army send me, and this time it's Germany.'

Around her she could hear people chatting and laughing as if nothing had happened. Paddy stepped in and steered the couple to a quiet corner. 'I'll be nearby if you need me,' he said, shooting an angry look towards Dean. 'You both need to talk.'

Annie sat down on a straw bale, not caring about her wedding gown, and tugged at Dean's arm for him to join her. Once they were side by side she took the beer bottle and threw it away then turned and hissed at him, 'What's going on, Dean? Ivy Rose and I are supposed to be getting on the ship in ten days to head to America. You told me you'd be there to meet us. How do you intend to meet me if you're going to Germany? Also, what about our honeymoon?'

'Sorry, Annie, it's all been cancelled by orders of the American army.'

It was Annie's turn to swear. He really was quite drunk.

'I don't think that's very ladylike. You'd better not say that word in front of my mother,' he said, getting angry.

'I know far stronger words than that one, and if you don't sort out this mess right now, you'll find my bedroom door locked tonight, wherever we might be staying.'

His eyes opened wide as he tried to comprehend what she was saying. 'Now look here . . .'

'No, you look here, Dean. I was unsure about marrying you, but you pleaded your case, and I fell for it hook, line and sinker. I thought we had a future even if it meant uprooting Ivy Rose and travelling across the world to live with people I've not even met. I had enough respect for you to think love would grow between us once we'd set up our own home and perhaps our own children came along in time. Now, I'm going to change into my going-away outfit and you'll come up to my room in half an hour and tell me what you're going to do.' She got up and marched away towards the house, unaware her dad was calling after her. As she went through the kitchen she bumped into her mum and Jocelyn.

'My dear, there you are. Jocelyn and I have a little surprise for you and for Ivy Rose. I was speaking to your store manager recently and he told me how uncomfortable it was going to be travelling on the ship that Dean and the American army had booked for you. We didn't like the idea of you both being so seasick, so Jocelyn checked out how much it would cost for you to travel on an ocean-going liner. After all, it is only one way.'

Annie shuddered at the thought.

'We decided to club together to treat our girls. Here are the tickets,' Violet said as Jocelyn handed over a glossy folder. 'It means you leaving a week later, though, but the journey will be quicker.'

Annie looked at the brochure and then at her mum and Emily's mum before bursting into tears.

'It's all been a bit too much for her,' Jocelyn said as she helped unpin Annie's headdress and veil as she lay sleeping on her bed. 'She's cried herself to sleep.'

Paddy put his head round the door of Annie's bedroom. 'How is she?'

Violet put her finger to her lips to tell him to be quiet. 'She's just dropped off. After the excitement of the last few days no wonder she's emotional.'

'It's not that at all. The blighter didn't tell her he's off to Germany with his regiment and won't be in America to meet her off her ship.'

'Perhaps now she's arriving later, he can be there?' Jocelyn said, showing Paddy the brochure.

'No, I've just been talking to one of his comrades. They're over in Berlin for six months minimum.'

'Perhaps we could get the money back and book a later date?' Violet suggested.

Jocelyn pointed to some words on the tickets. 'Non-refundable, so she loses the money.'

'No, I won't,' Annie said as she rolled over on her bed

to face them. 'Ivy Rose and I will go to visit his family on our own,' she said, sitting up on her bed. 'His family are my family now so there's nothing to stop us travelling on our own and he can join us later. Thank you for the tickets, it will be so much more enjoyable. However, I must give you some money towards them.' Annie found herself being scolded as her mum and Jocelyn refused point blank to even discuss money. 'Dad?'

'Don't get me involved,' Paddy said, backing away. 'I'm going to have another word with him before he's collected by the army truck. To be fair, he's taking a lot of stick from his buddies right now and having had a drink isn't helping him.'

'He doesn't usually drink,' she sniffed.

'And that hasn't helped either,' Paddy added. 'Not that he'd have been much use to you in that state . . . Sorry,' he apologized hastily at the furious look from his wife. 'But you know what I mean. Without a night together, your marriage isn't even valid, is it? Though of course you've got the certificate,' he amended as Violet now looked fit to burst.

Annie sighed and leant back on her bed. 'What a mess.'

'It's only a mess if we allow it to be so,' Jocelyn said as she reached for her handbag. 'Now, I have a couple of things to give you before you leave for foreign shores and as I won't be here for much longer, I may as well give them to you now.'

'Oh gosh, what do you mean?' Annie asked.

'Don't panic, I'm only going back to Somerset. Now, here are the details for the two accounts I've set up in your and Ivy Rose's names. You're both beneficiaries in my will, but in the meantime, I'll be topping up these accounts so the pair of you don't have to worry too much about surviving alone in a foreign country. Please don't say no; the house in Bexleyheath has been sold and my plan all along has been to treat the pair of you. There's also money for young Albie, so he doesn't feel left out.'

Violet was almost speechless. 'I can't thank you enough . . .'

'Please don't, you all feel like family to me. Oh, and there's this,' she said, taking an envelope from her bag. 'I bumped into Simon the other day, he's down visiting his father. I told him about your wedding, and he asked if he could give me a letter to pass on to you. We met for tea and that's when he gave it to me. You know he's very fond of you.'

Annie took the letter and tore it open. She could hardly believe what she saw. Inside was one sheet of paper where he told her he would always love her and had been a fool to walk away the day he saw Dean kiss her. He'd been a coward and all the time he was working in Edinburgh he should have got in touch instead of brooding over his lost opportunities.

'Simon, you are a fool,' she said as she placed the letter back inside the envelope. She'd never guessed that he'd seen that first kiss, and her head spun as she wondered what might have happened if things had gone differently that fateful afternoon. There was a second slimmer envelope and across the front he'd written *not to be opened unless you need me to help you*. She placed that back inside the larger envelope as well, knowing she should have tried harder to get in touch with Simon. They were both utter fools.

40

'This looks nice,' Annie said as they gazed around the cabin that would be their home for the next ten days.

Ivy Rose chewed her fingernail as she slowly moved around the space, peering in cupboards and looking in the fruit bowl. 'Don't they have any chocolate?' she asked.

'I'm sure there will be some somewhere. Oh, look at the tiny bathroom! It'll be fun using that.' There was everything that they might need, but cleverly designed to fit. All the taps shone and the tiles gleamed.

Ivy Rose shrugged her shoulders.

'How about you choose which bed you would like to sleep in?'

'The one by the window,' she said straight away, jumping onto the narrow bed and bouncing up and down to look out of the porthole. 'Can you open the window, please?'

'I don't think we can but when our steward returns perhaps you could ask him.' Annie knew that some of the cabins on the lower decks did not have the luxury of a porthole. 'In the meantime, I'm going to use that tiny desk over there to write a few letters. Why don't you draw a picture of the room, and I can put it into one of the envelopes to your nan, or perhaps Jocelyn?'

'All right,' she sighed, 'but I'll need my colouring crayons.'

'Darling, we packed them in the trunk. I did ask if there was anything you wanted to put in our hand luggage and you said no.' It was hard to be around the child these days and Annie often felt that if she said something was black, Ivy Rose would turn around and say no, it was white. The little girl just wouldn't co-operate, and she knew it was getting on everyone's nerves. She swore Paddy gave a sigh of relief when Ivy Rose begrudgingly walked up the gangplank. She hoped that given a couple of days her daughter would start to enjoy her new surroundings. She could but pray.

The ocean crossing was uneventful, and they were soon into a routine of wrapping up well for brisk walks around the deck followed by letter writing, reading and playing board games with the other travellers, who on the whole were older than Annie and fussed over Ivy Rose, treating her like their own grandchild. By the time they arrived in New York harbour having seen the Statue of Liberty, they were on first-name terms and had exchanged addresses with quite a few people. After going through immigration, they stayed one night in a hotel then caught the first of two trains that took them to Chicago. For Annie, who had heard of these cities, she found no excitement in finally being in America such was her homesickness. It was cold and snowing and they both felt thoroughly miserable. In Chicago they had to send a telegram to Dean's family to say what time their train would get them into Oregon City where they would be met.

After asking a carriage guard to notify them when they finally reached their destination, they both fell into a fitful sleep for half a day before waking to eat some of the picnic food Annie had picked up to save them some money. There was a small toilet in the carriage where they would freshen up a little, although Annie knew they would both be frightful sights by the time they met Dean's family at the station. The next day was very much like the first and it was a very bedraggled Annie and Ivy Rose who stood by their trunk waiting for Dean's parents.

An hour later they were still sitting on their trunk when a young woman approached them. She was a little older than Annie, and her wavy blonde hair was held back neatly, while her clothes were obviously well cut. She would not have looked out of place in one of Maisie's most upmarket creations. 'Would you happen to be Annie?' she enquired.

'I am, and this is my daughter Ivy Rose. Whoever was supposed to meet us is late.' Annie was in no mood for pleasantries.

'I'm sorry, that would be me. I'm Louise Carter, a friend of the family. My car had a flat tyre, and it took an age to repair.'

Annie could see how harassed she was and despite her irritation at being kept waiting after such an epic trip she felt sorry for her. 'Never mind, you're here now. Will it take long to get to Dean's family home? We both need a bath and a good night's sleep after our journey.'

Louise, who'd been waving to a staff member on the platform to help load the trunk, turned and laughed. 'We have a one-hour drive. It's normal for people to get the Greyhound bus, but I suppose with your trunk it would have been arduous,' she said as she opened the car door for them to climb in.

Annie felt as though she'd been chastised and kept quiet as she climbed into the front seat while Ivy Rose sat in the back. 'Dean never explained very much about the journey,' she said when she could no longer remain quiet.

Louise chuckled. 'That's our Dean all over.'

Annie wanted to know more about the man she'd married. 'Do you know Dean?'

'Know him? We were engaged to be married at one time.'

She inwardly groaned. Now she was trapped in a car with Dean's old girlfriend. Could life get any worse?

'Mum, I feel sick,' Ivy Rose called out.

By the time they reached the Delaney house, Ivy Rose was burning up and weeping. Annie had little time to take in her new surroundings as she was so preoccupied by her daughter's distress, and so failed to notice the grand old home and the generous gardens it was set in.

'We should get her into her bed and call a doctor. It's probably nothing, but better to have her checked over,' Louise suggested.

'You're right, thank you. I'm afraid our arrival isn't quite what I expected.' Annie at least had a moment to realize this was quite an understatement.

'Don't worry about it. Felicity is out today at one of her fundraising events; you can settle in and be refreshed before you meet your new in-laws. Come on, I'll show you your rooms,' she said as they helped Ivy Rose out of the car and into the house.

Annie hadn't expected to find herself in such a large and expensively furnished house and the rooms set aside for her and Ivy Rose included a bathroom and their own sitting room. She made a note to tell her parents about it when next she wrote. From what she could make out, the family had staff to care for them as well. It wasn't the small home with churchgoing family members that she had pictured.

She liked Louise, who she felt was not unlike herself in height and colouring; was this why Dean was attracted to her when they met at the Woolworths Easter party? The woman helped her unpack and arranged for the trunk to be stored away from their rooms, explaining that she worked for Felicity and so was usually on hand to assist in any way. She even arranged a meal for Annie and soup for Ivy Rose. After leaving them alone for a while she returned to inform Annie that a doctor would visit in the next hour to look at Ivy Rose and she was not to worry about his fee as the family had an account.

Annie thanked her profusely, knowing that her own family had always lived in fear of having to call the doctor because of the expense. She settled down by Ivy Rose's bed. The only worry she now had was meeting Dean's mother. She must have dropped off as she awoke with a start as the bedroom door opened and a larger-than-life woman with rigidly set grey hair entered the room followed by a man who must be the doctor, and then Louise who gave her an apologetic look.

'So, you're my daughter-in-law?' She frowned, not waiting for an answer. 'And this must be the child.' She peered at Ivy Rose, who had been woken by the noise.

The doctor pulled a stethoscope from his leather bag and started to thoroughly examine the little girl, asking questions of Annie as he did so. When he'd finished, he turned to Felicity Delaney. 'The child is just weary from the journey. Rest and plenty of fluids will have her back on her feet in a couple of days.'

'Is it not malnutrition? I've heard much about the eating habits of the British and warned my son about the possibility of not being able to produce me an heir if the women do not take care of themselves. I imagine the journey in the lower-class cabins on the ship did not help.'

Annie was livid. She was tired as well, which didn't help her control her tongue. She rose to her feet and met the woman's gaze. 'Excuse me if you think I am speaking out of turn, but I'd like to explain that most British women are not malnourished, and neither is Ivy Rose. Also, we travelled out on an ocean-going liner in a first-class cabin, which was not paid for by Dean or the American army; I have money of my own.' She finished by taking a deep breath. If Felicity thought she was a woman of means, she'd not correct her. There was a feeling of empowerment in acting as if she was a woman of importance.

Felicity stepped back as if she had been slapped. 'Dean never informed me of this.'

'Dean doesn't know as he was called away by the army even before we'd had our honeymoon,' Annie replied, trying hard to smile and be pleasant to her husband's mother, at least until they had a home of their own and she could create some distance between them.

'Oh, that's a shame,' Louise said before casting her eyes down to avoid Felicity's glare.

'Thank you, Doctor. Please send your bill in the usual way. I'll leave you to care for your daughter; you can eat here with her,' she said before sweeping out, followed immediately by the doctor and more slowly by Louise.

'Blimey,' Annie said as she collapsed on the bed next to Ivy Rose, who burst out laughing at her mum's exaggerated actions.

'She's someone to keep an eye on,' the child giggled, using one of Paddy's favourite sayings.

'At least we'll have something to write home about,' Annie said. 'Now, how about having a wash and I'll put you in a clean nightdress?'

Ivy Rose nodded her head in agreement. 'Can you read me a story, please?'

Annie gave a sigh of relief. Her daughter was already on the mend and their relationship was back on track.

41

Mid-May 1946

Annie looked up from where she was writing a letter to Jocelyn. 'How are you getting on?' she called out to Ivy Rose, who was sitting at their small dining table in their sitting room working on a set of arithmetic questions. Although she'd enquired of Felicity about a school for Ivy Rose there had been no response other than that it was something Dean should be involved in. Her letters to Dean had not been answered of late, and the few replies that had arrived did nothing to help her settle into her life as a wife and mother. So she decided to educate Ivy Rose herself for the time being. Thanking her experience at Woolworths of working with figures, she found that side of things easy; it was everything else she struggled with. Louise had come up trumps, bringing her reading books and investigating education levels for a child Ivy Rose's age. When the weather was agreeable, they set off for walks and she found the child's natural inquisitiveness about nature and the world around her was enough to instigate reading poetry and science books. Everywhere here was so different to the marshes where she had grown up; she felt as if she was learning it all afresh too, and she tried not to miss the scent of the Thames or familiar calls of the birds that nested along the riverbank. Annie was also insistent they kept up their letter writing as it helped them both to strengthen links with home and helped with Ivy Rose's handwriting.

'I've finished,' the child called back in a sing-song voice. 'Can you make them harder next time?'

Annie walked over to look at the calculations. 'You've done very well, but you might want to check your answer to question number five. You're like me in that you have problems with subtraction.'

Ivy Rose grinned up at her. 'I'm pleased I'm like you.'

The reply took Annie by surprise. This time spent together had certainly reaped dividends. 'I'm pleased you are too. You know, I was only a friend with your mummy Ruth for a short time, but we got on so well. I can see so much of her in you.'

'Did you know my daddy very well?'

Annie had expected questions about Ivy Rose's parents and had discussed as much with her mum and nan before she'd left England. They'd decided on the best way to approach the child's concerns. 'Yes, I knew your daddy, but he had gone away before you were born so I don't think he knew about you, but if he had, he would have adored you. Would you like me to explain how I'm related to you?' she asked, reaching for the child's sketchbook.

'I know you're my mummy, but it isn't straightforward like other families.'

'As far as I'm concerned, you are my daughter. First, I was your godmother when you were christened, but after your real mum went to heaven, I adopted you; it had been your real mummy's wish. Now, this is my nan and grandad,' she said, drawing two stick people standing side by side. 'They are Jasper and Ivy James. They had two children called Peter and Violet,' she said, adding a downwards line and two more stick people who she labelled with their names.

'Violet married Paddy, and they are my parents.'

Ivy Rose leant closer to the sketchpad in fascination.

Annie pointed to the figure of Pete. 'He met your mummy, Ruth, and they had you.'

'May I add me and Ruth?' she asked before carefully drawing in two more stick figures.

'Now, what can you tell from this?'

Ivy was thoughtful before replying. 'I was named after Nanny, and we haven't added in Ruth's mummy and daddy.'

'Sadly, we know that Ruth was an orphan so didn't know her parents. My mum, Violet, wants to investigate this to see if she can find out anything about them. What else can you see from our diagram?'

Ivy Rose beamed. 'Violet, your mummy, is my real aunty and that makes us cousins. So, you're my cousin and my mummy, and Violet is my aunty and my nan,' she chuckled.

Annie laughed. 'Now I feel confused, but Nanny Ivy, who you were named after, is still our nan. And this is called our family tree.'

'Gosh,' Ivy Rose said as she again stared at the sketch. 'I like you being my cousin and my mummy; it's like me having two of you. What does that make Dean?'

Annie frowned. She wasn't about to say it made him an absentee husband who never had much time for the child.

An idea started to form in her head. 'How would you like to take a trip into town after lunch?'

'I'd like that very much, Cousin Annie,' she grinned.

'Let's clear up these books and prepare for lunch then we'll be ready to head out,' Annie said, picking up a copy of *Treasure Island* she'd been reading to Ivy Rose and going over to a small bookcase set against one wall. She'd been informed this room had been Dean's when he was a child so the books would have been his. As she slid the book in place on the shelf she noticed a small photograph album. Pulling it out, she settled down to look, flicking through the early pages showing a young Dean with his mother. Felicity hadn't changed much, apart from growing stouter. Towards the back of the album there were photographs of Dean in his army uniform and one with Louise standing by his side holding out her hand. Annie sucked in her breath as she spotted the ring she was now wearing on her own left hand. She knew Louise had once been engaged to Dean, but this looked as though it was more recent than she'd thought. 'I'm just going to pop down to Louise's office for a minute. I'll be back before lunch is brought up to us,' she said, leaving Ivy Rose still working on her family tree.

'Can you spare me a couple of minutes?' she asked as she entered the small office where Louise kept the paperwork for Felicity's charity work.

'Of course, come in and take a seat,' she said, putting down her pen. 'You look worried.' She glanced to the album in Annie's hand. 'Ah, I wondered when that would come to light.'

'I discovered it in the bookcase.'

'Oh, Felicity must have placed it there. She does like to

interfere with things when they aren't going her way. I do want to explain a few things to you, but first, please ask me what you came here for.'

'I'm thinking it will be one and the same thing, although I have a few questions.'

'Fire away.'

She took a deep breath. 'Why are you no longer engaged to Dean and what made you stay here afterwards? Why have I been brought here when Dean is still away? He doesn't seem to want to correspond with me. Finally, why are me and Ivy Rose kept away from the main part of the house and not included in family matters?'

Louise gave a self-deprecating laugh. 'I loved Dean when we were at school together. When this position came up, I made it my goal to do a good job and have Dean fall in love with me. I love it here so working on Felicity's charities was a joy and I am good at what I do. Felicity came to rely on me – she still does – and she would pair me with Dean when we had charity functions to attend. It was when the war started and he knew he would serve overseas that he began to think about the future and how it would please his mother if we were to become engaged. Of course, I went along with it as I thought I still loved him.'

'And you didn't?'

'I was besotted rather than in love. I was caught up in the whole Felicity Delaney roadshow and, being an orphan, it looked to me like a pretty good family to belong to. Dean is like his mother. As his embarkation came closer, it was apparent he didn't love me and just wanted the whole package with a girl waiting back home. I gave him back his ring and said he was bound to find someone he would love more than me. I made it clear to Felicity that I would not be leaving my job, but recently I've felt my time here is over as Felicity resents me for ending the engagement. She was shocked when she found out he wanted the ring as he had found a girl to marry.'

'It wasn't Felicity who sent the ring to England?'

'No, he asked me to send it, no doubt hoping to upset me for cancelling our engagement. Just as he arranged for you to move here so quickly because he wanted to rub my nose in the fact he'd found himself a wife.'

'That makes sense, and I suppose I'm kept away from everyone so that Felicity's friends are unaware he has a wife and a daughter?'

'Yes, and that is what I wanted to tell you. I've given notice and Felicity is very angry. She's held on to the hope that Dean would return and fall in love with me; it was never going to happen as I've found someone else, and Dean is too self-centred to love anyone but himself. He is too like his mother.'

Annie sighed, trying to take in all this new information, although she had suspected much of it already. 'I'm sorry you're leaving as you're the only friend we have here. However, I'm happy for you finding someone you love and who loves you. I envy you that.'

'Which leaves my question: why did you marry Dean?'

Annie stood up to leave, but first she spoke the truth that she had often tried to hide even from herself. 'Because I loved someone else and let him go.'

She returned to their rooms to find lunch being served.

'You're quiet,' Ivy Rose observed.

'I'm just thinking about things, nothing for you to worry about. Now eat up and we'll take that trip into town.'

Annie remained thoughtful as they wandered around the shops, stopping to purchase sketching materials for Ivy Rose and a fresh notepad and envelopes for herself.

'The shops are boring, there's more in Erith,' Ivy Rose commented. It was true. The town was more spread out and there were few buildings over two storeys high. But in fact, there was far less to look at, or at least in terms of shops.

'You don't miss much for someone your age,' Annie said. 'Let's go down this street. We can always stop for an ice cream if nothing else.'

Ivy Rose burst out laughing. 'Look, there's a Woolworths store.'

They made straight for the large building and, stepping inside, Annie had never felt so disappointed. Yes, the layout and livery were like back home, but it wasn't home. For a couple of minutes as they'd headed towards the store, she'd expected to see Freda, Maisie and Sarah behind the counters and Mr Grant chatting with Betty Billington. This was like a nightmare she would never wake up from if she didn't do something to save herself.

Back at the house Annie picked up all her correspondence from back home and looked through the letters. She knew from Jocelyn that there was money in her bank account enough for two tickets home, but there was something else. She quickly came across the letter from Simon and pulled out the second envelope which made her heart soar.

'I'm just going to see Louise,' she called out to Ivy Rose, who was unpacking her new sketching materials.

'Two visits in the same day?' Louise laughed as Annie hurried into her office. 'What can I do for you?'

'Can you help me purchase two berths for England and also train tickets to New York? I have the money in my bank account.'

'I can do that...' Louise looked momentarily astonished, but recovered well. 'And Annie, I'm so pleased you're following your heart.'

'Is it that obvious?' she asked, putting a hand to her burning cheeks as Louise picked up the telephone to start booking the trip back to England. 'I do have some letters to write; would you post them for me, so I know they're on their way?' She knew everything would be a rush but now she understood that she could stay in this place not one minute longer than she absolutely had to.

'If you write them now, I'll post them on my way home,' Louise promised before starting to speak to the booking clerk on the other end of the line. Scribbling on a notepad in front of her, she replaced the receiver. 'I can reserve you two berths for the twentieth of June. If we allow five days for you to travel to New York, it means you'll be leaving here in three weeks' time. Does that suit you?'

'Oh, it does. Thank you so much.' Annie couldn't quite believe that she had found the nerve to turn her back on what she had hoped would be her new life, but now saw was nothing but a dead end. She had to follow this through and, as Louise had just said, follow her heart. It led in only one direction.

'My pleasure. I'll be leaving on the same day so I can drive you to the station. You can't take a bus with that large trunk.' Louise winked conspiratorially.

Gratefully Annie smiled back and then almost ran to their rooms, where she started to write her letters . . .

42

New York, June 1946

'Everything looks so different to how it did when we arrived,' Annie said as she checked her guidebook. It was still the busiest city she had ever seen, its skyscrapers towering above anything London had to offer, but now she was full of anticipation.

'It's a very sunny day,' Ivy Rose agreed. 'Look, is that what we're looking for?'

'It certainly is,' Annie said as she gazed skyward at the Woolworth Building. 'I'm glad Jocelyn told us to visit this place before we join our ship and head for home. It's not a sight we see every day.'

'I wish I had time to draw it,' Ivy Rose said as she looked up trying to see the top. 'It's so big, Mummy! I can't even count how many windows it has! And it makes my neck hurt even trying.'

'It was the tallest building in the world until a few years ago,' Annie said. 'And it's sixty floors high. You can't count to sixty yet so don't worry. Let's buy some postcards then you can copy them in your sketchbook. There's a stall over there.'

They walked through a sea of sightseers on Broadway all keen to look at the impressive building.

'Can I buy some souvenirs to take home?' Ivy Rose asked, her eyes opening wide at the array of gifts. There were miniature models of the famous skyscraper, with its grand tower on top of the first thirty floors.

'Of course, but don't spend all your money as we have three weeks on the ship.'

'I'm all right as I'll have twelve shillings and sixpence to collect from Grandad Paddy when we get home,' Ivy Rose announced proudly.

Annie frowned. 'Why is that?'

'He said he would pay me half a crown for every month I stayed in America.'

Annie roared with laughter and so at first she did not hear a man's voice close by until he repeated himself. 'Postcards, madam, only thruppence and sixpence?'

She froze, not wanting to turn towards the direction of the voice. She had to be mistaken. Surely her ears were playing tricks on her, trying to make her deepest wish come true? 'Simon, is that you?' She felt an idiot for even voicing the thought but then his hands were on her shoulders as he turned her to face him.

'You never replied to my letter. I thought it was too late, and you'd gone for ever . . .' Annie gasped, still unable to take it in. Simon was here, in the middle of New York, and he had somehow found her among all the teeming crowds. It was like a miracle.

'I was on my way to the airport as soon as I'd read your news,' Simon said, and he was more handsome than ever. 'Jocelyn told me she'd suggested you visit the Woolworth Building, but if I'd missed you, we would have met on the ship. Do you think I was going to allow you to travel home alone and possibly lose you again?'

'But I was coming home to you,' she said, looking up into his face, wondering how the familiar lines and his shining blue eyes could make her heart beat so fast. 'I've missed you so much,' she managed to say before he enfolded her in his arms and kissed her, as from the river she heard ships sound their horns inviting travellers to start a new voyage.

Elaine Everest

1953–2024

Elaine Everest died, suddenly and unexpectedly, in August 2024. Her cremation took place at the Kemnal Park Cemetery in Kent on 17 September. The room was packed with her family and friends, professional associates, fellow writers and ex-students, all as shocked and saddened by her passing as I was, but dressed in the bright clothes that her husband, Michael, had asked us to wear, because Elaine had always been such a lover of colour. I felt honoured to have been asked to speak that day, as both a close friend and a representative of the Society of Women Writers and Journalists (SWWJ), a very old and supportive society to which we both belonged. Needless to say, it was a very emotional occasion.

I first met Elaine on a writers' holiday in Wales around twenty years ago. We were both writing articles and short stories back then, both hoping to get a first novel published and both working as creative-writing tutors. On the surface, we had little in common beyond that. I loved cats; Elaine loved dogs. I was divorced; Elaine's marriage was still going strong, having wed at eighteen. I had children and went on to have grandchildren; Elaine did not. But none of that made any difference. We seemed to have a similar view of the world, shared many of the same opinions and beliefs, and soon became firm friends. We both had an interest in horse-racing, among other things, and at one time I believe we both owned a very small share – probably hardly more than an ear! – in the same horse. (Perhaps unsurprisingly, this never made us our fortune.) It even turned out that our birthdays were just ten days apart.

Elaine was born and bred in Kent, setting many of her stories around Erith, which she knew so well, and basing them around real-life events that her parents and grandparents had spoken about when she was growing up – from bombing disasters and paddle steamers on the Thames to small boats returning after the Dunkirk evacuation. In fact, the house on Alexandra Road, Erith, where some of her Woolworths Girls characters live, is the very house that Elaine and Michael moved into as newlyweds more than fifty years ago.

She was a long-standing member of the Romantic Novelists' Association (RNA), passing through its New Writers' Scheme (as did I) and later serving on the committee for a while. Over the years, along with several fantastic friends I might never have made if not for Elaine, we attended lots of events, meals and parties together, travelled on trains, sang our hearts out and gossiped the night away in RNA conference kitchens. We jollied each other along as we sought our first agents and publishers; we commiserated when things were not going well; and we celebrated our successes with great humour and, often, cake. Elaine was thoughtful and kind. She bought me flowers when I was sick and she came to my wedding.

In December 2023, Elaine and I both reached the age of seventy. She sent me a box of my favourite chocolates. I sent her a monogrammed notebook, which accidentally arrived minus the gift note that the online seller should have put inside the package. It was amusing to see her Miss Marple tendencies come to the fore as she spent a day or two frantically trying to work out who had sent it!

Elaine always invited her friends to her wonderful book launches. One was held in a garden centre restaurant; another in a 1940s-style tearoom in Ramsgate, where we ate wartime food and were served by waitresses styled with victory rolls and pinnies, as if we were living in one of her Teashop Girls novels!

When Elaine asked me to contribute a short story to an anthology she was putting together, it was to raise money for Against Breast Cancer, a charity that meant a lot to her since she had suffered from the disease herself when she was only in her twenties. When she asked me to be the judge for a short-story competition, it was in memory of a late mutual friend and to raise money, again, for charity. Elaine was so good at helping others. She spent a lot of time sharing her knowledge, passing on writing tips, and advising and guiding new writers – in her own writing classes at The Write Place, but much more widely, too.

Among the outpouring of tributes on social media when the news of Elaine's death broke, her close friend and former student Natalie Kleinman wrote: 'Elaine was a force of nature, outspoken in her opinions and ready to stand by them even when they were controversial, but she would be there front and centre if you needed her. I've never known anyone give so much of themselves to other people.'

Elaine and I messaged each other often, to share secrets, writerly gossip and news of our latest books or occasional betting successes. I know she harboured a desire to publish a crime novel, but, with her sagas in such demand, that plan was still on the back burner.

She loved holidaying in Cornwall and Switzerland, making an enormous effort last summer to return from the latter as quickly as possible when her beloved dog Henry fell fatally ill in kennels while she was away. Dogs and their welfare were always central to her life, so a wonderful pair of wool-and-flower creations, representing all twelve of her past dogs, took pride of place among the floral tributes at her funeral. Michael also made sure that the ashes of those dogs were included inside her coffin that day, so that they could all make their final journey together. Elaine would have loved that.

When it came to her writing, Elaine was a true professional, never letting her ill health get in the way of finishing the next book. She formed a fantastic partnership with her agent, Caroline Sheldon, and her publisher, Pan Macmillan, and together they published sixteen novels. The final story (this one!) was completed and delivered to her agent just weeks before Elaine died.

The Woolworths Girls books cover the war years and beyond, having just reached 1953 and the Christmas when Elaine and I were both born. The baby who was born to a mother in the next bed to Sarah at the very end of *A Christmas Wish at Woolworths* was in fact Elaine herself, as she explained in her letter to her readers for that novel.

Sadly, none of us will ever know what plans Elaine had for her regular characters, Freda, Sarah and Maisie, in the years ahead, but I do know that she would have made sure they all got the happy endings they deserved.

Elaine had so many regular readers who followed her series right from the start and who loved chatting to her on Facebook or attending her talks in libraries. It is hard to believe that this has all come to such an abrupt and tragic end.

I can honestly say that there was no one among all my friends in the writing world who I trusted and confided in more than Elaine. The SWWJ and the RNA will miss her. All her writing friends and her tens of thousands of loyal readers will miss her. And I will miss her . . . very much. I already do.

Rest in peace, dear friend.

Vivien Brown x

Elaine was a keen supporter of The Cinnamon Trust, which helps to care for dogs when their owners die or become too old or sick to look after them. A memorial fundraising page has been created where donations can be made: elaineeverest.muchloved.com

Discover the first book in the Woolworths series

The Woolworths Girls

Can romance blossom in times of trouble?

It's 1938 and, as the threat of war hangs over the country, Sarah Caselton is preparing for her new job at Woolworths. Before long, she forms a tight bond with two of her colleagues: glamorous Maisie and shy Freda. The trio couldn't be more different, but they immediately develop a close-knit friendship, sharing their hopes and dreams for the future.

Sarah soon falls into the rhythm of her new position, enjoying the social events hosted by Woolies and her blossoming romance with young assistant manager Alan. But, with the threat of war clouding the horizon, the young men and women of Woolworths realize that there are bigger battles ahead. It's a dangerous time for the nation and an even more perilous time to fall in love ...

More than 100,000 copies sold

Available now

The People's Friend
The Home of Great Reading

If you enjoy quality fiction, you'll love
The People's Friend magazine.
Every weekly issue contains seven original short
stories and two exclusively written serial instalments.

On sale every Wednesday, the *Friend* also includes travel,
puzzles, health advice, knitting and craft projects
and recipes.

It's the magazine for women who love reading!

For great subscription offers, call 0800 318846

@ TheFriendMag

PeoplesFriendMagazine

thepeoplesfriend.co.uk